THE RETREAT OF RADIANCE

THE RETREAT OF RADIANCE

A Novel of Revenge

IAN MOFFITT

STEIN AND DAY / Publishers / New York

First published in the United States of America in 1985
Copyright © 1982, 1985 by Ian Moffitt
All rights reserved, Stein and Day, Incorporated
Designed by Terese Bulinkis Platten
Printed in the United States of America
STEIN AND DAY/*Publishers*
Scarborough House
Briarcliff Manor, N.Y. 10510

Library of Congress Cataloging in Publication Data

Moffitt, Ian.
    The retreat of radiance.

    I. Title.
PR9619.3.M55R4   1985   823   84-40703
ISBN 0-8128-3020-2

FOR
MARGARET O'SULLIVAN

Part One

"... Quinn lives alone and rarely speaks to neighbors. Left of Center, but not considered violent. Has had psychiatric treatment ..."

Australian Security Intelligence Organization

Hua-shan, Shensi: My nineteenth birthday.

WE DESCEND LIKE A SLUG on a Sung scroll; we slime every rock as we wind down through this chilling mist. My poisoned hand is puffy; I imagine it glowing like a fungus in the gloom. We have stopped on this mountain for a brief rest. Keh pokes his head out of his sedan chair, shouts with terrible anger, sees me looking at him, gives the V sign, and pops back inside. A bitter wind burns my face; I want to tear it off like a mask and fling it over the precipice. The soldiers squat beside their packs, staring stupidly. I will bayonet my hand and spray them with yellow pus.

Later: I still can't quite believe it has happened. One poor simpleton sat staring at me, murmuring and smiling, and then he began to pluck gently at my sleeve, as if he were removing insects, and finally he began to push me firmly, and then harder and harder, toward the edge. I don't know what it was all about; I just don't know. Shiozawa shoved past me, dragged him back by the collar, pushed the Mauser pistol into his mouth, and there was this god-awful bang, and he sagged down with the blood pouring out through his small black teeth, and Shiozawa rolled him over the edge with his boot. I keep thinking of the sick whale I saw slaughtered on the headland at home; the river of blood flowing down through round black stones. I keep trying to think of the whale. I am trying to pretend this is something I'm used to. I can still feel my arm where he was pushing me . . . Everybody is laughing a bit now; they have perked up. I stood up a minute ago and pretended to stretch. He is upside down on a ledge about 12 feet below, with his legs over his head like a straw dummy. I closed my left eye so I couldn't see him.

11

West Ridge, New South Wales: My forty-ninth birthday.
Dear Rock, Dear Leaf Mould, Thank you for your cards. I am
quite well, thank you, and you? You never change. I caper before
the coffin—I shake a belled cap—but I know you are always there,
stretching away beyond the limits of my own little life. And you,
Dear Emptiness. How are you? Do you remember the last time
we swam together down in the gorge? Years ago now, wasn't it?
We clambered over the soft sandstone boulders, some flushed a
deep peach-crimson, others a rich orange, and we drifted quickly
down the creek, laughing as the gap widened between us. Then
over the little rapids we slid into the deep green pool, and we
floated there, gazing up at the caves licked out of the olive-green
bush; remarking on the medieval crossbows of the king parrots as
they flung themselves across the bland blue sky. Remember? The
rusted cans are still there tonight, caught in bearded flood-
driftwood in the rough tan river sand and I am beginning to think
these days that I have almost merged with memory itself. Perhaps, like you, I belong most truly in the world of crickets, of dogs
that bark faintly, far away, plucking the primeval chord.

ONE

AFTER HE RESURRECTED REVENGE FROM its hiding place and sent out messages in its name, changes began to occur, some in his own head, some in the world around him.

QUINN HALF-ROSE FROM his bed, one elbow jammed hard into his pillow. Someone was watching the house. He stared at the bedroom windows, his eyes alert for the quick blur of a face or knuckles rising over the sill; his brain and ears awaiting the creak of the bedroom door behind him. Faintly, far down on the highway, a truck whined down toward the city beneath a scatter of icy stars; he pictured a green rectangle of cabbages swishing briefly through the black wastes of bush. Nothing else stirred, but the oppressive awareness of a presence lay all around him; it had shaken him from sleep. He slid his feet onto the floor and sat quite still on the edge of his bed. The streetlight beyond his front gate lit the white trunks of eucalypts like the backdrop of an empty stage.

Quinn switched on the rickety yellow bedlamp that lay on a chair by his pillow. He was not ready yet for a confrontation: the sudden glow was a plea to intruders to melt away until he could face them on his own terms, in daylight. Somewhere a roof-beam cracked; he imagined a man crouching up on the rafters. Quickly he pushed his feet into a gaping pair of old desert boots that served as slippers and moved to the bedroom light switch. He stood alone now in faded pajamas: prepared, at last, to kick a groin if he was cornered, or to smash a nosebone with one backward swing of his right fist. The courage of the fearful buoyed him, and he pulled open the door into the hall with a brisk show of confidence.

No one. Quinn stooped swiftly through the cottage; opening doors, snapping on lights, peering beneath the empty beds in which his three children once had slept. He even gazed up at the manhole cover in the hall ceiling in case some intruder above had dislodged it. And after that, he took a flashlight and cautiously opened the front door.

The dark, damp shapes of the garden rose immediately to meet him; he flashed the beam on them imperiously, and then he began stepping slowly around the house—avoiding the far side, which was clotted too thickly for safety with oleanders strangling in a half-stripped tent of honeysuckle. Quinn stood at a corner of the house and flashed the light over them with a spurious aggression, ready to hurl the flashlight at a hostile body suddenly rushing toward him out of the black pit of his own fear—out of Kwangsi Province more than thirty years before. His inviolability now had ended, he knew; his long peace, of sorts, had shattered forever.

He stood for three or four minutes beneath the pale eucalypts, both inviting violence and rejecting it; indecision had shielded him from involvement for most of his life. A few moths clicked against the streetlight, but nothing moved in the garden. Warily, he walked back inside the house and flattened himself against a wall.

Only the welcome clink of bottles up the street ended his vigil: the slam of a van door as the milkman jumped in for his last delivery at Quinn's place on the edge of West Ridge.

He checked the rooms again in case someone had slipped in through the front door, and switched on his cracked electric kettle to make tea. The old refrigerator shuddered in a corner of the kitchen, and Quinn leaned on it until the water boiled, wondering who it was who had been crouching out there in the early-morning darkness.

"QUINN'S FINAL PHASE," as he called it then, had begun a few months before this. His cottage was perched on a bushy mountain crag at the end of a sandstone road, and its isolation confirmed his semiwithdrawal at that time from the human race. Few relatives or former friends called, and he rarely answered the door when they did. He played, instead, a queer game of hiding, squinting through the kitchen curtains at occasional callers who penetrated this far west of the city. He even lay in the hall one day and stealthily pushed back a *Watchtower* booklet that a Jehovah's Witness had just slipped beneath the door (trembling with mirth at the astonished silence of the disciple on the other side). To be going a bit around the bend in this anesthetized society pleased him secretly; the only worthwhile people, he had concluded during a brief bout of therapy, were a trifle mad.

Quinn had bought the cottage some years before. That had been the springtime of it all, when his children were very small; occasionally (half-hoping to find Aboriginal stone tools or convict manacles) he still dug up cracked, withered pacifiers that they had dropped when shrieking with glee under a distant summer hose: artefacts of a lost age that made him smile gently. West Ridge was a perfect place to remember: his backyard sloped down into the river gorge where once the whole family had swum together.

Each December the summer brushfires flared, heralding Christmas; he and his neighbors stood on their rooftops with hoses, guarding the residential sprawl along the ridge, while the sirens wailed and the sky boiled orange above them.

Now, however, it was really the winters and rainy springs that he noticed most: the water jerking heavily through the rusted gutter outside his bedroom; a faint stench drifting up through the snail-tattered leaves of the cannas that he had planted to suck up the septic overflow.

And yet it was a pleasant enough purgatory there: the spot for retirement and respectable termination. He had already stopped regular work, and some of his former colleagues from the defunct proofreading room of the *Star* down in the city—phased out, as he was, by automation—spoke of him as if he were already dead.

More and more he was being "driven in on himself," as the saying went—a process he recognized clearly as he existed on the dole and his dwindling savings. "I'm being driven in on myself," he chuckled one night, blundering down the hall and pretending to bump into himself and sagging against the wall, his dark hair graying fast, his green eyes dancing, laughing at the empty rooms. He liked to think that he was twenty-nine, not forty-nine.

Inevitably, he talked to himself: old family jokes scratching short on phantom records as he puttered around the rooms. Sometimes he teased a small pillar of air (his daughter) recoiling, grinning, against a wall, just as he had when her tiny fists had pummeled his chest with exasperated love. Occasionally he wrote letters to himself, or to the air and the earth and leaves, and sometimes at night he lay on trial in his littered bedroom, pretending he stood in a dock.

This was his second "Poetic Phase"—the first was in adolescence—and nobody then felt more Australian than he: oblique, defeated, the bitter lonely land itself, its ribs rubbed sharp as bullock bones. West Ridge deepened his gloom: few people ventured forth in his neighborhood except old men who limped down to the local bowling green in the awful stillness of noon. He watched them sometimes through his windows, vowing never to limp into line behind them.

Now, however, was the ultimate lonely period of his life, he surmised: the season when mortality crept into the bones to take up lodging, and an endless darkness began to press against the windows. He dreaded the half-century. The ego of youth had drained away, and for the first time he truly sensed his transience. Life seemed to be closing its pale circle, the trees crowding closer to outlive him, and all the songs he had ever loved destined to outlive him, and stretches of wet streets he had walked at night on the fringes of country towns, and factory walls he had known in the city, and gratings and the corners of buildings—all the second- and third-grade backdrop to his life, all destined to outlive him. Quinn MM, he sometimes called himself. "Q: Military

16

Medal?" he asked, pausing for the answer. "A: No, Male Meno-
pause," he replied. Once he even signed a conservation petition
"M.A. Angst." A middle-aged joke, he told the young widow
who presented it at his door, and he invited her in for a glass of
Riesling. Later they embraced, briefly and inconclusively, on his
sofa.

Quinn suppressed all thoughts of his former wife. He began
thinking quite a lot, however, about the dead—including his
father and Tony Doyle, although both had died in the fifties: his
father up the coast in their hometown of Wongbok—Wongbok!
It always rang like a cracked bell—and Doyle in the British Crown
Colony of Hong Kong, back in the days when Hong Kong
government officials still called it a "colony."

Two vivid pictures of his father usually surfaced. The first he
snapped off immediately: his father rose like a gutted cathedral
from his wheelchair to lean on the flying buttress of his mother
as she lowered him to the lavatory seat; his father's eyes then
became tall Gothic windows set with stained glass. In the second
image, however, his father sat in his wheelchair by the orange
tree in their backyard on the edge of Wongbok, coughing First
World War German gas as the Passchendaeles of ring-barked
paddocks stretched away behind him to the lonely coast. He had
tried to paint this scene, but it was better in his mind. In these
reveries, his father always tossed a tennis ball to him (which he
strove to hit straight back to him with a cricket bat in case he
toppled sideways from the wheelchair), and when a visitor
appeared at the side of the house his father turned and pretended
to inspect the orange leaves for aphids while Quinn gazed down
at him steadily through the dark tunnel of the years.

It was particularly difficult, on occasions like those, to separate
the reality of memory from the reality of the present. Sometimes
Quinn switched off the lights of his cottage at night and wandered through the empty rooms: cradling a glass, easing past
furniture, remembering the China of his teens. And what was
more real, he asked himself, when he did that? The spirits of his
children played unaware among the cracked yellow feet of the
Taoist priests from Hua-shan. And, somehow, it seemed that
Doyle and his father and Asia were linked with all of this, as if his

whole long life since those feverish days in China had been a dutiful dream; a long pause in an unfinished story that still burned for a conclusion.

QUINN BEGAN DREAMING vividly again about this time, and each dream, each day, became pretty much like the other. He dreamed early one morning that his children were running gaily down the hall, calling to him. "Don't run on the road!" he instructed them automatically while reading a book. "Don't run on the road!" But he was aware that a giant chasm had opened in the hall beside the kitchen door, and he failed to warn them of that. Their little figures, idealized in white nightgowns, began wafting gently down through dark space toward a landscape he could not quite imagine; he peered over the edge of the worn green carpet and watched them drifting to and fro a few meters beneath him in the darkness. Quinn placed moss on the bottom of the chasm to break their fall, but the wet black walls of rock were grinding together on their feet as he jerked his head away. He opened his eyes after that dream and switched on his bedside radio for distraction.

Week after week, month after month, through ten crowded years of marriage, and now a recurrence of the solitary gray ones of adolescence; even a return to the abortive one-night stands (after too much liquor) of his youth. Yet for three decades, Quinn had preserved one secret that he never babbled in bars, but that lit his brain with subliminal flashes while he was talking and laughing with his old colleagues from the *Star* or joking in bed with strange young women down in the city. Nobody ever suspected what he was seeing inside his head.

He painted this secret, suitably disguised, during his brief "Art Period" in the early seventies: a litter of golden starfish wilting in a parched bean field on a cracked plain, the misty mountains of traditional Chinese landscape towering above them. He called this painting "The Chinese Civil War," and entered it, like a murderer deliberately planting a clue, in the local Art and Horticultural Society's annual exhibition down in West Ridge village.

It was a bad painting. The judges agreed that it was clumsily executed, confused in intent, and not worthy even of a Merit Card—and they were right, as it turned out, for nobody bought it. Quinn carried it home after the exhibition and propped it on a

18

dusty chest of drawers. *He* certainly liked it, but then only he could hear the cries and songs from that bean field long ago in Kwangsi: the young voices floating up clearly through the morning bird calls; drifting sweetly around the walls of the Retreat of Radiance.

He never forgot that day in 1948, or the long ghastly night that followed before General Keh Shih-kai's Nationalist troops continued their flight south from the Yellow River toward the Golden Triangle. He painted this army as a slug, smearing a trail of slime down the cold peaks of his memory.

AND OF COURSE he remembered Larsen; Quinn never quite forgot Larsen. Most of the other China ghosts that haunted him were dead—like Tony Doyle—but Larsen was alive and prospering in Manhattan.

And, strangely, his hatred for Larsen became therapy of a kind: he could not slip silently into the crematory furnace at more than 500° C before he had resolved their story. The time had come, in middle age, to wipe the slate clean.

This fact did not appear in the slender Australian Security (ASIO) file on Quinn's career that Larsen obtained several months later, and neither did the final trigger of Quinn's journey: an unforeseen stroke of luck. One of two aged aunts—his father's sisters—died in a brick cottage of heart disease. She left him $15,000 (undeclared) in a plastic shopping bag and a black suit, tie, and hat that she requested him, in a final, spidery note, to wear in mourning: his penalty for accepting the gift.

This archaic request dismayed Quinn even more than her death, but it was a small price to pay: stroking an imaginary beard, he posed secretly during the funeral service as Modigliani's *Portrait d'Homme* (so blotting out painful memories of another church, two smaller coffins).

Later, at his surviving aunt's home, he smoothly comforted her over her prized plum cake and tea while sliding a strand of her gray hair from his saucer and slyly emptying the cup into the sink.

"Don't worry," he said, turning and patting her bony little shoulder. "You'll see her again." But it was the sort of comforting lie a father told a child.

Picking up the shopping bag, declining a second cup of tea,

19

"Bye, Auntie," he said. "Look after yourself." Because I'm afraid I won't be able to, I have to act now, or forever hold my peace.

QUINN BEGAN THE next day by unwinding some of the vines from the dark oleander branches in his garden, which the vines had crushed into barley-sugar shapes.

The work tired him; he was out of condition. The swifts were flicking back to northern Asia's conifer forests after their annual summer migration down the east coast of Australia. He watched them until he spied old Miss Bird, an elderly Englishwoman who lived across the road with a malevolent cat. Miss Bird, half-crouched behind a diosma bush, as always was watching *him*. She had spread her tattered underwear on the bush, trailing loops of elastic, to convey the impression, he suspected, that they were cleaning rags. He knew better: he had seen her bending over her zinnias.

Quinn waved cheerily to her and cried: "How are you?" and this confused Miss Bird greatly, for he had never acknowledged her before. She ducked around the back of her cottage to escape from him, and Quinn marched inside his house for a beer, well pleased with himself. He was beginning to feel liberated at last; the money had opened up a vast new world in his head. When the kookaburras laughed now, he chuckled too.

Sprawled on a couch, sipping a can, he realized suddenly that the rooms were suffocating in paper. Sagging cardboard boxes were jammed everywhere, stuffed with dust-furred newspapers and magazines commencing with the *Lifes* and *Looks* of John Kennedy's assassination; most of them charted the rise of conservation and the fall of Vietnam, when he, like so many others, had cared about the distant future of the globe.

He spent the next few days burning them. He tore up his old clothes and thrust them into garbage bags. He collected piles of his children's old gear, which had lain in drawers for years and thrust them into bags for the St. Vincent de Paul (tipped in hurriedly, afraid he might reconsider). He peeled their old sticky-taped drawings from the walls and placed the best of them carefully in his wallet. As for his wife, he had removed all trace of her several years before.

When he had done all that—when he had cleaned and swept his tomb—he was ready to leave it. He began jogging every day

20

through the bush amid the giant cicada shells of abandoned cars—sparring sometimes, his skin gleaming with sweat. The university lightweight quarterfinalist 1947 (KO'd, round one) was launching his comeback, he announced to the trees, and he stopped, leaning against a eucalypt, grinning at the absurdity of the mission that was forming in his mind.

At last he was ready, and that evening, Quinn took a small hessian bag from a filing cabinet in his bedroom and emptied it onto his kitchen table. Three tattered little 1948 diaries slid from the bag, followed by his ancient Vest Pocket Automatic Kodak and three red rolls of undeveloped film. He weighed the rolls of film in his hand like shotgun cartridge while Larsen's dry Midwest voice rustled back into his brain like rat paws in corn husks.

He wrote a very explicit letter that night to Larsen at his home in New Jersey, telling him precisely what he intended to do, with further letters to General Keh in Taiwan and to Lancelot Ming, Albert Porter, and Andrew Veitch in Hong Kong. Then he walked up to the mailbox on the corner and dropped the letters in.

As he was walking back slowly along the sandstone road, between cottages lit by the sickly blue glare of television, the eyes of Miss Bird's cat gleamed at him from her path, and he stopped. He became aware for the first time of a bond between himself and Miss Bird; she was softly playing "The White Cliffs of Dover" on her piano. Like him, she lived in the past: her war, too, had never ended.

FOUR WEEKS LATER—not long after he first concluded that he was under surveillance—Quinn stood at the doorway of his cottage holding a small sludge-gray suitcase. It was 5:00 A.M. in winter, and he stared back into the dark hall, the familiar shabby rooms beyond—ready to return to China.

"Bye, kids," he said softly, stooping to place his key beneath a mossy brick, and immediately his children pelted toward him out of the empty house: somehow four years old again, giggling, clutching his neck, bearing him down to their level.

Quinn disengaged them gently. "See you," he murmured, and he closed the door and walked out briskly through the photinias at the front gate. This morning—well, it was strange, perhaps— but this morning he felt light, almost jaunty: a cheerful man in mourning-black on his final journey down to the railway station.

Solitary figures were drifting silently through the mist toward the train: factory workers bearing sandwiches and thermoses and cheap thrillers in their greasy airline bags. Quinn fell into step with them, a shadow amid the shadows. He saw now, not the dark waves of eucalypts, but a vast calm ocean brimming deep to its horizon. Then, close up, he imagined a shark slicing like retribution through a wave—a bloody flurry in the breakers.

"I'm not certifiable," he whispered, grinning at the bone-white trees, and raising his left hand, he jiggled briefly in a crazy little dance.

That was the last time that Miss Bird, peering from her bedroom window with a painkiller and a glass of water, saw Quinn: he boarded a jumbo jet that day for Hong Kong. His key began rusting beneath the mossy brick.

TWO

"THE BASTARD'S NUTS," LARSEN THOUGHT. He sat in a large dun suite at the Manhattan Statler scattered with color brochures of gaping mouths. Sticky martini glasses studded the furniture, and the air reeked of gin and vermouth and tobacco. He picked up the phone and called Westchester, waving with queasy good cheer as the last of the dental convention delegates bellowed out with their aging women.

He could hardly breathe, sitting there watching the women with scorn: they were smoke-dried from too many hours in too many suites like this amid the fat phallic zeppelins of businessmen's cigars; their hair frosted as if powdered with cigar ash; the hair of dead old women. His hatred, he suspected, sprang partly from their inability to arouse him.

"Hi," he rasped. "It's me." His dry voice quivered faintly with fuzzy desire; the Biblical placards of childhood rose accusingly from his father's Iowa cornfields; the farmhouse with texts hanging over every doorway. He turned abruptly to the windows to snap off the thought: his balding crew cut now graying, his lean face ivory-white, his fingers flicking imaginary dust from his thighs.

"Hello, luvvy." It was a warm, rich English delivery, as if she were indulging a slightly retarded child. "Long time no see," she said, and chuckled.

Larsen flushed. "I've been pretty busy, I guess," he lied. "Guess you think I'm crazy."

"Course I don't, honey," she cooed, and then she chuckled again. "Only next time you'd better wait till it's warmer. I could have knocked your goose pimples off with sticks."

They had driven their cars out to New Jersey's Great Swamp National Wildlife Refuge one cold afternoon. Larsen, the meticulous Manhattan management consultant, the organizer of coups and conventions, had wriggled into poisonous black and crimson panties and bra and sung a few lines of "Mammy" for her there while she sat whooping with laughter behind her steering wheel, peeping through her plump fingers.

"It was a joke," he lied again stiffly. "Look, I want to talk to you."

"Talking's no good, luv—ooh, I can hardly move," she sighed, and he imagined her sitting down slowly in her gracious home, bruised and bitten from her previous night's adventures in Harlem or Long Island. He knew the succession of her black lovers by their first names now; even the penis size of the present one: a Georgia mechanic who had posed as a medico from Puerto Rico until she surprised him under an auto in Queens.

She held nothing back. Her laughter rippled again over the line, and then her voice dropped with mock concern, heralding the hushed tones in which she delicately revealed her crudest excesses.

"My body," she moaned. "I've got bruises all over—I mean, this fellow, the way he kisses. Both my breasts are, like, purple, they really are, and my back, all around my shoulder blade has got little bite marks . . ."

"He sounds like a hamster," Larsen observed acidly. "There's something I want to ask you . . ."

"Well, His Lordship will never see it, so that's all right. Let's face it, he's not going to see it."

24

She paused, her confessions were always breathless, broken sentences that jerked past like speeding trains; Larsen could only leap at the substance and hang on for a moment before tumbling off short of the destination.

"I'm so *sore*," she bubbled. "My shoulders, everything . . ."

"Bertha!" Larsen broke in. He wasn't sure how to broach the subject; he wanted only to stop her. "I have a suggestion . . ."

"The answer's no," she giggled. "Just a tick, luv—His Lordship's coming. I've got to wrap up. What did you want to ask me?"

"Don't worry," he said. "It doesn't matter now. I'll call you later."

LARSEN JOINED THE peak-hour crowds swirling mutely through Manhattan. He had decided to walk to the Port Authority; he needed time to think. Morosely, he threaded his way over Eighth Avenue, rode up the escalator, and joined the line for Suffern, clutching his attaché case, staring dully at the Short Line bus shuddering on the concrete track. It quivered as the line thumped aboard; he sank into a window seat near the back as the door hissed shut.

He felt ill. The bus rolled down toward the Lincoln Tunnel, and a group of girls began offering to exchange seats with each other. "We're all split up!" one wailed with pretended dismay, and a Dali vision of dismembered bodies spread across Larsen's Kwangsi sky: torsos floating over New Jersey, legs dangling above the George Washington Bridge, arms hanging in the smog above the Village. He determined to concentrate on the immediate threat: Quinn, who had risen so persistently from the past down in Australia.

The bus bumped softly out of the tunnel, as if on a lumpy carpet, heading for the cracked concrete of New Jersey's Route 17. *Tap Room* flared up in the gathering darkness; *Hideaway Bar; Opici (Say O'Peachey) Wine.* A grubby little sailboat sat by a crumbling jetty in the poisoned Jersey swamps, hinting of escape, and he leaned forward absently, as he always did, to ensure that it was still there; touching it like a talisman with his cold gray eyes.

Quinn's letter lay against his heart; the acrid warmth of the bus for once failed to soothe him. Quinn could ruin him if he talked. His career; his future strength in the Republican Party, if the local

25

power struggle came out right; the move from his modest Waldwick box to something sprawling and stylish over in Saddle River—all torpedoed. The guy was a walking time bomb who had tracked him down after all these years—shooting off unsigned cards each Christmas, which he had to pass off to Donna as jokes: "From all the kids. Sorry haven't written. Up to our ears." Something had to be done about Quinn.

An old man behind him was surreptitiously sucking a cigar, and suddenly he coughed harshly, laying on the dying air the metallic, livery scent of his own poisoned little marsh. Larsen shrank against the window from the stench of humanity and tried to immerse himself in Bertha, whom he had met by chance one morning on a crossed line and found himself, startlingly, flirting with.

Bertha—Lady Earnshaw—the wife of an English lord who had climbed out of the North of England pits to make a fortune in steel, and who was now losing a pile in Wall Street while Bertha mined her more lucrative market in Harlem. Larsen's own big, breathing ex-Gaiety Girl of the mind: a mother-aunt-wife-lover wrapped up in the opulent San Francisco saloon of his imagination—all crimson plush and gilt mirrors and ostrich plumes and ribald song, with Bertha swooping above it on a high swing while he attempted to lure her down into sexual extravagances that he had never dared. Larsen-Humphrey Bogart growling, "C'mon down, kid," with a garter belt hidden beneath his raincoat.

The fantasy did not work tonight; it was still surfacing in tatters as the bus swept at last around the lucrative landscape of Saddle River. Larsen stepped down at Waldwick with relief, watching the red lights burning between the oaks and maples as the bus trundled on toward Ramsey. His next task: to convince Donna that an unexpected holiday in Asia was a dream come true, for he could not arouse her suspicions by going alone.

He walked down Cherry Tree Place, controlling his dread, and turned into his white two-storied dollhouse with the sloping lawn. No one from the office had seen it, to his knowledge, although he couldn't be sure: a couple of them drove out this way to visit relatives occasionally, and their wives could have pressed them for a furtive look. His hand trembled, inserting the key.

"Hi!" he called. The living room was as dim and still as a museum. Donna was out, thank God; he had forgotten the

26

neighborhood get-together in The Magnificent Crêpe, which she helped organize and always attended alone. He dropped his attaché case beside an antique mahogany chair of Donna's, inlaid with rosewood and mother of pearl, and sat down in it, his hands still trembling, by the phone.

Larsen called an old CIA friend to trigger an Australian Security Intelligence Organization surveillance of Quinn, who he said was a suspected Communist of many years standing. "Anything you can get on him," he asked. "In strictest confidence." He also called Lancelot Ming, a private detective in Hong Kong, to bring him up to date and warn him of Quinn's coming arrival there. He even called General Keh Shih-kai in Taiwan. And, finally, he called Bertha again and wheedled her into agreeing to make the trip to Asia for a week or so. They could meet accidentally as business acquaintances on the plane, or in some hotel in Hong Kong or Taiwan.

Only after all that did he sit back and surrender himself to the peculiar sexual thrill of his empty house, imagining Donna's underclothes tumbled in her drawers upstairs. The mahogany chair transmitted a sensual mastery over her which electrified him only in her absence. He gripped two carved lions' heads on its massive arms and gazed around their phoney world.

She had created it in the sixties after an ecstatic visit to the Pavilion of American Interiors at the World's Fair: a tiny pocket of old Pennsylvania in Bergen County, overlaid with an Irish Catholic patina imposed by the aunt who had adopted her as a child in Mt. Airy. The sofa sprinkled with cannon and cracked Liberty bells; the sideboard crammed with crystal that jingled as he pressed his shoe on a loose board; the Biblical inscriptions on the Gothic gold-metal plates around the light switches; the Sacred Heart on the landing; the white café curtains and hobnail milk glass and bayberry candles and miniature eagles; the whole bow-fronted boredom of it all.

He substituted Bertha. Her red swing swished through the sanctified air past the Sacred Heart, and he pictured himself standing beneath her with his arms stretched wide. He jumped when the telephone shrilled beneath his elbow. It was Donna, to say that she was going to be late.

Larsen stood up to mix a martini and the sideboard sang. Neither of them was even Catholic; the house was just as much a

27

lie as their marriage. They hadn't made love for three years, and the last occasion was best forgotten.

He stood at the curtains jiggling his martini, absently watching the girl next door as she raised her sturdy arms to toss a ball for the family dog. It was all a mockery, but Quinn wasn't going to destroy the base he had built up for his final big leap.

He struck what he thought might be a characteristic Bogart pose at the window; the Bogart facade, he had decided, hid his ambivalance better than most.

Quinn, he growled to himself—Quinn had to go. Imagining the Hollywood movie cameras creeping closer around him; lights, camera, action, while Lady Earnshaw reclined on a waterbed in his luxurious trailer beside the set.

THREE

UP IN THE BLUE SKY, high above the islands of Hong Kong and its maimed dragon hills on the mainland, the hawks were circling. A curious stillness hung with them up there, a sense of silence poised to descend; it filled the space beneath their wings as they soared over Sanyo and Nikon and Pioneer Stereo and Revlon; over the doomed green crabs that sat winking in old women's baskets on Wanchai Pier; the bodies of refugees rolling in Mirs Bay and Deep Bay and the South China Sea.

Lancelot Ming had never watched the hawks consciously until today. Now they shadowed his brain; the silence they portended was too permanent to contemplate. He sat hunched in the stern of a motor boat as it chugged out into Discovery Bay from the high hills of Lantao Island. A Marine Police launch dashed toward a black witch-wood of masts in the green refuse-strewn water. Automatically, he averted his face to light a small Brazilian cigar.

This was the arrival point for the refugee armada of junks and motor-driven hulks that were streaming up from Vietnam in a gentle southwest monsoon; a faded blue houseboat had just wallowed in, slopping water over its sides. Women and children were screaming as it tilted: it seemed flimsy enough to capsize with the flick of a finger.

He watched the police launch throttle to dead-slow and nose toward it to reduce wash, and then he tossed a match in the water and expelled smoke through his rotten teeth. He felt, deep in his stomach, the first faint prickling of fear—not for the Vietnamese, but for himself. For not only had Larsen called from the United States, but Quinn had written to him from Australia, and both acts were eroding the cocky image that he had cultivated for so long. He called to the boatman for more power—not because he was in a hurry, but merely to puncture his mood. The boatman mumbled, ignoring him, and gently corrected the wheel. The cries of the refugees faded behind.

Water splashed his pink cotton suit as the boat bumped over the wake of the police launch. His wide silk tie, emblazoned with a green bead palm tree, flicked over his shoulder. He was certainly ugly, he knew that: his head too large, his body too small; the terrible teeth that he promised himself one day to plug with gold. But garish bravado had kept him alive for decades while others went under. A Japanese freighter loomed above the boat, the dreaded faces of the Devils peering down over the rail. He spat into the water.

"I hope the Dwarfs sink next," he called to the boatman, and leaned back, all four feet eleven inches of him, with pretended nonchalance. The boatman chuckled.

A lazy old Hong Kong Special Branch man with a bent for zoology had once told Ming that he resembled a harmless frilled lizard that snapped open a painted ruff to disarm his enemies (a careless display of erudition, before a sour superior, which precipitated the forced retirement of the Special Branch man during an efficiency crackdown; bewildered, he haunted Whipsnade Zoo until he died in 1965). But he was right and Ming knew it: his progression of pink suits, which he had worn since the Second World War, were as vital to him as the Chinese sex jokes that he squealed to defuse latent hostility; the dated thirties slang that he still affected; the sets of obscene photographs that he plucked from his breast pocket in bars—naked women pinned belly-up like frogs beneath the communal male lust. He might be a tiny card index of brothels and police contacts and Triad gangsters, strutting the blurred line between crime and the law, but he was much more than that. He was a survivor.

He closed his eyes and then opened them quickly: it had been just about here, in 1948, that Quinn had saved his life as they were returning from an outing to Cheung Chau Island with other habitués of The Vienna Restaurant: Tony Doyle, Andrew Veitch, Albert Porter, and the rest of them . . .

He overbalanced again, in memory, from the back of the boat—drunk on rice wine, unable to swim, apparently unseen in the darkness. But Quinn had seen him go; he had jumped in and swum toward him swiftly.

"Don't choke me, you bastard!" Quinn had spluttered, jolting him in the face and turning him clumsily so that he could grab him around the waist. And he had held him up until the boat circled and hands dragged them aboard (one old *gweilo* madman, he remembered, had tried to throw him back because he was undersized). And later, wrapped in a blanket in the cabin, Ming had stared at Quinn dolefully. "I never forget," he had said. "I am dead but for you . . ."

AN ANCHOR CHAIN rattled up ahead: one of the Keh syndicate's rusted black Panamanian freighters squatted in mid-harbor beneath the suspicious glare of the port authorities—its ownership disguised, he knew, its cargo suspect, the port of origin falsified. General Keh's drug business was booming; now he was supplementing it with new fortunes in the flesh trade from China and more than ten ports in Vietnam. The snake boat operators from the islands near Lantao had just agreed to Keh's instructions (which he had passed on faithfully) to step up the input of Chinese from Macao and the mainland while the Marine Police were struggling to cope with the Vietnamese. And yet his uneasiness persisted.

There were reasons for this. His own roles, for a start, were so ambiguous: a private detective (set up originally as a U.S. intelligence front after the Civil War, but never used or financed); a Hong Kong minion for Keh in Taiwan; a part-time funerals reporter and police and underworld contact for the *Clarion*, an old

English-language biweekly that still published around the corner from his agency in Wanchai. He wore so many hats each day that even he had become confused. He was about to take off his Keh cap and clap on his *Clarion*—after a quick check at his office to see whether anyone was desperate enough that day to require his services as a lawman. But now the separate compartments of his callings had disintegrated; when something erupted in one it spilled over into the others. And the latest eruption—following Quinn's and Larsen's communications—had occurred the previous day.

He had dropped into the *Clarion* with a little historical article that he contributed each month on the pioneers who lay around Tony Doyle's grave in the old Colonial Cemetery—and which the subeditors buried as deeply as they could. He did not pretend any writing skill, but he had held down his little corner there since 1946 as a link-man with the Chinese police and criminals who were too lowly for European cultivation.

He had been sitting in the newsroom, grinning bravely as a New Zealand subeditor picked up his deathly prose and held it distastefully at arm's length. "Any takers for the Crimson Curse?" the New Zealander had pleaded around the subeditors' table: a poor play upon this Ming Period that afflicted them so regularly. And then the telephone rang, and, to his surprise, the call was for him. The caller merely said in Cantonese: "Your work is being watched with interest on Taiwan." That was all, and that was enough.

The motorboat sidled into Wanchai pier; he sprang off without speaking and twinkled up to Gloucester Road. His office was a room on the first floor of a small building surviving redevelopment: a rotten stump, appropriately, in the island's gleaming new set of commercial towers, which smiled across Kowloon and the New Territories toward the feast of customers awaiting them in China. Peking was about to issue its long-awaited law permitting foreign investment; the multinationals were ready to barge in with samples under their arms after three decades in the waiting room.

He envied them, bustling into his own grubby little building. One day, perhaps, he promised himself. One day . . . A tangle of exposed electrical wiring was bundled like guts on a wall just inside the entrance, beside Chinese and English signs that adver-tised small firms. One, which he had painted himself, said: *L. Ming, Detective Agency. Upstairs Pleise.* He darted past it up the chipped stone stairs.

Solemn groups of small children were playing on the stairs; he picked his way up among them in two-toned shoes salvaged from a Vietnam veteran who had been killed in a knife fight in a topless bar up in Lockhart Road. On the first floor, he stopped in mild surprise: scraps of yellow paper, torn off his office door, littered the landing around a small empty cardboard box; its lid lay beside it.

Twirling his key ring, about to enter, he decided that the pieces of paper did not matter: they had been foolish charms that a grateful old woman had pasted there for extricating her daughter from a charge of theft without demanding a fee—well, not a monetary fee. That girl, he recollected, had been a helluva dish.

One slip of paper was a charm for opening doors when the key was lost—written, she vowed, with the blood of a woodpecker mixed with pearl dust. Another was a spell enchanting a woman to fall in love with him; a third a power that kept out evil. He had left them there rather than tempt ill-fortune by removing them, just as *gweilos* sometimes exposed religious medallions in their wallets while paying for liquor or women or small boys. Now he looked down suspiciously at the children, who were turning over a small object in their hands. He realized with horror what it was.

Sick with dread, he pocketed his keys and fled back down the steps. Outside, a slender young girl in a crimson cheongsam slit to the thigh was crossing Gloucester Road: a cocktail waitress from one of the big tourist hotels. He stopped distractedly to watch her: a gaudy little votive candle burning constantly before his lurid image of Woman; his eyes flicked an urgent SOS. "*Ai-yah,*" he whispered absently, but his heart wasn't in it.

MING HURRIED UP toward Queen's Road East to catch a bus to the Colonial Cemetery; he was already running late for a funeral that he had to cover for the *Clarion.* A bellow stopped him as he passed the bar next to the newspaper office: Senior Superintendent Rushton and a group of other old *gweilo* police and pressmen were gesturing at him through the glass. They wanted him to adjudicate another bet, no doubt. When did the British and American sailors die fighting the pirates at Kuhlan? When was the cholera outbreak? He went to the doorway.

"Lancelot!" boomed a fruity old English press hack who always ignored him when he was sober. "When was the Great Fire that spread to the ships in the harbor?"

Lancelot stared at him blankly. This was the knowledge, stored on gold-lettered marble in the cemetery, of which he was most proud: if he was a card index of crime, he fancied himself as a computer on death. But now his brain was empty.

"The Great Fire?" he echoed.

Rushton looked down at him, gaunt and eroded now, but still towering over everyone else; in from the New Territories border area for a weekly reunion with his old colleagues in Wanchai. Tony Doyle's best friend: a hero of the Kong Kong Police Force who wouldn't have lifted a glass with any of them once. "Tell them, Lancelot," he growled. "I've got the next round on it."

"Listen," Ming said. "I gotta go." He dived out the door. A roar of protest followed him as he fled.

He caught a bus to Happy Valley and picked his way along beneath the half-finished concrete overpass of the Aberdeen twin-tube tunnel. The tunnel stuck like an exposed artery from a tombstone-studded hill in one corner of the cemetery; the grave diggers were removing more than three thousand bodies to allow motorists to speed through the spine of the island in three minutes. It was this reorganization, apart from his fear, that sparked most of the errors in his memory bank: he paused, bewildered, and then skipped over summer rain puddles toward the burial ground. A Chinese truck driver was easing a load of steel girders over a rut; the driver crouched, wincing, over the wheel, as if the jolting crash might wake the undisturbed dead, and Ming followed him inside.

The cemetery, apart from this corner, was still peaceful. A young American in thick spectacles gazed keenly at Ming from his headstone—his photograph, impressed in marble, was as sharp and bright as if the Reaper had just popped in while he was dictating a letter to his secretary. Nearby, a Methodist minister announced silently that he was now with Christ, which was far better . . .

Far better for him, perhaps. Ming hesitated among mildewed

memorials marking the deaths of officers on the China Station, his eyes raking the monuments. A tunnel workman sat reading a Chinese newspaper on a marble tomb, his yellow hard hat perched on the small white cross beside him that marked Tony Doyle's plot. Sparrows twittered in the shrubs and trees, and a grave digger, wearing only jeans, was peering up into the lateral layers of a frangipani tree; he balanced a tiny cage containing a delicate green bird on his flat right hand. He seemed to be the only grave digger who was awake; the others were sleeping on the grass around a small chapel. Ming looked up the slope: a black clot of mourners had gathered around a grave at the edge of a jungle of bamboo and banyans and convolvulus that climbed several hundred meters toward white apartment blocks. This was his destination.

Ming circled toward them slowly, delaying his inspection of the cards on the wreaths until they departed; he did not feel up to the chirpy conversation today that *gweilos* always expected of him. Larsen's suggestion of violence—even murder—had shaken him. Murder belonged in his office filing cabinet with the best private collection of sex and sadism photographs in Hong Kong, if he said so himself. There were bulging folders of pictures stored there: priceless warlord executions during the Revolution of 1912, rare atrocities of the Japanese Time, unique postwar Triad victims hacked to bits in Hong Kong alleys—he had gathered death (and sex) with the breathless enthusiasm of a collector of coins. But they were merely the hobbies of his calling—photographic bait to impress the policemen he courted and the gangsters on whom he fawned. To endanger his own freedom over Quinn was madness. The prospect invested each object around him with menace: a Coke bottle floating in a lily pond, the arthritic roots of a banyan clutching the earth, the pitted trunks of tall palms—all spoke to him of grenades and strangulation, the tearing impact of knives or bullets.

"It's got to be around here somewhere."

Two large American women in floral pantsuits were fussing among the headstones near the chapel. Cameras were slung around their necks, and they were bending to check something written on a slip of paper. Each wore a large white circular badge on her breast, bearing the black imprint of a man's head. Ming read the words BING LIVES.

"Do you wanna go and wake someone up?" one asked. She pushed a damp strand of graying hair from her high pink forehead and suddenly spotted Ming. "Sir!" she called. "Excuse me, sir. I wonder if you could help us? We're looking for . . ." She bent over the slip of paper.

Ming smirked automatically. "The grandfather of Bing Crosby," he chirped. "Tea trade. Clipper ships."

Her eyes widened. "Nathaniel Crosby!" she cried. "You know him—I mean, you know where he is?"

Ming brushed past them among the tombstones and crouched by one so worn that the inscription was almost illegible. The diversion comforted him, despite the meaty odor of their bodies; they bent closely behind him, lifting spectacles on silver chains, as he scooped up a handful of orange clay and rubbed it into the weathered words. It was an excuse to hide; the mourners were drifting back down the path.

"See?" he said. "N-a-t-h-a-n-i-e-l C-r-o-s-b-y." He peeped around the headstone as he slapped more clay on the stone tablet. "H-e d-i-e-d . . . He died i-n g-o-o-d-n . . ."

"Goodness!" they cried together and laughed. One of them placed a stubby forefinger on the next letter; Ming withdrew his as if it might sting him.

"Goodness a-s h-e l-i-v-e-d," she spelled out. "He died in goodness as he lived. Won't the girls be excited when we show them this! We only found out about it yesterday at the Consulate."

"I tell *them*," boasted Ming. He stood up and brushed his hands lightly against his trousers. The path now was empty. One of the women backed off with a camera.

"We can organize a tour of clubs from the west coast!" she boomed. "A pilgrimage! The Road to China!"

She lowered her camera suddenly and frowned significantly at her companion, who began rummaging in a shoulder bag for money. Ming flushed with embarrassment and walked off quickly; no European had ever taken him seriously.

"Sir!" they called. "Sir!" but he waved briefly, without turning, and kept going. A grave digger was wandering down from the new plot up at the edge of the little jungle, postponing final burial, perhaps, until after his morning doze. The coast was clear. He passed two Indian security guards from the tunnel, who sat outside a hut marked "Danger—Explosives," singing to Indian music on a cassette recorder; one stopped and murmured to the other and they both laughed, following him with their liquid eyes. He ignored them, bending over the wreaths that lay beside the open grave. Furtively he began ripping off cards: "Always Remembered, J. Stope . . . Deepest Sympathy, Mr. and Mrs. J. Simpson-Nuttall . . ."

This death should have given him especial pleasure: the corpse was a retired British magistrate who had once surprised him squatting inside a hearse, copying the inscriptions on wreaths heaped on a coffin so that he could slip away early to an assignation. The magistrate had tugged him out by one ear and booted him into a flower bed beside the slender ankles of a Portuguese widow, long dead, who then conducted a funeral parlor (and whom Porter claimed to have seduced on VJ Night—her black dress crumpled up beyond the moon-mystery of her thighs—on the outsized coffin of a White Russian). Ming burned anew at the memory of his humiliation, but now a dark foreboding masked any joy he might have felt.

The sun was directly overhead; a little stream, foaming with detergent, was bubbling down into the cemetery from the heights above. All around him, the lush Indian music entwined the monuments with an alien sensuality, and the Portuguese widow faded gradually into the image of a girl unfolding a sari. For a moment he was lost in lust.

A sixth sense prompted him to look up. Above him, on a bank where the wall of undergrowth arose, a wounded angel was staring down at him blindly. Her mildewed wings rested against a giant cross, and her arms were wrinkled like the soles of laborers' feet. Only the stumps of a few fingers stuck from her outstretched hands.

Behind her, the Old Black Hawk also gazed down at him with hideous intensity through his one good eye; the other, smeared with an ugly custard of blindness, rested beside the stone eyes of the angel. Keh's lowliest employee of all: once a killer for the Triads, now a creaky messenger, an informant, a ludicrous warning from the old days. A scissor blade, Ming knew, lay somewhere beneath the ancient black oiled-silk that clung to his bony old frame.

He pretended that he had not seen him. He dropped his eyes to the scabrous arms, the maimed hands of the angel, and then he stood up casually. Bustling back down the path, he imagined the plunge of steel between his shoulder blades. He realized now, without doubt, why the children had been playing with the plastic replica of a human finger on the steps leading up to his office. Keh's twisted sense of humor again: a warning, absurdly left at his door, to do something about Quinn or else.

The American women still clustered around Nathaniel Crosby's headstone; the cemetery workers were slumbering around the chapel in the frangipani-scented air. But the game of violence had begun; Quinn had opened up a whole field full of graves, and already the little skeletons were climbing out to pursue them all.

"Sir!" one of the women called, but Lancelot Ming did not stop. Like Quinn, like Larsen, he was setting off down the road into the past. The Road to China.

Part Two

FOUR

QUINN'S TARGET, GENERAL KEH SHI-KAI, climbed Hua-shan, the sacred Taoist Flower Mountain in Shensi, one sunny day in 1948. No military history recorded the event: the eyes of the world were on the checkerboard of armies that wheeled and clashed two thousand meters below on the vast plains of north and central China. Chiang Kai-shek's Nationalist troops were crumbling fast under the judicious cuts of the Communist armies; the approaching fall of Mukden was to begin an accelerating collapse ending in the Nationalist withdrawal to the island of Taiwan the next year. The speed of that collapse surprised the Communists as much as it angered the U.S. military advisers who were trying to shore up Chiang's rotten regime. Massive injections of equipment could not cure a disease of the soul.

It was an ancient sickness, Quinn realized many years later; it had wriggled like schistosomiasis larvae down through the rich river silt of the centuries—human corruption, forever incurable. Chiang merely stamped the disease with his own brand: "graft" became synonymous with "Nationalist" before Seoul and Saigon popped up to wave the flag for dollar democracy. Histories of the American War of Independence had helped inspire the Chinese Communist leaders when they were young, but by then, ironically, the Americans themselves had become the Redcoats; it was their turn to begin the doomed process of supporting detested regimes. Chiang's seal-like face already was dissolving into a slide-smear of lesser puppets, propped up to counter the Larger Evil of Communism.

The struggle between the Nationalists and Mao Tse-tung's Communists had been in bitter existence for more than two decades before that morning in 1948—and the struggle for national freedom against foreign powers had been flickering for more than a century. But patriotism in any form did not matter that day—or any day—to General Keh, the thirty-one-year-old "boy commander" of the crack U.S.-equipped White Horse Nationalist Division (it was still a crack division, its American advisers joked bitterly, because it never engaged in significant combat). General Keh himself was a dangerous joke: sending a plastic finger to Ming, decades later, was the consistent height of his wit.

Patriotism meant only profit to Keh, a short, plump man who took parades during the Civil War on a stout little white stallion that he mounted briskly whenever photographers—especially foreign news photographers—showed up. They were twin obscenities, General Keh and his pudgy stallion: his bottom rose and fell on the saddle as he spurred it into sluggish motion for the cameras in village streets. Peering ahead, sometimes brandishing a German Luger, he liked to pretend that startled Red troops were fleeing like rabbits not far in front of him.

Newsreels and still photographs of that time showed him in action while his hungry soldiers squatted against the mud huts, making sly chopstick-gestures with their fingers as the rotund duo bounced by. Grandparents dropped their granddaughters down hidden tunnels (dug beneath the huts in the Japanese Time) and peered fearfully from their torn paper windows over the soldiers' heads as Keh went past—awaiting Keh bayonets at their withered throats, the discoveries of tunnel entrances, the rapes after Keh had posed for the pictorials. A French still-photographer (whom Quinn contacted three decades later) fluked just such a bayonet-at-the-throat threat to an old woman in the background of one of these General-Keh-charging-the-enemy pictures earlier that year; blown up, it hung on his study wall in Paris for years, until his shrewish wife tossed it into the Avenue Foch during an argument on women's rights.

Keh also tossed out what displeased him: he was building an image for foreign consumption that he parlayed eventually into a fortune in the sixties and early seventies; inessentials did not interest him. The Civil War itself, but for this, was an inessential. His grasp of strategy was lamentable, and his knowledge of military history worse; highly eclectic, he stole from the twenties and thirties only what could clothe his grandiose presence (as he saw it) in the forties. The result was a ragbag of contradictions: he stuck on bits of one warlord here, another there, secure in the knowledge that Chiang—who had feared and manipulated all those very warlords—would always love him as a son. Both knew then, apparently, that he was more valuable to Chiang when he was wearing the disguise of Chiang's enemies.

Quinn boned up meticulously in later life on Keh's military career—and also that of Shiozawa, Keh's Japanese bodyguard through the Civil War from 1946 on. Keh had served briefly as a young captain with a Chinese Nationalist division in Burma during the Second World War. He had distinguished himself there mainly with his sexual excesses, and he had almost certainly collaborated with the Japanese during his more comfortable "war" in China.

Shiozawa, in fact, seemed to be living proof of this; he had joined Keh in Shanghai late in 1945 after only brief repatriation to Japan, and they had been on opposing fronts in China for some time before that during the global conflict. Shiozawa was a big burly man, and although he was already approaching middle age in 1948 (when Quinn encountered him) he was the main driving force behind Keh. He had a huge, pockmarked face and bare spots as large as coins in the stubble of his head. He also had an even larger blood lust than Keh.

But Shiozawa was not merely a killer: it was he who suggested the symbol for Keh's division—a white horse. He probably borrowed this idea from one of his old Second World War commanders: a Japanese general who rode a white horse into battle in New Guinea (and drowned ingloriously in a river for the Emperor, who confined his own outings to prudent canters in his private park in Tokyo). If so, Shiozawa did not pass on this postscript to Keh, but he *did* commandeer a white horse for him—inferior as it was. And it delighted Keh: it was so fat that he knew it could not throw him in a fit.

Once he had the horse, Keh began to build a pastiche of other military figures around him. He pictured himself secretly in some moods as Chang Hsueh-liang, the "Young Marshal" of Manchuria, who had kidnaped Chiang Kai-shek in the Sian incident in 1936 (and who later became Chiang's pampered slave). He also strutted in the mighty footsteps of the "Christian General," Feng Yu-hsiang: another warlord enemy of Chiang's who was such an uncanny forerunner in word, deed, and appearance of Mao Tse-tung (and who died mysteriously on a Russian ship in 1948). Keh was not a patch on Feng, but he borrowed some of his maxims, and he even baptized his troops with a firehose one bitter morning in blatant emulation of Feng—a ceremony that reduced the White Horse Division's limited effectiveness that day to zero; eight men died later of pneumonia. But he was Chiang's man, through and through: a fellow Methodist, of sorts, on the make.

His success was assured: his father, a corrupt Shanghai merchant, had helped organize the massacre of the Shanghai Communists in 1927, cementing Chiang's superiority in the Kuomintang and clinching a successful career for the younger Keh.

On that day in 1948, however, the end for Chiang was approaching fast. He had lost more than 2,600,000 men in the two years since mid-1946: the phrase "wiped out," which Europeans assumed to be killed or wounded, covered massive Nationalist defections. Nationalist and Communist emissaries arranged the surrenders in teashops while the Nationalists pledged new Stalingrads—and salted away two billion U.S. dollars in private deposits in American banks.

Manchuria and North China were toppling, with Central and South China to follow; Truman's shattering victory over Dewey, coinciding so symbolically with the surrender of Mukden, was about to end last-ditch Nationalist hopes of a massive American intervention that could save their necks.

The war now was lost—it had been lost since 1947. And all of that meant to General Keh only that the time to make his fortune was running out. Which was why he sat on his small white stallion that day in the village of Hua-yin, Shensi, staring up at the sacred mountain of Hua-shan.

That was the first time that Quinn, jumping from a battered UNRRA truck, had ever seen him. He wished later that he had never set eyes on him, for Keh and China were to shadow him as long as he lived: shadows that stretched far into the future over his cottage on West Ridge where he spent so many lonely years reading and remembering.

QUINN'S STEAMER DROPPED anchor in the oily green harbor of Hong Kong about four months before he met Keh in 1948. He was eighteen then, and his top lip, he remembered, had swollen after an insect bite. He was practising secret smiles in his cabin mirror to exercise the flesh (One: Soldier Courage. Two: Gay Dog. Three: Wry Grin. Four: Sardonic) when an unexpected movement outside the porthole attracted him. A sturdy Chinese woman in black pajamas was standing in a sampan only an arm's length away. Her legs were braced apart, and she was rising and falling on the swell as the water sucked and slapped at the hull of the ship, her black garb stirring him as the sensible black bloomers of his female classmates had electrified him only two years before at Wongbok High School. He remembered her years later when he saw the first photographs of Communist propaganda posters looming above the city streets of the New China: giant females in righteous overalls exhorting their scurrying little sisters to storm the sterile heights of industrial production. Her sexuality trailed faintly around their blocky thighs, as discredited as the final whiffs of Chiang's cordite.

Quinn's parents traveled down second-class from Wongbok to see him leave Sydney in 1948: a family friend drove them all to the wharf in a Cadbury's Chocolate van that comfortably enclosed his father's wheelchair. The young Quinn grinned to himself, trundling through the early-morning streets, at the appropriate manner of his exit: "Soft-Centered Hero Departs for Asia." His mother rode in the front seat while he traveled with his father in the scented gloom of the interior, stealthily bracing his legs to stop the wheelchair in case it should slide toward him while rounding corners.

It was a bitter irony, that, he recalled later, when he stacked it up against the grudging snippets that his righteous mother had let slip of his father's wild youth: the bush timber cutter and horse breaker and occasional tent boxer who had stormed Gallipoli; the Catholic larrikin who had been excommunicated (that word! that unspeakable perversion which had whispered through his childhood!) after some devilish vandalism in a church behind the lines in France; the infantryman who had been badly wounded at Pozieres and gassed an hour later. His father had never spoken of this, but Quinn had absorbed him by osmosis— attuned to a silence that his mother (although she had ensured that he was Church of England, like her) could not share. And his father and he had absorbed the last of these silences in that van, clinging gratefully to trivia while the unspoken depths of their love yawned beneath them. Conversation with his father was like walking along the beams of a half-built house.

"You sure you're all right, then?" his father asked for the third time on the wharf. "I can always send a quid or two if you run into trouble."

"I'll be all right, thanks," he said. (What are you going to do? Sell the wheelchair?) "Good day to sail," speaking tightly at the sun.

"I can always raise a quid or two," his father repeated, and they stared carefully away from each other, balancing on the beams of their emptiness, while his mother hurried off to buy streamers. But already he was doubting the absurd fantasies that his father's example had inspired in him: the infantryman charging over no-man's-land with a picturesque bandage around his head (his throat bursting with a choking exhilaration to kill); the guerrilla jogging downhill to the Bolero with a flower stuck in his rifle.

His life, he was beginning to suspect, was to be a process of establishing what he was not—as his mother had sensibly warned him. And yet the juvenile dream of courage persisted like sexuality; the need to prove himself, as his father had done, remained dominant. Doubt, surely, was weakness.

LOOKING BACK, HE realized that this first journey to Asia was poor farce: a university dropout, imbued with the battle ethic, creeping slowly in the wake of the Second World War troopships to finish off the Yellow Peril. He went to China because it was staging a military struggle, and an Old China Hand in the reading room of the *Star*, which he had joined after leaving university, had arranged a job for him in Hong Kong on the *Clarion* (where that year he met Lancelot Ming for the first time). And so Quinn's ship crawled north for three weeks while he hunched over the mad fish-skitter of its wake, watching the weary steeplechase of the ocean rollers, willing the bloodshed to keep flowing until he could get in for his share. He counted porpoises and flying fish and floating logs while his father began counting his last months; they never met again. A letter from his mother awaited him at Manila, the first port of call: "I'm still tugging on to my streamer. Dad was blow-blow-blowing his nose . . . I've started reading some lovely books on China—*In a Shantung Garden* is one of them. So pretty . . ."

Hong Kong, jammed with refugees from China, was not pretty. He checked into the European Hostel in the British Colony's Kowloon slice of the China mainland; it was there that he first met Tony Doyle. Doyle lived two rooms down the corridor from him on the second floor; he managed a small import-export agency on Hong Kong Island for General Keh—the first time Quinn had heard the name.

Keh was establishing the basis of his business empire in Hong Kong as he prepared to withdraw his White Horse Nationalist Division troops from Northern and Central China; he spent almost as much time courting the Hong Kong British for business favors as he did in exasperating his American military advisers in Nanking, who were attempting to instill in him the quaint notion of the lightning counterattack. Doyle used to chuckle about Keh's devious business and military stratagems in those days, but then all of Doyle's life had degenerated into a bitter joke by then. He was an Australian who had fought in Greece and Crete as an AIF Sixth Division sergeant in the Second World War (and escaped from a POW camp in Germany); he regarded the war over the border, in which no British troops were engaged, as little more than a comic-opera sideshow. Inevitably, Quinn grew to revere him.

He never forgot the first time he saw Doyle at the hostel one evening after dinner. He wandered into the first-floor reading room: a little jungle of bamboo chairs and potted palms that screened shelves of mildewed books. Framed illustrations of elegantly posed British officers of the eighteenth and nineteenth centuries hung on the walls, and tattered copies of *Punch* were strewn on low glass-topped tables studded with ashtrays advertising Johnny Walker whisky. Doyle was flicking impatiently through a *Punch*, and—when he glanced up from this thicket of bamboo and palm—he transfixed Quinn with the pale gleaming eyes of a crouching tiger. Those eyes had burned into the nation's race memory from a thousand fading photographs of the boxer Les Darcy in a thousand Australian bars; they glittered with the empty cruelty of the golden eagle on the Church of England pulpit in Wongbok: the hard-chip Australian eyes of drought and war and Depression, instantly recognizable until the soft silt-browns of Asia and the Mediterranean began washing over the old gray-green Anglo-Irish quartz in the fifties and sixties.

"G-day, chum," Doyle said, sticking out a hand. "Tony Doyle." And yet even then Quinn sensed the brittle emptiness in him, the vast windy gaps beneath his surface certitude. Meeting Doyle was like coming face to face with his own stricken continent.

They talked for an hour that night—not that many words were exchanged; Doyle left him dangling in voids. But Doyle did reveal something unwittingly—or so it seemed, anyway. He must have needed company badly that night, for he was rarely as loquacious again. He talked of his halcyon days, as he called them, in Sydney's northern beach suburbs.

"Cocky young pup I was before I got tangled up in the war," he admitted. "Won every fight I had; open surf race champion at Freshwater two years running . . ."

"I got my Bronze up the North Coast. They dragged me in just before I drowned," confessed Quinn. "I think the bastards took pity on me."

Doyle grinned. "Jeez, I got pissed the night I got mine—we had an eighteen gallon keg. Declared on the whole bloody Collaroy mob. Hit-hit; I was pretty fit then."

And later: "The northern beaches—playground of the gods," he declared grandly—there was always something of the snob, strangely, in Doyle; obviously he had been forced to use whatever lowly material was at hand to elevate his status.

48

"The women—used to knock 'em off with sticks! A couple of mates and myself—the 'Three Men in Top Hats,' they called us. Down the Corso in Manly every Friday night. Top hats, coats, ties, no shirts. Up into French's Forest with the grog!"

"You come from around there originally?" Quinn asked, and Doyle's face began to harden.

"No, southern beaches," he said.

"Southern beaches." Quinn echoed politely. "Where abouts?"

"Engadine," Doyle said at last, and it was the final way he said it, the shutter snapping down, that made Quinn guess where Doyle had been living at Engadine. Boys' Town.

"COULDN'T TAKE AUSTRALIA again when I got back," Doyle said one morning. "Threw a party with an eighteen gallon keg and that was it."

He was scribbling with a large blue pencil in his cluttered office on the Island; piles of invoices and bills of lading around him were yellow around the edges.

"Bumff," he said. "Get through this little lot, and I'm off." Plates of dried curry and rice on a shelf, empty beer bottles in the wastebasket. Beads of perspiration on his face.

"You mean you left straightaway?" Quinn was puzzled; where had Doyle got his training? He was the most unbusinesslike businessman he had ever seen.

"Not straightaway." Doyle folded an invoice into a rough dart and aimed it toward an outer office. "Another one, Wong!" he called as it dropped to the floor.

"Ran a little country pub with a couple of mates for a few months, but they drank all the profits. Got out of that and got this old blue Essex. Started a bit of carrying."

He chuckled. "Demon Doyle's Deliveries. This big red devil on the side on roller skates—bird I knew did it for me. Made a quid for a while."

"What happened?"

"Diff. Went. Some cunt had filled it with bananas." His Chinese assistant picked up the invoice and stooped out, smiling faintly.

"Just got down to Darling Harbor when—kerfut! Didn't have the brass to fix it so I left it there." He tugged at a stuck drawer, slid his hand inside, and prized out a chopstick.

"You mean you lost all your money?"

Doyle speared the chopstick into the wastebasket. "I had twenty quid to my name. Made a fortune playing poker when I was a POW but couldn't collect my bets. Turned out for the best though." He began dashing entries into a ledger.

Quinn gazed around Doyle's forlorn little foothold in the business world; a storeroom behind him was jammed with packing cases and cartons that spilled straw and paper out into Doyle's office. The broken blue Essex with the red devil wasn't far behind. "In what way, for the best?"

"All my mates getting spliced, dropping off like flies. Wives didn't want to know you." He closed the ledger and tossed it aside.

"Anyway, I'm drinking down in Darling Harbor, wondering if some cunt wants to buy the truck for scrap, when I meet this old Sixth Divvy bloke who fixes me up as a ship's carpenter. Third trip here I signed off."

"So how did you get into the import business?"

"That's another story," Doyle said. "Bullshit beats brains," grinning cockily among the yellowing pillars of paper, the packing cases and cartons where his life already was spilling out.

IT WAS DOYLE who introduced him to The Vienna Restaurant on the Island; eventually he even arranged for him—despite clipped misgivings—to join Keh's troops at the front. "Clipped" was the word for Doyle: he fired a verbal shorthand over the abyss that divided him from his fellows; affection was an exasperated snarl or a dry chuckle, hard back in his throat, which he suppressed almost the instant it began. He was not tall but solid and always on the attack: the natural leader at every bar counter. And yet he was the most *alone* man whom Quinn had ever met. They sat on many evenings over the red-and-white checked cloths in The Vienna, divided by the immensity of the Second World War. Doyle, he realized later, had lived his life, whereas his was just beginning.

Thirty-odd years later, up on West Ridge, why had it all come back so clearly, driving him to return? Perhaps it was because The Vienna was not only where his Hong Kong life really began in those days: it was where his life had begun as an adult. The Vienna was a small haven for Europeans in a cobbled lane jammed with Chinese stalls near the Island waterfront. Outside, cubes of barbecued pork and glazed duck glistened as if varnished under fierce acetylene lamps near a lurid Taoist temple; cheap Chinese magazines were spread in the pools of harsh light, and poles of washing stuck out from tiny cluttered balconies above them in a ragged archway that concealed the sky. Inside, the clientele formed a *Debrett* of the defeated.

The restaurant was an evening hangout for mainly European bachelors who were delaying the cold coffin of the single bed; a few retired police and customs officials who had been East too long to return to the alien English winter; one or two local stringers for the London dailies, who had budded on little journals in the English provinces, and who hoped now for a few extra pounds (and instant flowering) with late Civil War disasters lobbed into Fleet Street; occasional British Army officers squiring plain nursing sisters fit only for the ranks at Home; the odd Westernized Chinese warming a European business contact slowly over minute steak.

In there one night, Doyle told him how he had met Keh a few weeks after arriving in Hong Kong. The old Doyle luck, it was, he said; he always turned up trumps.

"Broke again when I signed off," he said. "Had a run-in with this big South African engineer on board. Nailed the cunt, but I knew him and his mates'd get me on the way back. Wound up at the old Empire Hotel over in Kowloon my first night. Landed on my bloody feet.

"Big Vera's there. Prostitute. Wouldn't touch her with a barge pole, but she's straight as a die. Getting a hard time because she's not pulling in any business. I threaten to pull off this Chinese clown's head. They want to kick her out of her room there.

"Anyway, I round up a few of the Buffs and offer a cut rate and soon she's going like a house on fire. She stakes me to get my room in the hostel."

"The Buffs," Quinn murmured. "My old man used to like the Buffs."

Doyle signaled for more beers; other men's wars were as far beyond his ken as Doyle's war was to Quinn. With no reality to share, they were already doomed to banter, banality; more skeletal scaffolding with no roof, no floor.

"Couple of weeks later," Doyle said, "I'm in the officers' mess with the Buffs. By this time I'm practically running the whole box and dice. They waltz in with this little Chinese general they've discovered—he's doing card tricks. I show him two or three he doesn't know and before you know it he's hired me to run his business . . ."

QUINN OFTEN PICTURED The Vienna in later years, for what it was worth. Gus, the proprietor, was an honest little Austrian Jew, twice-displaced (Vienna-Shanghai, 1938; Shanghai-Hong Kong, 1948); he retired in 1974 to an old family villa beside the lake at Traunkirchen, in upper Austria; Quinn traced him there in the seventies, and they exchanged several letters. Gus by then was trembling to the clashing rhythms of Beethoven and multiple sclerosis, with a former Nazi neighbor's BMW motorcycle (which Gus had stolen in 1937 because the swastika painted on the headlamp offended him) still buried guiltily in his garden. But in 1948 he was at the peak of his powers: almond eyes gleaming, bald head shining, he liked to dart about the room in endless quest of the minutiae of service—which included a long, gray diseased dragon of beggars who lined up in the laneway each night. Gus used to detach Small Boy, the youngest waiter, to attend to them: at eleven o'clock each night Small Boy stood on the steps to feed the dragon with leftover bread heaped in a sagging tablecloth. Chinese fingers scrabbled silently in the laneway outside, while the dislocated personalities inside sat lamenting their exile; grief, like a full belly, was also a European luxury.

The Colony was the final poison port for the eccentric Old China Hands who were grumbling out of China before the Communist advance, and most of them bobbed up briefly at The Vienna before the tide of history swept them away forever. Occasionally a distinguished visitor entered. Ian Morrison of *The Times* appeared once: the classic Rupert Brooke adventurer with a handsome, tanned face, fringed satchel over his shoulder, blue eyes burning beautifully—Han Suyin's many-splendored lover, destined to be shattered like a priceless vase when a jeep hit a land mine in Korea. But the rest of them were the also-rans of life at best, plus a collection of demented exiles who had lost touch with reality and now spent their nights alone.

Andrew Veitch and Albert Porter were probably the sanest of them; Quinn met them both for the first time at Doyle's table one

52

night. Veitch, who was then with British Army Intelligence, was a local-born Scot with a dash of Portuguese: a lean, lugubrious bachelor with keen gray eyes and dour Lowland features, but with the distant lilt of Lisbon in his voice. He wore tweedy sports clothes—his usual uniform, whatever the weather—and he sipped whisky rapidly.

Porter was a lowly official in the Hong Kong government service, and he was on the slide even then—although he did not know that anybody had noticed. He was the son of a Cornish sea captain and a Chinese woman who had died after giving birth to Porter's sister Winifred: a plump roue with glossy black hair that he drenched lovingly with brilliantine—for he had something of a reputation then as a minor Don Ameche (his idol) in local amateur theatricals. The cuffs of his glistening white sharkskin suits were always greasy; he was forever straightening them and running his hands over his head as his eyes wandered (like Veitch's) for women.

Doyle was shaking a small bottle of San Miguel over his glass when Quinn joined them that evening; Quinn remembered it very clearly. "Bullshit!" Doyle snapped, brassing it out.

"Doyle, you have my solemn word," Veitch was remonstrating in his pedantic way. "Beneath a koko tree in Rangoon. Near the Strand Hotel." And he bumped down his whisky glass hurriedly, another memory striking him. "The orchestra was playing a Strauss waltz."

"Strauss assholes!" Doyle snarled, waving for a menu. "Keh couldn't hit a barn door at five paces."

"Well, I am telling you, Doyle. I was there," Veitch protested. "This soldier—Chinese chappie—couldn't start Keh's transport, and so he just shot him. Under the koko tree."

"You've been pulling your koko tree," Doyle said, but his voice wavered. "Boy! *Fidi*, uh?" He turned to Veitch: "When are you springing another party?"

"Soon." Veitch rolled his glass between his long fingers—a craftsman's fingers. Exiled from women during the war in Burma, he had carved a tiny fleet of Portuguese caravels; now his hands soothed a procession of one-night lovers (and occasionally his fiery Eurasian mistress). "Very soon," Veitch said. "I am inviting only top-drawer women. The cream of the crop."

"Cream of the fucking dregs," Doyle chuckled, but it was at one

53

of Veitch's parties, eventually, that he met the upright English girl he married. He ordered a meal and then drove home his attack—turning apparent defeat over Keh into an offensive on liquor. "You right for grog this time? Man nearly died of thirst last time."

"Of course." Veitch waved a hand grandly. "I am always 'right for grog,' as you put it. You know that."

Porter stirred, now that the dangerous subject of Keh was out of the way. "I shall bring some new dance records," he promised. For he loved to dance then, twirling partners for hours until the brilliantine trickled from his sticky hair onto the collars of his crisp white suits; his big moon-face flung back, straining for the light quips of his American idol in English almost as stilted as Veitch's. "I may also bring a new partner if she arrives on time. Quite important, from Home," and he fiddled absently with a fair facsimile of an old school tie.

"Don't give us that shit!" Doyle barked, and Quinn felt sorry for Porter, for they were all phoneys, to some extent, in a cockpit crammed with phoneys. But Doyle uttered a brutal truth later after Porter had swayed off into the night. "Poor bastard," he said. "He copped it in the eyes."

That phrase, and Veitch's accusation against Keh, insured that he remembered that otherwise undistinguished evening. But Quinn's eyes, meanwhile, were gazing toward the entrance of the restaurant, where romance and adventure might enter where the beggars could not—love and courage bursting above him like star shells; exalting him, magnifying him, enriching him!

Hong Kong, unfortunately, did not have too much love to spare at that time, and the war, compressed neatly into the headlines of the *South China Morning Post* and the *Clarion*, was almost as distant as if he had been back in Australia. He chafed in this asylum within an asylum, yearning for escape from the exiles around him who had left the best of their lives behind them while he still fretted to make his beginning.

ONCE QUINN WENT down to the Kowloon docks with Doyle before starting work at the *Clarion*. Doyle was checking one of Keh's consignments from Bangkok.

"Know anything about ornaments?" Doyle asked him. They

stood beside the rusting side of a freighter; a greasy garland of Lascars hung from the prow, chipping.

"Not much," Quinn admitted. "Ferns in helmets. Mulga wood ashtrays. The odd plate. That's about all we had."

"Dead fucking loss you are," Doyle murmured. He watched a thick rope sling jerking down toward the wharf, the coolies swarming around as it descended.

"We also had a porcelain lady with a parasol. Terrific little ankles. I used to draw her naked."

"Shut up," Doyle said. He swaggered forward and tapped a packing case in the sling with his umbrella. "Drop this," he barked, "and I'll have your guts for neckties."

He came back and stood beside Quinn. "Teak Buddhas," he said. "Coals to Newcastle." He checked a clipboard list. "Buffalo horn salad servers with silver handles. Who wants 'em?"

"I don't know," Quinn said. "You're importing them."

"Keh's importing 'em. I'm OC Operations." He bristled with a sort of frustration. "Storeroom's jammed with the bloody stuff." And he turned and looked at the Customs Office behind them. "These bastards don't even check 'em."

"Maybe there's gold in them," Quinn said. "Precious jewels, tiny nude women . . ."

Doyle gave him a queer look. "Wong's always ratting around in the storeroom" he said, half to himself. "Bastard won't go home . . ."

THEY WERE CERTAINLY a strange lot those days in The Vienna: Doyle joked once that if Gus replaced his restaurant sign he could go straight into the madhouse business with his patients already on the premises. It was odd, Quinn often reflected, how he had never forgotten them all, and how, perversely, he had even come to value them as he grew older.

Veitch and Porter were comparatively normal. They merely sublimated the social blemish of mixed birth in Portuguese and Chinese bedmates—although Porter even then was getting drunk and turning over rickshaws.

Both Veitch and Porter measured their morality in spare cash; their time was a dull trough between ejaculations; women who brushed past them in The Vienna triggered an instant gleam in their eyes, like the lights of wreckers luring pretty ships for plunder. Each night Quinn watched their banal ritual of conquest while the starving dragon lay outside in the alley. Veitch recording his running expenses on paper napkins before transferring the totals to a small black diary; Porter stealthily counting his money beneath the cloth before departing for imaginary assignations with imaginary high-born beauties from Home. But they were models of decorum compared with the rest.

DOYLE, FOR INSTANCE, led a goat into the Hong Kong Cricket Club on Anzac Day; the most ancient members watched, scandalized, but he was too formidable to tackle when on the crest of a binge. British troops out in the New Territories were intensifying their training for the remote possibility of an eventual Communist land attack; the last of the Colony's tired old Spitfires were dropping, one by one, into the sea. And Doyle's war, too, had finished.

"Tie him there," he instructed a waiter, who delicately tethered the goat to a pillar. Then he ordered a beer and chuckled as two crusty old gentlemen puffed out into the open air with their pink gins. "I've got an idea," he said.

The giant Rushton entered, a craggy Yorkshireman who had joined the Hong Kong Police Force after a bloody period with the Palestine Police. A grim man (he'd tired of pouring sugar into bags in a little corner shop in Bradford and wound up pouring his colleagues into larger bags in Palestine), he was a beloved friend of Doyle's. He was carrying his saxophone, a relic of his days with a boys' silver band in Bradford; later, quite drunk, for small bets, he'd play strangled requests: "Name a song! Any song!" and usually lose—Jewish terrorists had shattered his education in the hit parades. Now he laid the saxophone on the bar and glared at the goat, which promptly defecated on the floor.

A waiter swooped with a brush and tray, but Doyle gripped his wrist as he was hurrying out with the droppings. "I'll fix that!" he snapped, and he disappeared into the kitchen with the tray.

The old male joke; he emerged with a plate filled with sandwiches, cut into dainty triangular slices. "Shark Guts'll be along soon," he explained, placing the plate on the bar by his elbow.

Shark Guts rolled in half an hour later: a big-bellied Australian marine engineer who ate anything within reach of his brawny arms. He joined them, and it all went as Doyle, poker-faced, had planned.

He was reminiscing about a girlfriend he had had while he was on leave in England when he broke off; Shark Guts had just emptied the plate.

"How were the sandwiches, Shark Guts?" he asked casually—one of Quinn's happier, if crude, memories of Doyle.

"Aw," said Shark Guts, reflectively picking at a crevice between two teeth, "bit gritty."

And Rushton began to shake with long, slow, mournful laughter. Aw, bit gritty; that went the rounds of the bars.

LANCELOT MING USED to join them sometimes at The Vienna in the pink suits and loud ties that he had adopted as his trademarks—squealing stories of outrageous sexual escapades with never less than two or three women the night before.

It may have been Doyle who introduced Ming to Keh; he didn't know, and it didn't matter now. And it was the others, anyway, who interested him more at the time because they were beyond his reach (just as Doyle was beyond his reach); it was them he scribbled about innocently in his diaries before he began recording Keh's murderous excesses later that year in China. They were the cheap setting, he supposed later, for the paste jewel of Doyle that he came to treasure; the memories in middle age that only he valued as he sought to inject new meaning and purpose into his life.

For they never really left him after that, all those failures and madmen. He had brought them to live with him up on West Ridge: mental snapshots that never quite bleached away.

THERE WAS, FOR instance—what was his name? Anderssen! The old Swede who used to sit in his favorite corner near the restaurant kitchen, drawing diagrams of the assassination of Gustav III at a masquerade ball in the Stockholm Opera House in 1792. When he got to the actual murder—"Good evening, fair mask!" declared a black-masked assassin, tapping the king on the shoulder to identify him—he'd order Benedictine and deploy troops to round up the killers. What historian had ever recorded him?

Who cared about No Name, the Tartar with the mysterious background, who drifted down from Manchuria and danced on the Vienna tables until fishermen found him floating off Shaukiwan one morning with a bullet in the back of his head? And Riboud, the French soldier-diplomat (killed later in Indochina); a Japanese officer was about to behead him in Hong Kong in 1941 when Riboud discovered that they both loved Masefield. Riboud used to bring down the house in the restaurant when he sprang up and recited "Sea Fever" with a hissing Japanese accent.

Who remembered poor loveless young Greyville, of the Hong Kong and Shanghai Bank, who had bowled one season for Essex and died of leukemia before he lost his acne? Who remembered Williams—White Water Williams, because he was so dangerous; the trigger-tempered young third mate on the Shanghai run who boasted of a splendid education at Eton (hand over heart, eyes upraised, reciting *"Floreat Etona, et gens togata . . ."*), unaware that a peripatetic friend had spread the real news: Williams had been expelled from a red brick secondary school in Leicester, where his father (boozed every Saturday, bellowing for Leicester City at Filbert Street) had terrorized him in a council-built semi.

And there was Grantham, dear handsome old Grantham, who dropped in sometimes on his way home from his little passport studio to a mysterious hovel in Kowloon, where he spoke with affection to rats; Grantham was leading a British patrol one night in Flanders when a flare went up, and he and a German officer (both pointing pistols) pretended they did not see each other; Grantham was dead for a week in Kowloon before the police forced open his door, and who cared any more about him?

Quinn MM cared—up to a point. He still remembered them all up on West Ridge, where he riffled through his old diaries the night he posted the letters, puzzling over the drunken, lonely entries he had made so long ago. And yet none of them mattered so very much to him, if the truth were known; they inhabited the periphery of his mind, just as they had inhabited the margins around Doyle's table in The Vienna.

It was only Doyle who still called to him with any strength from the pages, like a drowning man beyond the last dark line of breakers; Doyle flinging down his ugly bone-necklace of phrases in bars and restaurants: "I could eat a dead dog with sore eyes . . .

You wouldn't know shit from clay . . . You wouldn't know if your asshole was punch-bored or counter-sunk . . ." Doyle insisting quietly beneath his crudity, long after they had laid him to rest in the old Colonial Cemetery in the fifties: "Remember me, chum. Don't let me down."

"WHEN'S KEH GOING to drop back to Hong Kong?" Quinn asked Doyle as they walked late one evening from The Vienna down to the Star Ferry wharf. Around them, the night murmured with beggars.

"Soon as the fighting gets too close. That division of his couldn't beat time."

Black shapes were detaching themselves from the darkness. A prostitute flared like a garish orchid in a wall crevice, hissing as they approached.

"Getting a bit bored with the *Clarion*," Quinn said carefully. "I thought I might do a few lone charges at the foe."

Doyle laughed, raising his umbrella with mock menace at an old woman who tugged at his coat. "Pissed myself putting on a counterattack once near Mount Olympus. Took the mob through a river so they wouldn't twig." He shot an amused sideways glance at Quinn. "You'd shit yourself."

"I'd fall in manure," Quinn protested. "Anyway, I'd find out. Where's Keh's division now?"

"Shensi," Doyle said. "Asshole of the world." Everywhere except in his immediate vicinity was the asshole of the world; alien places spelled danger, discomfort.

"I've got enough money to get up there and last a while. Just to have a look. Do you think you could fix it for me?"

"Fix what?" Doyle was serious now. "Look, the Communists aren't mucking around. They'll go through China like a packet of salts. I don't want to be writing any letters to your old man."

"I'll be a distant observer. And you said yourself that Keh's not going to get mixed up in anything too hot."

Doyle walked on in silence. "Keh's a wily bastard," he said. "Best to stay clear of him. I'm beginning to think he's not the full quid."

"Who is? Look, I'm going bloody mad in this place. I just want to get out for a few weeks."

They crossed the road to the ferry wharf. "Could you contact him? See if I could go up there for a while?"

Doyle stopped, digging for change. "All right. I'll see what I can do. On one condition."

"Anything you say."

"Get in and out quick. He's bad news. Bastard's up to something, and I don't know what."

"What sort of thing?" Quinn asked, but Doyle would say no more. Keh's heroin dealings became obvious later, but they didn't know then: both of them were innocents in their separate ways.

"COME AND HAVE a drink," Doyle said late one night, after rapping on the door of Quinn's room in the hostel, and they walked to a small European-run bar on Nathan Road.

Doyle was more tense than usual—but not shaken enough to reveal what evidently was beginning to trouble him. More surprising, he was cold sober.

"First one today," he said, lifting his glass.

"Been working?"

"Checking another shipment. Just in from Bangkok . . . I should have stayed in the Army."

"But then you lacked my incredible daring," Quinn said. "I remember outside Benghazi—or was it Pozières? Anyway . . ."

"Shut up!" Doyle snapped. "Enough fucking clowns without you."

"No really!" Quinn protested. "Often I'd be sitting in my trench, as calm as you please, humming a little tune, minding my own business, but cunning, see? I'd know what they were thinking: 'When's he going to try his next lone charge over no-man's-land?' So I'd put on the kettle, do a little flick here and there with the tea towel, and then—bang!—I'd be over the top, knees pumping high, the terrified Krauts fleeing everywhere. 'The white Gurkha!' they'd be screaming. 'The white Gurkha!' and then I'd be in among them with the cold steel."

"Belt up!" Doyle ordered. "You're over the crest."

But he had nothing serious of his own to add, beyond small talk; if he had intended to confide in Quinn that night, he seemed to have decided against it.

Only later, going home, he clapped Quinn firmly on the

shoulder as they were about to cross a road. "You're no threat to any cunt," he said softly. "You'll be all right."

And a few minutes later he paused at the door of his room. "You were right about that stuff from Bangkok."

"What do you mean?"

"Bastards are hollow," he said and closed his door.

QUINN DID NOT have to work too hard at the *Clarion*, which was owned by a retired British colonel. It was a marvel, with its polyglot staff of incompetents, that it ever came out at all. The latest jokes about the colonel and his local rag went the rounds of the bars every week: the colonel telephoning for a batman to report to his bungalow when he wanted a messenger to come to his hotel; the colonel stuffing menus—anything!—down the copy chute when he was drunk; the colonel spluttering with rage when his Chinese compositors placed a reference to Leopold III in the obituary column because they thought that he was "Ill" (and that was the same as dead); the colonel with his dotty old brain still anchored in twenties-India, just as Quinn's even then was fastening on forties-China. Hong Kong on the colonel's level was a boozy comic strip; only Doyle's brittle self-reliance seemed to embody any semblance of dignity.

Years later, he realized that he should have tried harder to break open this fatal carapace that had locked Doyle in such isolation; he had attempted to melt Doyle with jokes, and that was not enough. He even dreamed about Doyle one night at the hostel. Doyle was a dark tower; he joked at his front door, hoping for a chink of light at a tall window above—the twinkle of an eye, to show that he had been observed. He told Doyle this dream briefly (wrapping it in obscenities to make the confession palatable), and Doyle stirred uncomfortably. "Best fix you up with a little something," he said. He was a pragmatic man, Doyle; eight words was the average length of a Doyle delivery.

And so it was Doyle who arranged both his first woman and his first war: he would always owe him, in grim jest, for those. He would always owe him for accelerating his journey toward manhood, for it seemed self-evident then that the Gorgons of sex and violence guarded the path up into his eventual fulfillment; only by conquering them could the male of the species hope to win peace.

Life, meanwhile, was bedlam; his brain was cocked to counter each beggar, each rickshaw puller, each prostitute as he jostled toward romantic love and the mutilation of war, unaware of the ambivalence in his desires; hoping only that here at last was the place where he might leave his old self crumpled behind him like a discarded suit; all his doubts and fears and indecisions heaped up behind him forever: the lonely boring hours, the staring at faces in crowds for a soul mate, the shadow of the wheelchair by the orange tree of his childhood.

OFTEN WHEN THE Vienna was more depressing than usual, Quinn and Doyle used to end the night at the Empire Hotel, a sort of bolt-hole for the floating European male population—after calling in on the way to a Police mess where Rushton then presided. A fearsome man, Rushton: sometimes he playfully pointed his revolver at Doyle when Doyle announced his intention of leaving (although Doyle always kept walking).

Walking? "Swaggering" was a more accurate description, now he came to think about it; Doyle rolled slightly, taking quick little steps and brandishing a green oiled-paper Chinese umbrella as if he could not get used to moving without a rifle. He never had got to the essence of Doyle; Doyle's actions were always unpredictable, just as he had blown into Hong Kong on a whim and fluked his job in Keh's little empire—no doubt because Keh wanted a minor front man who could bolster his image with the British military. Poor, enigmatic, unpredictable Doyle: his life seemed to have begun when he was fully grown.

Doyle showed his unpredictability at the Empire one night. Very unimportant persons from most of the white nations on the globe were jamming the tables in a vast first-floor room: British soldiers from their camps in the New Territories, American and Australian airline crews, Scandinavian seamen, and Canadian adventurers, even a young German deserter from the French Foreign Legion in Indochina. Many of them were there for prostitutes, but most merely to drink and to talk; there was no music, no entertainment. They crouched over the tables in a haze of cigarette smoke, casually watching the lines of Chinese prostitutes who drifted in after midnight—pockmarks powdered, lizard-bodies rested, glossy handbags dangling from their brittle wrists. Some of the prostitutes joined men they knew and sat patiently by their elbows while the men ignored them; others arranged themselves like cheap art around the walls. Large fans writhed from side to side in the corners; when the waiters in grubby white coats began switching them off, everybody knew that it was approaching time to move on to the last dive of the night. They were switching them off when the first incident occurred.

A drink-maddened little Scottish soldier slapped Doyle's face twice and taunted him to fight. Doyle remained rock-hard in his chair. "I leave fighting to my dog," he said, and at last the Scot stumbled away, slurring his contempt. It was then that Doyle began to laugh: a dry, terrible laugh as a thin stream of blood trickled from his lips. He flicked the blood with one finger into his beer.

Ten minutes later a more sickening scene occurred—this time when Doyle went to the aid of the Empire's resident madman, who was also, ironically, a Scot. And Christ, what did it matter now? He was only another loser in the Quinn gallery of losers; couldn't he ever forget? But there was an elderly man there who always sat alone, his bubble-bright eyes glistening wildly as he sang snatches of arias with one hand cupped to his ear, or declaimed fragments of philosophy that were tainted with the decay of his reason.

He was shouting questions for himself this night amid the hubbub around him; he never addressed anyone else, and nobody ever spoke to him. "What is a bodyless head?" he cried. "Or a headless bod? Take it away! Take it away! All human flesh smells! You are what you are! You cannot make it go further!" Words limned with the phosphorescence of his own passing.

And then he stood up. "Look at me!" he cried. "Arrayed in white robes! And who the hell cares?" And sweeping out one arm, he knocked over a bottle of beer, which splashed the shoe of a large German who sat at the next table with two friends and the young deserter.

The German heaved himself up and stood over the ancient Scot. "Who ask you to cry out?" he demanded.

"That man there asked me," the Scot replied, pointing at an empty chair beside him.

The German then took a small bottle of Carlsberg from his table and emptied it over the old man's head. Turning, he laughed at his three companions and then grasped the Scot by the neck and forced his head between his knees.

"You drink!" he ordered. "You make too much noise."

Doyle stood up and tapped the German on the shoulder. As he turned, he butted him in the face and punched him four times as he sagged to the floor. The other Germans were half out of their chairs when Rushton—God, how happy Quinn was to see Rushton!—loomed up in the doorway in full uniform, one massive hand on the revolver in his black holster. The deserter melted away, and three minutes later the other Germans began half-carrying their friend toward the exit under threat of imprisonment.

One of them then turned, grasping the semiconscious man's arm around his neck; stooped, he looked up at Rushton.

"You do not ask all the circumstances," he protested. "I study the law for two years in Munich. Circumstances alter cases."

Rushton glowered down at him; the Stern Gang had taught him the futility of discussion. "Broken noses alter faces," he growled. "Piss off."

The room relaxed after that, and it became part of Rushton's tarnished legend, that phrase; from then on his juniors repeated it solemnly to raw recruits from Home, who flinched whenever Rushton looked at them.

As for Quinn, it taught him that despite his reverence for violence, the reality sickened him. He had performed boxing jokes for Doyle—"I'm Jimmy Wilde. The ghost with the hammer in his hand!"—but they were destined to remain jokes as long as he lived.

"Hey, I've realized something," he said. "I'm not so much like Jimmy Wilde. I'm more like Cornel."

That was the only joke that Doyle ever really laughed at; he threw back his head and chuckled so hard that the blood trickled anew from his lips . . . Another old, old memory, which only Quinn treasured.

DOYLE WAS ALWAYS a jigsaw puzzle with several pieces missing. His platonic friendship with Big Vera was a case in point: "Whitest woman this side of the black stump," he'd say, locked in this time when "white" meant "best." She joined them that night: a heavily built Russian-Chinese whose sagging body had received countless strangers, but who saw herself in the role of a wistful romantic—an ingénue peeped bright-eyed from beneath the brow of Marie Dressler. She was flirting hopelessly with Doyle, using dialogue from every bad movie she had ever seen.

"Ah, Doyle," she sighed. "I wish I could fall in love with you, just like that. I wish I were drunk. I feel like getting drunk tonight. I would like to go out to King's Park and run like mad till I'm so exhausted I forget . . ." That sort of thing: humming "Holy Night," offering wisdom—"Live full and die young. Get lots of experience"—even sinking back into her school days, when the teacher one day had said "classifier," and the Chinese students had run outside, believing that the school was about to go up in flames. Maudlin reminiscences and schoolgirl gaffes: "What's testicles, teacher?" Well, it had been too much for Doyle, with the old Scot in full cry again, bellowing about the nature of matter: "Ask Fleming! He'll tell you! It festers!"

Doyle took Quinn and Vera to a Chinese "club" nearby: a brothel behind a restaurant, although the members had to send out for their women. It was empty; Doyle roused the head boy and stood over him while he dialed numbers from a tattered address book.

"Looks like you get me," Vera murmured, resting her head briefly on Doyle's shoulder.

He chuckled. "You bring a pack of cards?"

"Listen." Quinn hoped his voice was not shaking. "I'm not that keen."

He took a glass of whisky out onto a tiny balcony and leaned over the railing to conceal his shivering body. Kowloon still crackled with life: neon lights were blazing, and the scent of magnolia blossoms drifted up from a flower stall, mixed with the stench of shit in wooden pails on the footpaths. That night did not bear much thinking about—the shit and magnolias and blur of neons overlaying his ignominious fear of the adolescent ritual. He selected the first girl who arrived to get it over.

Doyle and Vera left him alone in a room with her, he recalled; going out, Doyle kissed the girl lightly on the forehead, bequeathing her to Quinn as a gift. Amusement glinted in his eyes, but there was a solemnity there too. There has to be a first time. Why not now?

He turned at the door: Quinn always remembered that. "You've got to feed it, chum," he said. "It's too high to eat grass."

She was a nice girl, in her way; slipping out of a black cheongsam, she assured him of her status. "You meet someone on the street," she said, "tha's no good. Very cheap. Not nice. My friends very good. Very good. Ship's captain . . ." And sliding into bed, with sudden surprise: "Your hands like girl's. You no work?"

He never forgot the grinding sequel as she fulfilled her contract; later she slept with the simple trust of a child, exuding warm breath and cheap perfume in his face as he lay trapped in the stifling darkness.

He could not stand it; before dawn, he slipped quietly out of bed and padded into the hallway. Vera was snoring on a divan in a room at the end of the hall, and Doyle sat fully dressed with his head on a table. He was talking in his sleep.

He had not been joking about the cards; they lay scattered beneath his arms. And beside the cards lay a small black pistol.

WHY HAD HE felt such tenderness for Doyle all his life, when their association had been so brutal and so incomplete? Doyle had never sought tenderness; he had never asked for anything from any man. And yet he had dominated Quinn's Hong Kong; he had *become* Quinn's Hong Kong: "Doyle's Irish for Dark Invader. Move aside, you cunts." Doyle standing on the parapet of his last killing ground, barking mock-threats and scorn and desire and memory with the same rapid-fire velocity; a few bursts of bathos before he rammed in a clip of nostalgia.

Nothing distinctive; merely the obscene argot of the Second World War as he played out his life. "Tell him fuck him . . . I'll have your guts for a necktie . . . He wouldn't know you were up him till you dribbled on his neck . . . I'd draw her on like a Wellington boot . . ."

Doyle and his mats singing "J'attendrai" on marches through Palestine, and "The Wizard of Oz" as they attacked Bardia; Doyle fresh out of crutch when on leave in England because his lover's husband had returned ("Lovely kid, she was. Drink like a fish. Sit up at the bar—none of this nonsense"); Doyle cursing on Mount Olympus as the Stukas dived; Doyle fresh out of land in Crete when the German parachutes blossomed, heralding six months in the POW camp before he escaped; Doyle the harsh man with an empty core like their land, but surely a fragile loveliness in there too if only he could find it.

Well, he never had found it: rummaging, he had come up only with bitterness and regret; a few dry chuckles crackling like porcupine bush in the desert behind his eagle eyes.

DOYLE WAS THE Anzac, of course, that Quinn had wished to be; that was one simple explanation. He bludgeoned with words: "Come on. Spring off your ass, Lightning, or I'll smash you into the earth ... Shut up, you fucking wax borer. You couldn't knock a sick old woman off a piss-pot ..." Other men's words, already tarnished, but the force behind them was Doyle's alone. Doyle of the surf club punch-ups in Sydney before the war; Doyle "going down the mine" in the big green sets at Freshwater before the surfies called them sets; Doyle seducing girls in the backseats of Singers. Staccato memories ejected in Hong Kong bars.

Doyle, when maudlin, murmuring: "We few, we happy few, we band of brothers" at the blank golden faces of waiters; Doyle declaring: "Hound of the Mound, Pride of the Regiment, Hawkeye Doyle. I should never have left the Army," while they smiled and bowed and awaited the bill. Doyle when he had the taste, declaring: "There's a bloody drought around here ... I think I shall dunk the love-muscle tonight." A steady salvo of cliches to distract the enemy as he withdrew. Doyle, the common Australian enigma.

Quinn capered to hold him back. "I am Baldur von Schirach," he announced one night. "There are seven men standing outside who claim to be Baldur von Schirach, but I am Baldur von Schirach"; or: "See that hill up there? There's a Breda up there"— anything to penetrate the fatal armor and light up the eyes; anything to say: there is a human being out here who is trying to reach you.

But it was never enough; Doyle was going even then. He never made him laugh again. Because Doyle, he realized later, had been a man of his time, the thirties and forties, and his time then was almost up. "Fuckin' war ring-barks a man," he'd say, shaking the last drops from a bottle into his glass, and it was true: he was only twenty-nine, but already the shell of the man he was describing. The Passchendaeles of paddocks were claiming him as their own, just as they had claimed Quinn's father, just as they waited to claim Quinn himself, and he bound the three of them together with this secret knowledge.

Toward the end, Doyle reminisced more and more, but whether this was due to the drink or a growing trust in Quinn, Quinn never knew: he guessed later that Doyle must have felt the evening of death in his belly long before the *Clarion* printed his passing a few years later: "*(Died Suddenly.) Anthony David Doyle . . .*" The compositors placed it in the correct obituary column, but the *Clarion*, as usual, was not wholly accurate; as in most cases of this sort, Doyle had been dying slowly for years.

And somewhere behind his death, Quinn began to suspect as the years unfolded—not wholly responsible, perhaps, but certainly in part—somewhere behind his death strutted a jolly little murderer who did not reach the peak of his fortunes until the seventies. General Keh Shih-kai, a supporter of the World Wildlife Fund, a pillar of UNICEF, a merry prankster during horsey events each year at Olympia and Windsor (pretending to kick Mark Phillips's horse); the owner of a vast forest amusement park in Taiwan. Kenny Keh, beloved killer and corrupter, who prospered more and more as each decade unfolded while all the people who really mattered to Quinn were withering in exile or under the ground.

SOMETIMES, WHEN QUINN could not face the madmen in The Vienna, he used to drop into a Chinese restaurant around the corner to flirt mildly with the Chinese waitresses: a jaded facsimile of courtship. He spent his last night there before setting out for Shanghai—although he did not know this as he approached it that humid evening.

Rushton suddenly ran crouching from The Vienna alley and flattened himself against the wall of the Chinese restaurant, his revolver stuck out in front of him. Quinn stopped a few paces from him; his heart was pounding.

Rushton turned and beckoned urgently, and two Chinese

police with revolvers out loped into full view behind him, and then four more—bent forward slightly, their revolvers wavering.

Oh God, Quinn prayed. Let there be violence. "What's up?" he asked.

Rushton turned his craggy head slowly. "Training," he said. "In case we inherit some trouble here. I'm just trying to get through to these blokes."

He walked out into Queen's Road and began to gawk and peer in crude imitation of his men, his great chin stuck out grotesquely. They smiled sheepishly and looked at their black boots, and Quinn turned and entered the restaurant. His time had not come.

A plump young amah in a white jacket and black trousers laughed when she saw him, twirling her plait around a finger; he had become an object of merry curiosity among the girls there, who used him to practice their English. One of them fondled his hair sometimes and told him that he was a very beautiful man; she liked to press a toothpick beneath her front teeth and flick it at him archly so that occasionally it fell into his beer. He preferred another, Ah King, with more lady-like reserve.

Ah King's English was abysmal: she used a jar of Stillman's Freckle Cream in the belief, apparently, that it was an all-purpose face preparation. The restaurant closed each night at 12:30; at precisely 12:20 she used to sit down and dab spots of freckle cream on her face with a toothpick, humming in a thin hard-edged little voice as a *foki* plucked a sentimental song of war and parting on a p'ipa: *"The clock is asking you to hurry, Time will never come back . . ."* Porter had translated it for him: the court damp with dew, the lover clinging, the air filled with perfume, the shit pails outside on the pavement while the white dots marched across her face.

It was too early yet for that. She unwrapped a paper napkin to display a photograph of herself taken in the Hong Kong Botanic Gardens, and then she showed him a piece of paper on which a kind English soldier had written the words of "I'll Never Smile Again" for her to learn. He was about to study them when Doyle swept in and clapped a hand on his shoulder; Rushton must have told him that Quinn was there.

"Off your ass, Lightning!" he snapped. "You're on a train to Shanghai. I've cleared it with Keh."

Doyle saw him off the next day at Kowloon Station: leaning on his umbrella, laughing hard back in his throat at this joke he was springing on the Nationalist Army. A gray pallor had seeped beneath his skin, but the eagle eyes still glittered as he shoved a bottle of vodka through the window of the train.

"Give 'em hell!" he said, and Quinn leaned out to shake hands; already he could imagine Doyle's hilarious account of his departure the next time he dropped into the mess to see Rushton. He tried to think of something chipper to say, but all that surfaced was another phrase of Doyle's: "If there's a furry ball in your throat, it's your asshole."

"I'm Charlie McCarthy," he joked. "I think I'll change my mind," and then Doyle began sliding away into memory with the other ghosts in his head.

Rattling north through Kwangtung, he found in his pocket the words which the soldier had written for Ah King: a string of misspelled song titles strung together with four-letter words.

He tore up the paper, raised the window, and scattered the pieces over the soft green rice fields. The Anzac doll was heading toward a larger obscenity.

FIVE

SHANGHAI WAS FRAGMENTING LIKE AN overblown rose. Doyle had arranged a first-floor room for him above another of Keh's small export offices on the Bund. It boasted a camp bed set among sodden gray armchairs that had subsided down the years in the summer humidity seeping in over the Whangpoo River, the winter mists drifting in from the sea. There were dirty brown walls, a rose-wreathed china spittoon on which he dropped a folded copy of the *North China Daily News* to cover its viscous yellow pool, and a blackwood screen, inlaid with porcelain panels of birds and plum blossoms, concealing a sink. The room dismayed him: its only virtue was that it was free in a city of astronomical inflation, and he expected to be there no more than a week while Keh arranged a promised DC3 flight to Sian in Shensi. Doyle had contacted Keh from Hong Kong and informed him (tongue in cheek) that Quinn wanted to record his military exploits for the *Clarion*; Keh, after some hesitation, had agreed. He was on his way.

Of more immediate benefit: Doyle also had instructed him how to tip the Boys at the Cathay Hotel so that he could take baths each day in the half-empty suites. Each morning, awaiting Keh's summons, he lay in bathrooms as tall and white as the insides of monuments, contemplating his goal: only squeeze a trigger, shatter a skull, and—presto!—instant manhood. His own niche one day, perhaps, in the nation's mightiest monument of all in Canberra; his entrée into the myth. Beneath the tattered shoulder badges, the punctured water bottles, the dark Dyson drawings, a birth . . .

Eagerly, each afternoon, he asked Keh's Chinese clerks in the office below his room whether they had received Keh's invitation for him to enter the Civil War. "Maybe tomorrow," they always smiled apologetically. "Maybe tomorrow . . ."

One week stretched into two, and each day leeched his enthusiasm. The city was grubby with Nationalist generals and their concubines: the higher the rank the larger their girths and the more delicate their painted companions. They feasted in the hotels and restaurants and crumbling villas while a miasma of decay crept through the greasy black streets around them; corruption hung over the gray craft in the broken brown water of the Whangpoo as the corrupters swilled brandy and whisky and supervised the transfer of their riches to the United States and Taiwan and Hong Kong and Malaya. That broken water came to represent Quinn's own adolescence; he struck out desperately toward the calm harbor of a maturity that lay somewhere far ahead. Walking swiftly at night along the Bund, daring the trigger-happy sentries, he realized that he was still an antipodean child in a tainted world of alien adults.

"Give 'em hell!" Doyle had laughed; legs crossed, leaning on his umbrella. He flushed at the memory.

ONE MORNING IN his third week—his money dwindling, his ferocity fading—he was walking past Broadway Mansions, a red-brick pile that was swarming with distracted members of the U.S. Military Advisory Group; one of them, framed in a window, was gesturing in urgent conversation, as if he were trying to pick up a Nationalist division to hurl it at the foe. Up ahead, a strange young man stood watching him approach.

Although crew-cut, the fellow was decked out in the volumi-

72

nous shorts and long socks of the Britisher; although apparently American, and young, he wore the sneer of an Old World ancient, as if misplaced in time. He reminded Quinn instantly of a lanky country boy he had seen once in the main street of Wongbok, trailing behind elderly parents in short pants too long for him; of sad stork-daughters from the failed farms, who scuttled along beside the shop windows in their aunties' dipping, faded frocks.

"Hi," the young man rasped. "You Quinn?"

His skin was marble-white—as white as the ankles of the beach fishermen near Wongbok—and tiny beads of perspiration glistened on his forehead. His cold gray eyes bored into Quinn's face with the certainty of superiority; if he was odd, he did not appear to know it.

"Yes." Quinn was nonplussed. He took the hand offered him; it rested briefly in his, damp but edged with sharp callouses, before the stranger withdrew it and wiped it down one side of his shorts. He smelled of carbolic soap.

"Ed Larsen. I'm with UNRRA. I'm told you want to get over to General Keh's division in Shensi."

"Who told you that?" Quinn stiffened defensively; right from the start he did not trust Larsen; he was as uncertain as a wayward cell. He scratched an armpit, gazing at Quinn triumphantly. "Ah-ha," he countered, "top secret."

That was another trait that Quinn came to know very well in the time ahead; Larsen loved to invest the commonplace with mystery. Quinn stood watching him curiously, sliding his own hand down the back of his trousers.

"Let's go talk," Larsen said.

They walked along the Bund toward the Cathay; Larsen dived quickly between the groups of sauntering Chinese, forcing Quinn to walk faster so that he would not appear to surrender the initiative by lagging behind. Already, however, he was preparing to offer his destiny to Larsen, if he could help him, as he had surrendered it to Doyle. The main object was to get to Shensi.

The Cathay stared down on the Whangpoo, a dowager marooned in a slum; they entered an almost-deserted section of lounge near the Horse and Hounds Bar. Noël Coward had written *Private Lives* here; now the hotel's red carpets had faded around the overstuffed armchairs. A tall White Russian refugee in a frayed suit bristled by a window; he stared at them imperiously, ready to counter any attempt to eject him.

Larsen led the way to two armchairs drawn up around a teak coffee table; he ordered coffee without consulting Quinn. "This is on me," he said, and he rummaged in a satchel, laid a pearl-handled revolver ostentatiously on the table, and then snapped open a map of China.

Quinn glanced around him uneasily. The rotting breath of Shanghai seeped through the tall windows, and the White Russian was pretending to read an ancient book; threads of cloth dangled from its spine. He leaned forward, perched on the crumbling edge of an era. "Big gun," he remarked.

Larsen looked up briefly from the map, affecting surprise that it was there. "Yeah. Got it from a Marine," he said. "My 'Patton Special.'" Then he stabbed a finger into the heart of China. "I've got a truckload of supplies I've got to deliver to Sian. That's where you're heading. I'll see if I can get you along as codriver."

He drew back, folding the map, as a waiter set down cups and a heavy silver coffee service.

"Very good of you," Quinn murmured, his mind darting around the prospect for an alternative. "I've been in contact with them over there. I'm just waiting on the go-ahead."

Larsen laughed: a few sniffs through his nose. "You'll wait a long time." He was probably only a year or two older than Quinn, but his certainty was ageless. "Keh's agreed to it, sure, but that doesn't mean he'll do it. They say yes when they mean no. Have you heard from him direct?"

"No, not direct. It was organized from Hong Kong."

"That's what I mean." Larsen flicked a handkerchief from his shorts, rubbed it around the edge of his cup, and folded it neatly before he sipped: cleanliness obsessed him (which was ironical, as Quinn discovered later). "You don't know these people. You tell them, you don't ask. Fools ask."

Quinn registered his first stab of resentment against Larsen. "How did you find out about this?" he repeated levelly.

"MAG. They don't like Limeys. Leave it to me."

There was little mystery, it transpired later, surrounding Larsen's knowledge of Quinn's plan. He shared an apartment with a member of the Military Aid Group from his own state of

Iowa; Doyle had contacted an old friend in MAG to try to speed up Quinn's departure, and the news had leaked down to Larsen— a UNRRA misfit if ever there was one. It was weeks before Quinn discovered the truth: Larsen had persuaded MAG to cancel plans to squeeze Quinn aboard a DC3 for Sian so that he could undertake a gung ho journey with him in a UNRRA supply truck; like Quinn, it was violence, not good works, that had drawn him to China. Having persuaded MAG, he then pressured UNRRA into giving him the truck. No doubt they were glad to see the back of him.

It also transpired that it was Larsen who did not like Limeys, a blanket word which he used to cover Australians. The only comfort was that nobody, including his countrymen, liked Larsen. And yet Quinn and he shared one similarity during this period: both had been infected with the manly need to kill.

LARSEN CALLED INTO Quinn's room the next afternoon; in retrospect, his behavior was a rehearsal for the reality to come. He sat on the arm of one of the mouldering armchairs, swinging one leg, looking around him scornfully.

"Niggers got better shacks than this," he said. "I'll talk to someone. See if I can get you into Marlborough Mansions."

"It'll do for a few more days." Quinn was shamed; he cast about for a change of subject. "How did you come to join UNRRA?"

Larsen slid down into the chair, still jiggling a stockinged leg. "Iowa had nothing to offer me. I didn't want to farm." He lifted his shirt, elaborately casual, and eased a holster against his waist. "I don't know what I want to do yet."

"But why UNRRA?" An angel of mercy with a gun at his side; ambiguity was an area that Quinn understood very well.

"Why not? It got me here." Larsen's eyes flickered away from his own life. "Into the action."

"I know what you mean." The Passchendaeles of paddocks; staring at a blank horizon from the empty North Coast beaches while Valparaiso, Zanzibar, Samarkand burned in the brain. "The country gets boring."

"I didn't say it was boring," Larsen snapped petulantly. "I said I wanted some action."

He got up and began to stalk around the room, rubbing his

marble arms; he had ripped the short sleeves from his shirt to display them more fully. "I don't give a damn about UNRRA. It's a means to an end. Can you shoot?"

"Shoot? A few times with a .22, that's all. Rabbits—that sort of thing." Rabbits squealing away into the bushes to die, an old goanna clinging to a tree.

Larsen plucked aside the grimy curtain on a window that overlooked the back of the building. "Look at 'em," he said.

Quinn peered down over his shoulder. Rotting sampans jammed in a murky creek; squatting women and children; a hundred cooking fires.

"Never had a bath in their lives," Larsen said, and he shuddered. "Eat their own shit. Monkeys at the zoo. What use are they?"

Quinn opened his mouth to give a lame reply, remembering his mother: "Put that down. A Chinaman might have touched it."

If I had my way . . ." Larsen vowed, and he tugged his pearl-handled revolver from its holster and aimed it down through the glass.

"Hey," Quinn said nervously. "That might go off."

Larsen turned quickly with a look of contempt. "Hey," he mimicked prissily in an English accent. "That might go off . . ."

THEY SAT IN the Cathay late on several afternoons with a group of Americans from MAG and UNRRA. "Leave these guys to me," Larsen had instructed him. "I'm pushing it through."

They were large warm men with a capacity for swift action that their easygoing voices belied; sinking deep on their spines in the armchairs, they tossed lazy observations to each other while Larsen leaned forward, bristling, a chill on the edges of their conversation. None of them ever addressed Larsen directly, including the official whose apartment he shared; they sat him out while he threw words like stones into their genial pool before stalking off on brisk missions intended to point up their sloth.

"Watch that guy," one of them once confided to Quinn as Larsen disappeared. "He's got problems."

Quinn grew to dislike Larsen more than anyone he had ever known; Larsen, unforgivably, penetrated the very center of his immaturity. He used to lie on his camp bed at night, seething with anger at Larsen's latest slight while his sneer hung in the fetid air above him.

It never occurred to him that he could have got to Shensi without Larsen if he had been decisive about it; Larsen had promised a truck, and he transferred his hopes to it. And, meanwhile, he had some problems of his own.

WHAT DID IT matter now? Where did the pieces fit? Why was he cursed with such useless recall, such warped pity for them all—for the Polish-Jewish girl with UNRRA who lived on the floor above, next to the threadbare surgery of a little Austrian doctor; two more minor players who joined his secret life later up on West Ridge. Where was she now? He used to listen each morning for the click of her shoes down the stone steps; imagining her dark hair curled before her ears, the Phoenician profile, the full lips; instinctively avoiding what he most desired. He mounted the steps to the doctor's surgery only after she had gone, for he had developed the pathological fear that he had contracted a venereal disease in Hong Kong. How Doyle would have chuckled about that if he had told him.

The doctor was a kindly man; he owned a white cat that slept on a green cushion on a cane chair, and an old phonograph (pasted with the faded ocher stickers of shipping lines and continental hotels) that he played during consultations. Quinn assumed that he slept behind a curtain drawn across one end of the surgery. He used to hold glasses of Quinn's urine up to the light like rare wine, and then fuss gently over his smear tests and sulfa tablets and penicillin injections while Quinn joked—as Doyle might have joked: "I'm beginning to feel like a bloody dartboard." And all the time—as he grinned bitterly to himself—Richard Tauber was singing "Ah, Sweet Mystery of Life," over and over on the phonograph; his rich voice soaring out over the Bund; over the glasses of golden urine through which the sampans on the Whangpoo wriggled like spermatozoa.

"This is no place for a single man," the doctor reflected one morning, pausing with his head cocked sideways, a record balanced between two soft pink fingers. "I had an American in here with a sex life of forty years in America and other places. The first night here he gets three kinds." He put on the record: Joseph

Schmidt's "A Star Falls From Heaven." "Bulging," he said. "I had to operate to get the pus out."

Quinn remembered that many years later when he bit into a cream puff at a birthday party for his small daughter; he smiled gently to himself as he swallowed, and his daughter—believing that the smile was for her—smiled back. He never did have venereal disease, he came to believe later, but China was to remain for him (and for how many others?) a poisoned woman; a phantom flicker of pain in the penis of the West.

AS FOR THE Polish girl, she knocked at his door one evening with a brief message from Larsen: pack, it was all set for the next morning; he was getting the truck ready.

He asked her in for a drink; she hesitated, half-looking up the steps. "It's my birthday," he lied.

"I give you a clean bill of health," the doctor had said that morning. "You are free to marry," and he watched as she sat gingerly on one of the mouldering armchairs, sliding a shoulder bag to the floor and gazing around her.

"Regency Period," he interposed quickly. Turning his back, he wiped two glasses with a clean shirt.

"I've only vodka!" he called over his shoulder—Doyle's vodka. He splashed it quickly into the glasses before she could object and sat opposite her eagerly. "Cheers!"

She raised her glass absently. "You should not go with Larsen," she said gravely. "He is—how must I say it?"

"Nuts?" Quinn felt gay and irresponsible. "Well, we're all a bit nuts. It'll be a chance for a bit of excitement."

She stirred angrily, looking away into a corner, and lowered her untouched glass to her lap. "'Excitement' is what you call it. You come to Poland in the war. You come to Siberia."

"You've been to Siberia?" Gravity was the quick ploy now or she might slip away—and with gravity, anyway, he could cloak his naïveté. She sipped at last; he relaxed.

"In 1940, I was ten years of age." She looked again around the room. "I see him still when I enter a room."

"See who?" Quinn drained his vodka with bravado; the occasion was sliding away from him. She twisted her glass on her lap, staring into it, and then poured the vodka down her throat. He was faintly astonished.

"Every day for months. Can you imagine this? Every day the NKVD man comes and sits in our house. You know of the NKVD?"

"A bit." The VD part, anyway, smiling to himself. He refilled her glass.

"He never speaks. Only staring—staring. The red band on his hat. Can you imagine this? Looking, always looking."

"Why?"

"They wish to frighten us. My father is one of the chief rabbis of our town. People warn him when there is a deportation coming so that we may go to the country and hide, but after a time he does not want to hide, so they take us. The NKVD man goes away, and the next day they take us."

"To Siberia?"

"Thirty days on the train. My mother dies. My father is strong. They cannot kill my father." She brightened proudly. Her beauty, he saw, diminished the closer one approached her: her skin was drawn too tightly around her skull, and her big dark eyes were deeply shadowed. Ten years old: at that age he was eating his mother's roast dinners after Sunday school. He resented her for it.

She got up and began to step jerkily around the room, jiggling the vodka in her glass; stooping to peer with false interest at the birds and blossoms on the blackwood screen.

"It must have been a bad time for you," he said reluctantly, seeing the hands lowering her mother's body from a cattle truck, the long barracks buildings, the snow greased with the imprints of corpses.

"At least we miss the Nazis when they come to Poland. My grandmother, my uncles and aunts, my cousins . . ." She tossed off her vodka. "You hear the man scream in the night?"

"No." But he had.

"You know what is in the big building beside this one? The warehouse?"

"I didn't know."

"This company is the owner of that warehouse. General Keh's company. You know what is in that warehouse?"

"No." Quinn filled her glass again; the romantic interlude that he had contemplated so tenderly for so many days had degenerated into an examination.

79

"Our supplies. UNRRA supplies. We place them on the train and they go into China. One month later they come back for the blackmarket."

"What about the man who screamed?"

"Many people fight for these supplies. I tell Larsen, but he does not care of this. They all know. They cannot stop it. So I go away soon. America. Everyone is bad."

"I'm not bad." A last coy try.

She looked at him seriously for the first time. "You are a little boy." Then she rubbed her face with one hand. "Do you know what I see then?"

"What? When?"

"As I rub across my face. There is an old larch tree in the mountains in Siberia where we cut the grass on the collective farm. We sit under it each day when the guard brings us the soup. Long worms swimming in it—ugh! But the blue sky, the snow on the mountains, the tree. I look at them all the time and I swallow the soup and I think of God."

She left abruptly after another vodka, offering a stiff formal handshake. He never saw her again, but he never forgot her either: she was one reason that, years later, he married a part-Jewish girl himself. The need to share some concentration camp soup.

Larsen tooted below his window at dawn. He stole upstairs and placed the half-empty bottle of vodka at her door, wondering how old she was when she had learned to drink like that, and why.

He placed a note beneath the bottle. "From the little boy," he wrote bitterly, "who is about to grow up."

SIX

A NATIONALIST MILITARY ESCORT, LIEUTENANT Su, stood on the footpath beside the truck: a tall Szechuanese with the beaked profile of a minor bird of prey. He saluted Quinn smartly—too smartly.

"Glad to meet you, old chap," he announced in perfect English, as he slung Quinn's bag in the back. "All aboard for the Skylark." And Quinn stared at him, transfixed: in that seeping gray light he became certain of fiasco.

Larsen grated the gears, he remembered, as the truck started; he flushed when Quinn asked him what supplies they were carrying. "It's not the stuff that matters," he snapped. "It's showing 'em we care." Quinn found out later: they were loaded, ironically, with goods that the Nationalist blackmarketeer-officers in Shanghai did not want—cases of boys' yellow gridiron helmets for reasons beyond his comprehension; boxes of reject nylon stockings donated by a kind manufacturer in Manhattan's sentimental garment district; an assortment of high-heeled shoes from Rotary wives in Nebraska; two boxes of Scandinavian medical supplies that somehow had escaped confiscation. Even Larsen obviously was shamed.

The sun rose an hour after they had cleared Shanghai, bathing emerald fields and curved mauve roofs with a pearl-pink luminosity. Quinn huddled between Su and Larsen, straining one leg away from the gear lever and the small white skull of Larsen's kneecap; lurching against Su, who had removed his tunic and was softly singing Jerome Kern hits of the thirties as he rested one golden arm on the edge of the window. It was like one of his feverish dreams: three misfits, now, in search of a war. "I hope you remembered the toilet paper," he said.

Two young girls waved to them that first morning as they approached a village, and Su saluted them carelessly, wriggling his fingers. "Yeah, though we walk through the Rudi Vallee of the shadow of celibacy we shall fear no evil!" he cried, and giggled.

This minor incident, however, seemed to have begun a Freudian association in his mind, because a few minutes later he broke off a rendition of "Smoke Gets In Your Eyes." "Oh, bother!" he sighed. "I've forgotten my noisy bang-bang."

He was an excellent actor, Su, and, predictably, the most resolute of the three of them; it did not take Quinn long to discover that.

THEY SPENT THE FIRST NIGHT in the back of the truck beside a field of maize; Larsen and Quinn started at each rustle of wind while Su read a copy of *Macbeth* by torchlight.

Two planes droned over, very high and flying south; their lights winked a lonely farewell, speaking of the warmth of fellow humans, of the coastal cities they had left behind. "Witches at four o'clock," murmured Su.

Larsen spat over the side. "You're the funniest goddamned soldier I've ever seen. What about standing watch?"

"By all means," Su replied sweetly. "What do you suggest that I watch?"

"Shut up!" Larsen said. "I can hear something." Their ears strained: only the rattle of maize, the cry of a distant bird.

"Merge with the landscape," advised Su. "Release your fears into the streams. Don't be afraid of the dark."

"It's not the dark that worries *me*," Quinn confessed. "It's what's in it. You know this country?"

82

"He knows Tin Pan Alley," Larsen snarled. "That's about all he knows. I'll take first watch. No bastard's going to catch me asleep."

"As you wish," Su said. "But we may as well enjoy the journey while we can. Nothing like a blow in the country . . ."

Toward dawn, Larsen's revolver went off in his hand as he sagged over the back of the truck. The bullet struck the road and whined away through the maize. Quinn started up violently, white-faced among the boxes.

Only Su was unmoved. He opened his eyes slowly and regarded Larsen coolly for several seconds. "You're right, old chappie," he said. "I think I heard something too . . ."

A curious man, Lieutenant Su—too curious to succeed later in the United States, where he became a citizen.

THEY FOLLOWED A long looping route south of the Yangtze before the swing north to a shrinking Nationalist enclave around Sian— eating canned food and what vegetables they could get in the villages. Larsen and Quinn took turns at the wheel, and sometimes Larsen insisted on pushing on throughout the night.

Those nights—nearly a week of them—were the worst; a black dome clapped down, trapping them like insects beneath an upturned bowl; they rattled across a landscape where no open fires gleamed, no street lights ever shone; the dim huddle of a village, the occasional chink of light from a sludge-lamp in a hut, and then the ghostly antennae of the headlights were flickering again through inky wastelands of fields as they braced for a gleam of bayonets around the next curve; bullets shattering the windscreen.

The land was Nationalist in name only: the Kuomintang troops locked themselves in their blockhouses at dusk as the Japanese had done before them while Communist guerrillas ranged freely, dragging out local tyrants for execution. Only the unreal bravado of youth, and Su's documents, got them through: Quinn and Larsen went armed with their white faces before white faces became targets, sublimely confident that these magic emblems of superiority would stay fingers on triggers long enough for Su to smooth their path.

For it was Su who carried it off; unknown to his superiors, he carried two sets of documents—one for the Nationalists and the other for the Communists. They served him better than the weapons that he had deliberately (he confessed later) left behind; the uniform that he hid inside a pair of greasy overalls behind the supplies in the back. His Nationalist documents were too lofty for local brigands or Nationalist detachments to brush aside in their ceaseless search for plunder, and forged Communist credentials introduced him as a Party member from Szechuan (just returned from long study in France, so explaining his stilted local pronunciations). In each case, he explained airily to Quinn and Larsen, he was merely acting as their guide—to General Keh's Nationalist HQ or the Communist-occupied slab of Shensi, whichever was applicable. And laughed gaily.

Su, in fact, was Quinn's main memory of that journey. He had spent most of his life in the Lake District of England, not France; his father, a university professor, had taken him there as a child before the fiery province of his birth could claim him fully as its own. He had studied medicine for three years after Cambridge; he had joined the Army, he confided, only to qualify for a large inheritance from an ailing uncle in the KMT. Crazy old Su.

"THEY TOLD ME, Heraclitus, they told me you were dead . . ." That was Su bowing one afternoon to a goateed old gentleman in a shabby dove-gray gown.

They had stopped at a village pond to bathe. Su sat down first, threw off his shoes, and lowered his feet into the thick green water. Two rings appeared around his ankles.

"You know," he said, "I must seem very strange to that old man. Do I seem strange to you, Larsen?"

Larsen was peeling off his long socks, plucking bits of grass from his toes. He snorted with contempt. "Do you really want me to answer that?"

"How cruel you are," Su replied lightly. "But then you appear very strange to me. This phallic attachment to your gun— curious."

He watched two ducks waggling away across the pond. "To travel hopefully is better . . ." he murmured. "A cold coming we had of it."

Quickly he turned over and lay on his stomach, gazing at a jagged blue range of mountains. "I suppose I *am* strange," he
84

confessed. "Who wouldn't be? I'm a mess, a nomad. No base, no anchor."

He swung around and leaned on one elbow. Larsen was carefully scooping aside green scum, his soap and towel laid neatly beside him.

"You two," he said. "You have bases. I'm a leaf in a cataract. As soon as I get the loot from my dear old uncle I'm scooting back to London."

"Why London?" Quinn asked. "Couldn't you stay here?"

"Treasonable talk, my young friend. What have I to contribute to a new society? A Cambridge graduate back in kindergarten? Alexander Su, brick 1,569 in the foundations of a village urinal."

He gazed across at the village. "Besides," he said softly, "they'd tear me down. I prefer to let the slates slide off gently, one by one."

"You don't have many left," Larsen sniggered. "If you're a sample of the Nationalist Army . . ."

"Me!" Su cried in mock protest. "A common soldier!" He jumped to his feet. "I entertain you with a running fire of songs and poetry and literary anecdotes—few of them Chinese—and you accuse me of that! I am an oddity, I will have you know! I am a man of erudition, of passion!"

He struck a theatrical pose, his chest heaving with false emotion, and smiled and bowed again at the old man who stood watching. "I have just decided on my vocation," he said. "A psychiatrist. A passionate psychiatrist!"

"Passionate!" Larsen spat out the word like a poison pellet. "If you were passionate about your country . . ."

"What should I do, my dear Larsen? Rape the forests? Ravish the rivers? It is too late for that."

He began to cup his hands at various points of his body. "I am a passion machine," he said, glancing ironically at Quinn; he was enjoying his own performance. "A few squirts of Eliot and Shakespeare from here, a jet of Yeats or Joyce here, a trickle of *tz'us* here if I press hard enough."

A small crowd of peasants in patched jackets was gathering. "Oh," he cried cupping his hands over his groin, "if I could only pour myself in one long hot stream for Szechuan! All my love, spitting out a hundred wrong holes!"

Larsen was red with irritation now as if Su had touched the root of his own dilemma. Su sprang lightly onto the back of the truck and paused dramatically, arms extended like a ballet dancer on the wrong stage—the pale sexuality of Swan Lake amid the mud huts at noon.

"Positively my last appearance," he said, "before the great George Orwell Show!" And although his lips curved with sardonic amusement, his eyes strayed over the worn faces of the villagers with a distant warmth, as if some rich sense of being whispered faintly in his brain.

ONLY WHEN DANGER threatened did Su become grave, and then Quinn, at least, was grateful for his presence. "Mark up another victory to the cultural hermaphrodite!" he'd declare after negotiating them through each Nationalist roadblock. And sweeping along through the fields, watching the sturdy brothers and sisters who had been denied to him, he would laugh bitterly, humming the "Whiffenpoof Song."

Larsen said that he was a queer, gripping the wheel with such fury during Su's little concerts that his knuckles were white. Indeed, everything about Larsen seemed white, if not bloodless; he ran his hands up and down his marble arms as he prowled around the truck each morning and evening, as if to reassure himself that they were real.

Larsen's delight in his modest muscles expressed itself in a strange way although Quinn did not realize the significance of this then. Constantly, he cajoled or taunted Quinn or Su into bouts of Indian arm wrestling, which he always won; laughing, Su allowed his arm to flop over almost immediately before he dragged a book from his kit bag, and Quinn did not try much harder. On their second night out, Larsen forced Quinn's left hand on to the jagged edge of a can, drawing blood, before he released his grip. This seemed to work in Larsen like an aphrodisiac; he became flushed, and his eyes shone. As for women, they did not appear to exist for him in any special sexual sense at all.

THE APPEARANCE OF the Communist girl guerrilla fighter, south of Sian, was an example of this. Nationalist troops by then had stopped them many times at fortified villages, but it was only

86

there that Communist guerrillas surrounded them. They blocked them with pony carts at dusk in a narrow lane leading into a village.

"Be calm, my children" Su murmured as a dozen irregulars in motley uniforms swarmed down from the banks. "And Larsen. Keep that revolver out of sight."

The Communists leapt onto their mudguards; two of them flung themselves dramatically across the hood, pointing weapons through the windshield. Su raised his hands in a deprecatory gesture as Larsen stopped the truck. Smiling, Su then opened his door, forcing the soldier beside him to jump down again.

The soldier was a young woman. She wore a thin green cotton uniform that was too big for her, and she held a large pistol in her hand. She was small and slender; Quinn saw silver streaks in her straight black hair. A cap was pushed into her belt beside a giant holster.

Su steered her away from the side of the truck and disarmingly thrust his Communist documents at her; she fumbled with them and then pushed the pistol back into her holster as Su had intended she should. The males hung back, deferring to her: farmers, perhaps, leaving the paperwork to the local teacher.

In later life, Quinn considered that she was one of the most sensual women he had ever seen. She had an air about her that he could never define; sexuality, danger, her tongue flicking at her lips as she read, the sunlight glinting on the silver threads in her jet-black hair.

"If we get out of this," he said to Larsen, "I'll kiss Su's boots for a week."

Su was now blandly offering cigarettes all around; the guerrillas jumped off the truck and took them reverently, tucking them into their pockets. When she saw what they were doing, she spoke to them sharply, and they dropped them in the dust.

Larsen jumped from the truck and began to prowl up and down while the soldiers watched him warily—his irritation showing in his bouncy walk; every now and again he kicked at a tire. Quinn watched him anxiously. The girl was arguing with Su, her finger stabbing the documents while Su smiled and patted her arm; once she glanced at Quinn and he looked away. It had been like this at school: his spirit tagging boldly after the bushrangers while he was obliged to play the parson in a mock bridal set at a juvenile ball.

"Smile!" Su called to him. "Look cheerful and relaxed."

Quinn smiled a ghastly smile; the guerrillas seemed to be urging the girl to hurry, but she sat on a rock for several minutes, perusing the documents while Larsen muttered angrily. Two guerrillas began to study the boxes in the back.

Su appeared to make a sudden decision. He strode to the rear of the truck, dragged off a box of medical supplies, and laid it at the girl's feet. She argued the morality of this for another five minutes before she yielded; one of the men picked up the box and the girl waved them on.

Larsen steered the truck around a pony cart and revved the engine loudly; behind them, the guerrillas began filing up into low foothills past the graves of their ancestors; winding away forever up into the core of Quinn's brain.

"Another ten seconds," Larsen seethed, "and I was going to let the bitch have it!" A hollow threat which Quinn put down to his usual braggadocio.

SIAN: A UNITED States Army Advisory Group colonel sat on a bench beside a jeep, swigging a soft drink, sluggish with sediment, from a small bottle. His massive shirt was soaked with sweat, and his tiny Chinese driver lay curled asleep in the dust at his feet, his delicate hands bent like cat's paws at his chest.

"Hi." He was about forty-five and near the end of his tether. "Where you guys goin'?" he asked, gently shaking the last drop from his bottle onto his little companion.

"We're looking for General Keh's headquarters." Larsen jumped from the truck, ostentatiously easing his holster from his hip.

"White Horse Division." The colonel smiled: half-amusement, half-regret. "Most of the Division's here, but Keh's in Hua-yin." He gave directions and then began prodding his driver softly with one dusty boot, like a weary father saddled with a wayward child. "Hey," he said. "Hey, wake up."

Larsen stalked around him, bristling with a display of resolve. "How far are we from the front?"

"The front of what?" The colonel dropped the bottle in the

dust; a tiny crater spurted between his boots. "So many god-damned fronts, and they're all invisible."

Larsen went red. "How do you see it then? How's it going?"

"The war?" The colonel gazed away down the road. "The war's going great. We're advancing south wherever you look. Have 'em bottled up in Indochina in no time." He prodded his driver again. "C'mon, little fella. We got work to do."

Larsen was furious; the man had made him look a fool. "Maybe they're getting the wrong advice."

The colonel looked up at him with mock surprise. "Sonny, they don't need no advice. They got techniques nobody used yet. Why, jest yesterday I watched 'em strafing from two thousand feet. Now what other air force can do that? 'Course it ain't always effective, but you gotta admit it's new."

Larsen was almost speechless. "We trained 'em. We equipped 'em."

"Now I'm glad you mentioned that." The colonel prodded his driver again, and he sat up, stretching and blinking like a child. "All that fine equipment. Another army gonna destroy all that if they're retreatin', but not our boys, no sir. That right, Ling? Not our boys?"

Ling looked up at him shyly. "Not our boys," he repeated.

"You heard the little guy." The colonel held out his hands. "No scorched earth here. They got a better idea. You leave it in big shiny piles 'cause it's valuable stuff, see, and you don't destroy valuable stuff like that. Along come the Commies—sun in their eyes—and wham! they run straight into it. Ain't that the truth, little buddy? End of Commies."

"End of Commies," confirmed Ling.

The colonel stood up wearily as they were leaving and leaned in Larsen's window. "If you can't find Keh, jest ask for General Cornpone," he said softly. "Same thing, sonny."

Larsen seethed with fury as they roared off down the road. "That old bastard," he spat out at last, "was yellow through and through."

SEVEN

KEH WAS ABOUT TO DISMOUNT from his horse in Hua-yin after a sedate morning amble. He was decidedly not pleased to see them; they delayed an all-out assault on his breakfast, which was steaming on a table in the street outside a restaurant. His slender Shanghai concubine awaited him there; he joined her, tucking a napkin beneath his plump chin, while Su advanced to show Shiozawa his Nationalist documents. Shiozawa laid them before Keh, and the two men muttered together for several minutes while Quinn and Larsen waited beside the truck. Before them rose the sacred mountain of Hua-shan.

Suddenly Keh pushed back his chair and pattered toward them with a beaming smile. Standing before them in shiny boots, with a block of military fruit salad on his chest, he offered a soft hand and synthetic pleasure.

"Mitta Quinn," he murmured. "Mitta Larsen." It occurred to Quinn that he had never intended to call for him at all.

"We got up the mountain," he said. "We have information

there is a battalion of bandits on the top." He paused. "Suicide battalion."

He cupped one hand around his mouth and inserted a silver toothpick with the other, prodding between his large teeth as if he were already probing for the right path up through the towering walls of rock.

"A battalion?" Quinn spoke before he could stop himself. He glanced at a small detachment of soldiers who squatted in the shade of a wall. "How many men will you have?"

Keh waved the toothpick fretfully. "Plenty men. Plenty men." He spoke to Shiozawa in a low voice and waddled off, toes turned out, dipping his knees and plucking his trousers from his behind.

Quinn watched him go, absently sucking the cut on his hand which had become inflamed. He spat in the dust.

"There couldn't be a battalion," he said at last. "He's probably going to rat the poor boxes in the temples."

He did not know how close he was.

GENERAL KEH'S ATTACK on Hua-shan began soon after breakfast. It began slowly. He lingered with his concubine at the table while Larsen opened the last of their cans. The napkin was tucked beneath his chin, half obscuring the meaningless decorations. It was almost as if Keh were courting the resentment not only of them, but of his own men—a sudden rush at his throat, a greedy glitter in his eyes, and a few expendable soldiers twitching in the dust as a warning to the rest.

His troops squatted dully beneath the wall, wiping millet porridge and maize bread from their mouths: twenty-odd men, their rifles upright between their knees. Shiozawa walked slowly down their line, gazing at them with contempt. He was bigger than any of them, and although he had developed a slight paunch, his obvious cruelty remained intact. He took up a position a few paces behind Keh to show that he was ready to depart while the concubine popped a morsel in Keh's mouth with her chopsticks and murmured something that made him smile. The young general sat back and again began to pick his teeth, his eyes glazing already with the false somnolence of repletion.

Quinn remembered that scene later with particular clarity because it encapsulated so much of the war in a form that he could contemplate with limited distress: the greed of many Nationalist Kehs and their mistresses, the brutality at their shoulders, the troops they strewed behind them like straw. His mind often pushed aside the unbearable *later* to return to the bearable *then*: a final tableau of mock peace on that plain in Shensi before the cracking of the young girls' necks in Kwangsi; the round-mouth Os of the row of heads turning from side to side like roll-a-ball clowns at a fair; the cowardice of his own complicity.

And there was a loveliness in the morning, barely tainted then by their corruption. The sacred mountain of Hua-shan thrust up into a clear blue sky—not the solitary snowy peak of a picture-book Fuji or Kilimanjaro, but a cluster of gray-green peaks rearing from a massif chopped by a deep gorge from the body of the Chinling Range. Civilization lapped them like a shallow sea; distant temple bells tinkled faintly over the fields.

The temple bells were the tappets of a dusty Packard; laboring in the wrong gear, it crept around the corner like a sick beetle and stopped by the general's table. Steam curled from its radiator. The driver climbed out and saluted clumsily.

"Bastards have got tin ears," rasped Larsen. He unrolled a small white penis and began to urinate against a wall. Turning to speak to him, Quinn noted with mild distaste that he was uncircumcised. He had seen only one uncircumcised penis before: a fat orphan boy at school had peeled back his foreskin like a banana to enlighten his classmates. His distaste shamed him. He wanted to agree with Larsen about Chinese drivers, in private atonement, but he realized that this might offend Su. "Look, she's leaving," he said, welcoming the diversion.

The girl was climbing into the back of the Packard; a slab of her silvery thigh glistened like rancid meat as her cheongsam fell back. Keh closed the door and lifted his arm in a half-military salute.

Su wandered back toward them. "He's sending her back to Shanghai," he explained; he had been eavesdropping on their last moments. "A DC3 from Sian." And he pointed a slender foot at the dust with a tremulous gaiety. "We'll be off soon," he cried. "Let us make wing to the rooky wood."

Larsen became very excited at that point: an ominous sign,

when Quinn fitted it in with what came later. He pulled his so-called Patton Special from a holster and pointed it playfully at Su's foot.

Su withdrew his foot quickly and pushed away the pearl butt with a tiny touch of his hand. "Really, Larsen!" he protested. "You should grow up! How phallic!"

Larsen flushed with pleasure at Su's discomfort. Casually, he began sighting the revolver on the roof of a hut in a side street, and then he lowered it slowly toward the head of an old man who sat on a stool outside the hut—waving the barrel in a small circle as he settled on a center between his eyes. The old man looked back at him stoically until Larsen turned the revolver and began squinting at a wall. He had lost.

Watching him, Quinn realized that he did not truly want to shatter a skull. He and Larsen were not strong enough for stress. Their very presence was useless, absurd.

He stepped closer to Su. "Do you really think there is a battalion of Communist troops up there?"

Su eyed him with amusement. "Do you really believe, Quinn, that I would be marching up there if there were? There is another reason for Keh."

He was looking past Quinn's shoulder. A young Taoist novice in white jacket and trousers stood with bound hands in the street. A rope around his neck was attached to the saddle of Keh's stallion.

THE COLUMN MOVED out with Keh in front leading the boy; a sure sign that he considered they were in no immediate danger. The Communists controlled most of Shensi—indeed, Mao Tse-tung himself, pursued by erratic Nationalist bombers, had camped at the foot of the mountain only about four months before. Keh could not have known that then—and, as for Mao, the White Horse Division posed no threat to his vast design. It threatened only Hua-shan itself.

Larsen, Quinn, and Su walked in single file behind Keh; Shiozawa marched at the rear. Su sang a few bars of "The Lass of Richmond Hill" and laughed mournfully while Larsen's head jerked from side to side; fingering the butt of his revolver, he seemed to be willing Red bandits to bob up from every bush.

"At Halloween," he crowed, "I used to shoot the pumpkins. Now we might see the real thing."

"If they don't see you first," Su reminded him. "I hope my uncle is impressed by my exploits. I'm beginning to find this whole business rather depressing."

Quinn turned, speaking over his shoulder in case Keh over-heard him. "I don't understand. What's happening with the boy?"

"The same question," Su replied, "is exercising my mind."

At that point the boy stumbled and looked back at them—not with pleading, but with a steady curiosity. Quinn guessed that he was about thirteen. One of his cheeks was blue and swollen, and his white jacket and pants were smeared with dirt and blood.

He felt ashamed. A column of troops winding across a plain had been magic once: North-West Frontier Saturday matinee stuff, with eagle clusters of Pathans in the pitiless rocks; the Lancers jingling into ambush with bonehead British pluck while the Violet Crumble bars snapped with the filigree flintlocks. This was all wrong: it was obscenity, not glory. The troops shambled with the vacuity of mental patients on an afternoon ramble through autumn parkland. Small trees, aflame with vermilion and yellow, fluttered delicately in a gentle breeze; he half-expected to see a nurse pushing a wheelchair among the daisies in the tawny grass. There was no ambush. They entered a valley leading to the massive walls of rock. Three men waited by a stream that ran swiftly over pale smooth stones: a Nationalist soldier who was hurriedly shrugging a rifle strap over his shoulder, and two sedan chair carriers rising with sweat rags draped around their brawny necks. Keh dismounted and tossed the reins to the soldier, his absurd ceremonial exit from the town concluded; he stepped without a word into the sedan chair while the soldier tethered the boy to one of its shafts and untied his hands. Then the soldier slapped Keh's mount gently and began to lead it back to the town.

The column snaked to and fro across the stream on stepping stones as the water slid endlessly from a hidden gorge; several times the boy slipped sideways, jerking the rope fiercely into his inflamed neck. Remembering this many years later, Quinn was ashamed that he could have accepted such cruelty without inquiry or complaint; he contemplated his youthful docility, in middle age, with the same detachment as he had observed the smooth stones then on the bed of the stream. Then they began to climb.

They climbed slowly from the sunshine of the plain—up from the broken-walled villages, the green fields of maize, toward a belt of mist that hid the granite towers above. Small twisted pines began to climb beside them, and here and there fallen boulders blocked their narrow path. Keh remained hidden in his chair, shouting angrily whenever the carriers tilted him alarmingly, and then the mist enclosed them; the valley shrank toward an apex of rock and vapor and roaring water.

Nobody spoke from one hour to the next; only the carriers grunted and chanted and called instructions to each other as they clambered up through the valley; they, who seemed to have so little to sing about, now sang as if they had been hewn from the living rock itself and breathed into life. Occasionally, the column climbed past tiny Taoist temples. They were deserted; two steaming cups of hot water sat on a bench outside one of them, and two delicate heads peeped like rock wallabies from the boulders above. Keh's reputation had preceded him.

It was mid-afternoon before they reached the end of the valley. The column sagged there for half an hour outside another temple while Keh stretched his legs—taking quick little steps amid the rocks, bending his knees, plucking the seat of his trousers.

The carriers pointed and laughed; high above them a tiny monastery perched on the edge of a sheer precipice. They had not even begun the real climb.

Panting, marble-white, Larsen lay on his back with one hand on the butt of his revolver to show that he was prepared; Su dabbed curiously with a forefinger at a fluttering calf muscle, grimaced at Quinn, and, closing his eyes, rested his head against a rock. And Quinn inspected his hand, which had become a throbbing lump, and studied the boy, who was the only one who was utterly still. He lay on his side, his knees beneath his chin, gazing up at the monastery as if he were drawing its essence into an invisible ray that locked them in private contact. Bent in this fetal position, his face contracting to stone, he seemed to be allowing the last of his childhood to drain away before his final ascent into maturity.

Keh, at this point, was in a jolly mood; he had, after all, done no walking. The soldiers watched him nervously; merriment could be an omen.

He strutted over and smiled down at Quinn. "So! You are a friend of Doyle?" Standing so close above him, rocking to and fro in his shiny boots, that his stomach blocked the mountain. A small rubber spider dangled from a black thread wrapped around one plump forefinger.

Quinn ignored it. "Yes. I'd like to write about some of your campaigns. Put it in the *Clarion*." He dragged himself back a little on his elbow. "Whatever you feel like saying, of course."

Keh giggled. "Maybe I say nothing . . . Fight the bandits first, then talk."

"When will they be defeated?" Quinn remembered the young girl springing onto the road with her large pistol; the demoralized garrisons clustering in blockhouses as the shadows seeped down from the foothills.

"Soon. Very soon. Everywhere they run away. Field mice in the maize." His boots squeaked, his belt creaked; he stank of perfume and leather, the tang of rank nights.

"This suicide battalion . . ." Quinn began, but Keh had turned away. Reflectively, he jiggled the spider over the boy, prodded him with his boot, and then stomped away to sit on a rock.

"We drive them into the sea," he called—a rare feat from Hua-shan. And Quinn noted the knife edge of hysteria beneath his words: buffoonery on one side, violence the other. "Rabble!" he boasted. "They do not dare to fight."

"The very model of a modern major general," Su murmured, his eyes still closed, but Larsen sat up and laid his revolver on a ledge where Keh could see it: show and tell for the teacher, his bleak eyes flicking for red stars over the black rocks, the twisted pines, the cold water sliding out of the mountain.

"Bring on the pumpkins!" he said, tingling for a hideous Halloween.

THE FINAL ASCENT to the monastery took four or five hours; Quinn lost track of time. They climbed steps cut through crevices in the rock. Even Keh climbed part of the way when the carriers had to leave the chair behind; they pushed and pulled and piggybacked him for the rest of his incomprehensible pilgrimage up into the cloud peaks of the gods. They dragged themselves up clutching iron chains, on a path wide enough in many places for only one person: the carriers called out to warn descending pilgrims to wait until they could pass, but no one came down. Only the mist swirled around cliffs carved with giant characters that Quinn could not understand. "Worship," they instructed, "Worship," as the slug nosed its way up toward one of Keh's false footnotes in Nationalist military history. Quinn's hand hurt each time he gripped for support.

A long clitoris of stone bulged from the center of one crevice; it rose almost vertically and was notched with about thirty steps, each a meter high, with iron chains fastened on each side. They swarmed up that and then hauled themselves through an iron trap into a clearing beside another temple. The trap door guarded the only way to the summit—the priests bolted it down at night to keep out robbers and murderers, but now this temple, too, was deserted; no Communist troops waited there to slaughter them. They climbed up, edging around boulders, creeping along paths strung on the edge of the void, and struggled at last onto a narrow ridge. Perched on it was the monastery that they had seen from below; three or four tiny buildings jammed in a row. Their low roofs clung like scales to the dragon-back ridge.

Before them, the Taoist monasteries of Hua-shan straddled the razor-sharp ridges with terrifying precipices on each side. The path before Keh's column led straight through the nearest monastery buildings to the peak beyond it—the lowest of the five sacred peaks of Hua-shan—for there was no room to edge around it.

Further above them still, on the other four peaks, more monasteries sat sublimely above the smoking chasms of a monstrous crater in humble tribute to the Great Ultimate, and far beneath them they could see the mighty Yellow River glinting in the evening light as it flowed eastward to fertilize the North China Plain. Peasants had climbed up here for thousands of years to make burnt offerings for rich harvests and male children to Sheng Mu, the Divine Mother, the Goddess of Fertility, but now they were making burnt offerings to Mao and the People's Liberation Army. The vast landscape below was hazy with smoke; they were burning weeds to get ashes for saltpeter for the Communist shells.

Keh was waxen with fatigue, but he pattered ahead to the

monastery as if the next great Communist offensive was about to engulf the mountain. Shiozawa pushed through the troops, grabbed the boy's neck-rope from a carrier, and tugged him behind him as he followed his master. Going up the steps, he pulled out his Mauser.

The detachment sank down on the stone spine of the ridge; Quinn braced for a rattle of shots. Nobody could speak. Below them, a thin paste of sunshine still lay on the Yellow River as it bore its load of rich loess to the distant sea; China's Sorrow in flood and drought, but also the wellspring of her civilization. This river had awed him once in his sentimental ignorance (his feet curled around a hot water bottle in a rented room near the university in Sydney; his frozen lips intoning the English translations of *tz'us*). It had seemed too magnificent then for the tampering fingers of man. But now, the Shanghai newspapers had revealed, both armies were unleashing it as a flood weapon, just as Keh and his pathetic retinue were despoiling the mountain. Already the war made him feel dirty and cold. Up here it was already winter; Hua-shan and the Yellow River were threadbare concepts when he could not stop shivering.

He stood up, stamping his feet. "Fuck it," he said. "Let's get inside."

He led Larsen and Su toward the monastery; Keh emerged as they arrived at the steps. He was folding a piece of hide, marked with what appeared to be indelible blue pencil, and he pushed it quickly beneath his tunic and buttoned it up to the neck. His eyes flickered with uneasy resentment, but he forced a wide grin.

"Ah, gentlemen," he murmured. "We stay here the night. Come to the heat."

Inside, the monastery was dim and warm; Quinn paused in the doorway, allowing his eyes to focus in the gloom. The Taoist temple near The Vienna had been a gaudy little parlor compared with this retreat in the clouds. He had looked inside it once: it featured a ludicrous god who rode into battle on a black tiger, hurling exploding pearls at his enemies; another with his tongue on his chest and tears of blood rolling from his eyes—Luna Park lacquer for fishermen's families. But here the somber tones of antiquity, the glow of bronze and brass, the shadowed blackwood, cupped the contemplation of centuries; an accretion of humility darkened the room like the smoke of its fires.

He edged into the temple, straining to see, and soon a faint rustling and the gleam of an eye betrayed the presence of the priests: hair disheveled, beards straggling, they stooped in patchwork gowns enduring the ominous intrusion of the soldiers. Just as the carriers seemed to have been fashioned from the rock, so they were like fragments of life torn from the mountain itself: its earth, its grasses, its storms and silences. They did not look directly at Shiozawa, who pushed the boy down into a corner as if he were returning a stray dog.

Quinn felt ill. Mountains had never embodied magic for him: peaks were alien concepts in a hushed childhood drowsy with the cackling of hens at noon; each night the pale skeletons of the eucalypts around the town had lit the river flats for dramas that never began. No unearthly shadow had ever detached itself from the tree-line there; the mystery had tingled with unfulfilled promise in the bends of drowsy creeks (once, breathlessly awaiting a visitation, tensely observing the breaking of branches, he had confronted a Jersey cow). He had grown up there as a stranger, yearning for signs with all the other strangers—haunting a cemetery of departed essences, their schizophrenia had been complete. And in the end he had given up, just as the others had given up, bunched fists, and settled for less. Watched not for the supernatural, but for the slice of a fin, the glitter of a snake, the trap door spider in a shoe, the maniac crouched outside the tent. Because there—there, nobody belonged.

But here: here earth and peasant, priest and mountain, god and crop, plain and river, all merged. The priests crouched before Keh like the crooked pines, accustomed to mightier gales than this poisonous puffball who had blown in demanding shelter. He might kill them, but he was surely beneath their contemplation. Quinn stood there, watching them, and he saw earth spilling from their fibrous root-arms, orchids flowering from bayonet-holes in their throats, the rich loess streaming down the cracked watercourses of their withered necks. He realized that he was feverish; his throbbing hand had become so puffy that he could not close his fingers.

"Please! Please!" Keh beckoned them inside: he was all bonhomie. The priests retreated to prepare a meal, and with a puckish peep toward the kitchen and a finger to his lips, he tugged a brandy flask from his hip pocket and passed it to Quinn and

100

Larsen. They sat on a heated brick *k'ang* while Su dropped on the floor beside it, making soft little sounds of distress. Instinctively, Quinn kept his sickness to himself, in fear of revealing weakness to Keh and Shiozawa.

Outside the door, the troops huddled together, awaiting more millet gruel: hands pushed inside their jackets, heads shrunk to their chests as the bitter chill of night began to enclose the mountain. Shiozawa watched them coldly, a few paces from the *k'ang*. His pistol lay beside his right hand, and he rested his back against a plump idol of Sheng Mu; holding the vase of fertility, she gazed down on him reflectively, as if pondering the possibility of emptying its contents on his cropped head.

They ate vegetable dishes that night, and Quinn slept badly. The monastery was infested with rats; he dreamed that the largest of all was fastening its teeth into his hand, and he started up in fright while they squealed in the roof and behind the walls. The luminous dial of his watch said one o'clock. A shadow was moving on Sheng Mu's shoulder; he saw a snout lift slowly, quivering in candle glow.

Out on the steps a sentry crouched beneath the cold, his bayonet silhouetted against the mist; the other soldiers had crept in during the night and now lay bunched on the floor around Shiozawa, who slept sitting up against the idol. Keh was snoring gently on the *k'ang* beneath a padded quilt, and Larsen lay on his back beside him. The boy was a dim shape in the corner.

Su also was awake; he was whispering to a young soldier beside the *k'ang*. The candlelight glistened like oil on the soldier's throat which he was stroking softly, with long beautiful fingers, as he and Su murmured to each other.

Quinn closed his eyes and lay stiff and silent, remembering Christmas Eves as a child when he had pretended to be asleep; embarrassed that he had intruded on a sexual union.

"ALL RIGHT! WAKEE! Wakee! The next stage!" Keh was stamping around the temple when they tottered up the next morning to make the final climb.

"He can afford to be happy," Su groaned. "He's got another chair."

They climbed the final leg on a dizzy narrow path; it dipped and soared along the ridges above chasms with no ledge to break shrieking falls into the mist below.

Keh became terrified again; he climbed gingerly from the sedan chair and shouted at anyone who seemed likely to jostle him—edging his way over the perilous sections, he resembled a child who had wet his pants. An icy wind threatened to toss them like flies into the void, and crumbling stone posts and rusted iron chains were too dangerous to lean on. The column bent against the wind, creeping up giant stone staircases worn by pilgrims who had been sustained by faith, not desiccated by greed and bewilderment. For it was only greed that could have driven Keh as far as this. No battle or retreat could have drawn him up here from his rotting ease on the plain; the indelible blue markings on the piece of hide folded against his chest obviously explained his journey. He patted his tunic sometimes to make sure that the hide was still there: his talisman for a blessed future.

Su had discovered what was marked on the hide. They climbed a ladder set in a cliff; three soldiers refused to mount even its lowest rung until Shiozawa placed his pistol against their heads. Quinn went up first before his courage drained; besides, he felt a foolish need to wound Larsen by upstaging him. His hands were so cold that he felt no pain; conquering that crest, a joyous fire suffused his body—it was to be the last time that he ever experienced that electric loveliness of youth.

He felt like capering—like strewing flowers—but he turned stonily as Larsen's head appeared over the top. "What kept you?" he asked and was gratified by Larsen's murderous glance.

Su drew them both aside. "There is money buried up here," he confided. "Communist money."

They rested later in a mossy wood sheltered by three of the peaks; Quinn's brief elation had dissipated, and his hand again throbbed steadily. He and Larsen sat with their backs against a pine tree while Su dropped beside them and began to push gently with his toe at a pad of moss on a rock.

"One of the soldiers told me last night," he said, and Quinn once again felt shamed. "The boy's family lives in a village near Hua-yin—apparently he was visiting his home the other night. He's from one of these temples. Anyway, he saw three men up here with some boxes, and he told his family about it. He thought at first they were robbers—they'd just sent away their carriers.

102

"Well, his family and the village gossiped about it, and someone in the Peace Preservation Corps told Keh because one of his patrols killed three strangers down in the valley the next morning. They were all carrying grenades, and two of them had writing brushes and accounts."

He dislodged the moss and looked around quickly. "They were Communist bankers, obviously, burying their reserves. Gold or silver."

Quinn glanced at Larsen. "You mean the Communists hide bullion in the mountains?"

"What else can they do? Chiang has the cities—well, he's losing them all now. They've got to back their currency. The mountains are their vaults. Do you know the latest exchange rate?"

Quinn did not understand exchange rates. He gazed at the novice. He sat with his uninjured cheek resting against a maple tree; with one arm curled around its trunk, he was peering through the trees toward a small temple on the edge of a cliff.

"No," he said. "What will happen to the boy?"

"Ten thousand of Chiang's dollars to one of Mao's. The boy?" Su picked a blade of grass and flung it at the rock. "The Communists will be rather annoyed with him if Keh finds their gold, and Keh . . ."

"Yes?"

Su tossed another blade of grass. "Keh will want to get away as quickly and as quietly as he can."

"What does that mean?"

"Really, Quinn . . ." Su sighed with mild exasperation. "You and Larsen . . ."

WELL, WHAT DID it matter, decades later? Hua-shan was merely the beginning—notable only because it was there that he first witnessed violent death.

It happened suddenly. Keh and Shiozawa led the boy into the temple while the detachment squatted in the dripping wood; now and again the soldiers worked the bolts of their rifles desultorily, or hawked and spat in the sparse wild grass beneath the tortured pines, shivering in their worn cotton uniforms and wriggling their feet in the assortment of canvas shoes and slippers that had carried the White Horse Division so often beyond the range of enemy gunfire. A ragged priest sat outside the temple, painting

103

elaborate characters on a board with an otherwo`ldy absorption that seemed to shield him from the present, and high on a flat rock, stark against a boiling white cauldron of mist and clouds, two others thrust and parried in a ritual battle of shadow and light. While they did so, Keh and Shiozawa were staging their own demonstrations of darkness against the doomed boy inside.

They did not take long to wrench the exact hiding place from him. Keh hurried out and shouted at the troops, who scrambled up and trotted to the temple, laying their rifles with a clatter on the stone slabs of one of its courts. The court ended at the very edge of the precipice; a tall open gateway beckoned suicidal strollers to take their final step into infinity. It was here that Shiozawa stood, resting one boot on a large rusting chain that hung over the edge. He was speaking rapidly in a mixture of Japanese and Chinese while pointing down into the mist.

"There is a hermit cave," whispered Su. "The boxes are down there."

And it was true, as they were soon to see: three Communist bankers with a lingering affection for the gods had given General Keh the very cornerstone he needed to build his business empire.

SHIOZAWA POINTED TO two soldiers. They tried to speak, but their lips worked without sound and their knees sagged; they half-turned in dumb entreaty to their comrades, ducking their heads as they nuzzled blindly toward the safety of the herd.

Shiozawa did not wait: he stepped forward, clutched one man by the collar, and flung him with one sweep of his arm into the swirling sea of vapor.

A dreadful stillness chilled the group; the other soldier bent slowly and took up the chain, grasping it fiercely as he lowered himself backward over the edge, his feet scrabbling for footholds. He moaned as one of his slippers dropped off.

Shiozawa nodded briefly to another soldier; the poor wretch climbed down when the first soldier reached the hermit cave. And in the next half-hour they sent up four boxes in a thick rope sling lowered to the cave while Keh threatened instant death if they spilled any of the boxes into the abyss. The giggle had become a scream, just as Veitch had tried to tell Doyle.

"Did you see that?" Larsen hissed, edging close to Quinn.

104

Shiozawa's sudden ferocity had shattered even him. "Did you see that poor bastard?" Pushing his revolver more firmly out of sight beneath his jacket in case it should trigger a challenge. And Quinn nodded, white-faced, trembling as he had trembled in the brothel; his desire for adventure turning in on itself like a sick dog curling to sleep.

Keh ordered the boxes to be placed in the temple, smirking as he bustled past the novice to supervise the procedure. The boy leaned weakly against the wall of the temple; blood now was running from his nose, and one broken arm rested against his chest.

Then Keh and Shiozawa stood over the boxes while two soldiers prized them open. They contained not gold but ingots of silver, and while Quinn and Larsen craned to see, Su turned to look at the boy.

He said later that he saw him walk calmly to the gateway, pause, and then step out into the billowing clouds. He thought he heard him cry out briefly, as if his terrified childhood had suddenly rushed back into his mouth, but it could have been the whistling of the wind; the breathing of the Great Being, as the Taoist philosopher Chuang-tzu had put it in an inscription carved above the temple entrance.

Su translated the inscription later while, inside, Keh hooted with laughter and plunked himself down on one of the boxes: "Wind is what we call the breathing of the Great Being . . . When it blows, old caves begin to howl. Have you never heard this howling? The slopes of the mountain forests, the holes in old trees, they are like nostrils, like mouths, like ears, like roof beams, like rings, like mortars, like puddles, like ponds. There is a howling, a cursing, a hissing, a panting, a calling, a mourning, a banging, a biting . . . Have you never felt this swinging and swaying?"

Quinn scribbled it in a notebook, fighting to keep his grip. He noticed that Su's eyes were wet, but he appeared strangely serene for the first time, standing there on the steps of the temple, as if he had briefly returned at last to his beginning.

THE GREAT BEING howled all that afternoon and night, buffeting the temple and delaying their descent from the mountain. They huddled inside. Quinn watched the soldier's body fly over the precipice a thousand times and bounce back on its feet like a trick shot in a movie; his toad hand pulsed and the temple swung and swayed with the load of corruption in its belly. He wrote "Keh" in his notebook and underlined the word, staring blankly into the darkness: sullied and incriminated if he did not speak out; in danger if he did. Baffled that Keh did not care who observed his excesses.

He slept badly again, numb with shock and cold: two smoking charcoal stoves gave no warmth as the storm raged. He staggered up on the dawn of his nineteenth birthday.

Keh, for once, was already up, supervising the distribution of the silver ingots into equal loads for the troops. Speed was essential now, for he could not hope to keep the seizure secret for long. He sent one man ahead to alert carriers to meet them at the foot of the mountain; the laden soldiers shuffled miserably into line and began the descent.

An icy wind raged as they staggered down the mountain; Quinn's head thumped with fever. It was on this occasion, while they were sheltering amid a tumble of rocks, that the first soldier who had climbed down to the cave quietly went mad and began prodding him inexplicably until Shiozawa shot him through the mouth and pushed him over the edge. Shiozawa forced Su to carry the man's pack until Su's legs buckled, and then Shiozawa carried it himself.

They reeled out onto the floor of the valley late that afternoon, and it was not until several days later that Su told him why the four priests at the temple had not emerged to watch them leave. Dangling his spider playfully in their faces, Keh had ordered the priests to climb down the iron chain to the hermit cave as dawn was breaking. Two soldiers had then unbolted the chain and dropped it over the edge.

No doubt they died humbly, said Su, contemplating the void that filled them, their bones fragmenting, as they had always intended, inside the sacred mountain; their spirits beyond life and death, just as Chuang-tzu had said they were.

"They're happy," he said. But Su never sang any Jerome Kern hits after that. He never sang at all.

EIGHT

THE COMMUNISTS GOT WORD OF the seizure within hours, for irregulars launched a heavy attack that night on Sian airfield, forcing Keh to abandon his plan to fly from there to Shanghai with his booty. He ordered the main body of his division in Sian to cover his withdrawal, gathered one hundred men in a truck convoy, and loaded the silver into two makeshift armored cars at the head of the column—ugly relics of the war against Japan, they were built on the reinforced chassis of trucks. Larsen edged the UNRRA truck into the middle of the column as Keh climbed into the first armored car; the last truck in the line pulled a horse float containing his fat little stallion.

Ten minutes later they began roaring south as a frantic White Horse artillery barrage erupted around them. The great chase had begun; Keh now was on the run from the war in earnest, about to translate his genial ruthlessness into what the world's finance writers later lauded as business enterprise.

He struck south on a wild zigzag route which he altered on

sudden whim or rumor of Communist ambush. A simple cunning spiced his fear: the Communists, he surmised, would assume that he would try to race down the main road and rail routes between the large provincial centers, and so he veered off on cart tracks, doubled back on his trail, and even crawled up into mountain areas that the Communists had held since the twenties. His lunatic luck held. The grotesque armored cars labored up narrow passes where farmers rolling boulders and dropping grenades could have shattered his column.

Quinn's fever had worsened. His muscles and joints now ached constantly, and a distressing diarrhea bubbled in his bowel. He slumped in the back of the truck, plucking the yellow gridiron helmets from their boxes and defecating in them before he dropped them over the side: a Johnny Appleseed, he joked to himself bitterly, spreading new waste disposal techniques throughout the remote regions of Szechuan and Hunan. It was all that kept him going sometimes, that joke: earnest peasants gathering around his helmets in the ditches, as if they had dropped magically from the sky; the elders pontificating over the mysteries of foreign plumbing in the villages at evening. He moaned with laughter—at least they were down off the mountain.

There may have been a chance to break away from Keh in Hua-yin or soon after leaving there. Stronger and wiser men, he supposed, could have chanced it on that vast landscape and lived—tried to make contact, perhaps, with MAG in Sian, or with one of UNRRA's polyglot teams in the area—for Larsen still had not placed himself beyond the UNRRA pale. And yet Quinn could concentrate only on holding himself together, and to stay with Keh appeared safer, in any case, than turning his back on him. And so, like Keh's soldiers, he clung to the known, awaiting deliverance; convinced that the murder of a European witness to Keh's crimes was above Keh's station. He even determined to simulate friendship with Keh—or admiration if necessary—so that he could totter back to The Vienna eventually and wryly thank Doyle for such a lovely outing. "G'day, mate!" he'd say. "Look, you really shouldn't have gone to so much trouble on my account . . ." And he pictured Doyle chuckling with the steel of Greece and Crete in his belly, with the surf club keg in his belly, with the skinned knuckles outside dance halls in his belly: a
108

paid-up member of the vast club of suffering men who might usher him into the foyer, if he were lucky, and enroll him as an associate.

THEY ROARED INTO Szechuan one morning—electrifying Su, who barely remembered his early childhood there; his excitement was so vivid that Quinn dragged himself up beside him. He never forgot those first few minutes in Szechuan. A mighty life force irradiated the province and its people; it flamed in the peasants' faces and burst from the earth in banana and bamboo, mulberry and banyan, sugar cane and camphor: the richness of Su before the West subdivided him. Su was quivering like a deer scenting its heartland as the column careered through the villages, scattering children and old women and chickens; sucking it all into his veins, just as the great bamboo wheels scooped up the rushing water of the rivers for the irrigation channels between the fields. High above them the mountains marched westward to Tibet, ramparts of granite and ice echoed in the cheekbones of the people who watched them pass, and Quinn lay back and watched Su absorbing it all while the breeze streamed over his hawklike face, melting his years of exile.

He tried to find light relief in his plight to counter the awful fear that he might be dying—for when Su opened the remaining box of medical supplies they found that it was empty: cleaned out in Hua-yin, no doubt, while they were up on the mountain. He even developed a whole scenario starring the organisms in his bowel: they became tiny Nationalist secret agents in black oiled-silk and Western felt hats. He imagined them already gathering for departure at his body's exit—chittering with anger because they had not conquered him; rolling up their plans irritably as they prepared to jump off and thumb for another victim. Sometimes he wheezed with false laughter as he contemplated them—freezing suddenly as the poisoned river stirred again. Su pointedly turned his back on these occasions while Quinn groaned and groped, wondering what he had eaten or drunk that had afflicted him so badly. Even danger became irrelevant; the prospect of death a relief. All that mattered in the end was the jolting of the truck against his ravaged haunches; the desperate scramble to drag down his trousers; the sweating and delirium each blazing day and black night when they stopped in the villages.

109

One evening when his fever was high the sky seemed livid green, and a diseased rat crept slowly along a broken village wall with a ruby of blood gleaming in its side. He watched its delicate paws stroke the crumbling mud while bamboo creaked and a naked baby boy stood watching him gravely, his dirty hands folded on his swollen stomach. A radio boomed a snatch of "Don't Fence Me In" from Crosby until someone shouted and it snapped off; he lay in the gloom, his head whirling so sickeningly that he wished he could drain his skull. If Keh wanted to kill him now, he was welcome.

He vaguely remembered Shiozawa standing over him as he lay on one occasion beside the truck; he was laughing, and Quinn looked up at the gold fillings in his teeth and drew comfort from them because they represented cities and civilization. He was beyond hostility and too sick to dream; his brain clutched for support at the corner of a hut, a leaf, a wheel of the truck; each object on which he could focus was a step in a long staircase that climbed from the bubbling pit in the center of the earth, the deepest interior of his brain.

Keh, meanwhile, was flouting every rule in the textbook of military withdrawal as he twisted like a fox trying to spoil the aim of an invisible hunter. Unexpectedly, however, a fierce new resolve began to fill his men: they were heading in the right direction at last, and nobody was going to stop them. They even fought off a local Communist attack one night at a village in southern Szechuan although the Communists bottled them up there until dawn, killed three men, and blew up two trucks.

It was what Quinn had awaited all his life, but he was not up to the occasion. He lay on the cool cobblestones of the village marketplace, propped on one elbow, drooling, while the night erupted in an ear-shattering roar, and Larsen wriggled under the UNRRA truck, wagon-train-style, and poked out his revolver.

"Great help you were!" Larsen snapped at him the next morning, obviously well pleased at the night's bloody excitement, and Quinn smiled wanly, the effort of defense beyond him, mildly watching Larsen run his hands up and down his arms and absently scratch away at his armpits while they laid out the bodies of the dead.

SU CAME TO his aid; he solved the mystery of Quinn's sickness, just as he had shepherded them safely to Shensi. He stared closely at Larsen one afternoon in Szechuan as Larsen stood beside the truck in his underpants, soaping his white body with water from a wooden pail.

"Do you notice the pusy pimples beneath his arms?" he whispered as Quinn raised his head. "I am sure that there will be more on his body"—he paused delicately—"where we cannot see them. Larsen is a source of pseudomonas organisms."

Contemplation of Larsen's pimples made Quinn feel worse; his head thumped back on a kit bag. "Listen," he said. "I'm sick enough as it is."

"Let us assume," Su swept on, "that he scratches his armpits—he is always scratching his armpits. He cuts your hand—remember?—while you are arm wrestling, and in this way he infects your cut. You suck it some days later, perhaps, and the infection enters your bowel. Ten and sixpence, please."

Quinn folded his hands on his belly. "What does it mean?"

"It means that you have Shanghai fever. After thirteen days—something like that, I think—it will pass away."

He patted Quinn's knee. "You will not die. I will care for you as if you were my own child," and he snorted with bitter laughter. "My Anglo-Saxon child."

And from then on, while Larsen drove, Su nursed him tenderly: spooning salty broths into his mouth; bathing him with lukewarm water; wrapping him in a sheet to reduce his fever. And at night Quinn lay watching the blurred outline of Su's head as he translated *tz'us* to him by torchlight, wondering at the gentleness that remained beneath Su's cultural chaos; lulled by the images of a China that neither of them had ever known. A land without soldiers, where old men drowsed over their wine, and maidens languished at night on cold pillows, listening to the scrape of *wu-tung* leaves in empty courts, the dripping of water clocks, the beating of their hearts.

THAT WHOLE JOURNEY was a sick, confused dream, even as it happened, but two grotesque incidents occurred that Quinn had cause to recall many years later.

The first was the Day of the Hideous Monkey, as he dubbed it at the time to blunt the edge of its horror. The column swept into a large market town in Szechuan at the foot of a sharp green range of hills: a Nationalist stronghold, fortified with pillboxes, it guarded one end of a pass. Crowds thronged the marketplace: cheerful people, ignoring the soldiers, they were chattering over piles of vegetables and sugar cane as the black crop of Keh's guns suddenly sprouted among them.

At one side of this lively market-clatter, however, a small group of people were peering silently into a bamboo cage at the mouth of an alley near the truck. Drawn by their stillness, Quinn looked down over their heads.

In the cage was a big pig-tailed monkey that was staring sullenly back at the crowd. It was playing in a desultory fashion with a large torso—now shaking it, now pushing it away in boredom. It was a human dummy: the skin of a human stuffed with straw, which was spilling from a jagged hole at its base. A cap bearing a Communist red star was tied with thick twine to the skull, which sprouted only wisps of black hair and rolled wildly on a flap of neck. Above the monkey, nailed high on a bamboo rod, protruded a withered rosette of genitals.

The second encounter, near Ningsiang, north-west of Changsha, in Hunan, was èven more bizarre. The first armored car swept around a narrow bend, braked, and skidded sideways into three ox-carts jammed high with tables and chairs and piles of bedding. The load crashed to the roadway—also spilling, in the process, China's last batch of eunuchs, who had been perched on top, and now fell before Keh's column as if shaken from a time warp. An old man with the wrinkled face of a prune crouched clutching a battered tin trunk to his chest, and a dozen shaven-headed young boys in long gray gowns clustered around him, sobbing so hard that tears streamed down their tender faces, and urine trickled on to their feet from severed penises that they had not yet learned to control. From a bank above the road, a local detachment of the Peace Preservation Corps grinned down over fixed bayonets.

Even Su was shaken by this anachronism. He jumped down and attempted to calm them, but his hands quivered as he laid them gently on the shrilling boys and guided the old man over to the shade of a willow to question him softly. The old man squatted, placed the trunk on the ground, and gently opened it. He began fussing with rows of small glass jars inside as Su bent over

112

him. Behind Su, blood gushed from the neck of one of the oxen as it sank down on its forelegs.

Only Keh was delighted—after he had confirmed that his armored car had sustained little damage. He strutted up and down, questioning the Peace Preservation Corps men above him on the bank, who were tossing the last of the eunuchs' possessions down onto the pile of broken furniture on the road. When they had done this, Keh ordered his own troops to hurl the upturned tables and chairs and bedding into a ditch beside the road, and then he shot the injured beast and directed the column to keep going.

The young eunuchs pelted with odd little steps beside the column for a short distance, crying and hurling umbrellas which clattered harmlessly against the metal sides of the trucks. Behind them, Quinn caught a last glimpse of the old eunuch: he was backing away from two soldiers under the willow tree, still clutching his small tin trunk. That was another thing he never forgot.

THE COLUMN STOPPED that evening on a rise above a village. Su now had recovered his composure; he pulled a book from his kit bag and sat beside the truck as the troops milled around over cooking fires.

Quinn leaned over the edge of the truck above him. "Who were those people?"

Su looked up and tried a laugh. "The eunuchs? The old man was dotty. One of the last of the Imperial eunuchs—the Christian General kicked them out of the Palace in Peking in the twenties. Most of them must be dead."

He slipped a finger inside the book he was preparing to read. "He's got this bee in his bonnet that the last Emperor is coming back to the Dragon Throne to overthrow the Communists. Pathetic, really, but that's what the silly old dear thinks. So he decided to get together a palace bodyguard for the big day."

"You mean those kids?"

"He bought them from the peasants around here for castration." Su spoke airily, but his voice shook. "They were all living up near Ningsiang until the Peace Preservation Corps sent them packing. Probably ran out of bribes."

113

"You mean he castrated them?" China seemed to arrow back so swiftly to the penis.

"He or someone else." Su glanced shrewdly at Larsen, who was hanging around close by, listening intently. It was unlike Larsen to betray his interest in this fashion.

"Any questions, Larsen," he called, "before I rejoin the classics?"

"Questions? Me? No," Larsen stuttered. He plucked absently at a corner of the truck.

"Only . . ." he began, and he stopped quickly.

"Only what?" Su opened his book.

Larsen took the plunge. "What did that old guy have in the box?"

"The box?" Su now was pretending absorption in the pages he was turning; this was the first time that Larsen had assumed the position of a suppliant.

"Yeah. That little trunk. It had jars in it."

"Ah, the jars." Su placed his finger back in the book and closed it gently. "What do you suppose was in the jars?"

Larsen was pink now. He licked his lips but looked away carefully to disguise his interest. "How would I know? Medicine?"

"Medicine?" Su was toying with him and enjoying it. "Well, not quite medicine. Medical specimens. Yes, much closer to medical specimens. Why do you ask?"

"Oh, no reason." Larsen gazed keenly at the sky and glanced at his wristwatch. Then he gave in again. "What kind of specimens?"

"The 'precious,' they call them," Su laughed. "Precious specimens."

"What kind of precious specimens?"

Su glanced at him mockingly. "What would you say were your most precious specimens, Larsen—excluding the brain, of course?"

Larsen flushed bright red. "The heathen bastards!"

He stalked away, and Su smiled impishly up at Quinn. A few seconds later they heard him dry-retching behind a clump of bamboo.

KEH HALTED THEIR mad dash for nearly a week in Hunan (although it was Mao's birthplace) while he negotiated the next stages of their escape route. They holed up in the Retreat of Cloud Dreaming Perfection, a large Taoist temple with glazed yellow roof tiles south of Changsha; sweeping views over a misty valley allowed excellent cross fire for the nests of machine gunners that Keh sprinkled in and around the building. The main Communist armies were far north of here, but the local guerrillas were active.

Keh's radio crackled day and night in a room behind the altar, on which a gold-lacquered god sat behind red curtains and pillars entwined with golden dragons. Although now a murderer of priests, Keh lit firecrackers each day before the altar; Methodism alone obviously did not hold the key to his salvation. With Shanghai blocked off, he had hoped to ship the silver from Canton to Hong Kong or Taiwan, but circumstances now combined to prevent this. Not only was he afraid of strong Red guerrilla forces in Kwangtung Province and swarms of pirates in the Pearl River estuary; he was fearful of his compatriots as well. Hanging around, Su again got the story. Two Nationalist commanders in Kwangtung were holding their divisions for the stand-and-die battles that always melted away at the eleventh hour; more to the point, they were demanding a share of Keh's loot in return for safe passage through their lines. Keh fumed behind his radio operator—cuffing his head whenever he lost contact; oilily polite whenever he got through to his equally treacherous colleagues. It was almost slapstick: Oliver Hardy tweaking Laurel's ear.

At other times during this period, however, Keh was unaccountably jolly: murder and merriment, sitting side by side in his head, sprang up unpredictably when the relevant incidents triggered them. One morning a small girl (egged on by two unkempt priests who were stooping behind a cluster of azalea bushes) sidled up and presented Keh with a small jade horse: an appropriate gift for the Division. Keh beamed, tugged her shining black plait fondly, and bustled away to his armored car.

Ten minutes later he popped up beside the UNRRA truck and offered Quinn a cigarette which was sticking out of a packet; it was the first time that Keh had spoken to him since the ascent of Hua-shan.

Quinn waved it away weakly, but Keh insisted, standing there smiling, prodding at him with the packet.

115

"Very good cigarette," he said. "Best quality."

Quinn pulled out the cigarette to please him, and a tiny rubber snake shot up and bounced off his face. Keh shrilled and stamped with unrestrained glee while Su stared away stonily into the distance, and Quinn pondered the possibility of slipping feces into the general's soup.

IT WAS A minor demonstration, that incident, of Keh's instability: more evidence that some necessary linkup had not occurred in his brain. But that evening—joyous, perhaps, that his deliverance was at hand—Keh capped everything with a final display of his twisted talents.

"He wants to see you." Quinn and Larsen were sitting together in uneasy silence on a stone bench above the valley; they looked up to see Su standing beside them in the dusk.

"Wants to see who?" Larsen asked. His hands went immediately to his arms and began to rub them softly.

"Both of you. He wants to show you something behind the temple."

Quinn groaned; his belly, which had been recovering, began to ache again. "What's he up to?"

"He's fussing around in his armored car. I think he wants to show you some more tricks."

"Jesus!" Quinn stood up slowly. "He kills people and . . . Are you sure it's all right?"

"I'm not sure of anything . . . But he just put a tin inkblot on one of the ancient manuscripts. The monks are still recovering."

They walked carefully around the temple. Soldiers lounged over machine guns; far down on the floor of the valley the peasants were harvesting rice. They heard water rushing through a grove of ancient cypress trees behind the temple buildings.

Quinn stopped at the corner. "Where is he?"

The armored car was poking from the dark grove into the ornamental gardens that surrounded the buildings. The trees seemed to be moving: cubes of darkness shifted silently in the branches, and a musty odor drifted toward them over the flower beds. In the dim light, something snarled.

"Monkeys," said Su. "Bearded monkeys."

116

The grove was alive with them; large savage creatures that swung higher into the branches as they approached, chittering with rage, young clinging to their backs. Just inside the trees stood Shiozawa. He turned to face them, holding a large sword.

"Stand here!" he ordered and raised the sword menacingly at the monkeys.

Small curtains, striped red and black, hung from a bamboo frame fitted over an escape hatch at the back of the armored car. Inside, shrill voices began to argue like testy gnomes, and they heard Keh giggle; the scratch of a needle as he put on a record. A blare of music wavered up and died as the needle rasped across the disc. "No matter!" Keh called. "No matter!"

A minute's silence followed before the shrill voices started up again. Then, poking up through the curtains, up from the Middle Ages in Europe, the church fetes of his childhood at Wongbok, appeared the grotesque head, the huge curved nose of the hump backed Punch—the little master of violence, of cunning and cowardice, bowing merrily in his tasseled hat, his ruff, his red and yellow coat.

"Ladies and gentlemen, how do you do?" he squeaked at the dark wood, the yellow-berry eyes of the monkeys burning in the branches. "If you all happy, me all happy too," and Su turned and leaned his head against a tree. Quinn looked at Larsen: he was as white as a skull.

"Stop and hear my merry little play. If me make you laugh, me need not make you pay . . ."

There was a pause, the rustle of a script, and then the curtains jerked open and Punch and his victims were dancing to Keh's tune, with scenes misplaced, lines hanging in air, only a ghastly zest holding them together: the dog and Scaramouch and Judy and the baby; the hangman and the Devil.

"How you do, Mr. Toby? Me hope you very well, Mr. Toby . . . Bow, wow, wow! Bow, wow, wow! . . . Let go my nose! My beautiful nose! . . . Ah, Mr. Scaramouch! What you got there? A fiddle? That look like a stick, Mr. Scaramouch! . . ."

He had blotted out most of it: the thud, thud, thud of the stick on Judy's head as it lay over the platform; Punch's sly retreats from danger to the edge of the curtain; the hangman poking his head in the noose. And with each death: "That's the way to do it!

117

That's the way to do it!" screeching out into the clotted trees. It went on for fifteen minutes.

Then up popped Keh. "You enjoy the performance?" He held Punch in one hand, the dead Devil drooping from Punch's stick in the other. "You like my dolls?"

Only Shiozawa was grinning; he removed the stage and helped Keh clamber down to the silent group.

"A surprise, uh? Me—I—buy this from the English soldiers in Burma. I like the Englishmen. I have an English nanny when I am a boy. Very special. This one, this Punch," he tapped the nose, "the beak of the macaw. Liberated from the Calcutta zoo but it die. Now I show you more things."

Keh reached up and pulled down a small box. "Ship's captain in Shanghai give me," he said. "German." And reverently he laid small objects in their trembling hands: mock dog-turd, a fake cockroach, a trick glass of beer, the inkblot, several rubber spiders. The sort of articles that were to endear him to England's horsey set in the more settled years ahead—and even, it was rumored, to one or two of the Royals, who had inherited a little Teutonic buffoonery themselves.

"The magic general!" he declared, and his eyes glistened with joy while the bearded monkeys stared balefully from the wet black wood, and the water roared like death in their ears.

NINE

THE MASSACRE, LIKE ALL MASSACRES, was unnecessary. Approaching Kweilin, winding easily around the base of a crescent of limestone peaks, Keh suddenly swung the column again up into the mountains. His destination was the Retreat of Radiance, a Buddhist monastery with a distant view of the city on the plain beneath it. Perhaps, having twice touched base with the Taoists, he wanted to borrow a little luck from the Buddhists, just as pilgrims rubbed copper coins against incense urns and hung them around the necks of their children. Perhaps he just wanted to pause there with another good field of fire while emissaries negotiated a welcome for him down in Kweilin: all men, under Chiang, were decidedly not brothers. But that was where he went—standing like a conquering hero on the side of the lead armored car as it nosed up into the courtyard.

The Retreat of Radiance was only a short distance above the plain; isolated enough in that seemingly endless scroll of peaks around Kweilin, but far beneath scores of other temples and

119

pavilions that studded the mountains soaring above it in the mist: retreats of Splendid Wisdom and Omniscient Transformation and Heavenly Peace, where the monks chirruped like crickets in cages, awaiting their sublime release. Most of the temples were not visible for much of the day: they appeared sometimes for a few seconds and then faded uncertainly into memory (a trick of vision, perhaps?). Like tropical islands remembered, or imagined, by old sailors, they seemed to beckon from just beyond the edge of reality. Only the Retreat of Radiance seemed real in that unreal world: a spacious building behind high white walls inscribed with large black Chinese characters. But when they entered the main hall, two great figures obliterated all sense of space. They looked up at the God of Universal Light: a bronze figure, clutching a scroll, who stood on an elephant with a jewel glowing in a single shaft of sunlight on its forehead. Keh bowed when he thought no one was looking.

The location of the monastery led to the murders. The monks had built it on a crag at the end of a pathway which was widened into a motor road in the thirties by a local warlord; he liked to be driven there in those days to consult the deities before gobbling ice cream with his concubines in an old Humber Snipe on the terrace. Occasionally, when he felt grandiloquent, he threw a fat dog from the edge of the crag onto a village below, a gesture that led to a long tradition of resentment among the villages toward gifts that rained from the skies. The village became a minor Communist enclave in the forties although its old people continued to climb on pilgrimages into the clouds.

Keh was a fitting successor to the warlord. Once again, he deployed his troops in and around the monastery; machine guns poked from balconies and from large limestone caves around it that had been inscribed for centuries with gracious Buddhist graffiti in praise of the gods. Then, faced again with only vegetarian fare at the monastery, he sent a patrol down into the village to grab chickens or pigs while an old abbot stood behind him, wincing with disapproval.

Quinn was walking shakily around the monastery at the time, regaining his strength; he was carrying his camera for the first time. To his surprise, he saw Larsen tagging behind the patrol, and so he sat down against a rock at the end of the crag, hidden from the monastery, but with a clear view of the plain below.
120

It was a lovely morning for pictures. The air was scented with the fragrance of sweet osmanthus shrubs; their white, yellow, and orange flowers blazed on the mountainsides above the village vegetable gardens, and birds were singing in the valley below. He could see Larsen stalking importantly down the village street while three or four soldiers began to enter the huts.

A footstep scraped behind him; it was Su. Su sat down beside him, hugging his knees. "I have been looking for you," he said. "I was beginning to get worried."

Quinn was fiddling with his camera. "Been taking pictures. What about one of you?"

"Perhaps later." He paused. "The Master in Lunacy is resting. God knows what he's planning . . . What is Larsen doing down there?"

Larsen was wheeling around, his hand flying to his revolver. Nothing more happened for a few seconds, and then a soldier slowly stumbled backward from a hut, dropped his rifle, and sat down in the dust before pitching over sideways. A young man clutching a knife in his right hand suddenly streaked out of the hut, doubled behind it, and began running for the mountain through a field of beans.

He did not get far. From immediately beneath them, Shiozawa stepped out into a row between the bean poles, aimed slowly, and shot the man in the face. He pitched forward as soldiers began shouting with alarm in the monastery grounds. Quinn and Su flattened themselves on the rock as another line of troops began stumbling and sliding down a track from the monastery into the bean field.

What happened after that—what Keh and Shiozawa and Larsen did after that (and what he did himself)—did not bear much thinking about. It had taken him a lifetime to wrench his head back to face it.

"HEY, YOU GUYS! Get down here!" Larsen was looking up from the bean field, beckoning with his revolver.

Su stood up. "It's probably the safest thing to do. Look as if we're joining in the fun." He waved in acknowledgment.

Soldiers were falling in clumsily before Shiozawa. He shouted at them, and they fanned out through the huts. Firing from doorways; shambling inside.

Quinn stood up. He was shaking. Larsen was following the soldiers again—crouching by the stabbed man as if to borrow a dollop of drama. Troops began dragging children out from the alleys between the huts.

When they got down to the bean field, Shiozawa and his men had lined up fifteen young women and small girls—a bedraggled parade awaiting General Keh. Some of their faces were already wet with blood and tears.

They stood at the edge of the bean field, looking down at the orange earth. A mangy dog slunk between them, wagging its tail.

Keh's arrival was almost a relief. He rode slowly into the village on his fat horse from some point that allowed gentler access than the steep track down which his soldiers had clattered. On his left wrist he wore two watches, and he was shaking his arm and pressing them against his ear with an absorbed expression on his face. Behind him rose the peaks of fragrant osmanthus.

The other villagers were dead or had fled; even for Keh, this was a miserable haul. He did not look at them directly—just sat there squinting up at the sky while time ran out for his victims.

"Commies," Larsen explained, waving his revolver down the line. The last Commie was about seven years old.

Shiozawa knew what to do. His troops dug a long trench down the middle of the bean field, smashing through rows. He made the victims turn to watch while they prepared it. And he pushed them all in one by one when it was deep enough—except for one child who climbed in herself.

They stood in the trench facing the village while the soldiers heaped the earth on them. In only a few minutes it had reached the necks of the smaller children. One of them worked her left elbow free, and leaning on it, she began lifting herself earnestly from her grave, until a soldier drove a spade into her arm.

The orange clay smeared their mouths and noses, their heads wagged like clowns; sitting on his horse, Keh stared dreamily over the ring of soldiers. Some of the girls shrieked, and some straggled into a song of sorts, choking on clods. Quinn took pictures.

There was one girl—God, there was one girl with her eyes shut and her head lolling sideways. Quinn suddenly found himself kneeling in front of her, pushing up the earth to straighten her head, and then Shiozawa planted his boot beside him, and he worked it under her neck, his Mauser resting against Quinn's head, and there was a crack of bone as her eyes flew open for the last time.

Quinn stood up and—from somewhere behind him—Larsen fired. Fragments of bone scattered from her head, and then Larsen rushed away behind a hut to vomit and Shiozawa strode away down the line. Most of the girls were underground now; here and there he pointed at the top of a head, a hand.

Only the heads of the four tallest girls remained above ground; a soldier wearing a baggy pair of mustard-colored trousers pretended to sit on one, making his comrades laugh. They were in no hurry to bury them while a little sport remained.

It was at this point that Shiozawa—who was glowering at Quinn—spoke to Keh; there seemed little doubt what he had in mind. Quinn and Su slipped away behind the huts, and then climbed back up to the monastery, tensed for bullets in the back. They hid among the rocks while the girls sang their last song.

Larsen had disappeared; hours later they saw him in the distance, circling down toward Kweilin. They spent that night high on the mountain above the monastery in a limestone cave chiseled with the piety of pilgrims. Keh sent fiery dragons after them—weary troops searching desultorily with burning brands in the monastery grounds, the village, the plain beside the river. They did not sleep.

Wedged behind the damp stone statue of a Buddha, Quinn scribbled in his diary. Keh seemed to be everywhere, he wrote—a gigantic Punch with a head as big as a mountain, shrieking: "That's the way to do it! That's the way to do it!" He added: "I feel guilty, dirty, smeared forever. I was loathsome. I didn't want to be next. I pretended it was—entertaining."

TEN

THERE WASN'T MUCH MORE. KEH and a heavily armed bodyguard fled south to Hainan the day after the bloodshed, and Keh flew his silver (and his horse) from there to Taiwan. He left Shiozawa and the rest of his men to establish a bridgehead in Yunnan—not to oppose the Communist armies when they arrived, but to grab a share of the burgeoning opium-heroin trade from the Golden Triangle. The remnants of his White Horse Division joined Shiozawa there in 1949 before they all fled over China's southern border with 25,000 other demoralized Nationalist troops.

Larsen got back to Hong Kong a few days before Quinn and Su. Lancelot Ming met him there, on Keh's instructions, and arranged a quick passage for him on a President Line ship to the United States, so that he would not have to wait around to answer any embarrassing UNRRA questions. The *South China Morning Post* accidentally recorded his departure in a group picture of Old China Hands sailing into exile. He stood beside them at the rail, still rigid and unapproachable in his abominable Eastern pantaloons.

Keh then summoned Ming and several Hong Kong Triad leaders to Taiwan for a briefing on his expanding business interests, and so Quinn and Su did not run into Ming when they reached Hong Kong. Su did not wait for the inheritance from his uncle; he sailed to London, where he finished his medical course at St. Bartholomew's Hospital Medical College, and eventually disappeared into psychiatric practice in Arizona, of all places; perhaps Arizona was the final savage incongruity, the ultimate act of masochism he sought to cap his private chaos. Quinn left for India and later rejoined the *Star* in Sydney.

Before he left Hong Kong, however, he slipped into The Vienna, where Veitch and Porter presided: Doyle was absent in Shanghai. They were more interested in their sexual conquests than in tales of his travail in China, but Porter did promise to take care of a series of statements that Su had collected from the survivors of the massacre in Kwangsi the following day—eyewitness accounts that Porter could stow away safely while Quinn pondered (as he pondered for many years) on the best course of action to take. That he entrusted the statements to Porter, he knew, was hardly testimony to his resolve to act quickly, but at least Porter was remaining in the area. And Porter did not have a destructive mistress (like Veitch), who might toss them out; he lived with his sister Winifred (whom Quinn had met once or twice), and she appeared to be a very sensible person.

The Nationalists, meanwhile, had begun the interminable last act of their own wartime farce. It was the beginning of the end for Chiang and Madame. She began dispensing tea and wisdom to the grateful representatives of El Salvador and Macon, Georgia, at her table of polished banyan while Chiang fed his carp and pledged endless Returns to the Mainland, between rumored testosterone injections. And plump Nationalist generals commenced toasting a line of visiting U.S. Congressmen deep in their underground cave HQ in offshore Quemoy—down where the loudspeakers boomed "This Land Is Mine" (safely out of Communist earshot) while propaganda units above gently patted bright balloons bearing biscuits and bloodthirsty leaflets toward the long yellow haze of the Fukien coast.

It was the end of the beginning, however, for Keh. He prudently contributed a sizable proportion of his silver for the defense of Taiwan and (Veitch hinted to Quinn) began negotiating a murky agreement with the newly formed CIA in the Golden Triangle area: Nationalist spies into Yunnan; heroin out to Hong Kong.

As for Doyle, Quinn never saw him again. He left a letter for him at the hostel telling him what had happened in Kweilin and on Hua-shan, but Doyle did not reply until several years after Quinn had returned to Australia. Doyle must have suspected that he was going to die when he wrote. He scrawled "Burn This" on the top of his letter, but that was probably for Quinn's protection: he included references to Keh's drug dealings that he would not have recorded if he had looked forward to a comfortable old age—plus an assurance that Porter was still holding the Kweilin documents that Su had gathered.

"Remember big Vera?" he wrote. "She croaked the other day." Eight words over the abyss. "Still with Keh. Would have left long ago, but he's got me by the balls." Another fifteen to tell him that, somehow, he was trapped. And then the jokey stuff: an account, with bitter humor, of the demise of Shiozawa, who had returned eventually to Hong Kong to strong-arm Keh's operations there among the Triad gangs. "Incredible, chum," Doyle wrote. "Keh even wangled Shiozawa into a Masonic Lodge although he was going mad fast—untreated syphilis, Rushton reckons. Used to wave his bloody great Samurai sword when he was Outer Guard instead of the ceremonial weapon—you can imagine how *that* went down with the Jardine Mathieson mob. Anyway, one night he choked on a fish bone during a dinner in the Great South and went west—it was a pretty big room, and none of the Masons got to him in time. Probably frightened of getting septicaemia if they stuck their fingers into his mouth."

Doyle also included, without explanation, a receipt for a sum of money bearing the stamp of a psychiatric center in Kowloon. Quinn thought that he might have slipped it into the letter by mistake, but he tucked it back into the envelope and stuck it into one of his old China notebooks.

He never did burn Doyle's letter. "For how," he once asked his empty house, "can I destroy this last link with my Ideal Self?"

Part Three

ELEVEN

QUINN PAID OFF A WORN-OUT Mercedes taxi outside the Foreign Men's Hostel in Kowloon. The hostel was exactly as he had remembered it: a squat gray Victorian building sheltering behind ancient banyan trees plugged with green-slimed cement. It hid in a sleepy cul-de-sac near Minden Row, beyond the main tourist bustle of Nathan Road; closed and boarded up in the fifties while its aging White Russian owners awaited an impossible sum for the site; eventually reopened in the seventies in an eccentric (and niggardly) bid to cash in on the global swing to nostalgia. A nub of the past, still more or less intact.

He mounted the hostel steps swiftly in his black suit, clutching his gray suitcase in one hand, his priestly black hat in the other; thankful that no one darted forward to help him, for he did not know what to tip. The heat, he noticed, had seared most of the ancient gold lettering from its glass doors (Foreign Men's Hostel. Ping-Pong, Library); they were kitsch of a type now, like the large fans that sliced slowly through the humid air of the foyer in front of him. But at least, like him, they had endured.

He pushed open a door; demolition could not be far off. A Sikh watchman had guarded the building in the old days with wooden plugs sealing both barrels of his shotgun, bellowing at the beggars who lay like spent gray moths on the steps, coldly ignoring the cocky, wrinkled rickshaw coolies who shouted happily over elephant checkers beneath the banyans—orange peel for chariots, spent matchsticks their only cannon. Now the steps and forecourt were deserted. The hostel obviously did not run to a Sikh these days, and the beggars and rickshaw-pullers had gone. Time and the tourist tide had swept them all away: the ragged children pushing up empty tobacco tins ("No poppa, no momma, no chow-chow! Ten cents! Ten cents!"); the starving babies, the cripples. Only the hostel remained, moored in an historical backwater for mainly Caucasian drifters: hippie kids wandering between Bangkok and Katmandu; dislocated locals who had given up grappling with the present.

Quinn knew them in his soul. Gently he set down his suitcase before the desk of a withered little Portuguese reception clerk. Electric with a new tension, his eyes raked the foyer around him.

"Quinn," he murmured, as if he were afraid to shake the foundations. "Room 29. I sent a letter."

The foyer had barely altered: the rows of dusty potted palms on the red tiles; the curling notices of recitals and church services and ping-pong matches drooping from the green felt boards; the same faded old photographs of Hong Kong rugby teams frozen in stilted imbecility on the walls. The heat had wilted them all, just as it had drained him on his first arrival by ship from Australia in 1948: the streamers snapping in Sydney; his father blowing his nose in the wheelchair on the wharf.

"I hope you've got it," he joked. "I don't want to have to go back."

"Ah." The clerk scrabbled among the papers on his desk, extracted one, and motioned Quinn to sign an old brass-bound ledger. It was almost filled: write the final signature on the last page, he thought, and the whole bloody building might dissolve in mossy gray rubble. He scratched his name slowly, listening for the past, for the subsiding of walls, while a Boy in a grubby white uniform (were they still called Boys?) bent and picked up his bag.

Quinn followed him into the gold mesh cage of the hostel's

creaky old elevator and stood behind him with a sudden hollow jocularity, a tentative smile on his lips like something dropped to disguise his aloneness.

The elevator doors crashed open on the second floor; the pungency of floor polish instantly sharpened Quinn's memory. Two old amahs leaning on mops giggled gold-toothed at him from a doorway; the amahs in the hostel had always been beyond sexual contemplation. He bowed ironically and began walking down the dim coir matting corridors toward his old room: treading back through shrinking arteries toward his youth; through veins that once had pulsed with sexual excitement; blood that the prospect of war had quickened with a semblance of courage.

He passed Doyle's old room, No. 27, before the Boy unlocked the door of 29, placed his suitcase on the floor, and departed abruptly; the tip, Quinn supposed, came later. Quickly he locked the door and leaned against it, breathing deeply. He had made it! He was back in the same small brown box that he had rented while waiting to get to the Civil War front. Alone again with the iron bed, the wardrobe, the chest of drawers, the white sink in the corner near the window; a color TV set against a wall was the only new adornment. The same old brown linoleum—it must be the same!—lay pitted and worn beneath his new black shoes, and harsh white light was striking in through the foliage of a banyan.

He sniffed; the room was still musty after years of disuse, and on the sink by a pumice stone crouched a large cockroach—so large that he could see that one of its legs was missing. Its antennae turned slowly to meet him like the blind and ominous guns of a battleship.

Quinn stole forward, knocked it into the basin with his hat, and screwed on both taps as its remaining legs drove back and forth in a grinding fight for survival. It disappeared slowly down the drain while he loomed above it.

"Got you, you bastard," he murmured. "Quinn 1, Cockroach nil." And grinned again, uncertainly.

Then, turning, he stabbed a straight left into the air as he had done when he was clowning with Doyle in the old days, on visits to Keh's little import-export agency over on the Island.

"Face of a choirboy, heart of a killer," he announced, and somewhere close by his elbow the ghost of Doyle wriggled impatiently on a chair. "Will somebody take this young bastard away?" Doyle snarled. "I'm trying to work."

Quinn walked to the window. He felt fearful, triumphant: he had forced the arc to return to this room where his life had begun to unravel. He leaned out, suspended once more between two worlds. The clang and crash of Cantonese opera had assailed him here once: the strange shouts and high wails of the beggar-moths heaped against the walls below as more than a million and a half people fled into Hong Kong from the warring armies; the crying babies nuzzling flat breasts; the dying scrape of wooden clogs as he lay alone on his bed late at night, praying for murder. The bad time . . .

And now? Now all that had changed; now they had tamed Hong Kong. He had washed up amid a sanitized cluster of tourist shops in a network of sunny little streets: it could have been a Hollywood set. The leaves of the banyans at the hostel entrance framed a little Chinese girl in a pink party dress who was hopping up and down the steps of a beauty salon next door with a music box pressed like a transistor to her ear. It was tinkling "The Sound of Music." Here beneath him was a cellophane-wrapped sample of Asia only a few minutes walk from the Peninsula and the Miramar on Nathan Road: fur traders, dress shops, jade factories, watch and jewelry stores; Revlon and Florsheim Shoes and Bally of Switzerland; silver fox furs and beach balls erasing an agony that existed now only in his mind. He left the window and switched on the TV set. Two fat little Cantonese boys were licking their lips over chocolate bars: portly consumers already where for so long he had nourished the memory of starvation. He turned off the set and sat on the bed, wondering exactly why he had returned; where he belonged. He could see his haunted face in the mirror above the sink, drained by drink and strain; the mauve half-moons beneath the eyes now permanent, thank God; the deep lines hiding his naïveté at last.

His green eyes stared back at him; he pressed his fingers into his cheeks, briefly erasing the lines. He had savored this moment for decades; his mind had returned again and again to this room. He had imagined himself leaning out of the window, just as he had done now, while the old aromatic mixture poured again into

134

his eyes, his nose, his ears—permeating his bloodstream; rekindling the dormant fever.

And yet the chemistry had not sizzled as he had hoped: like Hong Kong, he, too, had changed. He was no longer afraid of Asia for one thing; even the vermin did not disgust him these days. Two small cockroaches began marching along the edge of the sink, all danger apparently past, and Quinn turned to greet them, dropping his hands from his face.

"Hello, little chaps!" he called. "Done your tiny homework, have you?"

Well, he smiled to himself, at least they didn't answer. A grave psychiatrist had told him, when he was under his greatest strain, that his logic was impaired; he had recommended a drug that concentrated the mind like a laser. "What do you mean, 'impaired?'" Quinn had asked him—troubled for a moment, and the psychiatrist had sucked impressively on his pipe. "You're still making imaginative leaps," he had pronounced, and Quinn had shaken his head in wonder and never gone back. That man was madder than he was.

So fuck psychiatrists. He was back! Back with his memories—the old phantom-baggage he had carried on a jumbo jet flight as dull as sitting in an insurance office awaiting a policy renewal; a Japanese businessman on one side of him printing cables in large English capitals (THEY HAVE HEAVY STOCKS . . . POSSIBILITY FOR NEW YEAR), and an elderly Australian woman on the other side fiddling with a diamond and ruby ring and toying with a gold necklace and straightening her slacks and saying, archly, that her friend was looking after her house while she went to await her daughter's baby in Hong Kong, where it was very crowded now, and the people rushed everywhere like little ants, and was he going on business?

"More a holiday," he had said. "Looking up old friends." For how could he explain his mission, even to himself? How could he have said over the plastic cups, the toy food: I'm going back to where my life began to go wrong. Back not merely for revenge, but to acknowledge the dead; back to tether himself like a goat for the tiger. Back to the ghosts of Doyle and of himself when he was young and of the loveless prostitutes in the old Empire with fictitious daughters in the Sacred Heart. Back to the ghosts of the frothing-drunk Scottish soldiers who had spat venom at them sometimes outside the dives and the rickshaw boys who trailed them gently through the early-morning streets with shining eyes and dovelike entreaties to couple with girls or boys and the mutilated Nationalist soldiers fleeing from history and the diseased dragon of beggars who lay in wait outside The Vienna for bread. How could he have made her understand? They were the ghosts of the failed and the forgotten, with whom he celebrated in silent brotherhood. The voices he dragged behind him, just as the jet had dragged the ghost sound of its engines.

He lit a cigarette and stared at his suitcase. Quinn the loser. A string of crackers exploded down the street; he flinched but he did not get up. Memories of love and beauty and death: the comforting smell of his father's gray overcoat as he hugged him in his wheelchair after his first visit at nine to the dentist; a young Indian girl gliding gravely across a jungle clearing once in Bengal in 1949 and melting forever into a wet green wall of trees; Doyle snarling, "Keep your head up!" in the Hong Kong dives before he lowered his own in Room 27 and pointed the pistol at his temple. How did they all fit together, these jigsaw pieces which he had collected: And did Doyle's blood still stain the linoleum?

"Ah," he thought, "I'm a morbid man." He flicked the cigarette into the sink and walked to the window again; the darkness of evening now clotted the banyans.

A tiny Chinese in a pink suit stood on the steps beneath him speaking to the desk clerk, the perennial cigar glowing in his hand. He felt no surprise: he had been awaiting this moment for thirty years.

"Lancelot!" he called down. "Is that you?"

Two blurred faces lifted quickly toward him before the clerk scuttled back up the steps and the pink figure withdrew beneath the trees. A minute later a taxi moved quietly away up the cul-de-sac, a door slamming as it went.

Quinn stood there alone. Out in the harbor a ship hooted mournfully, and he shivered suddenly, as if shedding a life.

TWELVE

SUNLIGHT WAS BATHING HIS ROOM when he awoke. He lay thinking about Doyle, holding his image up to the light like a piece of broken beer bottle—only glass, certainly, but warm and rich with the sun in its heart. "I want to know why he killed himself," he said aloud.

Then he swung naked out of bed, wrapped a towel around his loins, and sat on the edge. "Fool," he growled. Why must he be a repository all his life of the unimportant? Because that was what he was; his suitcase contained the proof. His old 1948 diaries. They still sealed him from the present—just as the eucalypts bristled in his head while the convolvulus blossomed outside the window. Everything close to him touched by death.

Savagely, he dragged the suitase toward him, took out a cigarette carton, and shook the diaries from it onto the bed sheet; the old "Burn This" letter from Doyle fell with them. He hated the diaries: his tiny tombstones.

But he opened them. He riffled through them even more

carefully, in fact, than he had that night of decision up on West Ridge, and in fifteen minutes he failed again to find anything of human significance. The people he had grown to worship then in Hong Kong and China were not only no gallery of greats: they crept out like illegitimate peasant children who had been locked for decades in basement dungeons—wax-white, squinting in the stab of sunlight, the glare of eyes and arc lights.

Sitting there half-naked, he lit his first cigarette of the day. No, they were not even children; they were dried mice trickling dust in an ancient cupboard. He had recorded a time without grace or love or dignity, that was all. A blur of drunken evenings in The Vienna and the dives of Kowloon while the globe changed color; a shoddy saga of crumbling colonials who had communicated, like Doyle, in borrowed words and songs—their private pain all that was real. Only the scribbled notes on Keh were relevant—first on Hua-sham and later in Kwangsi, and they occupied only one book. He tossed it onto his hat.

The rest were irrelevant. As irrelevant as the men in wheel-chairs; war dead stacked in mouldering greatcoats; the pyramids of baby skulls; the flesh of women chewed under the mucky tracks of Great Ideas. And he had become irrelevant himself while life bloomed around him. He crackled like an ancient radio with its receiver jammed open. He registered urgent messages decades after the callers had died.

He washed his face and looked out the window; groups of European tourists were laughing below. So what should he do now? Say: "Do you worship the dead? Am I the only poor bastard who's receiving them?"

Quinn the nut case. The guilt of the survivor in a generation bred to die. They'd toss him into the loony bin if he talked like that.

The tourists were peering into the windows of a camera store; they wanted color prints, not his gray visions of the dead. He had to shake them off—and, to his surprise, he found that a strange thing indeed seemed to be happening. Not only had the sour scent of feces whipped into the cabin of the jumbo jet before it stopped rolling the previous day at Kai Tak, but so had a whiff of almost-forgotten adventure. Lancelot Ming by now must have reported his arrival, and yet for the first time in his life he felt wholly unafraid.

HE HAD A shower in the bathroom down the corridor from his room, comtemplating Andrew Veitch, who now lived in retirement on the Island. He had boasted once that he had amassed a huge file on Keh during the Second World War in Burma and China—and he had always kept a well-stocked liquor cabinet.

Happily, he padded back to his room in his towel, dressed, and placed a chair beneath the lamp shade. Peering into the dusty bowl, he found that it was littered with the crumbling bodies of moths. It should do. He took the old rolls of film from his suitcase and placed them in the bowl; only a faint shadow betrayed their presence when he switched on the light. Next, he slid two Hong Kong diaries and Doyle's letter beneath his mattress before he placed the China diary in his inside coat pocket. Only then did he step out into the corridor, carrying his hat.

Doyle's door swung open as he approached; for a jolting moment he expected him to swagger out in his quick, cocky way, chin up, his oiled-paper umbrella slung over his shoulder like a Lee-Enfield. Instead, a middle-aged Chinese was backing into the corridor, slipping the strap of a pair of field glasses over his head. He wore a Royal Randwick T-shirt, shorts, long socks, and sandals; he must be losing, thought Quinn, to be reduced to the hostel.

"Hey, Harry!" the Chinese yelped in a broad Australian voice. "Can I borrow that hair restorer of yours when we get back? Siddie tells me he was bald before he started using it, and now he's coming up."

"Crikey, take it," floated an identical voice from Room 27; Australian-Chinese agents from the Sydney vegetable markets, perhaps, on their annual Qantas package tour. Their simple pursuit of pleasure cheered him; he quickened his pace as he drew level, fired for the first time by a ridiculous optimism, and as he caught the man's eye he jerked his head and clucked his tongue against the roof of his mouth in wordless Australian greeting.

"G'day, Father!" the man called after him, and Quinn felt surprised eyes boring into his back. He walked on, pressed the elevator button, and then chose the stairs in case the men followed him and cornered him for conversation. A fat European was already asleep in an armchair in the library, a newspaper resting on his belly, and a table tennis ball clicked in the game room beyond the tearoom. In there once a drunken English soldier had smashed his ten-cent cup of weak brew on the table, sitting silently, oblivious, as thick dark blood welled slowly from his hand. Now the tearoom was empty, jammed with buckets and mops.

The foyer, too, was empty; the little Portuguese clerk who had been whispering with Lancelot Ming stood outside at the foot of the steps, taking the air. Descending, Quinn suddenly clapped a hand with murderous piety on his stubbly head. "Lovely day," he observed, watching the clerk's cockroach-brown eyes scuttle from side to side under his hand to see whether anyone was observing his humiliation.

Then Quinn took his hand from his head, grinning down at him with malicious sweetness. "Tell Lancelot I'll be calling on him," he said and felt his adrenaline pumping—a spurt of amusement at his ersatz daring.

He stood for a few seconds on the footpath, marveling faintly that no beggars clustered around him. Slowly he walked up the cul-de-sac, and no assassin sprang forward, pointing a pistol; no car ran him down. Even the odors of Hong Kong seemed to have drained away here: the vast envelope of musk scent that had once sealed the crowds had evaporated. When he looked back, the clerk had scurried inside.

Quinn crossed Nathan Road and rounded the corner of the Peninsula. Fountains splashed at the entrance; the little pageboys in white caps and white uniforms were still fiddling with their white gloves near the white lions, just as their grandfathers had done before them. Only the guests had changed: an overseas Chinese in a gray striped suit was posing for a photograph with a proprietorial hand on one of the hotel's Rolls Royces; he pointed with his other hand at the Spirit of Ecstasy to ensure that his friend included it.

There was a pedestrian subway now beneath Ashley Road, and the Kowloon Star Ferry terminal (just ahead, as he had remembered) was encrusted with glittering new gift shops. Outside the wharf a fat Chinese was bending over, shaking so much with laughter that tears were popping out of his eyes, and Quinn gazed at him with a sudden remembrance of pain. One night in 1948, a Chinese deckhand had fished a dead female baby from the oily green water here; laughing, the deckhand had hooked her aloft on a long bamboo pole as a glittering stream fell from her cap of black hair onto Quinn's shoes, completing a circuit that now sparked faintly again in his brain.

He rubbed one shoe absently against the back of a trouser leg and was queuing at a turnstile when he saw a crowd of tourists peering down at a fishing boat beside the wharf. He left the queue to look over their shoulders.

Two fishermen were rolling their main catch onto the pier: the first mainland refugee of the morning. He was a young Chinese in blue cotton shorts with a deflated motor tire still twisted around his ribs, and dead eyes that stared up at the Nikon cameras dangling around necks, the gay Hawaiian holiday shirts, the Florsheim shoes; the glow of capitalism that had beckoned to him over the black water from some dreary commune.

An Australian woman trod on Quinn's foot as she blundered away out of the crowd. "Disgraceful!" she muttered angrily. "It shouldn't be allowed . . ."

Quinn took her mentally by the throat. "No," he agreed. "We don't pay good money for *this*."

He turned and descended a ramp onto the top deck of the ferry, and it throbbed out quickly, cutting a scar across the harbor toward the Island; a scrubbed white naval launch dashed toward an American warship as if escaping from contamination. Beside him, an elegant Chinese woman suddenly hawked and spat, smearing the spittle in an arc with one dainty shoe: the old Chinese national anthem, "Symphony in Green." It had disgusted him when he was young and callow, but now that he was old and callow he grinned at her and pointed at the Please Do Not Spit sign, making her suffer because he had just seen a dead man on the pier. She edged away along the seat.

Ahead, the Peak rose above the office towers and plush hotels and mighty apartment blocks that now marched at its flanks; spider webs of bamboo scaffolding draped giant new buildings that were sprouting where once only modest Victorian stone had crouched. The crowded fringe of bat-wing junks and sampans that had tiptoed at the Central praya had disappeared (except from the travel brochures); only motorized junks hurried by now under bare poles—heads down, like preoccupied little spinsters on shopping excursions in the High Street.

Quinn stepped ashore into a new world of concrete overpasses and pedestrian bridges and tunnels and plazas and air-conditioned restaurants and stores where the beggars once had jostled. He sat for several minutes on a curved tiled bench beneath the lacy green and gold layers of a young jacaranda, marveling that nobody accosted him. The hostility, the despair, had drained away.

A Chinese girl walked past wearing a red T-shirt. *I Like Hong Kong. Hi Pal!*, it said, and he watched her until she disappeared. Then he caught a taxi down to Happy Valley to see Veitch.

THIRTEEN

A STEEP FLIGHT OF STEPS in Ventris Road led up to a row of houses; Quinn clanged a brass lion-head knocker on a house in the middle of the row.

At first there was no answering sound inside, but eventually he heard a distant shuffling and grumbling, a small object falling, and finally the slow progress of an old retainer to the door.

There was a thump and a scuffling before Veitch edged it open. He had shrunk into a yellow old man with glasses pushed up on a thick mat of gray hair; an old brown woolen dressing gown covered striped winter pajamas, despite the humidity, and another pair of pajama pants were hooked over one slipper. He shook them off and pushed them into a heap against the wall before he opened the door fully; standing sideways, prodding at the pajama pants with his foot; absently extending a limp right hand over his left arm to shake.

"Good morning, Quinn," he grumbled as if they had not met

for a week. "I got your letter. Damn drafts. They come straight under this door and onto my neck."

A walking stick hung on his left arm, and he transferred it to his right hand and leaned back on it, motioning Quinn inside.

Quinn entered; he observed cracked egg stains on the lapels of Veitch's gown. "Well, how have you been?" he asked breezily, his heart already sinking, for Veitch, obviously, was past it.

He was now closing the door and pushing the pajama pants against it with his walking stick. He prodded at the cloth deliberately as if he had already forgotten that Quinn was there. "New buildings," he complained. "They funnel it. They funnel it," and he gave the cloth a last testy little poke. "Come in and sit down."

Quinn stood aside to let him pass, and Veitch shuffled ahead into a small living room past a fallen coffee table that Quinn placed upright. Dusty models of Veitch's Portuguese caravels sailed along a shelf above an old armchair gaping horsehair; brittle brown palms stood in tubs littered with cigarette butts. Everywhere, books spilled from shelves over a nondescript carpet, and the walls were hung with photographs of British soldiers crouching outside tents in Burma, the crews of DC3s posing eternally beneath their propellers.

"The old place, eh?" Quinn tried with spurious brightness. "You had some good parties here." Remembering the last one: Veitch's mistress had nearly scratched Veitch's eyes out.

Veitch did not answer. Grasping his stick, he flicked a folded newspaper crossword puzzle from the armchair onto the carpet and, turning, sank down slowly as Quinn perched on the edge of another chair, unwilling to descend into the malaise that had obviously overcome Veitch. Only Veitch's eyes were much the same: keen gray flints fighting a final rearguard action as the flesh collapsed around them. He had always been a pedant and a hypochondriac, but youth had kept these traits at bay. Now only the eyes awaited the final coup de grace; the faint twinkle of Rat remained in a lugubrious Badger.

"You look OK," Quinn offered lamely. It was as far as he could go.

Veitch waved away the attempted compliment. "It's boring," he said. "I have all sorts of troubles, all sorts of things. Little things, you know?" He twisted a hand around the back of his neck. "I had a rash on my neck. Now the rash has gone, and I've had boils—boils! I haven't had boils since Burma!"

"How's your diet?" Quinn asked; bleak despair edged the underside of his words. To think of the old days: Veitch had tossed off a million whiskies then; his lovers had included the best whores of southern China and Hong Kong—or so he had claimed. Now, beside Quinn's chair, a translation of *The Lusiads* lay on a stack of ancient *Playboys*, with several lines underscored: "Just as dawn was breaking gently overhead, the ships all spotted together the Isle of Love . . ."

"My amah has left me." It was almost a whine. "She said she is too old. She has made a fortune out of me. Oh, I cook eggs, and sometimes I go down to the Football Club for dinner, but there's the traffic to cope with, and the stairs. I can't get about too quickly."

"You used to be a pretty fast mover." A little joke.

Veitch leaned forward. "And I never go out at night. A friend of mine was mugged last week at the Star Ferry wharf. The Star Ferry, in Central! He'd been to a meeting of the Philatelic Society. He's still in the hospital. Broken collarbone."

"You could get taxis. You shouldn't moulder away." His own cottage surfacing amid Veitch's crisp palms; the ravaged gutters, the key beneath the mossy brick, the spirits of children playing in empty rooms. "You've got to get out."

"It's easy for you to say," Veitch protested. "Would you like a whisky?" Old newspapers stuffed now in the liquor cabinet.

"What about you? Can I get one for you?"

"Not for me." Veitch studied his wristwatch. "I have one at evening—two on Sundays if friends call. Doctor's orders."

"I won't bother." Quinn suppressed his resentment. "There was no counting the trees as they soared skyward, all laden with fragrant, luscious fruit . . ."

He didn't want to know what was wrong with Veitch, and perhaps Veitch sensed it. He roused himself briefly from his absorption with his body and waved around the room.

"Everything's broken," he complained. "The TV set only works properly for ten minutes and then I have to switch it off. The switch of my reading light doesn't work when I go to bed. I have to pull it out of the wall. Where are you going to get people to fix things? You can't get tinkers. There are no tinkers these days. Even the street sweepers wear sunglasses."

"Tinkers." Quinn smiled despite himself; Veitch lived even further in the past than he did. The parties he had held here after the races! Gin and French records, that was how long ago it has been: BOAC hostesses and English nursing sisters from the Queen Mary Hospital, swaying to Edith Piaf on heavy hocks; Portuguese magnolia blossoms from the banks; tiny Chinese dolls with the souls of Siamese fighting fish. And Veitch's fiery Eurasian mistress locked alone in the bedroom aflame with jealousy as he flirted with others—crunching his galleons to her breast like the shells of cicadas; pounding his reading glasses to white powder with a small brass Buddha while Veitch tapped gently on the door, telling her not to be a silly girl.

Well, no woman's touch lingered now; she had taken off long ago, no doubt, leaving Veitch to rummage for his sex in the sixteenth century. ". . . The air was redolent with the odor of delicately moulded lemons, like a maiden's breasts."

"Do you still go to the races?" Quinn asked, wondering if the lock on the bedroom door was also broken.

Veitch half-turned toward his windows overlooking Ventris Road, the racecourse beyond, the old Colonial Cemetery behind it where the Veitch family mausoleum had once been visible from here.

"I used to be able to see the glow of the night meetings on my bedroom wall, but they've stopped all that—saving energy," he said plaintively. "Are you sure you won't have some coffee? We could make some coffee."

Quinn gauged the expenditure of time in the task. "No, don't worry about it," he said, and he sank back into his chair. The day was lost. "We had some good times," he lied.

"You know something, Quinn? I'll tell you something. I haven't had a woman for seven, must be eight, years. I can't get the old fellow up any more."

"That's not like you."

"I went to my doctor the other day. I had this rash on my whatsit. I said to the doctor: 'Doctor, before you go on, I'll tell you one thing it couldn't be.' I said to him: 'Doctor, I'll tell you one thing it couldn't be.'"

146

He consulted his watch again. "Do you think you could pass me those tablets there?" He tossed them into his mouth, sipped from a glass of water, and made a notation on a pad.

"You remember that file you had on Keh?"

Veitch dropped a pencil gently on the pad.

"File? What file? I never had any file on Keh. Keh's a very big man, Quinn. He's in all sorts of things these days. Big business."

"I can imagine. But you knew him in the war, didn't you?"

"Keh?" Veitch stared away into a corner; over the Hump into the days when he had danced in Delhi and conducted houseboat races in Srinagar with the most meticulous set of rules devised by man. He had explained them in boring detail on many nights in The Vienna.

"He was with Wingate for a time," he said at last. "He was mad, but he knew what he was doing."

"Wingate. He used to sit in his tent, dripping sweat—quite naked except for a pith helmet. I can see him now, dipping into a tin of olives. He loved olives."

Quinn sighed, almost ready to give up. "You fought with him, didn't you?"

"I didn't fight!" Veitch rallied briefly to defend his status. "I was Intelligence. I just brought him olives. I didn't slither around slicing up Japs."

Veitch suddenly became very crotchety. "What do you want to know about Keh? Everybody knows about Keh. I don't know anything about him. I lost interest years ago. I've retired. I just want a quiet life."

He jabbed at the crossword puzzle with his stick. "A few creature comforts, that's all I want," he said. "My amah left me. Twenty-seven years . . ."

Following several long silences, Quinn said good-bye. No doubt relieved that the meeting was over, Veitch pulled himself upright at the door and gripped his hand more firmly.

"You never married?" Quinn contemplated the cracked egg stains.

Veitch grew indignant again. "Why should I marry? Why should I double my expenditure? Do you know what you pay for steak these days in the supermarket? Here, look, I've got my grocery list somewhere . . ."

147

"I believe you," Quinn protested, holding up a hand and forcing a laugh.

He waited a few seconds after Veitch had shut the door, listening while he prodded the pajama pants back against the crack. So much for Old Contact No. 1: the air already seemed redolent with the odor of failure.

FOURTEEN

QUINN CAUGHT A TAXI BACK up into the Central District and wandered into the Hilton Hotel's expresso restaurant. Sliding behind a table, he marveled mildly that the hotel should be there at all; he remembered only chaos.

He ordered a bottle of San Miguel and sipped steadily, thrusting aside the aches in his body. Veitch had tossed in the towel; already he had crumbled completely into the past. Porter was his next mission—but not yet. He was grateful to be alone: submerging slowly, where once he had jittered with nerves, in the fluids of the plastic Hilton womb.

Opposite him, an American woman was ordering hot dogs for herself and her two teenage sons; her face—abnormally taut, the skin stretched over the bones—betrayed a new lift. "Two no nothing. Right?" she directed; one of the youths added, "Newburgh-style," and she laughed and then stopped suddenly, her mouth half-open, as if gaiety might open her stitch-lines.

He watched her absently. Hong Kong also had undergone a

face-lift. How many times, late at night, had he fled through this area from The Vienna with Doyle on their way to the Star Ferry wharf: brushing past the cupped hands of the black-garbed beggars; the aged, half-bald women who had clanged tin cups on cobblestones beside him in the darkness, jolting his heart with shock? And everywhere the rickshaw coolies, gaunt and tubercular, wheeling like great flapping bats that folded their dark wings after midnight beside the phlegm-splattered gratings, the police patrols stepping among them with a dainty brutality, prodding them with shiny batons. But now—nothing! All the beggars and prostitutes had vanished, just as they had been swept from the main tourist area of Kowloon. Only a token cluster of rickshaw-pullers sat patiently, with civic blessing, down at the wharf: a touch of color for the visitors. The tourists sauntered without fear of repugnance or the distraction of pity, unaware of the torrent of misery that had spilled so wildly through these streets.

Quinn studied his glass. Well, that was his Hong Kong, not theirs, he could see that plainly now—he could even smile about it in this last quarter of his life. It had mocked his adolescent naïveté and corroded his schoolboy idealism, traded fear of syphilis for love, degradation for narrow decency: the usual swap. He ordered another bottle, sinking gently amid the soft lights and subdued music, a glossy sterility that once he had despised. For it was pleasant for a while to linger in the familiar artificiality of the Hilton—just as Hong Kong now was familiar to him not because he had lived here long ago, but because its metamorphosis echoed the other cities around the globe: the concrete expressways curving into the mass-consciousness; the pudgy TV children touting for capitalism.

Most of all, however, he could feel safe here for a time while he considered his next step: reality surely could not reach down into this adult playpen. The area's new plazas and fountains, the concrete overpasses and expensive boutiques, all shielded him not only from the underworld of his youth, but from the subterranean forces that he had set in train. The only menace in Hong Kong was of his own making.

"PORTY? THIS IS Veitch. I just had Quinn here. Quinn. Asking about Keh . . ."

"Arrived, has he?" Porter grumbled "He sent me a letter."

"He's odd," Veitch said. "Looks like a priest. Asking a lot of questions."

"Look, I can't talk now. I'll ring you back."

"Have you got someone there? Who is it? Not that widow from the bank, is it? The one in foreign exchange?"

"No," Porter said. "I'll ring you back."

"All right, all right. Phone me back . . ."

SIGHING WITH EXASPERATION, Veitch shuffled to answer his telephone. It was Porter, his voice raised above the traffic jam beneath his flat on Queen's Road East. "Veitch? I just got rid of her."

Veitch picked up the telephone and sank back with it into his armchair. "Was it the widow?" Beginning to undress her himself.

"It was my sister," Porter said. "She just dropped in. Telling me her troubles."

"I didn't think Winifred ever had any troubles." Disappointed, Veitch plucked his gown back over his knees. He'd tried to seduce her when they were young; she'd dropped a dictionary in his lap.

"Wants me to take her on a holiday. Home," Porter grumbled. "Husband's getting her down." He paused. "What did Quinn say?"

"He wanted to talk about Keh. Digging up all that old stuff. I told him I wasn't going to get involved."

"I suppose he'll be on to me next," Porter complained. "I've a good mind not to answer the door."

"Well, he's not welcome back here," Veitch said, huddling deeper amid his memorabilia; a tatty little Isle of Love in Ventris Road was cosier than a sack in the harbor . . . "If you see him, tell him I'm a sick man . . ."

IT WAS ONLY mid-afternoon. Quinn tipped his hat over his eyes and walked down Queen's Road Central and then up Battery Path toward St. John's Cathedral—laying a lazy trail to see if he was followed. He gazed fondly at its facade: the church failed on a much grander scale than he could ever hope to achieve, and that was worthy of some affection. He took off his hat and entered.

A few Chinese were dozing or praying, and he sat behind them amid the sheaves of flowers, the miniature shields of British regiments, suddenly realizing what had drawn him there. *Doyle: Doyle up on the altar.* The golden eagle gleaming on the pulpit; its neck impaled by a microphone, its beak shrieking at him soundlessly; the shallow glitter of Doyle's eyes delivering the true Christian message: kill. For whatever its origins in Ezekiel or Horus that eagle had always spoken to him of blessed violence, not the dove—it was as much a lie as Wongbok's clergyman, who had rested his sermon on a similar bird when he was not (the townsfolk whispered) resting his belly on the verger's ungainly wife. The tattered battle banners on the church walls in Wongbok; the white marble digger bowed over his rifle in Wongbok's main street; his father's helmet brimming with maidenhair fern—these had been the real symbols, not the Cross; the *Champion* and *Triumph* comics that arrived in convoys from England had been more precious than any Bible.

He stood up suddenly and stared at the eagle, trying to think of a prayer for his father: his father singing, "I'm INRI the Eighth I am, I am," until his mother upbraided him for blasphemy; it was years before he realized that he had not been singing "Henry." Strange, that: death had infected their Christianity for as long as he could remember. Not the crucifixion of Christ: at least Jesus had died quicker than his old man. No, the cleansing Blood of the Lamb had mingled with the slaughter at Mons; Calvary had been an anagram for the Light Horse; Christian piety merely the icing on a Christmas cake that was rich and dark with the fruit of sacrificial war.

He grinned, remembering the comics, and bowed his head. "Rat-tat-tat-tat-tat-tat-tat," he prayed. "Rockfist Rogan, RAF, zoomed his Spitfire in a steep dive at enemy territory . . ."

The true Living Flesh drew him out again into the sunlight: a beautiful Indian girl in a tracksuit was padding past a window, a carry bag suspended from a hockey stick over her shoulder. When he emerged, however, she had gone.

He meandered up Garden Road toward the Botanic Gardens, turning sometimes to look behind him. Once, when he was young, he had marched up here swiftly to demonstrate the physical prowess of the European to Chinese families on Sunday afternoon strolls from crowded tenements: how they must have smirked behind their fans at the clockwork Foreign Devil cleaving

152

up through their ranks! Now, however, he took the sharp slope slowly, loosening his tie, slinging his coat over his shoulder; leaning against a wall, his face damp with sweat, as groups of teenagers streamed up past him. For that's what they were, teenagers: the Chinese no longer were insulated in black oiled-silk; no longer as alien to him as insect creatures from another planet, but a global middle class among whom he felt at home. He gazed at them now with a fatherly affection: one student's spectacles, another's jeans and sneakers, a crucifix around a young girl's neck—all reassured him briefly of normalcy and decency, of hope and imagination.

His Cantonese, too, was coming back: they were chattering not of blood and revolution, but of flirtations and record albums. And he knew that they wanted what everyone wanted, love; they were dreaming the dreams that he had dreamed; they were willing romance and adventure to burst above them like star shells before reality closed its jaws as it had closed its jaws on him.

He bought a small square pack of warm sugar cane juice from a vendor at the Garden gates and sucked it slowly through a tiny straw. Pink and white flamingos stepped delicately beneath the mauve blossoms of a bauhinia tree, and a cluster of Chinese schoolgirls were photographing a glossy black statue of King George VI in full regalia; he looked as if the Public Works Department had just dipped him in a fresh pot of tar.

Quinn sat on a seat for a while near the monarch, gazing casually now and then down the path leading up from the gates as if he expected to see his own destiny rising to meet him. Once, beyond the flamingos, he thought he saw a deeper splash of pink, but he was not sure. He watched an old Chinese shuffle by, gripping the arm of a nurse in a white uniform; his bodyguard strolled behind, his coat slung over one arm, the bulge of a holster beneath his shirt. And later an elderly Australian tourist-couple paused near his seat. "The begonias go mad here," the woman said anxiously, as if they were about to leap up and savage her ankles, and Quinn regarded her gently, with faint regret, across the gulf that divided them.

"HE'S HERE!" MING squealed when Larsen answered in New Jersey. "He come in last night!"

153

Larsen rolled closer to the bedside phone; behind him, Donna stirred drowsily. "Lancelot? What's the matter?"

"He's here! Quinn arrive in Hong Kong!"

Larsen cupped his hand around the mouthpiece. "What do you mean?" he hissed. "Quinn's not due till Friday your time!"

"He check into the hostel last night!"

Larsen paused. "What's he doing?"

"Sitting in the park. Getting drunk."

"Has he talked to anyone?"

"Veitch. Only Veitch. There's no worry there."

"Who's Veitch?"

"Forget it, I tell you. Look, what am I gonna do? When you come here?"

"Just a minute." Larsen turned to Donna. Her golden head lay on the pillow, turned away from him, but he sensed by her stillness that she was listening.

"I'll talk downstairs," he said. "A business contact."

"Who is it" she murmured sleepily—or with a pretense of sleepiness.

"A mess-up with the booking," Larsen said, sliding out of bed. "Don't worry. I'll fix it up . . . Lancelot, are you there? Wait for a minute. I'll come back to you."

He padded downstairs past the Sacred Heart and picked up the phone in the dim living room. It was 5 A.M. "Lancelot? Now listen. What the hell's going on?"

"Quinn, I tell you! Look, I don't wanna get mixed up in this!"

"You're in it whether you like it or not. We're all in it . . . Is he alone?"

"Sure, sure. Alone. Out in the bars."

Larsen breathed out shakily, trying to summon up some Bogart authority. "I guess you've had instructions from Taiwan?"

"Sure, sure. Instructions. When you come here?"

"You go nowhere. You meet my flight on Friday. I want to know everything he's doing. Don't let him out of your sight."

There was a movement at the top of the stairs: Donna, muzzy, half-awake, was padding softly to the bathroom. The nightgown which clung to her slender body shone like silver.

He turned away irritably; why couldn't she ever cover herself up with a robe? "I've got to go," he said curtly. "Meet me at Kai Tak."

EVENING: THE TOURIST hotels glittered now like magnets in the Central District. Quinn thumped down in the Mandarin Hotel's Clipper Lounge and ordered a brandy. Already he was beginning to regret his morbid preoccupation with the hostel: the blood still bright sticky on the floor of his memory; the ghost of Doyle swaggering into the corridor.

There were no ghosts here; a photograph of a ship's sextant on the menu was the only reminder of the days of the clippers. A dried arrangement of Pan-Am hostesses sat in the next booth discussing moisturizers to counter their pressurized cabins. Their brown skin hung in slender folds; he heard the word "constipation" as they lowered their voices. Hey ladies, he wanted to say, catching their eyes, let's paint the town beige.

He raised his glass to one of them and smiled; a large V of annoyance appeared on her forehead. He knew why he was getting drunk tonight: he needed to tip back the balance of fate for a moment; to make the living dance against the gray backdrop of his dead. He dissolved so quickly into the past, that was his trouble—his dead still chuckled with the living; the landscapes of youth and middle age, of China and Australia, fused in one endless scroll, no matter what concrete and tar the Public Works Department was pouring outside the windows.

Nearby, a flushed American in a crumpled gray suit was trying to sell a satellite navigation system to a Chinese. The American had a heavy cold; he looked as if he had been traveling all night. "OK," he said, plucking a glossy brochure from an attaché case beside him on the floor. "OK," clicking a gold pen and blowing his nose. "As you can see, Series 28 looks very much like Series 29. Hardware-wise, the only difference is this . . ."

Quinn took out a pencil and began doodling on a coaster— gravely, drunkenly, playacting the investigator. One: Whatever material Veitch had gathered on Keh during the Second World War he had dumped or left behind long ago when he retired. The British, in any case, obviously were not interested: they or the Americans no doubt had extracted other favors from Keh after he reached Taiwan—or he could not have got within shouting distance of the reputable circles that he now disgraced. Two: Porter, he trusted, still had the Chinese eyewitness accounts of the Kwangsi massacre that Su had collected. He'd see him tomorrow. Three: His own undeveloped film lay in the lamp shade, and his own scribbled descriptions (written on a slow train to Canton) were in the China notebook in his coat pocket. Four: The Clipper Lounge, and playing spy, quickly began to bore him.

The hostesses were easing out of their booth, smoothing down their skirts and sliding carefully neutral glances across his face; the salesman still snuffling bravely. "ITT," he was saying. "The United States Government . . . "

Quinn moved on to the next watering hole: a goat, he thought again, in search of the tiger.

A SHINY RED display rickshaw sat on the marble floor outside the Lau Ling Bar of the Hotel Furama. Inside an Asian group was finishing "I Left My Heart in San Francisco" as Quinn slid onto a stool. The Chinese essences were leaking through a pinhole in the bottom of the globe while the Western anesthetic seeped into the top. It was both comforting, on the surface, and deeply sad: the same tunes dribbling everywhere, as ubiquitous as sparrows and lantana and jeans and plastic name badges and internal combustion engines; everyone was at home everywhere and nowhere.

"Good old song," he said to a European who sat beside him and tensed for a rebuff: the stranger might mistake his advance.

"I was just thinking," the man said, swilling a drink gently in his hands, "I'll be there tomorrow." He was a lean, tanned American: his hair silver-gray, his voice lazy and friendly like the voices of the MAG men in Shanghai, the colonel in Sian; it curled like wood smoke from the hidden certitude of his position. Nice men if you shared their beliefs.

"Been on holiday?" Quinn was not really interested. Soon he must leave these protective capsules and chance it on his own.

"Business in Pakistan." The American half-turned toward him. "What about you?"

"Holiday," Quinn lied. "Looking up old friends. You staying here?"

The American laughed dryly. "Just for the night. My wife

156

asked me to stop over and get her sunglasses fixed. The lenses are scratched. Otherwise I'd have gone straight through."

He studied Quinn's black suit, the battered black hat on the bar, the black tie tugged away from the collar. "You with some religious organization?"

It was Quinn's turn for a dismissive laugh. "No," he said, stripping the honeysuckle again in his garden. "Horticulturist. Should be writing to the kids but I'm having a night off."

The American flipped three color photographs from his breast pocket onto the bar: three small black boys wearing red football helmets. They all held footballs, and their teeth gleamed through the bars. A blonde woman stood behind them, her hands spread proudly, as if they had sprung from her loins. Quinn saw "Mike's Missiles" stamped on their chests.

"Adopted," the American explained. "I can't wait to get back. This one's American, this one's from Honduras. This little feller's from Pakistan. Want one more Pakistani and that's it."

"You like Pakistan?" Quinn felt unreal; they bent over the snaps like matrons on an excursion.

The American pushed the photographs back into his pocket. "Pakistan is the only strong area parallel to North Vietnam," he pronounced solemnly, "and I'll tell you why. Pakistan is the seat of the Moghul Empire."

"Yeah," Quinn said, "yeah. I never thought of that." Wondering about the Taj Mahal, he instead asked, "What line of business are you in?"

There was silence for a few moments while the man made up his mind. "Air defense," he said at last. "Hughes Aircraft. Civilian advisers to the Pakistan military."

"You mean Howard Hughes? He was madder than I am." It was out before Quinn could stop it.

The American straightened, faintly protective. "Howard Hughes was always a shy man," he conceded. "Other people had to go out and get his girls for him."

They drank together for a while; the group oozed into "Memories." Quinn's head was spinning.

"Well, I'd better be off," he said. "Fall into a heap. So what's next in line for you?"

The American swirled his drink gently. "Well, maybe not for

four or five years, but you know what's in the back of my head? You know what I'd really like to work for? I really think it would be a great challenge to defend China."

"Be terrific," Quinn said. "Well, it's been nice to meet you."

Swaying out to the lavatory, the room dissolved. He fought for air, drowning in "Moon River."

LATE THAT NIGHT, blundering down the corridor toward his room at the hostel, he saw that Doyle's old room was empty. The door was open; moonlight shone through the window onto the linoleum.

He swayed in the doorway. "Couldn't you have waited, you bastard?" he mumbled. "Couldn't you have given me more time to understand?"

He staggered to his own door, unlocked it clumsily, and switched on the light. Chaos. His mattress had been half-dragged from the bed and was sagging on the floor; the clothes he had left in his suitcase were strewn everywhere. He pulled the mattress onto the floor and tilted it over before throwing it back on the bed. The Hong Kong diaries, and the old "Burn This" letter from Doyle, had gone.

Quinn dashed water on his face and neck and leaned against the wall. In Australia, you could never be *sure* that you were being watched—only that you were on the wrong side.

He had never been *sure* of the signs in those last few weeks at West Ridge: a presence in the early-morning darkness; a black car turning slowly one evening outside his house; two cigarette butts in the canna patch; a closed window that he could have sworn he had left open. For each suspicion, there could have been a simple explanation.

But this—this was real. Gazing around him, he felt reassured.

FIFTEEN

QUINN SLEPT TILL NOON BEFORE he gingerly stood on a chair and confirmed that the ancient roll film was still in the light bowl. They had missed nothing else in their clumsy search: the lining of his suitcase ripped open; travel brochures scattered; even toothpaste squeezed from a tube in pursuit of God knows what . . . Three hours later he was back on the Island outside Porter's address in Queen's Road East. It was an old stone building, and it was on fire: brown smoke billowed from the windows, and crowds of Chinese were milling around a fire engine.

He pushed through the crowd to the foot of a flight of steps; a Chinese policeman shouted, motioning to him to go back, but Quinn sketched a sign of the Cross and smiled, lowering his eyes, as if to say: I am here on God's command, in case of human need. He felt invulnerable in his black armor. "God's work must continue," he said.

The policeman scowled and pushed back two amahs who were jostling with baskets; one spilled two eggs, which splattered on

159

the footpath beside a fire hose. She wailed in protest and clutched at firemen as they ran up the steps.

From the windows above the main entrance a tongue of flame darted out before a large cloud of steam overwhelmed it. The road now was jammed with honking cars and clanging trams, and Chinese were scurrying out of the building clutching bedding. One was wrestling with a half-open suitcase as a fireman shoved him in the back, and he slid down the steps, scattering clothing. The crowd laughed, looking eagerly up at the entrance for more entertainment.

Suddenly they fell silent. A rotund Eurasian in a crumpled white suit was looming out through the smoke and steam, turning to argue with the firemen as they nudged him gently toward the top of the steps. He was vastly overweight—striving to assert his dominance, but hesitant, like someone just shaken awake; he edged back toward the center of the confusion, as if only there could he begin to understand it. He came down the steps reluctantly, and in his bloated face, the gray hair, the Chinese eyes, Quinn recognized his own past descending slowly to meet him.

The face was a travesty of Porter's. Unaware of Quinn, he stood close by on the footpath like a baffled bull elephant, his back to the building, staring at no one. His suit was blackened with cinders, and his arms hung slightly crooked by his sides. But it was exactly the way he had stood when drunk so long ago outside The Vienna—about to swing around and hook over a rickshaw by one wheel while the coolies scattered: Porter blind-drunk with the Eurasian miseries upon him, and the coolies circling behind him slowly, bearing no grudge, calling to him gently while he fumbled glaze-eyed through the money in his pocket to see if he had enough for a woman. Only in those days his hair had been black and glossy, his suits crisp and white, the mustache trim, his belly taut. Don Ameche? He was Orson Welles.

Quinn pushed back across the road and leaned against a wood-carver's window. He smoked two cigarettes jerkily before the crowd began to break up. Porter climbed the steps again with two Chinese policemen and disappeared inside; he emerged a few minutes later and again stood dazed at the entrance, his hands bunched in his coat pockets. Quinn dropped a third cigarette and crossed the road.

He extended one hand as he mounted the steps. "Porty," injecting a spurious lift in his voice. "What happened?"

Porter looked through him; he did not shake hands. "Quinn?" he mumbled. "So you've arrived. You're responsible for this."

It was a disaster; one could only dance on top of it—pretend it wasn't there. "I haven't done a damn thing," Quinn protested with mock gaiety. "I was just on my way to see you."

"I've lost everything because of you. I don't even have the price of a drink." He studied Quinn closely. "They tell me you're a priest."

"They tell you wrong." Quinn took off his hat and pushed it under his arm. "Come and have a few on me."

Porter stopped a taxi and muttered to the driver; it headed back into the Central District. A few minutes later, walking down a small geometric cement street near the harbor, Quinn realized that they were on the site of the cobbled lane that had led to The Vienna.

Doyle had bustled down here with his umbrella over his shoulder, briskly ignoring the gray dragon of beggars, tapping Gus gently on the head as he entered the restaurant. And now Gus was at his last gasp in Austria, and The Vienna had gone too, replaced by the Jet Bar Steakhouse.

They walked between new office buildings that had supplanted the old tenements, the magazine stalls, the gaudy Taoist temple. A black Lancia 2000 sat half on the narrow footpath outside the steak house, bearing Playboy Bunny stickers; signs flared above it— Bang! Bang!, Piaget, Park 'n Shop . . .

"Who owns this now?" Quinn asked as he followed Porter up the steps, but he did not want to know; he was merely sprinkling words into another chasm.

Porter grunted and pushed open a hissing glass door into the steak house. It was air-conditioned and decked with horse brasses: a haven for businessmen and their clients on expense account lunches—a few still lingered over wine and coffee. Quinn was preparing to walk deeper into the restaurant when a waiter pulled out chairs for them at a table near the plate glass windows. It was exactly where they had sat in the Civil War days.

"Still at the old stand, eh?" he asked lightly. The waiter now was switching on a metal fan set in an alcove beside Porter although the air-conditioning was excellent; it bore a brass plate inscribed Porter's Fan. And still Porter did not speak; he seemed to be nearing the end of his road. Soot and perspiration trickled grittily over the collar of his coat, and when he lifted his waxen moon-face, his swollen neck, to meet the sudden rush of air, Quinn saw a red heat rash stippling the folds of flesh above a look-alike old school tie. It dawned on him slowly: Porter had become a mutant of Empire stuck up like an exhibit for the tourists; a beached whale expiring in his folds of blubber. One day they might hang his vast skeleton, like a prize museum exhibit, from the mock-Tudor plastic beams. "What's the story?" Quinn repeated.

Porter roused himself—a dainty little twitch of the shoulder as the waiter set down two small bottles of San Miguel. Buried in Porter, there had always been his daintiness: the decisive little motion with which he lifted a glass, as he lifted it now—a suggestion of gay, smacking pleasure, of life lived to the full, where there had been a parody of it.

The waiter placed the afternoon's first bill beneath a bottle and it fluttered like a flag in the fan-air: Don Ameche had inflated into a greasy white Buddha, a glass wedged in the center of his being.

"I was reading," he mumbled. He had never mumbled. "The door flew open, and there was a whoosh of flame. They must have thrown in a bucket of petrol or something. I'm lucky I wasn't burned to death."

Quinn stirred uneasily. "Who would have done it?"

"Who do you think? Why do you have to dig all this up? You're going to get people murdered."

"Ah well, it'll be a bit of a change. Ease the boredom," Quinn said with a thin smile, and then he leaned forward quickly—this wasn't the time to pretend to joke.

"I only want to get the story straight. I was too young at the time—wet behind the ears, you used to call it." He hesitated. "I'm sorry, though, about your place. Surely they wouldn't be stupid enough to . . ." He broke off, not wanting to say it.

"You're still wet behind the ears." Porter motioned for another bottle and tugged at his tie. He rubbed his neck with a paper napkin. "You're a carrier. They should lock you up in quarantine. What are you now? A missionary or something?"

"A death in the family." Quinn dismissed it quickly. "Look, you

162

remember those statements Su collected? Well, I owe you an explanation. My room was robbed last night. They took an old letter of Doyle's saying you had them. I'm sorry. I shouldn't have kept it. Maybe they read it and decided to burn you out."

"'Maybe,'" echoed Porter, extending his snoot-smeared arms. "There's no bloody 'maybe.'"

"I guess not. You didn't have them there, did you?"

"That's the joke," Porter mumbled. "They weren't there. They've burned all my things, and they were somewhere else."

Quinn sighed and sat back while Porter sank another deep draft of beer, his hand flicking up and away as he set down the glass. "They're at my sister's place," he said.

"Winifred? I remember her." But Quinn was registering faint alarm: he had assumed that Porter would have hidden them away somewhere in the Government archives.

"You should. She used to fancy you."

"She was a nice girl," Quinn replied cautiously. And who had wanted only nice girls at eighteen, whatever one's desire for good?

"You made her cry. It was the only time I ever saw her cry."

"Me!" Quinn protested, and instantly remembered. Winifred curled weeping on a blackwood chair in the flat she shared then with Porter; it was the second (and last) occasion on which he had met her. The tears lay plainly on one polished arm, for the blackwood did not absorb moisture; she was weeping because he had told her jokingly that she was too young for him. Then Porter had come in, and she had scrambled up, protesting "I'm not crying!" as Porter lifted one teardrop on his finger.

He remembered now all right—he remembered the glance of hatred she had flicked at him. "I don't remember that," he said.

"Well, it happened." Porter's hand floated up from his glass. He seemed drunk already.

"I always thought she was a nice little thing," Quinn said. "Little" being the operative word; she had been small and frail. "Did she ever marry?"

"Married a dockyard chappie. Got their own place. Kowloon-side." And Porter rubbed his back to and fro against his chair to ease an itch, his face splitting into a devilish mask. "I'll have to stay there tonight. You can come over with me."

"If you don't think it would be an imposition."

Quinn waited at the table while Porter lumbered up to phone Winifred. A girl in a sweeping gray hat—Gene Tierney?—gazed up at him enigmatically. "You're a spy, aren't you?" she murmured, and then she melted away among the legs of the tables.

THEY TOOK A taxi through the harbor tunnel to Kowloon; he glanced at Porter as they swept out onto the mainland. He sagged beside him with his window rolled down, his bleary face nuzzling the night. His drunken spurts of frustrated anger had been isolated in the old days: the brief flash of a macaw through a jungle slowly decaying under pads of moss. But now he jiggled his feet fretfully and kicked sideways at Quinn's ankle—a new petulance that Quinn pretended not to notice.

"I shall have all the bands in Kowloon and Hong Kong," Porter grumbled suddenly. "The Argylls, the Leicesters. Ah, phone up the morgue!"

"Don't be morbid," Quinn said righteously. "You'll be all right. You'll live for centuries. Like me." The empty cottage in his brain; his body mouldering in bed for a week before the police broke in; Miss Bird and her cat leading an avid group of neighbors on the corner, grateful for the interruption. "We're survivors," he said.

"You'll be lucky to survive this." A half-turn of Porter's head. "I know these people. They'll drop you in the harbor for a dollar."

"What people?" But Porter was nuzzling the night again, and Quinn realized that he was humming the "Dead March" from *Saul*. "They won't drop me in any bloody harbor."

The taxi stopped outside a small house on the outskirts of Kowloon. A light shone at the front door, revealing a long porch enclosed with iron bars. Thieves, thought Quinn, until he saw a small women bending over a large white Chinese chow. Its snarling snout stuck through the bars.

The woman was Winifred. She was clutching the brute's collar as she spoke to it soothingly; with her other hand she was unlatching a gate in the bars.

"Hullo, Quinn," she called coldly. "He won't hurt you if he knows you're a friend. Will you, Princey?"

Quinn walked up the path and sidled in behind Porter, his hands stiffly by his sides. "Playful little fellow, is he?" he asked. Its teeth glinted in the light; the organ-stops of Winifred's spine stuck up beneath her dress.

Winifred patted Prince roughly. "Come on. Settle down, snookums," she coaxed. "Settle down. These are friends, see? Friends." For a moment Quinn thought that she was going to spell it.

"There's your Uncle Albert," she crooned. "Say hullo to Uncle Albert."

"You ought to shoot the damned thing," Porter grumbled, pushing his fists into his coat pockets.

Winifred flushed. She was still small, cold, and curved: an ivory figurine of the Goddess of Mercy with a silicone chip for a heart. She did not look as if she had cried for a very long time.

"He's my lovely boy!" she retorted. "Go in and sit down."

Her husband Herbert stood in the hall: a lumpish man who shook hands, mumbled in a Lancashire accent, and then plodded back into the kitchen.

Winifred shuffled in crabwise with the dog, and a phantom of Quinn sprang upon it, his thumbs pressing deep into its jugular. "Nice place," he said with bright insincerity.

Winifred ignored him. "Sit down so he'll get used to you."

Porter and Quinn walked to armchairs in the living room; Winifred's spirits seemed to rise as they reached their seats.

"There, Princey!" she declared brightly. "We're all friends, right? How about a whisky and ice?" Releasing its collar.

The chow clicked quickly across the polished floor and nosed their legs.

"You haven't changed a bit," Quinn observed with phoney gallantry over its massive head. "I'd have known you anywhere."

Well, *you've* changed, Quinn," she retorted. "I wouldn't have know *you*." The first dagger. She turned to her brother: "You'll have to stay here."

Porter grunted as Herbert placed drinks on coffee tables beside them: an all-purpose response to both gestures.

Winifred turned away. "I'll get us something to nibble on," she said, and she followed her husband back to the kitchen. "Not *that* way!" they heard her snap as a spoon fell to the floor.

A large clock ticked on a sideboard that carried two photographs of Lancashire cricket teams; a battered ball rested in a silver mounting. Out in the kitchen the bowler was taking a pasting: every now and again he shambled sullenly into view, clutching a tea towel, putting his feet down carefully as if they hurt from trundling down too many pitches.

"Remember those games we played against the Indian Merchants?" Quinn asked with a fake cheeriness: Doyle fielding suicidally close in slips, tossing the ball high in the air after a catch. "Dorn't you bowl me out! I give you three yards of silk if you dorn't bowl me out!"

Porter's red eyes opened. "I top-scored," he said. "Twice."

He reached for his glass, and the dog sprang, bristling, its fangs bared inches from his hand. Porter withdrew his arm sharply as if he had touched a hot plate. "Evil brute," he growled, but softly, so as not to provoke it.

A few minutes later, when Quinn reached for his glass, the dog swung on him. He and Porter sat stiffly together in silence, their hands on their laps, while Winifred and Herbert hissed and rumbled over the dinner.

Winifred delivered hors d'oeuvre eventually on two small plates that they did not dare touch; dinner followed nearly half and hour later. Quinn was pushing saffron chicken miserably around his plate when Porter asked Winifred about the documents that he had been guarding for Quinn.

She put down her fork. "You mean all those old papers and things in that cardboard box?" she asked. "I threw them out years ago. Albert," and her eyes, wide with innocence, held Quinn's for several seconds.

"You never looked at them," she said. "They were just cluttering up the place . . ."

Quinn's heart sank, but he asked her gently to look again. "No, they're gone," she announced triumphantly when she returned. "That's where Princey sleeps now . . . I don't believe in keeping old junk, Albert, you know that. You should have kept it yourself if you wanted it."

Porter pushed back his plate and rubbed his heat-pricked neck with a grubby handkerchief. "It was Quinn who wanted it," he mumbled. "I think I'll go to bed . . ."

Herbert stood up with him. "I'll get you some sheets," he said. It was the first time he had spoken.

166

Quinn and Winifred were alone; the clock ticked loudly. Almost immediately, her eyes lighted on the hors d'oeuvre on the plate beside the armchair where Quinn had been sitting.

"Goodness! You didn't have any savories!" she cried, and she darted over and picked one up. "You watch Princey do his trick!" and before Quinn realized what was happening she had placed on his head a biscuit bearing cheese and an olive.

"Get it, Prince!" she commanded, and the brute sprang and snapped up the delicacy. A paw scratched his neck as the dog dropped back to the floor.

"Good boy!" Winifred enthused, patting it heartily. "Who's my good little boy?"

Quinn stood up shakily, a cold anger forcing its way up through his fear. Winifred hung on like a mongoose. "I guess I'd better go," he said. "Could you show me where the bathroom is?"

Winifred directed him down the hall; the dog clicked silently behind him as he braced himself for a tearing wound in the calf. In the bathroom he urinated and dabbed his neck: James Bond, as usual, had crumbled into the victim. He steeled himself and walked back to the living room, his arms stiffly by his sides as the dog stalked him.

"Well," he announced at the doorway, "I'd better be going."

"Oh, really?" Winifred replied. "So soon?"

He waved aside her offer to call a taxi, imagining a long black hearse sliding up in its stead. Winifred held the dog as she opened the barred porch gate, but it managed to fight free just as he reached the end of the front path. He had to slam the street gate against its snout.

"I'll be off!" he called with pretended levity. "See you again!" and he walked up the footpath and stopped quietly, hidden by a clump of bamboo in Winifred's front garden. He heard her call several times to the dog before she went inside, and he waited, stock-still, watching its snout snuffling through the bars of the gate.

Then Quinn bent and prized a large loose brick from the base of the iron railings that enclosed the house. As he straightened, he saw Winifred, to his surprise, emerging cautiously from the porch with something in her hands.

"I won't be a minute!" he heard her call. "I just want to burn off some garden rubbish."

Quinn watched her through the bamboo. She shook papers from a cardboard box onto a small pile of branches, tossed the box on top, and struck a match.

He guessed what she was burning. The fire flared for a few minutes and then died down. Winifred poked the embers with a stick several times, called again to the dog, and at last went inside.

"It's a lovely night," he heard her say as she closed the door.

The dog knew that he was there. Quinn crept up almost level with it before it spotted him and leaped up snarling, its paws on the gate. He lifted the brick and brought it down with all his force on its head. The bean field in Kwangsi rocked violently in his brain.

His heart now was thumping so loudly that he feared Winifred might hear it. The brick had fallen. He picked it up, slipped it back into the wall, and walked swiftly away through the long dark streets toward the distant hostel.

Behind him, he pictured the chow lying stiff and dead in the moonlight: its soul swimming inexorably up a shaft of light toward a doggy heaven somewhere high above the Nine Dragons —its snout uplifted, its legs driving back and forth like the legs of the old maimed cockroach.

"Quinn 2, Other Nationalities nil," he announced.

HE WEDGED A chair against his door that night and slept badly. Toward dawn, he dreamed that he stood beside a dark copse on a common at evening, locked in a strange ambivalence—the result, perhaps, of some minor fault in his circuitry. Blip! He turned to the wrong controller: a shadowy figure who stood in dripping rain in the copse, his gaunt face gleaming, a small black coffin humming in his hands. Quinn tried to recognize him, but he was half-hidden beneath the shadows of a tree, his sodden felt hat pulled well down, his raincoat collar turned up; only a bar of his face shining in the gloom. The rain was not falling on the common, but the sky was white and violet, and thunder rumbled faintly overhead, like furniture being moved in a factory. It was the traffic beginning to roar in Nathan Road.

SIXTEEN

MING BLANCHED PASTY-GREEN WHEN Quinn barged in on him the next day. He swung his little legs off his desk and banged down the phone.

"Quinn!" he shrilled. "*Ai-yah!*" Dancing to his feet, he shot out a small soft hand with a long sexual nail on the forefinger. His eyes darted past Quinn's head. "You come back!"

Teetering before an empty chair, he flapped both hands to say sit down, sit down, and then he dashed to the door and closed it with a final panicky look down the stairs.

"You come back!" he cried again. "Hey, you look old! You get old!"

Quinn smiled and sat down, arranging his hat on his knees. "A heavy night," he said. "You haven't changed." The long hairs still sprouting from the mole beside his mouth.

"Sex! That's what does it!" Ming perched on the edge of a swivel chair, his hands gripping the edge of his desk as if to stop himself falling to the floor. "Last night I have this doll, see, and when one bed gets too hot we move to another! *Ai-yah*, I tell you!"

169

He was so jittery that he knocked an ashtray onto the floor and bent beside his desk to retrieve it. Quinn thought melodramatically: he might come up with a gun.

"I get you a woman!" Ming squealed wildly. "Soochow girl— helluva good!"

Trembling, he was trying to unwrap a cigar; Quinn reached foward and peeled off the cellophane for him. Ming bounced up and grabbed a book of nightclub matches from the top of a filing cabinet.

"Where you stay?" he cried, shaking a match and blowing a ragged stream of smoke. "Hong Kongside?"

"Kowloonside. You know where I'm staying." Quinn eyed him with amusement; it seemed impossible that this absurd little man could tinker with his destiny. "I saw you talking to the desk clerk the other night. You know why I'm here. I put it in the letter."

Killing the dog had calmed him; he tossed his hat on the desk. "Relax," he said. "I just want to talk."

He was playing the role well; only when alone did he sink into his introspective swamp. He sat back and looked around Lancelot's meager little office: two Chinese girlie posters, cluttered files on a small table against one wall, a large filing cabinet overstuffed with photographs, a half-eaten bowl of noodles by the phone on his desk. He could imagine the grubby little cases he scrabbled up here before they seeped into the police courts.

"We can't talk here!" Ming yipped. "You're a helluva dangerous man. I get my head chopped off for you!"

"You're exaggerating," Quinn replied. "This place is still British, don't forget. I've got friends."

He got up and sauntered to Ming's grimy window above Gloucester Road. Below him, a young Chinese had released a moth-eaten German Shepherd on a narrow strip of enclosed grass dividing the streams of traffic; it was sniffing the meager blades tentatively, as if they were some acrid new plastic. What friends? he thought. Two spent forces, Veitch and Porter? Winifred and her bloody dead dog?

He suppressed his fear, but the burning building thrust up in his mind, Porter protesting: "You're going to get people murdered."

170

"I saw Porter yesterday," he offered. "His place was burned out."

Lancelot jiggled his cigar. "You don't know these people. They do anything."

Quinn grinned and sat down again. "I'm a man of peace. How are your kids? You had some kids, didn't you?"

Ming looked blank. "One son," he conceded at last in a small distant voice. "A doctor in Canada."

"And daughters?"

"Yes, daughters . . . Listen, Quinn. Let me tell you, uh? I know what people do." The telephone rang; he picked up the receiver, dropped it back on the cradle, and then removed it. "I tell you," he repeated, sucking his cigar.

"Nanking, uh? I am a small boy when the Japanese come—1937. *Ai-yah!* You never see such many bodies—the soldiers all drunk. Stabbing, shooting! I hide in the reed beds two days."

"I know," Quinn said: "You told me in 1948."

"There is this coolie—very strong neck, very strong arms." He posed with his hands over his shoulders to illustrate large muscles, and then he struck one side of his neck with the edge of a hand. "The sword does not go through—very strong man from carrying the loads, you know? All the meat coming out. I get behind him under the bank when the Devils come. When he make a noise I hit him." He executed a swift little uppercut. "So. I live."

And you've been sheltering beneath your outrageousness ever since, thought Quinn; the neck gristle bulging from your childhood: baby Lancelot, undiscovered in the bulrushes. He watched him with mild affection: the guarded interest one retained for a dangerous toy.

"Second World War!" Lancelot cried. "I work for the Americans if they give me money! I work for the Japanese if they give me money! I don't work for the Chinese—no money! So they put me in the prison—my own people!"

Quinn smiled faintly; he was still telling the same old stories. Lancelot crouching in a corner of a Nationalist cell for two weeks while he arranged a bribe for the guards to get him out (like Galileo, it had been necessary only to show Lancelot the instruments of torture to inspire wild devotion for Chiang's cause).

Lancelot yelping once in The Vienna (with a vicarious blend of brutality and desire) of the young girl Communist whom the guards had dragged from the cell every night until they tortured and shot her; when she came back shiny and clean every morning all the prisoners knew where she had been. He even knew the aftermath of that one: Rushton had got it from two Chinese police who had spied on Lancelot one night in 1948; the story had entertained the restaurant regulars for several nights. Lancelot had dressed a bemused Wanchai prostitute in a mock-Communist jacket while the police had grinned and licked their lips at their peepholes. Then: "Die!" he had squealed, and the prositute had begun to giggle helplessly beneath him while he lay mortified, impaled on his own absurdity.

"I've heard it all before," Quinn said. "So what's your point?"

"I say this." Lancelot stared at his dead-man's shoes. "The Japanese kill! The Chinese kill! Everybody kill!"

Even me, thought Quinn. The shattering crash—the bloody pebbles of glass on the intersection; the small lolling heads. "I just want to talk," he said, shutting it out. "Do you still work for Keh?"

"Keh?" Ming echoed. "Years since I see Keh! Keh live on Taiwan. What about Keh?"

"No doubt you still work for him."

"I don't work for Keh! I am an investigator—private eye. I work for the Clarion."

"OK, OK." Quinn dropped it wearily. "Tell me something else. You remember Doyle? Was he in hospital before he died?"

"Hospital? Doyle? No, no hospital. Doyle shoot himself."

"I know. What do you know about the Precious Peace Psychiatric Center in Kowloon?"

"Nothing. I know nothing. Look, you gotta get out of here! Someone kill you if you stay in Hong Kong talking nonsense!"

"Nobody's going to kill me," Quinn said gently. "I'm Australian. I'm the moonlight on a rock. I'm the silence. Kill me and you only add to the emptiness. What's the gain?"

Ming stared at him, dumbfounded. "You've got a fucking rat in your head!" he said at last.

Quinn smiled. "There's another thing I want."

"Look, I'm helluva busy, I tell you!"

"I want to see Doyle's grave."

"Doyle's grave in Happy Valley? OK, OK. Maybe I take you to see Doyle's grave. Get you outa my hair."

He stood up and stubbed out his cigar. "I go first. You come when I give the sign." And he went to the door and opened it quickly, urgently motioning Quinn through, as if to motion him out of his life.

Quinn waited on the landing while Ming locked the door and trod carefully ahead down the steps. He hovered for several minutes at the street doorway, peering out, before he beckoned Quinn and they piled into the back of a taxi. His eyes were everywhere: the taxi traveled quite some distance before he relaxed.

"What about Rushton?" Quinn asked.

"Rushton?" The prospect of luck—even someone else's luck—cheered him. "He OK. Lucky man." He took out another cigar.

"Why lucky? What do you mean?"

"He make a lot of money. Squeeze. But they don't put him in jail."

"You're joking." For the first time Quinn felt momentarily deflated. "He was always as straight as a gun barrel."

"Not joking. The ICAC are on to him until they drop it. The amnesty, 1977."

"I read about it in *Time*," Quinn murmured: Hong Kong Police fleeing in droves as the Independent Commission Against Corruption cracked down on them—until the police forced the government to draw its fangs. "But how do you know he was guilty?"

"Everybody know," Ming said gaily, and he dropped a match on the floor. "He live up the Peak now. Indian wife—very big!—and her brother. Big spenders. Idi Amin kick them out of Uganda. And the view! Million-dollar view!"

Quinn gazed out the window. Rushton the giant of stone, who had smashed men with a fist or a look, the pillar of Empire, the aging hero of the Hong Kong Force. Doyle's drinking mate.

"I don't believe it," he said. But he did.

IN THE OLD Colonial Cemetery, Quinn stood by Doyle's bland little cross, and he knew immediately that he wasn't there, any more than his own father resided in a neat slot in the brick crematorium wall near Wongbok that allegedly contained his ashes. Doyle existed everywhere but here—in a tote ticket in the racecourse over the road, not beneath this sickly cake of marble; in a glass on the bar, the crack of disputation, but not this insulting piety. He turned away from the pallid sheet of white graves; the tiers of dead faces reflecting the live ones over in the racecourse grandstand: a landscape to paint from a helicopter.

"Let's have a look at the races," he said, and he gripped Ming's elbow firmly to stop him twinkling away like a clockwork toy.

"Quinn! I tell you! I gotta go!" Ming wailed. "Why you come back?" There was a midweek meeting in progress, and Quinn steered him inside through the crowds and up to the rails. It was not the races that drew him, but life.

He placed his hands on Ming's shoulders. "Why did I come back? Because I've been an also-ran all my life, Lancelot. I thought I was about due for a win."

Ming's eyes darted around him like the hostel clerk's. "Quinn, I know you save my life once. But we talk another time, uh?"

Quinn turned and leaned on the rail. "I'm not afraid," he said. "I've nothing to lose."

Out on the track, glossy horses were prancing delicately toward the barrier; they dabbed their hooves at the turf as if it were burning hot. A champion jockey from Sydney—G. Someone; they were always G. Someone, as if their mothers had christened them with initials—G. Someone bobbed past with long curls framing his puckered face. He resembled an ugly little girl.

"Keh was a great horseman," Quinn said, and he laughed, but in the jockey's departing curls, it was his daughter he saw, not Keh. Once in a dream, he had searched for her for hours through the mossy earthern corridors of a mouldering mansion, because he feared that she had curled to sleep on the floor of some dim Victorian room cluttered with bric-a-brac—beneath a brocade chair, perhaps, which crumbled to the touch—and when he stumbled out of the mansion he stood on a vacant allotment with rusted car springs sticking out of the sour earth, watching the taillights of departing cars: wondering if she were being borne off safely inside one of them, or whether she was still lost alone in the catacombs of the mansion, with hours more to search before the kookaburras began laughing outside his window. "About time the bastard had a fall," he added.

"Quinn, what you trying to do? Commit suicide?"

Quinn turned his green eyes from the track. "What are you trying to do? You still work for him. I knew that as soon as I saw you at the hostel. Who firebombed Porty? Who robbed my room?"

Ming straightened his tie and brushed his little pink suit. "I work for plenty people. Business is business. . . . It's bad for you here, I tell you!"

"Listen, Lancelot, it's bad for me everywhere. And I'm enjoying myself here, in my way. I feel alive. It's like getting a charge of electricity up through the soles of my shoes."

Ming looked at him doubtfully: the beginning of hope. "You joke, uh? You are telling the jokes? The investigation about Kwangsi—it is a joke?"

"Maybe," Quinn said bleakly. "I suppose it is a joke, really."

"It *is* a joke," Ming repeated firmly, but he frowned at the end of his cigar. "Quinn, I know you from the old days—OK? But other people . . .?"

"Other people might think I'm serious. I know," Quinn replied smoothly. "What are they likely to do?"

"You're a helluva crazy man." Exasperated, Ming fiddled with his tie. "Go away! Screw the women! Larsen . . ." He stopped.

"Has he arrived yet?" Quinn paused, lighting a cigarette, trying to still the quivering of his hands.

"I talk to him in the States," Ming confessed. "You still got time to get out."

He had a choice then. The uncertain danger of a knife thrust in Asia or a slow puncture at home: a bullet in the brain or a fist squeezing the heart; the old staghorn, cancer, quietly sucking away in the belly. Distant alternatives to dangle lightly.

"Thanks," he said. But when the field jumped, when the crowd pressed close to the fence, he knew that it was vainglory that was winning—the urge to risk destruction just once before they lowered him into a wheelchair too. Because he'd escaped at last from the gray landscape of West Ridge, from the fibro box with his China ghosts dangling over the roof and the spirits of the

Aborigines moving in the wet creek clay down in the gorge. The sadness of acquiescence had almost overwhelmed him there: he had been dying like the explorer Wills in his humpy at Cooper's Creek: not unpleasantly—with even a certain stoicism—he had swallowed the paste of nardoo, of resignation; he had played his old Sinatras and Kingston Trios and Roger Millers; he had sung his favorite hits of the forties and kissed children who weren't there, obediently awaiting his turn. But now he'd broken the pattern. He wasn't going back.

The horses thundered by but he did not look up. All his life, until now, he had had a bit each way. . . . Now he hesitated, considering a plunge.

"Quinn?" Ming was plucking his elbow; he looked concerned. "I tell Rushton you here. OK?"

"OK," Quinn echoed absently. And he watched him wriggle away through the crowd, a little fish trying to get off the hook, while G. Someone raised his whip in the air, and the shovels flashed up and down in the old Colonial Cemetery.

SEVENTEEN

THE BUNGALOW SPRAWLED BEHIND HIGH iron railings on a slope above Kowloon City. Its slate roof was holed in two or three places, and the gardens were rank and overgrown; a crumbling satyr, one hoof snapped off, hobbled after a mossy nymph who was fleeing in delicious terror through the weeds.

Three strands of barbed wire topped a rusty ornamental gate and the railings; affixed to the gate was a dull brass plate inscribed Precious Peace Psychiatric Centre: Dr. Nepean Wong. The plate was screwed to the letter N in the BLENHEIM, which curved in pugnacius metal relief, signifying some eccentric English owner, no doubt, whose dreams of glory had withered with his death. Just below the wire, wedged high in a crevice of the gate, reposed a large torn fingernail.

Quinn pressed a cracked ivory button in the gate, waited a few minutes, and pressed it again. A Chinese in a sloppy khaki uniform with brass buttons eventually ambled down the path, the weeds swishing against his trousers; he could have been either guard or patient, his expression was so vacuous, his purpose so aimless. Off to the right, at the side of the building, a shapeless figure was rocking urgently beneath a bauhinia tree. He pushed a piece of paper through the gate bearing his name and a request to see the superintendent.

"*Fidi*, uh?" he demanded brightly, squaring his shoulders; switching on the shallow stoicism he had learned from Doyle. The attendant studied the paper solemnly and slopped back up the path.

He felt absurd at first, being unsure why he was there, but the decay of the place drove out his uncertainty. He despised Dr. Wong and his ramshackle psychiatric center before he bustled out the front door and motioned to the attendant to open the gate.

Dr. Wong was a plump little Cantonese butterball in a white coat; he was smiling merrily, and the sun flashed on his gold-rimmed spectacles. "Mr. Quinn!" he cried, placing a soft warm hand in Quinn's as he came up the path; the thought struck Quinn instantly that he might judge him to be a prospective patient.

"Doctor," he said firmly, and he saw the little man blink suddenly at his authoritarian tone.

"Come in!" Dr. Wong invited nervously. "Come in!"

He motioned Quinn into an office off a hallway at the front of the building; brown water-stains had coiled on an ornamental ceiling above a desk, discoloring small bunches of plaster grapes and a chain of vine leaves.

"You must please excuse the mess," he said. "We are not up to peak yet. Sit down."

Quinn sat before the doctor's desk. It alone was spotless: a few typed sheets of paper pressed neatly beneath a glass top; a pad and a container of pencils. A desk to receive visitors, not documents.

He beamed at Quinn but began to fiddle immediately with the band of a gold digital watch. "What can I do for you?"

Quinn dropped his hat on a carpet of indeterminate shade, wondering where to start. "This is not a government institution?"

"Charitable." Dr. Wong pressed his plump fingers together as

178

he slipped into his professional manner. "We have a long way to go, but we are making progress. You live in Hong Kong?"

"Visiting," Quinn said. "I'm up from Sydney."

"Sydney!" He laughed delightedly. "I am an old Grammar boy! Tell me. I have a bet with a friend. I say Grammar won the Head of the River in 1955 and then 1978. He tells me 1977. Who wins the bet?"

"I'm afraid I don't know. I don't follow it too closely."

"Never matter," the doctor said briskly. "I go back to my unit on the Gold Coast for a holiday next week. You are enjoying a holiday?"

"Sort of," Quinn said cautiously. "I used to live here a long time ago. I wonder if you can help me—although it must have been before your time. I had a friend—Doyle, Anthony David Doyle. I think he was a patient here. In the early fifties."

"The fifties! I only come here in 1975," the doctor said, breathing his relief. And then guardedly: "Why do you require this information about your friend?"

"Oh, there's no trouble," Quinn said, groping for a lie to reassure him of no litigation pending; no tax-dodge stones to be upturned; no mental health regulations clamping down.

"It's a personal thing, really. He has a family in Sydney,"—a fictitious family—"and, well, he died some time after he left here. It was nothing to do with his time here. But they've often wondered what happened to him, and as I was coming up here, I said I'd make a few inquiries. It's not of importance, really, to anyone except them, but I thought you wouldn't mind."

"Anthony David Doyle. Well, I'm sorry, Mr. Quinn, but I don't know what I can do." The doctor was losing interest now that no immediate benefit or danger confronted him; so Quinn leaned forward with another lie.

"As a matter of fact, he was an old Grammar student himself," he confided. "His family would very much appreciate it . . ."

"Doyle," murmured Dr. Wong. "Sister!"

An elderly Chinese nursing sister entered from a room across the hall; she wore a white cap crookedly on her head as if someone had just tried to knock it off.

"Sister." He scribbled Doyle's name on his pad, ripped off the sheet, and instructed her in Cantonese to check old records of the early fifties for such a name. Then he began fiddling with his watchband again.

"I am not here all the time," he apologized. "Very busy life," and he paused at the sound of a quick scuffle down the corridor; the slamming of a door. "Very many patients to see," he said, and smiled a sickly little smile.

"I'm sure," Quinn murmured. "Very good of you," and he gazed around the room, picturing the doctor's pudgy face beneath a Grammar boater as he marched across the willow pattern bridge into the medical profession; smiling to himself because all his life he had sat stubbornly outside the structures that ensured social and monetary success.

"My unit on the Gold Coast": he'd taken about four seconds to slip that in. He was probably into real estate, restaurants, a horse stud . . .

The silence between them grew heavy; the doctor bustled out and returned a few minutes later.

"As I say," he said, "no record of a Doyle. We go back to 1949. Maybe you try somewhere else."

Quinn picked up his hat. "I'm sorry," he said, and then the sister was at the door holding a bulging red folder. She spoke rapidly to the doctor and he returned to his desk, flipping through it.

"There is a patient," he said, "who had a—what do I say—benefactor of that name. Long time ago."

"Another patient?" Quinn echoed. "You mean Doyle wasn't a patient?"

"Many names," the doctor murmured, flipping over a card. "So many names . . . England, United States, South Africa, Australia, Canada—so many names. Very strange business."

He shook open a wide brown envelope, and a bundle of letters slid out, all addressed in the same large careful hand. The doctor pushed them aside and studied the other documents in the folder with a sort of jerky anxiety, as if he spent his life preparing for distractions.

"You see," he said at last, "in 1951 this is an orphanage—private church orphanage. Later, new owners from time to time, and more emphasis on psychiatric care. Very difficult cases . . ."

He started as a shadow fell across the doorway; it was the elderly nurse returning to her room. Absently, he began to pinch a small white scar on one plump cheek; he seemed reluctant to continue.

"There is a patient," he began again, "admitted in 1951. Small boy for adoption—two years old. Eurasian: Russian-Chinese mother. She died of heroin overdose. Father of baby unknown. Very bad case."

"And he's connected to Doyle?" asked Quinn. "What happened to him?"

Dr. Wong stirred uneasily. "Some patients, if you apply the treatment early enough, there is a chance. But this one; very difficult. Very aggressive. He rejects the treatment."

"You mean he's still here?"

"Still here!" Dr. Wong echoed with a too-easy laugh, and then quickly he retreated into the medical jargon on a sheet before him: "'Projectile vomiting, no doubt psychosomatic in origin. Rejection of authority-figures . . .' Still here!" He smiled nervously.

Quinn dropped his hat again on the carpet, leaned back, and crossed his legs. "I don't understand. The many names."

"Ah." Dr. Wong turned back to the cards. "Each month for many years they all send the money to keep the boy here. All these men. You see here—all the way through the fifties; lesser, lesser in the sixties. Maybe they die, maybe they forget." He giggled. "Maybe their wives put their feet down. Anyway, now there is only the one," and he tapped the letters.

"And Doyle was one of those who looked after him?"

"Doyle," the doctor said, flicking back to the front of the folder, "is the main one. The catalyst, you might say."

"And the mother? Does it give her name?"

"The mother," Dr. Wong said. "Vera Koshnitsky, Empire Hotel, Nathan Road. Died O/D 25/12/51." He paused. "This is confidential information."

"Of course, I'll be discreet." Poor old Vera. "What's testicles, teacher?" . . . "Ah Doyle, I wish I could fall in love with you, just like that . . ."

"I'd like to see him," he added slowly. "Just for a minute, if I could."

"I think maybe not possible," Dr. Wong replied, shuffling the papers together. "As I say, a very bad case."

"Doyle's family is fairly wealthy," Quinn lied. "Land developers and so on. I'm sure if there is anything they could do to help . . ."

When the doctor got up and left him alone again, he tugged several of the letters toward him. The envelopes clipped to them were all postmarked Hattiesburg, Mississippi, and the pages still clung together: the checks plucked off swiftly, no doubt, before they were consigned, unread, to the files. One of them had been written in 1964: "You should have seen them Goldwater nuts, kid, running around with gold dust in their hair. We could do with a bit of that . . ." He turned to another, 1968: "You must be getting pretty big now, kid. Look after yourself . . . I got a new job in town . . ." 1974: "Old legs giving me hell. Just as well I dont have to jump out of airplanes no more . . ." Dumb farmer kindness in words that looped as large as furrows, and a blurry color photograph taped to one letter: it showed a big shapeless man with a shock of white hair, hunched smiling on a tractor; a gray farmhouse sagging behind him among a few slash pines and a litter of what looked like junk machinery. He pushed back the letters as footsteps approached. Some old POW friend of Doyle's, perhaps, or another relic of those polyglot nights in the Empire . . .

"You can see him for just a few minutes," the doctor said. And Quinn followed him down a short corridor into a courtyard behind, wondering at this band of aging brothers whom Doyle had recruited so long ago to support a prostitute's son.

Purple lantana flowers had spilled from a tilting Grecian urn in the center of the courtyard; now they were creeping away over the flagstones. On three sides were padlocked red doors; fingers curled from beneath one of them, gently stroking the morning air. Quinn stood by a barred trapdoor in the flagstones, praying that the fingers were not those of Vera's son.

"Very bad case," the doctor apologized again, and, unexpectedly, he squatted beside Quinn and peered down through the bars into blackness. The attendant pressed a light switch on the wall beside the back door.

Beneath them, a creature was pacing swiftly up and down a cell that contained a small wooden table and chair; a roll of bedding lay beside a wall plastered with the bright posters of airlines. He wheeled around and glared up at the sudden burst of illumination, and for a moment Quinn feared that he might see the burning cold eyes of Doyle, of Les Darcy, of the gaunt Australian bush itself, but there was nothing of Doyle in the broad Eurasian face below him, the flat black hair, the narrow brown eyes beginning to focus on a target.

"You've been a naughty boy," Dr. Wong said, and he smiled his frightened little smile, wagging his finger puckishly over the bars.

OUTSIDE, OUT IN the street where he could breathe, Quinn reached for a cigarette. Behind him, the attendant slowly began to lock the gate, puzzling over his keys.

Later, he remembered a car sliding into the curb and an old beggar in ancient oiled-silk clambering out of the back: it seemed vaguely odd to him at the time, for kind souls did not give lifts to the needy in Hong Kong. He also recalled the maimed cockroach on his sink as the old man stooped across the footpath behind him, but it was the car that really attracted his attention: the motor revving loudly, the rear door swinging open.

A blow on the back of his neck dropped him to his knees. He staggered up and turned to find the old man dancing grotesquely in front of him: he had only one eye. A second blow to Quinn's temple knocked him unconscious.

He awoke several minutes later; he was propped against the psychiatric railings. Dr. Wong was bending over him and the adenoidal attendant was peering over the doctor's shoulder. A stethoscope swung like a metronome before Quinn's eyes.

"Who did this?" the doctor asked.

Quinn stared up at him, bemused, but a ridiculous joy had begun exploding in his brain: the delicious realization that a geriatric had felled him with such ignominy.

He wanted to grab the stethoscope—to bark: "This is Walter Winchell broadcasting to you from Radio City Music Hall!" Instead, he sat up slowly, gingerly feeling his head; he had never felt better in his life. "That bastard," he said, "must have been 108 in the shade."

But an hour later, back at the hostel (holding a damp handkerchief to his head) he telephoned Rushton; even a corrupt policeman on his side might be better than none at all.

Rushton was having a party that afternoon at his house on the

Peak; it was his wedding anniversary, he said. He gave Quinn the address.

"FOR GOD'S SAKE, Donna!" Larsen fretted miserably at the front door, jingling his keys, the taxi ticking at the end of the drive. "We'll miss it if you don't hurry!"

"I'm coming," she called. "I'm just collecting my makeup. Did you check the back door?"

"I checked it. Everything's checked." He waved to reassure the driver and looked at his watch: Donna had never been on time anywhere in her life. He heard her now upstairs on the telephone, uttering final glad cries to one of her women friends—a warm, light tone that she never used with him. Agitated, he ran his hand over his cropped, half-bald head; imagining Bertha sweeping grandly out of Westchester, the jet taking off without him. "If you don't come now I'm leaving without you!" he grated.

Calm and poised, Donna suddenly appeared at the foot of the stairs, her force-field wrapped around her. "I'm ready," she said coolly, selecting a trigger-phrase that was certain to enrage him. "Keep your hair on."

EIGHTEEN

RUSHTON'S BROTHER-IN-LAW, SATAJIT, A HAGGARD Indian with restless eyes, flung open the foor of Rushton's apartment on the Peak. He made jovial noises of welcome as he clasped Quinn's hand and drew him inside, but his eyes were roaming over Quinn's shoulder to the empty elevator behind. His most desired guests, obviously, had not arrived.

He steered Quinn to the drinks table and then turned away distractedly. A few middle-aged European and Indian couples were dancing decorously to rock music, moving their hands and knees gently lest they puncture the membrane of their status. Quinn poured himself a brandy and looked in vain for Rushton, the great stone profile against the sky; Rushton had always reminded him of rock. He was not there. Lean Indian men darted through the party with a grisly gaiety while their stout wives stood in small groups, dabbing their plump faces as they murmured to each other. They seemed to be melting like chocolate popsicles beneath the ice-green coatings of their saris.

Quinn grasped the brother-in-law's elbow. "Is Rushton here?" he asked, but it was several seconds before Satajit turned his head. He was hovering at the edge of a group of Europeans, laughing automatically when they laughed to prolong their merriment, his haunted eyes raking the room for further signs that the party was alive.

"He is very busy," he hissed at last. Distraught, Satajit watched the dancers, flicking his fingers and tapping a cracked white shoe in electric imitation of joy. The party was flat: middle-aged Indian doctors and lawyers; a few middle-level English and Australians in the government service; perhaps an off-duty policeman or two; Quinn remembered the mix. He left his host and sauntered around the room, picking at cashews, cradling his glass, keeping on the move so that he should not seem too obviously alone, wondering which imposing matron might be Mrs. Rushton. He felt like a crow sitting on a fence; the party was not merely flat, it was dying, its bones thrusting through.

He poked his head around the kitchen door. Rushton was not in there; duty must have kept him from the celebration of his own anniversary. Ill at ease, Quinn wandered between the balcony and the living room, simulating a keen interest in the sweeping view below of the island and the harbor and Kowloon. Now and again he stopped to pretend admiration for the sumptuous furnishings of the flat—a consultant's package-design that the intrusion of cheap brass ornaments betrayed wherever he looked. A policeman's pay certainly could never explain this extravagance unless Rushton had married money. And there did not seem to be much money in Satajit and his cracked shoes; he watched him throw back his head and laugh gratefully to conceal his misery. He reminded Quinn of a beggar he had watched one cruel day in Calcutta. The beggar had waved a stick at a monkey that wore a faded floral skirt and sat on a jam tin. "English dance! English dance!" he had chanted, and, shrilling intermittently with rage, the monkey had got up and begun to waltz, just as Satajit jittered now at the edge of the floor, darting savage glances at the door and consulting his watch.

He found himself pinned in against a wall as three Australians jostled to tell jokes. "So, anyway," one was saying, "Brookey gets this big Henry the Third, shoves it in a box, and posts it . . ." and they all staggered back slowly, gently shaking their heads from side to side and slopping their drinks in their merriment. Quinn stepped quickly through the gap and found himself at a bedroom door. It was ajar: inside, a large Indian woman in a lollipop-pink sari sat at a picture window, brooding down on Hong Kong.

Quinn tapped lightly and edged into the room. "Mrs. Rushton?"

She inspected him without interest. Large tears streaked her cheeks, but she made no effort to brush them away; her grief was as abject as a child's. "What do you want of me?" she asked dully.

"I'm Quinn. An old friend of . . . your husband's. He asked me to come today."

She turned away. "There is plenty of eating. Plenty of drinking."

"I'm all right, thanks." Quinn gazed at her curiously, "Is there anything I can do?"

She turned back to him. Purple circles beneath her eyes lent her a moody beauty; the richness of bruised, overripe fruit. "What could you do? There is nothing to do."

"Is he here?"

"Today he made me the promise. Without fail."

"He's held up somewhere?"

A telephone buzzed on the carpet at her feet; her eyes bulged as she bent to pick it up. She listened solemnly, occasionally sniffing and murmuring her distress, and then she thrust the phone at Quinn.

"Quinn? Rushton. Look, I was just saying—I can't get in there. Got a spot of bother with some squatters—could be trouble. How's the party?"

"Oh, OK. Fine . . ." He paused. "I was just asking where you were."

"It's that bad, eh? Poor bitch is always chasing high society and they never turn up. The brother's worse." He paused. "I'll be tied up out here for hours. Would you like to come out?"

"Whatever you think. I'd like to talk to you."

"There's a car picking up one of the Chinese Information chappies. Be downstairs in ten minutes. And Quinn?"

"Yes."

"See if you can sweeten her up a bit before you go."

Quinn put down the phone, contemplating the damp saddle-ridge of Mrs. Rushton's bowed neck. "He does not love me," she complained.

"I'm sure he does. In fact, he was just saying that you were magnificent. There was no one like you. He's . . . stricken that he can't get here."

The lies mollified her; she shot him a grateful look as Satajit darted into the room, tossing a peanut into his mouth.

"The bastards!" he hissed. "The bastards! We ask everybody above and below—all the neighbors around—and nobody comes!" He darted out.

Mrs. Rushton sighed; Quinn pictured their English neighbors withdrawing discreetly to the Cricket Club pool until the embarrassing coupling of color and corruption had concluded.

"The body," Mrs. Rushton confided suddenly. "He enjoys the body. But next year I am starting at the university. I am having the BA."

"Good for you." Quinn flushed: if Satajit was Calcutta, sex with Mrs. Rushton suggested the heaving birth of the Himalayas —the brown earth crumpling as India thrust up into the soft underbelly of Europe; the geological hawsers creaking over the fault line like the ancient stays that bulked through her sari.

Satajit rescued him; the car had arrived. He opened the door for Quinn and then reached back inside to turn up the record player full blast.

"Play louder!" he shouted. "Play louder!" glaring wild-eyed up and down the empty hall as Quinn stepped into the elevator.

NINETEEN

A BLACK GOVERNMENT MERCEDES WAITED downstairs; Quinn climbed into the backseat. Beside him reclined a slender young Information Officer who introduced himself curtly as Xavier Chen. He wore a sports shirt patterned with delicate blue flowers and gold-rimmed spectacles that he prodded continually with a forefinger.

The Mercedes swept down the mountain, heading for Kowloon and the New Territories beyond. BEWARD OF THE CARS, proclaimed a large sign outside an apartment building as they rounded a corner, and Quinn glanced at Chen. He was barely twenty, but he lounged in his corner, apparently unaware of blemish, with all the arrogant assumption of the misspelled sign. Beside him lay a clipboard of papers and a small red book.

"Mao Tse-tung?" Smiling, Quinn pointed at the book to break their silence.

Chen flipped it over carelessly with a slim golden hand; it was a *hugo Italian Dictionary.* "I go to Italy soon for a holiday," he said airily. "My brother do his diploma course at the Istituto Centrale del Restauro in Rome."

He paused, having successfully negotiated the phrase. "Art, physics, chemistry, microbiology—all to save the Old Masters," he said, and laughed briefly. It was not clear whether or not he approved.

"You like art?"

"Of course. I paint very well. Landscapes, seascapes, portraits, whatever you want."

Quinn's head began to ache. He withdrew to his corner of the car and dozed as it sped through the harbor tunnel and Kowloon into the New Territories. He awoke with a start as the driver accelerated wildly around a laboring cement truck. "Plenty of power," he said, concealing the blip of fear in his belly.

"Eight horsepower," Chen declared proudly. "Eight horses. Eight horses!"

He turned, his face suddenly aflame. "Eight horses! You fail to see the connection?"

"I'm sorry." Quinn looked at him blankly. Dab-dab, went the finger quickly; perhaps the gold frame was heating up in his excitement.

Chen lay back again in his corner, luxuriating in his secret knowledge. Then he crossed his ankles and began to tap a fake Gucci shoe urgently against the back of the front seat. An unconscious semaphore, perhaps: You've seen the spectacles. Now take a look at these.

"You question me on my knowledge of art," he said at last; it was an accusation dragged out of nowhere. "You are a Catholic?"

"No," Quinn replied, mystified. "No." What was he? A wedding car studded with pink paper flowers swished past; raw concrete apartment blocks festooned with bamboo scaffolding marched across reclaimed land toward a village which had scuffled up under the lee of a hill. "I'm nothing much, " he said.

"I am educated by the Jesuits. My father send us all to the Jesuits. He say: 'Whatever you do, you always right. Always come out on top.' I win the school's Gerard Manley Hopkins Prize for Poetry two years."

"So you're a poet too?"

Chen scowled "Easy," he scoffed. "You can trick up Jesuits." He curled his hands in a sinuous motion, like the movements of a snake. "They think they so clever, but you surprise them."

He snipped his fingers, apparently severing the head of the invisible Jesuit serpent. "I use a medical dictionary and a report on the mining of quartz," he boasted. "Throw in some old Chinese poems and some things about God and mix them up! Easy!"

He hawked loudly into his handkerchief and sat staring carefully at the phlegm, turning the cloth slowly in his hands to catch the maximum light.

Quinn looked away; the Chinese preoccupation with inner health and harmony had never appealed.

"What about the eight horses?" he asked tightly.

Chen folded his handkerchief slowly and slid it carefully into his pocket for later contemplation. He seemed moody now, as if he had just read his future and found it wanting.

"There was a painting, *Eight Horses*, in our classroom, by Lang Shih-ning," he explained. "Lang Shih-ning, alias Giuseppe Castiglione. A Jesuit at the Manchu Court. A surprise, uh?"

He jiggled his shoe and prodded his spectacles, in the grip of an agitation that Quinn could not fathom. "I might as well be drunk," Quinn thought. "Why do I attract the insane?"

"The Jesuits," Chen explained, "go everywhere. Plenty of money."

"Well," Quinn replied, with happy malice," you're one yourself now."

Chen shot him a savage look. "There are seven beautiful horses under a very old tree," he said. "A very old tree—hollow and rotten. And the horses are very fat, you know—very plump. There is a man brushing one of them. And behind the tree there is one very thin white horse. Very starving. The ribs . . . " He sketched semicircles in air. "I ask the Brother: 'What does this mean?' And he say to me: 'Think. Think what this mean.' He never tell me, never tell me."

"Perhaps the horses are symbols," Quinn suggested. "The artist is telling you something else."

"Horses are horses," Chen snapped. "Men are men." He turned, frowning, to the window; he seemed a very long way away.

After a while he cheered up. "Yes, we are all very artistic," he said, affecting a deep sigh. "My sister is with the police. Yes, a police officer!"

He pointed his fingers in imitation of a gun. "Very good dancer, too. Very good. Next year she do the ribbon dance at the Edinburgh Tattoo. You dance?"

"No," Quinn replied gravely. "I don't dance." Whirling around the room again with his children, collapsing on beds, cuddling small bodies.

THE FRONTIER POLICE station sat on a ridge facing the misty mountains of China. It was a squat concrete building with a flat roof: a sort of two-story red blockhouse set amid bauhinia trees, which dropped soft piles of mauve blossoms on the square in front. A brand-new Union Jack snapped from a white flagpole like a sticky illustration in a boys' comic; the faint crowing of roosters and the distant barking of dogs drifted up on a fresh breeze from the paddy fields below.

Quinn climbed out of the Mercedes as a young police officer clattered out of the building, looking up at the roof. "Mr. Quinn?" he inquired politely. "With you in a jiffy."

Quinn stared up with him at a human gargoyle wedged over the parapet; its gold-flecked eyes glittered in blankly at some crystal vision deep within its head, and a long sticky thread of spittle hung, swaying, from the lips. A black boot was forced into the man's neck, and a hand reached out and straightened the beret on his head, as if military decorum could exorcise madness.

A rosy faced English army officer looked over. "It's perfectly all right," he called down. "No damage done. Lie him down there, Corporal . . ."

The face was dragged back; the spittle broke and dropped to a windowsill.

"Gurkha," the police officer explained. "When they go, they really go. Demons everywhere."

His voice shook slightly with shock or pity; he continued to look up at the roof as a hand placed a *kukri* on the ledge. "Poor bastards like to do some killing," he said. "Here they have to cop everything the refugees throw at them. Bloody shame."

"What will happen to him?" Quinn sensed Chen at his shoulder, prodding his glasses, and he felt angrily defensive: the foreign interloper shown once more at a disadvantage. All these people had to do was wait; judge and wait.

"Ship him back to his mountains with his transistor and his sewing machine," he said and turned to Quinn with a fair facsimile of bonhomie: all at once widening his eyes, sketching a smile; trying a cheery light tone.

"Sorry for that interruption. Rushton told me to direct you down into the valley. Bit of a show on there with some squatters the Court has to evict. He could be some time."

He led Quinn and Chen around the building. In a guardroom at the back, still wearing handcuffs, three young refugees from China crouched on a wooden bench watching a crime drama on color TV: it was probably the first set they had seen. Gurkhas were unloading another group of prisoners from a truck.

The officer pointed down a concrete pathway that dipped into a thicket behind the building. "Only a few hundred yards," he said. "You can't miss it. I'd show you myself, but I may be needed here." And he gazed anxiously at the Gurkha command post on the roof; two soldiers in camouflage uniforms bent there like rigid cutouts, watching soberly through telescopes for the human dragons trickling down the slopes to see television.

QUINN LED CHEN down through a little forest of mossy trees; convolvulus decked their rotting branches with purple flowers, and doves cooed in the shadows. Four or five Cantonese in shorts and thongs sat in a rattan factory in a tin shed, chatting as they delicately maneuvered the canes; Quinn waved casually to show that he came in peace, and one waved back. He crossed a narrow footbridge over a wide shallow stream that frothed through rocks as big as heads; old scraps of cloth and fragments of plastic were caught in the rocks, and two bloated white fish spun upside down in a purple eddy. Beyond rose a green hill that was creased with the swollen tribal scars of abandoned tea-rows. Down this hill now spilled the ubiquitous gray lava of squatters' huts: an illegal village that had slid to the edge of the stream.

Chen hesitated as he stepped off the bridge. "Better we go back to the car. We wait there," he said. He was watching a squad of police in glistening black helmets; they were fitting on gas masks and beginning to clump heavily at the double around the huts.

Striding to and fro in front of them, slapping a cane against his thigh, towered Rushton, his craggy profile uplifted as if he had just torn himself loose from Mt. Rushmore.

"We'll be all right," Quinn said, slapping Chen softly on the back and pressing him gently foward. "You can lead the charge. Besides, how can you give the official version unless you have a look at it?"

Rushton's presence immediately reassured him; he had a better backup, for one thing, than the squads he had trained in Hong Kong during the Civil War—mimicking their stupidity near The Vienna as they smiled sheepishly at their boots. And this was almost the setting for a game: the chief bailiff, in top hat and Pickwickian frock coat, might stride forth at any moment to commence proceedings by hammering a supreme court eviction order to a Flame of the Forest tree. The minutes ticked by to the whistle; Rushton towered in the sun.

A strapping Englishman in a Singapore Lion T-shirt was striding around the police perimeter, whirling a knobbly cane as his eccentric symbol of authority. He was obviously Special Branch: the short haircut, the ex-military bearing of the squaddie who had risen in the world, the confident manner and casual garb—all shouted his new calling. The red Singapore lion snarled on his chest, and a tattooed dagger dripped crimson down one forearm, but he appeared brisk and cheerful at the prospect of violence: he slung the cane over his shoulder as if he were about to referee touch football. Only the European spectators did not seem to be enjoying it: a knot of government officials clustered miserably beneath a tree, caught in a no-win situation; in enforcing the law, they were supporting the rich against the poor. Their eyes turned anxiously toward a rotund little Chinese TV cameraman who was leaning against a police van, dozing with his eyes closed. "This is going to look bad on the evening bulletin if the noise wakes him," one murmured.

Chen clutched his clipboard like a shield against his chest. "These people are rubbish!" he exploded. "The owner try to get them to go. All the time they ask for more money."

Up on the roofs of the huts, shouting defiance at the European and Chinese police, stood small groups of youths. They began tying cloths around their faces as the police fitted on their masks, and Quinn saw bottles and piles of stones at their feet. He found that he was standing behind a row of miniature women police in helmets and trousers and tiny black boots: plump little Cantonese whose bottoms bulged as they fiddled with their masks. They were like obscene crabs. In front of them stood three or four aged women who were speaking sharply at the policewomen's round blank faces. The old women's heads were gray and balding, their features wrinkled with the ancient wisdom of China, and now and again they rubbed tears from their eyes with dirty cloths.

Quinn looked at them, remembering his righteous mother, although he could never have told her that. And yet they seemed to have been cut from the same square brown block; even their obvious testiness was reminiscent. Here, surely, in another form, was her earthy Anglicanism, the matriarchal love of Wongbok, the roast dinners, the apple pie . . . "What are they saying?" he asked Chen.

Chen edged closer, wrinkling his nose; prodding his glasses as he leaned to listen. When he turned back to Quinn his voice was as expressionless as the policewomen's faces.

"They say you are a disgrace to your race. They say your mother should have pushed chopsticks into her cunt. They say you are a whore for the filthy fat *gweilo* pigs. They say they would like to hold you down and burn the hairs off your cunt. Is that sufficient?"

Suddenly tear gas shells began exploding among the huts. Doors splintered and glass broke as lines of police smashed through flimsy barricades into the village alleys; the youths flung down bottles and stones before the police were up on the roofs among them, pulling them down. The villagers sobbed and screamed as the police dragged them out into the open through the clouds of tear gas; men, women, teenage boys and girls, half-conscious, were pushed against the sides of vans for identification photographs with arresting officers; the police prodded up their chins and held numbered cards against their chests before thrusting them inside. A girl collapsed on the ground at Quinn's feet, drooling into an English inscription on her T-shirt: "Ever For Ever Love You." Nearby, a middle-aged man seemed to have

fallen into, or been dragged through, broken glass: he lay unconscious, his undershirt soaked with blood, while a woman knelt
beside him, weeping.

It was a minor sideshow, all over in fifteen minutes bar the
shouting. Police drove the last of the villagers from their huts and
herded them behind barricades. Quinn glimpsed Rushton striding around near the vans and men and youths sagging in handcuffs; the government officials picked their way into the now-
deserted village and he followed them, avoiding Rushton until his
job was done. "Thank God he hasn't filmed that chappie lying on
the ground," one official was saying. "Go down well with dinner."

Whiffs of tear gas stung Quinn's eyes; he walked down a
narrow muddy alley. Scrawny chickens stared from coops almost
as large as the huts themselves, and paper Communist flags and
magazine color photographs of Mao were pasted on outside
walls. Inside the huts, however, jammed with beds and tables and
chairs, were their deeper concerns: tinted portraits of daughters
in mortar boards and sons in school ranks; it was the god education who beckoned to the good life, whatever the flags
proclaimed.

When he came out he saw Rushton arguing with a small boy
who was threading his way continually through the mob of police
around a van. The boy was wailing and wringing his hands:
Quinn had never seen anyone wring his hands before.

"Don't take our houses! We have no money!" the boy was
crying again and again in Cantonese, but it was Rushton's reaction that startled him as much as the child's grief. For all the while
that the child was sobbing; circling and sobbing and pleading for
mercy from an authority that could show him none; all the while
that Quinn imagined the boy's childhood withering inside him
like the novice on Hua-shan, the girls in Kwangsi; all the while as
the adults played out their game of power and money, it was
Rushton he was watching. And instead of ignoring the child, or
directing the women police to quiet him, Rushton was bickering
with him like a harried parent in a mixture of English and Cantonese, snapping at him like a frayed housewife each time he
appeared before him.

Quinn saw the Special Branch man leaning on his cane, watching Rushton with cold contempt. Then: "Tell him to piss off!" the Special Branch man told Rushton, and Rushton flushed and began to bluster. "Yes, piss off! Piss off!" he ordered, waving his cane at the child, and Quinn turned away in case Rushton should catch him observing him in this moment that revealed that he, like Veitch, was a spent force, his nerve failing in sideshows.

But Rushton had seen him, too. "I'll catch you up in the mess," he called gruffly, and turned away.

CHEN SAT ON the low wall of the police station, consulting his Italian dictionary and his Chinese handkerchief, while Quinn inquired the way to the first-floor mess. Already behind the bar was a large wax-white police officer whom he had seen frog-marching a Chinese from the village; he poured two beers when Quinn told him that he was waiting for Rushton.

"The old chap, eh?" he said. "He'll be along." He had a soft Belfast accent with a hard edge that put Quinn on guard: he watched him drain his beer, pat his belly, and belch. He was only in his thirties, but puffy and overweight; small beads of perspiration on his pallid face betrayed the many days and nights he had spent in here.

"That's better," he said. "I needed that. Frisky little monkeys, weren't they?"

"You had it organized well," Quinn replied, slipping deceitfully on side. "A lively day."

"Like taking the screaming kids to mass." He sipped his second beer and began pouring two more as they heard voices upraised in the corridor. The Special Branch man stalked in coldly and took a stool at the far end of the bar; a few seconds later Rushton loped in and silently shook Quinn's hand.

He hooked out a stool beside Quinn, spread his giant legs, and plunked his hairy arms on the bar. Lifting a frothy glass mug to his face, he was the cliff above a wild river—but an eroded cliff now. His eyes held the peculiar gleam of a dying man.

"Bloody 'ell," he said. His attempt at humor. Rivulets of sweat had dried on his craggy face: Queen and someone-else's-Country had made too many withdrawals of his strength, and the ICAC investigation and his belated marriage had probably sucked up what was left. He had become a shell of authority now; law and order had eaten him out from within.

"You've earned that," said Quinn with false levity. "How about a few blasts now on the old saxophone?" Thinking: he couldn't manage a comb and paper.

Rushton bumped down his mug. "I'd like to shove a saxophone up the arse of the bloody landlord who pulled us in on this to do his dirty work! Every bastard will be doing it. Send for the pigs!"

He pushed his mug across the bar for a refill. "That's what we are—the brutal pigs! There'll be questions in the House of Commons tomorrow."

The Irishman leaned over Rushton's mug, watching the fluid rise. "Ah well," he murmured casually, "better new questions than the old ones," and his eyes flicked in malicious communion to the Special Branch man. Even here, beneath the plaques commemorating the old police forces of colonial Africa, the framed print of Sir Robert Peel above the gin bottles, the canned music dribbling behind a bamboo screen, there was no sanctuary now for Rushton. The pink tide on the map had ebbed back down the drain in Whitehall; he floundered like Gulliver in the last Asian puddle, the butt of sly inferiors.

He turned to Quinn and was about to speak when the Belfast man broke in. "By the way," he said, affecting an Indian accent, "your wife rang a couple of hours ago," and he glanced again at the Special Branch man, courting his approval.

"Could we talk?" Quinn asked quickly, sliding off his stool to muffle the insult. How ironic, that he should want to protect this broken giant from further hurt, when it was he who had come for assistance. It was obvious that he could not lay his burden now with confidence at Rushton's feet: there was no one to trust, not even himself. Rushton stared long and hard at the Irishman. "Why not?" he said at last, and he picked up their mugs and strode to a glass-topped bamboo table beside a small bookshelf; the table was strewn with new le Carrés, and tattered old copies of Saki and Dashiell Hammett that were circled with the ancient brown imprints of glasses. He put down the mugs and stalked out onto a small balcony above the main entrance of the building.

"Young Chen down there, eh?" he said, jerking his head at the figure seated on the wall, and Quinn followed him outside, away from the ears in the bar, as he knew Rushton intended.

"Funny world," Rushton said and leaned on the parapet. "Old man smuggled him in here in '62 with a gold bar stuck up his arse. Now they own factories."

Quinn followed his gaze to Chen. "I thought he must be local-born. He doesn't seem to have much brotherly love for the squatters."

"They'd sell their own grandmothers. Farmers around here are making a fortune hiding refugees," Rushton said. He paused. "Nobody does anything for nothing."

Quinn hesitated. Was anything to be gained, or endangered, by confiding his muddled mission to Rushton; how much weight did they carry now, those nights they had both shared with Doyle so long ago? He went back into the mess, picked up the mugs, and handed one to Rushton. He was finished with caution.

"I liked your wife," he said. "She seems pretty fond of you."

"Met her in Africa years ago," Rushton said quickly, "Nice little thing then." An apology for her bulk.

Rushton sprawled in an easy chair and kicked another toward Quinn with his boot. Inside, the Special Branch man had left his stool and was fiddling with the books on the shelf near the open doorway; Rushton lowered his voice.

"Buried a fortune in Uganda, and she can't get back to dig it up," he said and smiled bitterly. "You can't say the Indians don't put their wealth back in the country. Place'll be like a bloody molehill if they let 'em return."

He tilted his mug, absently holding it up to the light. "You married?"

"I was." The deep green pool, the children's laughter; the blowfly tow trucks converging on the small bodies of his sons in the crumpled car down on the plain; a crippled daughter playing hopscotch, on crutches, in Tel Aviv.

"Been a bachelor all my life until she popped up again out of the blue. Poor bitch. Still thinks I'm number one."

"What do you mean?"

Rushton stirred restlessly. "The system. How are you going to change the system? It was going when I arrived, and it'll be going when I leave."

Slowly Rushton was circling around his confession. He leaned forward. "Say there's a violent crime. How do you think we pay our informers?" He rubbed a mighty thumb and forefinger together.

"Squeeze," said Quinn. "I read about the ICAC investigation. Did it affect you?"

Rushton barked a laugh and rubbed a hand like an earth-mover claw over his face. "Me and a lot of others. Black marks, naughty boys. Taking money from brothels and gambling joints, they say. How the fuck else can you buy information on the big ones?"

Or lavish flats up on the Peak, Quinn speculated; could love have led Rushton, the unassailable Rushton, to that final indiscretion? Love or self-mutilation? "The old British Vampire has sucked me dry. See what luxury you have reduced me to before I go?"

Quinn put his beer on the floor. "Look, if I tell you why I'm here you won't think I'm crazy?"

"I know why you're here," Rushton grunted. "Ming's running around in a blue funk from one side of the fence to the other. Hiding in the shrubbery last night to yammer at me when I got home. Even Veitch and Porter have been on the phone, wetting themselves. What are you trying to do?"

"What did they say?"

"They say if you don't knock it off Keh will have you knocked off. I know the bastard myself. Nothing's beyond him."

"Did you hear about last night? Some old clown hit me on the head."

Rushton had not heard; Quinn decided to tell him all that he knew. He began with Hua-shan and Kweilin; told him of the letters he had written to Keh and Larsen and Ming seeking discussions on old times—the vague suicidal threat they could not miss behind every line. He told of the theft of Doyle's old letter and two of his notebooks; the boy in the psychiatric center, the attack outside. Rushton stood up slowly and went inside for more beers.

Down in the square, squatter women were wailing for the release of their menfolk; inside, the Special Branch man was joking about the inadequacy of their handkerchief-masks. Rushton emerged and stood over him, frowning.

"They don't take you seriously," he said. "They're playing with you. Otherwise you wouldn't last five minutes. Why don't you pack it in?"

"There gets to be a point," Quinn said, "when you have to make a stand before you die," and he wished immediately that he had not said it. "Anyway," grinning, "I'm not ready for fucking lawn bowls."

He stood up, walked to the parapet, and sat down again. "And I've been thinking a lot lately about Doyle—wondering why he did it. Thinking about Keh. I've been thinking for thirty bloody years."

"Pack it in," Rushton repeated quietly. "Keh's got plenty of clout. Who do you think owns that land down there we're clearing? Wants to build another factory."

"Christ," Quinn breathed. "The bastard's everywhere . . . But look, don't you understand? You've been in the middle of it all the time. I've never come out of my corner."

"You said you'd invited Larsen to meet you in Taiwan. Is he likely to come here?"

"It's possible. Even probable. I gave him the dates I'd be here—well, the wrong dates. He could lob in on the way to liaise with Ming."

"Don't worry about Larsen," Rushton said. "I don't like the sound of the bastard. I'll put out a few inquiries—he might strike a few problems if he arrives. Lean on him a bit."

"What about Doyle?" Quinn asked. "Why did he do it?"

"Doyle's dead. You'll be on your own in Taiwan. It's off my patch . . . Doyle's dead. Don't dig him up."

"I want to know."

Rushton sighed. "There wasn't just one reason. You knew him. Drank too much of this stuff. The war made him, the old battle days. He couldn't handle the peace."

"Was that all?"

"No, not all. I don't know it all myself. No one ever will. But Keh speeded it up—his death, I mean."

"In what way?"

"Sucking him in on the drugs racket. Doyle didn't know what

was happening at first. He was the last to find out. Barred from a couple of officers' messes before he woke up. I had to tell him."

"Jesus."

"You saw Vera's kid, that was another thing. Keh got her hooked and started her pushing. I've got a theory about that."

"What theory?"

Rushton wiped his mouth. "He always loved to get at people through their friends—anyone close to them. I saw him do it a few times. He liked to undermine 'em, isolate 'em, get 'em in his paw, and squeeze 'em. He squeezed Doyle til he snapped."

Quinn leaned forward. "If someone tried to bring Keh down, what could he do to them?"

Rushton stopped with his mug halfway to his mouth. "Put it this way—no one can do anything to me. I spread the word long ago—unless I die peacefully in my bed the axe is going to fall on a lot of people around here. But if you're talking about you, I told you. Forget it."

"I don't mean shoot-outs in the main street. I mean legally."

"He's too big—it's not going to happen. He's got backup from the CIA down to every Green Beret who ever went bad. The Triads—everyone. Christ knows how high he goes. Out of my league."

"It'd be nice though," Quinn murmured, "for Doyle's sake, if someone did do something. Discreetly, if possible . . ."

"Yeah," Rushton snarled. "Like a chopper between his fucking ears."

A woman shrieked beneath the balcony and Rushton swore and bumped down his mug. Rising from his chair, his face drained white with shocked fury, he swayed like a great tree about to fall.

He looked over the balcony and then headed for the doorway. "Keep in touch," he said. A blue vein was quivering in his temple.

He turned at the door. "Doyle's wife married a big global wheeler-dealer. Steinway, Repulse Bay," he added, and was gone.

TWENTY

DOYLE'S WIDOW LIVED IN A cream two-storied mansion set on large lawns at Repulse Bay. Frangipani and Flame of the Forest trees softened the high stone walls, studded with broken glass, that enclosed it. A pink Rolls Royce stood in the driveway.

A few tables and beach umbrellas decked the flat roof, but no one was up there; below, a cool sitting room, hung with graceful bamboo scrolls, displayed the same water view. Quinn found her in there: a handsome blonde woman on the edge of stoutness, but still firmly controlling her flesh. She stood at the windows, presenting a proud profile as she lightly sprinkled a decorative Spanish galleon, fashioned of cloves, from a tiny red watering can. The scent of the cloves spiced the air as an amah ushered him through a glass door at the side of the house; he wondered, cynically, if she had timed the ritual prettily for his arrival.

"Mr. Quinn." She put down the can and extended a firm hand. She emanated composure and discipline amid plenty—it was impossible to relate Doyle and his ragtag world to her presence.

"Tony used to talk about you," she said, and then she picked up the can again. He understood the gesture: this meeting will be light and brief.

Quinn shifted uneasily, twisting his hat; her dominance made an apology necessary. "I feel I shouldn't have come."

She glanced at him with faint amusement, faint reproach. "It *was* a long time ago," she murmured and bent over the galleon in a rehearsal for dismissal.

Quinn switched course. "That's a beautiful ship. I saw Veitch the other day—I don't know if you remember Veitch. He'd love one of those."

"Filipino," she replied coolly. "What was it you wanted to talk to me about, Mr. Quinn? Would you like a drink? Tea? Take off your coat?"

"No, I'm right, thanks." He tried to suppress his faint resentment at her wealth and assurance: this privileged platform on which she seemed so content while Doyle reposed in the cemetery. He failed.

"I'm told your husband is a big global wheeler-dealer," he said, and he felt a twinge of pleasure as she winced slightly: it seemed wrong that she should appear so . . . complete.

She laughed softly and sat down on the sofa—suddenly dissolving before his eyes into a warm woman, her performance over. "Is that what they call him? I should have thought he was more that that. I can assure you we don't spend our days and nights counting piles of money."

Quinn backed into an armchair, groping for firmer ground. "I wanted to talk about Tony. I've thought about him a lot down the years—ghosts in the head." He paused. "I always liked him a lot. I suppose I loved him in a way," wrapping the confession in a spurious laugh. "A man can say that now."

She looked at him simply, directly, for the first time. "Say everything, Mr. Quinn, before it's too late. Say everything. I try to tell that to Angela. She's so like Tony was. Very hard to reach."

So they had a child.

"You've other children?"

"Just Angela." She raised her head and stared away into a corner. "There's always something of Tony here when Angela's home."

"She's not married?"

"Divorced." She smiled sadly. "Twice. She's here from Geneva for a few weeks. Keeps me company while my husband's away." She hesitated. "The global wheeler-dealer."

Quinn smiled ruefully. "I deserved that . . . Tony married you after I left. I never saw her."

"Neither did Tony. I wasn't sure that I was pregnant—when he died, I mean. I've always been sad about that, wondering if it might have changed things. But she's never wanted for anything, apart from that—anything that I could give her. I don't mean money."

Quinn looked at her. How could he utter it? Why did you break up? Why did Doyle go back to the hostel? Why did he shoot himself? "He never seemed the settling-down type," he said.

He watched her as, absently, she began to smooth down a cushion. With what clipped tales could Doyle ever have won her? Soaking up curries on twelve-hour shifts in his office after days absent on the booze and birds; propping up police bars with Rushton; chatting to whores in the Empire; fighting old battles in the messes of the King's Own Scottish Borderers and the Royal Inniskilling Fusiliers. He could not even imagine them in bed together. With nursing sisters and BOAC hostesses, yes, but . . .

"I was nursing at Queen Mary," she said, straightening the gold threads of the cushion into neat rows. "I could always paint reasonably well"—she lifted her head briefly at the bamboo scrolls—"and I began teaching the other girls the traditional style. Cheeky, I suppose, but it caught on.

"Anyway, we met one night at a party at your friend Veitch's place, and after that Tony used to come along and sit up the back, painting these ghastly groves of bayonets." She flashed a brief smile. "He knew it made me angry. Perhaps it was the war, or"—daring it—"some castration complex. Anyway, we got married. Exeter, that's all I'd known. All rawboned and apple-cheeked from Home. It didn't work from the start."

"He had a pretty tough life. The war and so on."

"Tony had . . . problems," she volunteered softly. She crossed two of the gold threads and patted them gently.

"How do you mean?" Quinn leaned forward slightly; he was beginning to feel grubby. "What sort of problems?"

She looked up suddenly. "How well did you know Tony, Mr. Quinn? It doesn't seem fair, talking about him like this."

But she wanted to talk. She tossed the cushion aside. "Tony," she said slowly, "was a man's man. The Army—all that. He had been a POW, and before that—before that it had been something the same. Mother died when he was three; father disappeared. Women were just . . . beyond his experience. He was always alone on stage, Tony."

"I don't quite understand." Quinn was pressing her gently, anxious not to stop the flow, but despising himself. She swung away swiftly and looked out the window at a large luxury cruiser moored in the bay beneath the house.

"I have a good husband, Mr. Quinn. He works hard, he's earned everything he's got. He's proud of me. Proud of what we've done. And he's an affectionate man." She gave a little laugh. "Never forgets an anniversary or a birthday—in fact, he'll remember before I do. A loving man," and her voice dropped in gentle rebuke, "if you can say that of someone with the capacity to make large amounts of money. Whereas Tony—Tony was . . . unapproachable."

Quinn exhaled gently. "I know. The last of the straight-backs."

"Tony had difficulties with women. Oh, there were no men— nothing like that. But when he drank too much it was only men that he really loved—soldiers he'd fought with. I felt so . . . redundant. He couldn't relate. That's the modern word, isn't it?"

Quinn looked carefully beyond her. "You mean emotionally?" he asked quietly, meaning sexually, and she nodded quickly, giving the cushion a final thump.

"And now," she added, her voice bright and empty, "are you sure that you won't have some tea?"

"Well, there *was* another thing. Keh. How did Tony get on with him in the end?"

"That awful General Keh. He should never have got mixed up with him."

"Why do you say that?"

She stood up and fiddled with the leaf of a camellia. "There were all sorts of stories about him. Tony couldn't sleep at night. He'd sit up drinking for hours after he got home; terrify the amah. He used to make her try to sing with him. 'J'attendrai.' Can you imagine 'J'attendrai' in Cantonese French? It might have been funny if it wasn't so ghastly."

"What was it about Keh that upset him?"

"Oh, drugs, those sorts of rumors. He felt . . . implicated. Some woman he knew died. And the funny thing was that he wouldn't even take a headache powder himself."

She sat down again, absently smoothing her dress. "He hated props—props of any kind. He'd never had any, except drink."

"Did he ever say anything specific about it? The woman, I mean."

"Specific? Tony? No, I just heard stories, mostly from other people. But Keh is flourishing now, isn't he? Hobnobbing with the queen. Did you see the *South China Morning Post*?"

She pointed to a newspaper folded on the floor beside his armchair. "Her Majesty the Queen chatting with General S. K. (Kenny) Keh at the Royal Windsor Horse Show," stated the caption on a page-one picture, and there was a shrunken Keh, beaming with just the right degree of subservience tugging down the corners of his mouth while the queen stared frostily over his head.

"I don't know how they can bear to let him breathe the same air as she does," she said. "I always found him . . ."

"Repellent?"

"A ghastly man."

"But Tony never gave any details?"

She hesitated. "Well, I wasn't being quite truthful. The woman was some prostitute, I gather . . . Now what about that tea?"

Through the windows, Quinn saw a red Alfa Romeo roar up the driveway past the pink Rolls and screech to a halt; a young blonde woman jumped out and called imperiously to a servant stooping in a bed of jasmine.

"There's Angela," she said. "She'll be interested to meet you. Don't mention any of this."

"I won't stop." Quinn stood up quickly and stepped to the glass door. He had enough ghosts without adding another.

"I have to be going," he said, sliding it back. "But I'll be in touch. Thank you." Intending never to meet her again in his life.

The girl ran up the steps as he trotted down, and he shot her a quick smile: the same eagle eyes as her father, gleaming from a lonely aerie; pinpoints of instant decision without depth. He looked up from the foot of the steps, sketching a wave, and she was staring down at him curiously.

"I'll have you driven back," her mother called over her shoulder.

"I'll be all right," Quinn protested, but she was insistent. She came down the steps and opened the back door of the Rolls. A Chinese driver in a matching pink uniform sat stonily behind the wheel. "Tell him where you want to go," she said.

The driver switched on the ignition, and suddenly it was Doyle laughing at this last bitter joke of the Rolls, the harsh chuckle back in his throat. Doyle lived on, then: shaking the spray from his head in the prewar surf at Freshwater; singing "J'attendrai" with spurious sentiment as the long brown columns cleaved through the melting monuments in Palestine; clinging to the slopes of Mount Olympus as the Stukas dived; staring from his daughter's gray eyes as she stood ramrod-straight above the bathing tents, the soupy water of Repulse Bay, waiting for life to scream down and break her too.

"Kowloonside. European Hostel," he said, and he waved again as the car slid down the driveway. Then all at once he was weeping quietly; staring out the window and weeping for Doyle and for himself and for their children; roughly brushing the tears from his eyes with the back of his hand.

"I'm Quinn," he wanted to say. "I'm back. I'm sick in the head. Where are you? Why did you toss it in?" And he knew that Doyle would haunt him as long as he lived, just as his own land had always haunted him; they all merged with the silence that whispered just beyond the perimeter of understanding, the One. Doyle would be waiting for him if he ever went back: lingering over the surf on hot days sticky with sun-oil; sighing in the long dark waves at night; clinging to soldiers' uniforms in city streets, and in smoky bars wherever the talk was clipped and empty—concealing, never revealing—his laughter the staccato bark of the old Vickers.

Fitted together, they might have made a whole; apart, they were lost. The cores of emptiness in their brains had been shaped by a mystical land too complex for white mathematics; they had joked in crowded rooms with dried dams in their eyes, not the

208

cosmic wheel of star and bush and rock and animal. And Doyle, in the city, had been even more alone, despite his bravado, than he was. He curled through the memory-banks of Quinn's brain; he rustled in the suburban trees, and in the screeching wake of party cars skidding through empty junctions at three a.m., stirring the cigarette wrappers in the local government gutters. For the saddest thing was that Doyle had never been earth. He had been the geometry of fence posts.

AT KAI TAK, with Donna, Larsen struck four obtuse Hong Kong Immigration officials who purported to find puzzling discrepancies in his passport and visa. One even conducted a minute examination of his travelers' checks when he rested them on the counter, and when he accidentally dropped his New Jersey driving license in his agitation, the official laboriously began to inspect that, too, until Larsen snatched it away.

Finally they delivered him up to their Customs colleagues, who nudged him into a corner like persistent beetles and spread the contents of the Larsen suitcases for fifteen meters around them, shaking each item with soft little cries.

Donna waited patiently, immersed for the first time in the Orient. The large English lady whom Ed had met on the plane was queening it over everyone, and Donna began to study her more carefully, for it was not till half an hour after she had seen Ed surreptitiously drop a note in her lap, when returning from the aircraft toilets, that he had suddenly affected, with mock surprise, to spot her up the aisle. Lady Earnshaw—certainly an odd business acquaintance. And Ed (for how long?) had been having an affair with her. Donna watched her sailing grandly through the barriers in a caftan patterned with hibiscus; suddenly she cannoned into a small Chinese in a pink suit who was talking to Ed, and she whooped with laughter, brushing a shower of sparks from her imposing breast. The Chinese offered up a strained smile and ground out a bent cigar under a two-toned shoe.

The suspicion that this was more than a working holiday for Ed to touch base with prospective Asian clients had occurred to her in New Jersey; the early-morning phone call about Quinn had placed her on full alert. Now she was certain, but who and where was Quinn? Ed had denied that it was the same Quinn who sent them the Thanksgiving and Christmas postcards, but she always knew when he was lying: he rubbed his arms.

He wasn't rubbing his arms now; he was dancing around the suitcases, white with fury. Not far away Quinn was standing at the doorway of his room for the last time, tipping his hat to the large maimed cockroach as it clambered laboriously out of the sink.

"You're like me, you bastard," he said fondly. "A bloody stayer."

TWENTY-ONE

PORTER DROVE HIS BROTHER-IN-LAW's battered little blue Datsun fast and badly out from Kowloon into the New Territories. He steered jerkily, whether drunk or sober; the white center line wavered beneath him until each oncoming vehicle forced him to swerve violently toward the edge of the road. He rarely used the car, a fact that certainly had prolonged his life; it was a clattering appendage from which he tried instinctively to free himself, like a man who has lodged his shoe in a child's toy. His crimson face bulged as he strained against the metal, and he stabbed the accelerator savagely, as if each thrust might precipitate a glorious explosion.

Porter was sober today—or as sober as he was likely to be—and as dangerous as ever. A Volkswagen Beetle rounded a corner ahead and suddenly squeaked with fear as it saw the Datsun charging for it. It scraped against a rock wall and careered out of sight around the next bend, the waxen faces of four European priests burning Holy Shrouds in its glass.

"You really must teach me to drive, Albert," Winifred declared, clutching an ancient picture hat to her head.

Porter shot her a guilty look. She was not being accusatory; obviously she had not noticed the Volkswagen as she relished the breeze and the view on her left. Winifred was not programmed for danger; death, when it came to his cold little sister, was likely to be an electronic pfhut; a final twitch of the limbs as the light blinked out.

"I could take poor Princey for picnics," she said, and she turned to pucker a kiss at the Chow that Quinn believed he had killed; it sat cross-eyed on the backseat, a bandage lumped precariously on a wound on its head. "I'd love to get my hands on the fiend who did that," she vowed.

"We're having a picnic now," Porter growled. "Keep a lookout for the turnoff to the temple."

The New Territories spread soft and green around them. A kite dipped and fluttered above a nearby hill, and wading birds stepped with elderly arthritic grace around the margins of a small lake. Porter felt uneasy, not because he made such a large-game target when drawn out of the spurious cover of crowds, but because the absence of people so often made him doubt his existence; he needed the solid soundings of other warm-blooded creatures to bounce back constant reassurances of his presence. His great legs thrusting before him in crumpled white, one arm bulked on the edge of his window, he floated in the netherworld of his fragile identity: a hillock of flesh, a frill of eczema, the moist gray eyes blinking a few heart-starters of San Miguel, his fake old school tie stained with last week's dinners.

"Look! A stork!" Winifred cried, and he looked and saw their aged, sanctimonious father pacing in his Bible-black coat in genteel retirement from the China trade in Cornwall; scrawling his spidery letters down the years (on hoarded ship's notepaper), which always added up to the same conclusion: I think it inadvisable that you come at this stage . . .

Porter's mind flapped heavily over Turkish minarets and Spanish castles and dropped in the Home they had never visited, among the relatives in London and Cornwall whom they had never met—a shamed family constructed laboriously, in a sense-vacuum, from photographs and letters sent to them dutifully down the decades. Their father's whines and warnings (of the money-grabbing socialists) from Penzance; the Christmas cards from aged aunts who shook the dry little trees of their years on pale afternoons by the Serpentine, lamenting the rotten fruit that had fallen in Asia. That was all that he and Winifred were: guilt-edged insecurity, whispers in the park, damp photographs plucked from withered black handbags.

"We've passed it!" Winifred squealed. He had to reverse.

A dirt road snaked up to a grubby little Taoist temple, tucked in against a hill, which was devoted to the worship of the ten Kings of Hell; hawkers crouched outside offering warm Coca-Cola, and seedy wild birds huddled in small bamboo cages. Winifred's picnic basket teetered on the backseat beside the dog, promising for her a resurrection of childhood, and she leaned out eagerly, holding down her hat, as they braked and slithered up into the edge of a silence that lapped from the wastes of Siberia, seeping in over the vast plains and mountains of China until it broke up at the edge of capitalism in Kowloon.

Porter ground his teeth. It was an absurd place to meet, but Ming had been so insistent. The area had frightened him since 1962, when the first mass of refugees had begun flooding in to escape famine; long lines of them winding down into the Colony's paddy fields, calling to their waiting relatives. Now they were flooding in anew; last night he had dreamed that he was drowning in brown bodies and he had awoken to find Prince curled on his bed. He skidded to a halt near the temple, his head jerking forward over the wheel.

"Well!" Winifred breathed, already spreading the tablecloth in her mind. "I've got your favorites! Egg tarts!"

"I have some business," he said, "with Ming."

"Oh, Albert!"

"It won't take long," he grumbled. "About Quinn. Nothing you need to go into." Wanting to share the burden.

"What about Quinn?"

"I'll explain later," he said. "You find a place and put the things out."

HE HEAVED HIMSELF out of the car and clumped up the steps to the temple, ignoring the hawkers. Gold-painted statues of the Kings of Hell sat against the walls offering a variety of tortures; the King of the Ninth Hell glowered at his elbow, guarding the Death-by-Accident City deep in the core of Hades, where condemned suicides were reenacting their grisly departures forever.

Ming was not inside. Porter came out and lumbered around the side of the temple. A long workshop and office had been built in the courtyard; inside, painters were bowing over pieces of porcelain, with boxes addressed to Detroit, New York, London, heaped around their slippers.

"Porty!" Ming popped out from behind the building. "You late! *Ai-yah!* This is bad, I tell you!"

"Why the hell did you drag me all the way out here?" Porter complained. "What's up now?"

Ming drew him in toward the workshop doorway. A Chinese girl typing out invoices gazed at them blankly and switched on a transistor radio. "Tonight's the night," Rod Stewart rasped at full volume; a painter dropped a plate and cursed.

"They ask us to talk here," Ming hissed, and he pointed one thumb at his own chest so that it was not visible from behind.

Porter looked past him through a cement moon gate that opened onto the hill behind the temple. Three men were crouching beside a cluster of boulders up on its crest. They had daubed several symbols that he did not recognize in red paint on the boulders, but he knew at once who they were; the stench of the underworld, of the grimy police court, seemed to drift down the hill.

"Triads!" he blustered. "The little bastards! They're pathetic. I'll ring their necks!"

Ming laid his hands gently on Porter's chest. "Listen," he pleaded. "Things are getting hot! We talk before we see them, uh?"

Porter bunched his big soft hands in his coat pockets. "Talk about what?"

"We gotta do something. Quinn's crazy, I tell you! If Keh really get mad . . ." He drew Porter closer against the workshop wall. "Quinn got these little books and a letter from Doyle."

"Doyle's been dead for a century. What little books?"

Ming squeezed the mole by his mouth; for once in his life he was momentarily speechless. "I tell you, uh? Quinn got these diaries—all about the old days. He got this letter from Doyle, all
214

about . . ." he dropped his voice and looked around him, "you know . . . drugs. All about some statements you got about Keh."

He tugged Porter's sleeve. "The guy's a time bomb, I tell you! We gotta do something!"

Porter rubbed a chill of fear from his face and shoved his hand back into his pocket. "I don't have any information about Keh—nothing! Quinn left some stuff in 1948—I never looked at it. Winifred threw it out years ago. I don't know anything."

Ming looked around miserably. "What we gonna tell 'em? They got this stuff from Quinn's room. I tell 'em it's nothing, but they get another guy to translate it. And now Quinn talks to Rushton. He goes to Doyle's wife—the amah tells these guys he asks questions."

Porter lowered his head: a large sick elephant at bay, with nothing left but a final blather of despair. "I'm not his keeper," he protested. "I'm not responsible for him. He came out of the blue. I wasn't even a friend of his."

"Well, he better stop," Ming said. "Taiwan tells me I gotta send him home or else!"

He looked up the hill at the little group among the boulders. "I tell you, sometimes I think Keh's more crazy man than Quinn! He send this old man, following me around—every morning, every night: 'When can I kill him?' *Ai-yah*, I tell you! Yesterday I say OK, OK, just a little tap. Nothing big. A warning. Maybe Quinn go away."

"I don't want to know about it," Porter boomed. "Don't tell me!"

"OK, I don't tell you," Ming hissed, but he could not help himself. "Anyway, he's dead!"

Porter grabbed a lapel of Ming's pink coat, half-lifting him off the ground. "Who's dead?"

"The old man!" squealed Ming. "The Black Hawk. They have a getaway car, but they hear a police siren and they take off. He chases 'em for two blocks, knocking over stalls!"

"And what happens?"

"He has a heart attack. First time he run for years."

Porter lowered Ming gently; the little man smoothed his coat and straightened his tie. "We better talk first, OK? See what they say?" Chirping with his own sick bravado.

"Five minutes," Porter said. But he meant fifteen.

Ming bustled ahead up the hill and stopped before three young men who sat in the grass beside the boulders, sipping cans of soft drink. They were already wizened by poverty: petty criminals in their best cheap white shirts and dark trousers, with extortion and chopper-murder the heights of their calling; the lurid patriotic ceremonial of the ancient Triads now debased into a hasty pricking of fingers and a muttering of vows on staircases and rooftops and in urinals as they dragged prostitutes and hawkers, shoeshine boys and drug peddlers into their protection racket—small fry using garbled bits of tradition for their own minor ends, just as Keh had borrowed military glory, at the peak of their criminal pyramid, for his.

Even Ming looked down on them—until one of them stood up: a junior George Raft with liquid almond eyes.

"Your hair is still wet," he observed in Cantonese.

Ming straightened his tie and cleared his throat. "My hair is still wet," he squealed with embarrassment. "I was born late. My family was poor, and I did not study the Five Classics." He hesitated, groping for the right words. "I hope you will tell me who, at the Flower Pavilion . . ."

Porter loomed up at his shoulder, panting, mopping his neck. "Do we have to go on with this bloody-mumbo jumbo?" he rumbled.

He thumped down on a rock and stood up again immediately, a small smear of sticky red paint on his seat. "God fuck you all!" he bellowed.

The little George Raft Cantonese glanced at him murderously, murmured to Lancelot for several minutes, and then sat again on the grass, his aides crouching dumbly behind him.

"He says . . ." Ming began.

"I know what he bloody well says!" Porter lowered himself miserably to the earth and lay propped on one side, gazing away into the distance with blind sorrow and rage. His chest heaved as he fought to calm himself; his home destroyed, and now this. He wanted to smite Hong Kong into powder and pour it like salt into the sea. "I don't know why I have to answer to riffraff."

Ming started nervously and patted him on the shoulder. "It's OK," he said and squatted fastidiously so that he would not dirty his suit. But his mind raced, knowing that it was not OK: the reed-beds of Nanking rose silently into his brain. Keh wasn't worried now. He was leaving it to the small fry. But if he got concerned . . .

Porter turned suddenly; his Cantonese was workmanlike, but he decided not to use it here—English might keep them at bay beneath him for a little longer.

"As I've told you, I know nothing about this business," he said. "I don't want to know. And if anyone touches me the whole damn government will come down on them. Tell them I don't know a damn thing!"

He stared morosely down the hill at the lake where his hated stork-father stepped delicately through the clinging weeds. Winifred suddenly appeared at the Moon Gate, holding a vacuum flask.

"Will you be long, Albert?" she called. "I'm ready to pour the tea."

He flopped a hand to signify that he would be coming soon while Ming and the Cantonese conversed, and then, unobtrusively, he stuck a plump finger in his ear.

"They are nervous," Ming said eventually, but it was he who licked his lips. "They want no harm to Europeans, but they get instructions. They think maybe you spill the beans to someone."

Porter removed his finger. "Tell them I know nothing, and they have my solemn word that I will say nothing. And if they kill me or Quinn, they'll swing for it."

Ming duck-walked over to him, jittery with anxiety. "They say I gotta do something!" he whispered urgently. "Maybe chop off his arm or they gonna do it!"

Porter heaved himself to his feet, nodded curtly at the Triads, and began lumbering off down the hill.

"Porty!" Ming cried, running after him, grabbing his arm. "There's another thing I don't tell you! Larsen arrive today! I just meet him at Kai Tak!"

Porter felt ill, but he fought to keep himself in control. This miserable little lot weren't likely to get to Quinn now; what frightened him was what they might do when they realized that they had failed.

"Play along with them," he said. "Get a little time. Tell them you'll work something out with Larsen."

Ming almost moaned. "Don't go, Porty! What am I gonna do?"

Porter laid a big moist hand briefly on his shoulder; further down the hill, beside the road that ran up to the temple, he watched Winifred spread a tablecloth on the grass near the car. She began arranging herself on it beside their picnic basket.

"If I were you," he said solemnly, I'd pack my bag."

"I SAY, OLD girl," he began gruffly, standing near her as she unfastened the basket. "I've been thinking."

"Thinking what?" Reaching into the basket, Winifred hesitated, feeling a faint flush of pleasure suffuse her face; it was so long since he had called her "old girl."

"Well, it's really time we took some proper leave. Went Home."

"Oh, Albert! You don't mean it! You mean, really Home? But what about father? I mean, won't he . . . shouldn't we . . ."

"We could see the old man," Porter continued doggedly. "Do some sight-seeing. Look at Buckingham Palace. You always wanted to see Buckingham Palace."

"Do you think we could? Oh, Albert, it would be marvelous!" She felt young again, dumping her husband on the path back to innocence. For she knew what Albert meant: the secret dream that they might be leaving Hong Kong together forever lay unspoken between them. Herbert hobbled behind them, dwindling in distance.

"When could we go?" she asked. "I'd have to get some clothes." Then carefully: "And what about Princey?"

"Herbert will look after him," Porter said. "They deserve each other."

"Albert!" she cried, frowning with reproach, but there was the soft warmth of girlhood in her voice, a gleam of undared excitement in her eyes. He had not seen her like this for years. "How long will we be away?" she asked tentatively.

"We could stay as long as we like," Porter answered levelly; it was important to maintain a neutral tone in case she took sudden fright. He paused: "The old man's done well . . ."

Winifred sighed, lifting out the egg tarts and holding them in her lap. "Oh Albert, I'll never forget this day. First the picnic, and now this . . ."

"We could go in a day or two," Porter said. The old bastard

owned half of Cornwall; the empty cottage at Mousehole might do for a start—the first step in a long process of revenge. At least he could thank Quinn for that.

Winifred looked up at him doubtfully. "Albert, there's nothing wrong is there? I mean, everything's all right? That fire *was* an accident, wasn't it?"

"Of course it was a bloody accident," Porter grumbled. "Christ Almighty, we've never been! Never got a penny from him! He can't keep us out here forever!"

She sighed again. "I'm sure you're right," she said in a small voice he had almost forgotten. "I mean, we're grown-up people. We can make our own decisions."

"We might even be able to spend a few days in Paris," he added: a grudging concession to clinch the matter.

"I can't believe it!" she said. "Did you hear that, Princey? We're going Home! If you're a good boy, we might be able to bring you too."

"We'll see about it when we get there," Porter said shortly. And he looked away toward the mountains over the border; a fine misty rain was coming.

"Quinn's gone," he said abruptly. "He rang while you were shopping. He left for China this morning."

"Oh, what a shame." Quinn wavered like a dark comet in Winifred's memory and then vanished. "I wonder what the weather's like now in London," she said.

Part Four

TWENTY-TWO

GENERAL KEH—UNCLE KENNY, AS he had been affectionately known since the early seventies—was catching up on his business affairs after his return from England. He sat at a long curved desk in his circular home in the mountains of central Taiwan, with a helipad on the roof and sweeping views over a large triangle of rain forest beneath him. The sensuality of that rain forest still stirred him, but these days it was more an itch of memory; the brutal carnality of his original vision had dissipated somewhat in blueprints and concrete. He was now sixty-five, and the juicy lover beneath him had become a demanding wife.

Lover, because that was the way he had first seen this area—as a sleeping woman. It was the day of Kennedy's assassination, he remembered clearly: the great powerhouse of the nation was shuddering in Washington, peasants were weeping in the fields of the world, humanity frozen in the blackest gloom, and he had waddled up to his copter pilot and instructed him to take him aloft—not merely to study the proposed site for a new dam he was dickering for, but to ponder what profit might accrue to him from this unexpected development in Dallas. He seemed to be the only man *alive* that day, peering down over the pilot's shoulder with a map on his knees! And then he had spotted the pubic rain forest, the round folds of her thighs, the peaks—one of them needed rock-fill—of her breasts, and he had dropped all thoughts of the dam and Dallas. He had ravished everything else—now the earth.

It was a long love affair that had languished for several years during litigation (and the negotiation of several hefty bribes), but he had never wavered in his dream. This was to be his monument, his culmination, his glory, his ultimate cover: a massive resort complex where he could launder his drug-millions and court the popularity he craved. Stage 1 (the belly area) was already functioning, Stage 2 (the breasts) on the drawing board, Stage 3 (the lower limbs and feet, which he had decided to subcontract and lease) still unplanned. As he giggled once to a Japanese industrialist: "There are more urgent projects than the feet."

His plan was bizarre. He visualized revolving casinos on each peak in Stage 2, with possibly a vast sculptured head as an extension of this. (Lakes for eyes? Parking in nostrils? He wasn't sure of this, any more than he had set a deadline to finish Stage 3.) But Stage 1 had been virtually completed since 1977, and it was already a major tourist attraction. Not the glittering James Bond fantasy he had pondered at first—and which it might yet become—but a workable mix of recreational facilities for the family. Most of the visitors, lacking not only helicopters but his peculiar insights, did not realize the true significance of the forest, although he had coyly alluded to the gentle feminine aura of the site in an interview in the *Free China Weekly*. In this way, it appeared as a vague conservationist tribute to womankind.

His house sat on the sleeping beauty's navel: a large knoll with steps descending gently into the rain forest in front of him, down through the mossy boulders of an ancient landslide. There were cliffs on the other three sides. Around the house on these sides he had laid out an eighteen-hole golf course for (mainly Japanese) visitors, who were to be penalized a stroke if they hit over the unfenced edges into space. The course faced the twin peaks to the north, which were behind him where he sat, with a tiered series of rice paddies ascending between them like a great jade staircase. Sometimes he regretted that the house did not revolve so that he could also contemplate the peaks from his desk, but, on the whole, he preferred to look down into the forest.

His office was a command post linked to each area of the complex with closed circuit TV screens he never watched: he left security to his large staff. Armed guards, wearing blue American-style helmets and shoulder patches designating them as guides, patrolled the whole complex with walkie-talkies, and nobody regarded this as peculiar on the rigidly controlled island; indeed, it merely enhanced the martial atmosphere that Keh presented to display himself as a defender of the Free World. Visitors entered through tableaux honoring his service in the Civil War; his picture hung with Chiang Kai-shek's and Sun Yat-sen's in a resort hotel he had built just inside the entrance gates. Keh the Hero.

The office, however, was also the focal point for his major business interests, both legitimate and illegal, around the world; here he played with telephones and telex machines while subordinates in Taipei did most of the work. The photographs on the walls here reflected his fleeting moments with the Great: introductions to Her slightly pained Majesty at the Olympia International Horse Show; pudgily peering over Prince Philip's shoulder at a wildlife conference; patting a horse with Ronald Reagan before he became Governor of California—even an old Second World War photograph of Bob Hope clowning with him at a concert in Honolulu after he had wangled his way onto a Nationalist mission to the States. Keh the Celebrity-Comedian. And Keh the Lover of Nature: Siamese fighting fish flicked and wriggled in large tanks inset in the walls and in a ferny pool in the center of the room, where butterfly specimens rested on mossy rocks and rain forest logs: *Ixias pyrene insignis, Cepora nadina eunama* and *Catopsilia pomona* pinned like paper flowers to disarm the gullible.

The red telephone buzzed: Hong Kong. It was several minutes before Larsen came on the line—deferential, anxious.

"General Keh? Larsen. I just thought I'd let you know that I've arrived in Hong Kong. With my wife. We'll be over there next week."

Keh had to think for a moment or two before he placed Larsen:

another minnow, like Quinn, surfacing from the past. He stood up and reached for a folder at the far end of the desk—priority zero.

"Have you seen him?" he asked, flipping over the pages.

"That's what I wanted to talk to you about. He's checked out of his hotel. Nobody knows where he is."

"He said he comes here next week also. So we wait. Better not talk."

"Sure. I just wanted to let you know that I was here."

Keh hung up on him, placed his gouty right foot (ascribed to a Japanese mortar attack) on a stool, and flicked with mild irritation through the folder, wondering how much Quinn was going to ask.

His staff had placed in the folder photostats of all the information they had received on Quinn from Larsen, Ming, and Quinn himself, plus the letter from Doyle that Quinn had never burned and a report on the diaries stolen from him in Hong Kong ("Nothing useful"). Ming and the Triad minions had bungled what should have been a trivial matter not requiring his second attention; it irked him, but it was still of minor concern. He dozed off a few minutes later; there was plenty of time to prepare.

TWENTY-THREE

AN HOUR AFTER THE LARSENS (and Lady Earnshaw) arrived at Kai Tak, Quinn left with twenty-three other people on a conducted tour to Kweilin. "No," he had scribbled on a form asking if he had visited China before—not this China, anyway. He shuffled aboard a China Air Service flight with a mixed bag of tourists: three or four German doctors, two Australian homosexuals who pushed each other playfully in the queue, several American couples with Polaroids, an English clergyman with large yellow teeth and a greasy red crease where his collar bit into his neck. Quinn shrank from them all as the plane took off: nursing his memory of murder over the soft green landscape of southern China; half-disappointed that Lancelot Ming had not erupted onto the tarmac to semaphore his disapproval in front of the nose cone.

"You go to China before?" A young overseas Chinese woman sat beside him in a pale blue pantsuit and gold sandals. Turning to him, smiling at him uncertainly, he saw that she was almost beautiful—only her teeth, too long and protruding slightly, marred her exotic appeal. She was taking large knobbly rings from her handbag and slipping them on to her fingers: several diamonds and emeralds, a large opal shot with red and blue fire. It was the opal that gave her away.

"No." He watched her push it on; instant arthritis blossomed above her knuckles. "Are you from Australia?"

"How you know that?" Her left hand flew, quivering, to her bouffant coiffure: an emblem of Western emancipation, of privilege and status to elevate her above the lowly dangers ahead.

"The opal. I just guessed. They're beautiful rings."

"You don't wear rings in Hong Kong," she said, hard-mouthed. "Someone chop off your hand for them." She closed her handbag with a snap. "Hong Kong people very tricky. Not like Melbourne. Melbourne people very good."

"The best," Quinn agreed gravely. "I'll bet you've got a beautiful restaurant down there."

"You know the restaurant!" She was pleased. "Very expensive business. I just go to Taiwan—order the glass panels for the walls. Six thousand dollars Australian money! Not counting the ceilings!"

She took out a mirror and began to study her smooth face for the elusive shadow of a line. "Hong Kong people tricky—you expect that," she repeated; he noticed that her fingernails were painted with delicate red and gold stripes. "But now in Taiwan, all changed. They look the same, but underneath they are very tricky too. Trying to . . ." And she curled her fingers gently in the air, seeking the right word.

"Con you," he said, and for the first time the possibility of somehow deceiving Keh occurred to him as an alternative to possibly bloody confrontation. "Are you going on to Kweilin?"

"See my mother," she said. "My grandmother. My husband say: 'Don't go! Too frighten!'" She laughed suddenly. "If I go alone and disappear—who knows?"

"You're too beautiful to disappear," he said, gently contemplating her thighs.

She stowed away her mirror. "Costs money. You can't look ugly, smelly, for the customers," and she laughed again. "My husband say: 'Stay in the group! Don't go nowhere!' I send money to my mother to come to the hotel."

"You'll be all right." Quinn gazed down at the green and silver land through which Chiang Kai-shek's demoralized columns had shuffled for embarkation to Taiwan: clouds of dust drifting up into silence with the ringing promises of last-ditch battles. His private in-flight movie screened below the wings, the pity almost leached from it all now, the action out of synch, but the guns still puffing soundlessly from the past. Keh's artillerymen twinkled around their field pieces with the demoniac gaiety of his puppets; they bowed slightly to each other in grotesque minuets of massacre, their arms bent slightly, as if tugged on strings; Keh's tiny infantrymen in ragged puttees crept to Quinn's brain to die. "At least there's no Civil War now," he said.

"Only baby then," she replied. "War bad for business. My father take me away. My name Ruby Ho."

"Quinn. How do you do? Your mother will be glad to see you. Does she like it in China now?"

"Of course she like!" The question astounded her. "If you don't like . . ." and she made scooping motions in the air with her hands, "you like to dig?"

CANTON WAS NOW Guangzhou, but it sprawled as of old around the muddy delta of the Pearl; mildew-streaked buildings under giant posters shouting for progress; stocky little southerners overflowing the streets while their chocolate river sucked restlessly at its crowded banks. The party's hotel rooms were not ready; a testy guide took them on a brief coach trip to Shameen Island. "Stay together!" he cried. "Not to get lost!"—and Quinn, contemplating the time bomb he was preparing to trigger in Kweilin, sauntered over the little bridge with the rest of them, straggling behind while Ruby Ho fearfully crowded the guide's elbow.

Shameen, like a mollusc, seemed to have absorbed the Revolution—its crumbling little yellow church had become a small factory of sorts, but the island's rich decay was intact. This was exactly the way it had been when he and Su had walked here after fleeing from Kweilin, trying to shake the horror from their brains while they awaited a night train to Hong Kong, staring hard at shadows in the doorways, under trees—assassins whom Keh might have sent after them. But now the sun was shining. A few unarmed Communist soldiers crouched chatting under a mossy banyan, their green uniforms and green sneakers blending mildly with foliage and trunk, and youths in bathing trunks were clowning for the tourists' cameras, pushing each other in the water, crying, "Hullo!" and "Good-bye!" as the Americans clicked their Polaroids.

Up ahead, the guide was listing the construction dates of new hotel wings, the size in kilometers of Guangdong Province, and Quinn's memory slid away to older facts that now mouldered, mossy with age, like the ancient banyans, the buildings.

He walked by weed-grown clay tennis courts, their nets in black lumps, and stopped to watch a ginger cat on a balcony, its body half-eaten away by disease, as it curled painfully to scratch. Beside it, two little girls in the red scarves of the Young Pioneers gazed down at him, giggling and waving as he blew them a kiss.

"AH, GOOD MORNING! Mr. Quinn, isn't it? I believe we're sharing." The clergyman, greasy with perspiration, was standing in his room. Tall and bony, with damp gray hair, he towered there in bare feet and red braces, trying to light up pale blue watercolor eyes in welcome—prurient eyes with the faint wash of a faded English seaside resort in them; he evoked a tang of donkeys on the sand.

"Millithorpe," he said, extending his hand. His smile twitched briefly like the edge of a lace curtain.

Quinn put down his suitcase and shook hands; the reverend's wet palm reminded him of Larsen. "Quinn," he said unnecessarily, concealing his distaste at sharing. "Apparently they're not geared for single rooms."

"Well, we're here, that's the main thing," the clergyman said. He had planted his suitcase on the bed nearest the window; now he was placing objects on the dressing table—an old warped tortoise-shell brush, several bottles of pills, a blue comb from which a tuft of hairs protruded. "And we're certainly blessed with lovely weather."

Quinn walked to the window to escape him. "It's great," he said. Outside in the corridor, the instructions to the staff were inscribed in large English letters on a board: *Taking care of old and young persons in various ways. Keeping our attitude toward the guests politely and not roughly. Standing up to reply questions* . . . Keeping his attitude politely and not roughly toward the Reverend Millithorpe was going to be a trial.

"Are you taking the whole tour?" he asked hopelessly. In the dressing table mirror, he watched his companion sit on a bed and bend to dab tenderly at a corn.

"Indeed I am!" He sighed and lay back against his pillows, crossed his legs, and then half-sat up as a sudden thought appeared to strike him. "Er, you wouldn't like this bed, would you? Forgive me. I wasn't thinking."

"No, I'm fine," Quinn lied. He could smell the reverend's socks. "I don't suppose we'll be spending much time in our rooms."

The Reverend Millithorpe settled back. "It's just that, living alone, one tends to settle into routines. Forget other people's needs." His eyes met Quinn's briefly in the mirror and then slid away. "I've been a widower now for seventeen years."

"That's no good," Quinn said lamely, yearning for the lunch gong.

"Oh, one can't grieve." Millithorpe's cheeriness fluttered softly, a gas fire in a draft. "There's always the young. Fresh new souls for Christ . . . I must say I'm very impressed with the people we've seen so far. Splendid physical condition."

THAT NIGHT, AFTER a tour of the city, a banquet in a restaurant, the group straggled back into the lobby from their coach, with no decadent bar, no nightclub, to prolong the evening. Quinn lingered in an armchair in the lobby; Millithorpe was no inducement to go to bed.

The members of the group were sorting themselves out, the Germans and Americans politely exchanging information on lenses and light meters, the few Asians drifting together, the gentle Australian homosexuals beginning to charm the old ladies. Nationalities blurred; the comfort of the middle class cushioned all. He got up reluctantly when they had ascended to their rooms and followed. The hotel was new, but letters already had fallen from signs; rubbish choked a fountain.

Millithorpe was rising from his prayers; his gaunt haunches, enclosed in outsize shortie pajama pants, were backing toward Quinn when he opened the door. "I'll let you in on a little secret," Millithorpe said jovially, looking over his shoulder.

231

"Oh." Quinn paused politely, deciding to undress in the bathroom.

"I've been here before." Millithorpe turned and displayed his large yellow teeth as he measured Quinn's stony face for surprise. "Oh, I don't mean just another tour—long before. Nineteen thirty-nine. It was like another world."

"It *was* another world," Quinn said, emptying the contents of his pockets into his hat. All at once he remembered that his mother had given him a New Testament before he sailed; he had lost it rapidly. "Corruption, famine, foreign interference," he said. He stopped short of "missionaries."

Millithorpe seemed disappointed by his curt response. "I mention it," he said, faintly aggrieved, "because I've been persuaded to write some articles for the parish magazine on the changes as I see them. I thought I'd pop a little one in the post tomorrow. I hope my reading lamp won't bother you?"

"No. You go ahead." Quinn went into the bathroom; when he came out Millithorpe lay stretched full-length on the bed near the window, a Crusader on his tomb, holding a bright blue toothbrush on his chest like a cross.

"I've just been thinking," Millithorpe murmured. "What does China mean to most people, I wonder?"

"Foreigners, you mean?" Quinn sat on his bed. He had decided on his manner: gruffness. "It's whatever you want it to be—sort of a territory of the mind you can reshape without touching the original. Depends who you are—politician, soldier, businessman, missionary—depends what you want. You don't have to *know* China, just make your own facsimile."

"That's a very cynical view." Millithorpe lifted his head to regard him curiously.

"I'm a very cynical man. But I believe it. You don't need the reality—wouldn't get any history written then. Easier to use it as a model for our changing needs. Bingo! There's your China! Rush up and show the teacher."

Quinn slipped into bed, propping himself up against the pillows. "I'm no different myself, but at least I know it." He unfolded a brochure and pretended to read it. He had never been as rude to a stranger in his life.

He heard Millithorpe uncurl silently, pad into the bathroom, and begin to brush his teeth. He emerged at the bathroom doorway, the brush still in his hand, white paste on his teeth. "The Church has a mission to bring souls to Christ," he said. "Who was it said last century—there is a great Niagara of souls passing into the dark here? They are still pouring into the darkness, Mr. Quinn."

"Whose darkness?" Quinn tossed aside the brochure, watching the souls glint like fish in the roaring white water. The weight of his mother's piety suddenly oppressed him from the grave: the weight of her cracked ivory-bound Bible on his earliest awareness of missionary China, extinguishing its essences, sealing the spices of the Middle Kingdom beneath the pale lacquer of Protestantism. It had not been war, not romance, that had brought him here first; the Wongbok parish magazine had killed any prospect of romance. Killed it in stilted old photographs reproduced on glossy little pages pimply with type, snapshots of long-skirted missionary women posing with parasols amid little mandarins in button caps, unaware of the sly self-interest in their subservient faces. Those bony European women had become his China just as Doyle, a decade later, had become his Hong Kong. Darkness! The darkness had lain beneath their skirts; he had pictured dying circles of grass where they had planted themselves in frozen sexuality for the Cause. To plumb the true mysteries of China, after that, had become as unthinkable as lifting the hem of his mother's dress. "What makes you think you've got all the answers? Those kids swimming down on the island—they hardly seemed satanic to me."

"Oh, certainly their lot has improved materially," Millithorpe conceded. "I'm not disputing that. Fine young fellows. But they are being denied the Word of Christ. There's a lot of work to do, to catch up . . ."

"Jesus," Quinn thought, "they can't wait. The war men in scratched sunglasses, the satellite salesmen, the Christian fifth column." And yet he was no better himself. China for him was a poisoned woman, for Keh a treasure chest—in each case, a receptacle to plunder. As Porter had said, he was a carrier.

"Have you considered " asked Quinn, "that you might just be spreading another form of infection?" In the dressing table mirror, he saw Millithorpe redden, his collar dangling from his neck. "A minor one, certainly. I mean, it's a joke, isn't it? Archbishops trotting around in funny hats while—you know. The diatoms

233

sink to the floors of the oceans, storing salt. The black holes suck in stars."

Millithorpe laid his collar carefully around his tortoise-shell brush and arranged his pill bottles in a neat line. "Perhaps it might be better if we were to make other sleeping arrangements tomorrow. It would seem that we are incompatible."

"Ah, don't mind me." Quinn affected a fake cheeriness. "It's just that I'm tired of bullshit. You're peddling your wares like all the others. Divine Love and Suffering marked down. Guilt on special." He realized that he was practicing aggression.

"I am sorry for you, Mr. Quinn. I really am." Millithorpe sat on the edge of his bed in a pool of light, a writing pad resting on his knees. He unscrewed a fountain pen; Quinn saw that his hands were trembling. "The more science uncovers, the greater the mystery."

"Well, maybe you're right." The quivering hands moved him; Millithorpe was too easy a target. "Were you here long in 1939?"

"Just a few months with a couple of chums from Cambridge. We did a little pilgrimage in the steps of Auden and Isherwood." A pained, dry expression to show that it was a joke. "They were our heroes then." Betraying more, perhaps, than he had intended.

"What I mean," Quinn explained, "is that I'm glad I'm not crippled with the gift of faith. I'd rather make it on my own. I don't have the extra Christian chromosome."

"Pride." Millithorpe sighed, and Quinn was content, knowing that he had handed him back his ascendancy; all he had to do now was sift the odor of sanctity from the aroma of socks.

"Light not bothering you? I shan't be long," Millithorpe called softly a few minutes later.

"Go for your life," Quinn said.

After a while he heard Millithorpe switch off his reading lamp and climb heavily into bed. Quinn lay breathing evenly in the darkness.

He slept tensely that night, or tried to. A rank old camel with Millithorpe's head plodded hour after hour through a Biblical desert, bellowing hosannas of halitosis at the distant date palms. Quinn walked beside him, a little apart, carrying a rubber knife, painted silver, beneath his gown.

"ED. THIS LADY Earnshaw. Who is she? What does she do?"
234

"What do you mean? What does she do?"

"Well, I mean, what do you know about her?"

"She's married to some Limey lord up in Westchester. I met her on a fund-raising campaign."

"When was that?"

"When was what?"

"The fund-raising campaign."

"Some time ago. Last year, I don't know. What's it matter?"

"What was the fund-raising campaign for?"

"Jesus, I don't know now. That hospital on Long Island. Something like that. It's not important."

"It seems important to you."

"What do you mean, it seems important to me?"

"On the plane you passed her a note."

"What note?"

"Ed, you're as red as a turkey. On the way down the aisle, you dropped a note in her lap. I saw you."

"I didn't pass her any damned note! What are you talking about? I might have dropped something. I didn't pass her any note!"

"All right, you didn't pass her any note. Here's one I made up myself, see? I've copied your handwriting."

"What's that? Give me that!"

"In a moment. 'My empress, I adore you. We will be together soon. Your devoted slave, Marcia.' Marcia?"

"You bitch. I hate you, you bitch. Where did you get that?"

"From her seat while you were dozing. She'd gone off to sit on her throne. So let me ask you again. Who is she? What's going on?"

"You wouldn't understand . . . It's a joke. I didn't tell you I knew her. I thought you might get the wrong idea."

"So what is the right idea?"

"She's theatrical. There was an amateur performance at this function. The fund-raising. She played the empress. That was part of the script. It was a joke."

"I see. And who played Marcia? Or shouldn't I ask?"

"One of the office girls— I don't know who it was. Now may I have that?"

"Take it. I notice she's staying here at the Pen. Small world, isn't it? Do I assume she's also going to Taiwan?"

"As a matter of fact, she is. Look, this is business. You wouldn't understand. I've got a lot on my mind. I could be ruined. Her husband's loaded. I might be able to swing something . . ."

"You should have told me you knew her. How long has this little affair been going on?"

"What affair? I'm not having an affair!"

"Ed, you're twenty years older than I am. I've never pestered you for . . . affection. But I don't enjoy being humiliated like this. What do you want me to do? Puff out my cheeks and put on half a ton?"

"You're being silly. It's business . . . She's—a very nice person."

"She's grotesque, let's face it. Still, it will be interesting to meet her."

"What do you mean, 'meet her'? You don't want to meet her."

"Oh, but I do. I most certainly do . . ."

TWENTY-FOUR

THE AIRPORT WAS SWIRLING WITH tour groups; wavelets of Westerners were washing in and out of the terminal under "Serve the People," emblazoned in gold, a vast scroll of Mao's poem of the Long March. Loudspeakers played Beethoven's "Song of Joy" while Millithorpe hurried around anxiously, belatedly trying to buy a stamp for his first dispatch from the Middle Kingdom.

The group boarded a battered Yak airliner for the flight to Kweilin; Quinn tried to hold an aisle seat for Mrs. Ho, but Millithorpe plunked down in it gratefully. "Ta very much," he said, slipping off one shoe.

He looked very old—already waxen with fatigue, perspiration beading his bony face. Imprisoned beside him, Quinn felt stifled, chained with him in mock piety while murder moved in his brain.

"You had a good old chat in your sleep last night," he said.

He had woken to find Millithorpe half-risen from his bed, one arm stretched toward the window, grinding his teeth and speaking strongly in bursts of incomprehensible words. He had decided not to tell him.

"Oh dear, I'm sorry. I didn't know I still did that." Millithorpe's right eye gleamed at him wildly. "What was I saying?"

"Nothing I could make out." Quinn affected interest in the tarmac. "Sounded like you were delivering a stirring sermon." Christ's frugality before tucking into a Sunday roast, he thought unkindly; thou shalt not covet thy choirboy.

"Very possibly." Millithrope was making an effort to turn the other cheek; his thin smile wavered at the corners. "My wife used to find me very trying on Saturday nights. Tossing and turning."

A hostess with long plaits moved gently down the aisle. She wore a white jacket, black trousers, and slippers, and when Millithorpe held up his seat belt to her to show that its buckles were missing, she made a little tying motion with her hands as she whispered past.

"Fix it with fencing wire," Quinn said. The wastes of the Outback were a more appealing prospect than Millithorpe's rumpled marital bed. "Presumably they're not overwhelmed with spares from Russia."

But Millithorpe tugged him back. "I lashed out once in my sleep and struck her on the forehead. Awful bruise." Happily, he picked at a knuckle. "Are you married, Mr. Quinn?"

"Used to be," denying him the satisfaction of further knowledge—and fearing that exposure to Millithorpe might tarnish the memory.

"Difficult to balance with a vocation. I had begun a study of the allegory of the *Song of Solomon* when I married. Took me thirty years to finish it." Miserably, he laughed, cloaking the dagger thrust into the corpse of his wife. "Hullo, we're off!"

The plane roared down the runway and lifted over the city, the mountains. Quinn imagined him solemnly peeling open every word, masticating each syllable of the *Song* until the juice trickled down his jaws. "Did you say 'allegory'?" he asked.

Millithorpe turned toward him, eyebrows raised. "Why, of course, 'allegory'! The marital union between Christ and His Church. Plain as a pikestaff, first time I read it . . . Like a sweet?"

He took some Chinese toffees from his pocket and offered them in his moist red hand. Quinn shook his head, and Millithorpe popped one in his mouth.

"The perfection of love," he said. "Quintessential worship.

Supreme sublimation in death," picking a fragment of rice paper from his tongue. "Matters for you to consider one day, Mr. Quinn. What is death, for instance?"

Quinn shut his eyes and did not answer. The bush had been a vision of death for as long as he could remember—bristling in the back of the brain, impervious to puny human achievement. *I'm waiting for you to fail*, it had told him in childhood. *You will fail. Travel as far as you like. You can never escape me.* He had spent his life fizzing like a dying rocket at the gray wall of trees.

He didn't say anything, pretending to sleep; he had nothing but his own emptiness to offer, and he treasured it more than Millithorpe's maxims. He was probably wrong. Perhaps it was not merely the bush that had eroded him—or a cosmic finger that had bruised him in the womb. Perhaps it was a simple vitamin deficiency, the chemistry of his blood or of his father's failing sperm. Yeah, that was it. He grinned, tipping his hat over his face: Type A, Pozières.

But the bush was bound up with it—the bush and war. At school, he could have told Millithorpe, they had sat under peppercorn trees electric with cicadas while their elders slipped slender moons of ice into their hot little mouths. Keats and Shelley—it had been schizophrenic. All that misty vapor while he could hear the timber cutters chopping down the flame trees up on the hill to make ammunition boxes and the last stands of coachwood behind them to build Mosquito bombers. So for every suck of Shelley another deposit of Anzac had lodged like Strontium-90 in his bones.

He opened his eyes only when Millithorpe jabbed him with his elbow. The clergyman was sitting forward anxiously as vapor poured into the cabin through a faulty system.

"I'm sorry," Millithorpe apologized. "I thought for a moment it was smoke."

"I hope not," Quinn said. "I'm not ready yet for supreme sublimation."

TWENTY-FIVE

AN ORANGE GLARE STRUCK THEM as they shuffled from the belly of the aging Yak; squinting, pushing on sunglasses, the tourists descended into a thin soup of humidity. Three hundred million years ago, there had been an ocean here; now the silver fins of MIG fighters, laid like fish in neat rows, glittered on the orange earth of the river plain. Above them, half in mist, rose the furry limestone peaks of Kweilin—what remained after the ocean bed had thrust up and eroded. When they were quiet, several thousand years ago, the Chinese had climbed up and dropped delicate pagodas, like caps, on their heads. They still wore their little caps.

"Kinda pretty, uh?" Backing from the plane, one of the Americans began to photograph them as if the scroll suddenly might wind up and disappear: bam!, next set of views, a hydroelectric project. The tour party straggled through the terminal to a coach; Ruby Ho had revved up into a hopping half-run to ensure that she remained in the center of the group. She sat near the back of the coach, grimly clutching the seat in front.

The Americans and the Germans were last aboard, clanking with equipment; one day they might sprout new shapes, their eyes in boxes, their ears in their hands, scanning the bleached globe for impulses with suckered feet, an elusive whiff of vegetation through an elbow. Quinn sat alone at the rear watching them with a smoky old magic lantern in his head: cherry-red flames, painted glass, the black pits of mouths singing soundlessly. And yet he continued to feel *alive*; that other Quinn melted quickly in the bright morning. The closer he got to the Retreat of Radiance the more his old horror and guilt receded: luxuries of loneliness, they did not belong here. The phantom Retreat had hung unchanged in the night air above West Ridge; the reality a few kilometers away was probably a bicycle repair works now—or perhaps a factory where the monks manufactured lenses. "It's the same with the Leicaflex," an American was saying.

Another guide popped up in front, as bright as a Disney cricket in spectacles; he looked as if he had jumped out of a crack in the rich earth. "We can't get to our rooms because other guests still get off," he announced, "so we go to a hill." He smiled. "But it's very nice hill!" And the coach trundled off through vivid green vegetation creeping close to the earth, small twisted firs, tiny water buffalo, shaggy little ponies, heads down, tugging loaded carts. The miniature world of the Chuang minority that the Han Chinese had subdued, the retreat of the Sung painters, the carvers in caves, a backdrop for the Polaroid. He did not recognize it. Kweilin had now become Guilin, and the autonomous region of Kwangsi was now Guangxi.

"I sit with you." Mrs. Ho, clinging to seats, advanced up the aisle and thumped down beside him. She had begun to chew the striped polish from her nails; a tiny gold fleck gleamed on a front tooth. "Why we not go to the hotel?" she hissed. "You think this is a trick?"

"It's just that our rooms aren't ready." Her knee pressed his, a meaningless juxtaposition of the meat.

"They say not ready. Maybe a trick." She clasped and unclasped her handbag, turning to look through the rear window as if she feared an armored column. "Maybe take us away."

"They want your money, not your body." He did not want her body either. Peace filled him, water rising in a glass; in the

242

golden-green rice fields on each side of the road peasants were stooping among the grave mounds of their ancestors. Only the starfish hands broke through his strange content—skeletal now, the flesh shredding from them as he remembered, almost fossils from another age. Bone or stone, it was of little moment either way—they were merely fertilizer or impediments to a plow, something to pick from the earth and drop aside, like a fleck of gold from a tooth. Who knew or remembered? And by what presumption, anyway, did he mourn, when they were her fragments, not his?

"I take only little money," she said, grasping her bag. "Few travelers' checks."

"No, I mean foreign exchange. Money from tourists." He looked in vain for landmarks, a pinnacle of fear to fix his mood, but the earth preached content; in the carved caves, in the memory cells of the mountains, the pilgrims had breathed love and longing through the centuries; Keh's hatred had beaten against it ineffectually, a tiny blinded bat. But Keh needn't have bothered; the Great Spirit by now must have expired in the new indifference. This was the content of the dead, a cemetery of atrophied veins encrusted with tablets, something for incomprehending foreigners to—click!—gawp at and stick in albums.

"I look at nothing," she said. "I go nowhere. I see my family, that's all.

THE DIVERSION TOOK a couple of hours. They drove through the fringe of the city, the streets crowded with cyclists, a few olive-green trucks of Second World War design, strange agricultural machines (with handles) adapted for the roads. The cyclists and drivers were the privileged; among them, straining forward, inches at a time, men and women tugged and pushed carts piled with huge logs or padded swiftly with loads on poles while the white faces at the coach windows floated above them. Yet, again, there was not the resentment that Quinn had expected; the brown faces lit up with unguarded delight when they spotted the tourist as if virulent hatred of the West, bred in post-Revolutionary nurseries for generations, had been expunged from their memories or had never been dispatched here from Peking.

And there was another thing that struck him. Up on the first floor of a crowded tenement, several people were fighting. A man clutching a small stool in his hands was being forced over a balcony by another man while a screaming woman beside them flailed at someone out of sight. The scene startled him; he had assumed that only state-sanctioned violence had existed in China for three decades, that Communism had eliminated personal passion, babies had been conceived without lust, theft eliminated with prostitutes and flies, random murders abolished by decree. That China had frozen into one vast political kindergarten after he (and Keh) had left it, new brothers and sisters sitting sweetly together at their lessons, their minds universally attuned to Marx. Looking back, as the coach swept on, he saw the man with the stool slowly turning over in the air, spelling out his ignorance.

"Charming," commented one of the homosexuals in front of him, wriggling upright, plucking his Bali T-shirt. "I told you we should have gone to Greece."

They left the coach and straggled up a small steep hill that rose straight from the plain like hundreds around it; in the cool mouth of a large cave halfway up, old men sat at round stone tables beneath black Buddhist tablets, playing chess and cards like ancients everywhere who had learned the falsity of institutions, the betrayal of faith, ending their lives now, as they had begun, in little games. Quinn was eager to get his bearings; up on top there was a small pagoda, and the tourists clustered inside it and lined a stone wall ringing the crest, gazing down at the city scattered beneath them through the peaks. Quinn stood beside three young soldiers at the wall; one of them was covertly sketching the strangers, slipping a landscape over his pad whenever anyone craned to see his portraits.

Millithorpe joined Quinn. "The Garden of Eden, eh?" he wheezed, leaning on the wall; already, like the photographers, he was enclosing the peaks in a frame: See the rich pastures we must sow again in China. "I wish I were forty years younger . . ."

"Chaplain to the Red Army," Quinn said cruelly. "You wouldn't have a lot of competition." Blocking him out, he cupped his hands, binocular-style, around his eyes; the Retreat of Radiance was a few kilometers from the city, hidden by peaks beyond a curve in the Likiang River. Slender bamboo rafts drifted downstream between the Muppet-mounts that had chilled him so long ago. The crop that Keh had sown mouldered in his memory. Perhaps

244

the old men, playing chess and cards, knew of its existence, but it was not on the tour itinerary with the caves and the river, the pottery works and film and theatrical performances, the panda in the local zoo. He would have to slip away by himself to reach it again—skulk in his room, pleading a minor illness, until the coach had departed on a lengthy excursion. There was no immediate hurry.

"They'll see the light," Millithorpe said comfortably. "Jesus lives."

Quinn dropped his hands. "He died in Kashmir. He never got this far." He had seen the little whitewashed building containing his tomb in a back street in Srinagar in 1949; inside, behind a fretwork screen hung with dead fairy lights, was a dusty catafalque draped with faded velvet. Outside, a young boy had sidled up to him and lightly touched his penis.

"Shot through when they fixed him up after the Crucifixion," he added. "Settled down with a Kashmiri girl."

"You don't believe that nonsense?" Millithorpe was red with rage.

"Of course I believe it. Ask the Moslems." But he did not believe anything; his few prayers had always clotted in the branches of the gums. "More probable than that rocket launch business you mob go on with."

"I will say some prayers for you," Millithorpe said tightly.

Quinn turned away. Ruby Ho now was clinging to a red pillar of the pavilion as if she longed for chains. "Do me a favor," he told Millithorpe. "Don't."

But he did not request a room change when they assembled later in the foyer of the hotel, and neither did Millithorpe. They sat on opposite sides of the coach on excursions that day to the pottery works, the grubby little zoo, cherishing their separate fantasies.

"Here I am," Quinn thought, "the last comic reinforcement for the Second World War, wandering lost, in middle age, behind the lines. Even I've got to admit there's a funny side to that."

THERE WAS ALSO a funny side to a young Japanese on the tour, Mr. Ochi, a cheerful bachelor on holiday from an electronics firm in Hong Kong.

He was standing on one leg in the foyer of the Likiang Hotel when Quinn encountered him that evening. A party of Japanese tourists had arrived, moving like hard-shelled insects across the marble floor in one glistening mass, pouring up the elevator shaft, swarming into their rooms, but Mr. Ochi paid no attention to them. He shut his eyes. "If you can close your eyes and stand on one leg for thirty seconds you are still young," he said.

Quinn waited until he had finished. "I won't try," he said. "I might get the wrong answer." It seemed significant that he should meet Mr. Ochi here, where the hulking Shiozawa had overshadowed his life.

Mr. Ochi studied his watch. "I am very young," he pronounced at last: like their baggage, his English always arrived late, but intact. He was probably in his early thirties: a little plump, but dapper in a striped T-shirt, blue shorts, white walk socks. A gentle quizzical humor played about his face—a vague abstract air, as if he were tuned to a secret transistor.

"You might meet your fate," Quinn said. "A beautiful woman." Ruby Ho was huddled with her mother and other ancient relatives in armchairs in a corner of the lobby, flourishing her striped nails while they stared at her dumbfounded, a visitor from another planet. "That Chinese lady likes you, I think."

Mr. Ochi followed his gaze. "The very tigerish lady," he murmured mildly at last. "Why do you give me this information?"

"I've been talking to her. She thinks you look pretty good," he lied. He wanted to jolt her off the rails as he had wanted to jolt Doyle's widow, to see what humanity lay beneath.

Mr. Ochi closed his eyes again briefly, raised his arms, and teetered thoughtfully on his other leg. "Do you consider we might make a love match?"

"You could try. You can see she's from good solid stock. Murmur 'catties per hectare' in her ear. She'll probably swoon."

"Ah, but you see," Mr. Ochi said, "perhaps I am not worthy. My ancestors come from the convict ships."

The group strolled down to a cinema that night for a special film screening. A sign in the foyer advertised two English-language attractions, *The Kid* and *Monsieur Verdoux*, but it was a Chinese movie they saw. It was a melodrama, hung on little Hollywood clichés, about a tragic love affair: dramatic shots of hands playing Chopin, a schoolboy tying a girl's pigtails, the heroine suddenly catching a ball tossed her way as the hero—their eyes meeting!—played with the schoolchildren. Debbie Reynolds with slant-eyes; he had grown up on it.

Filing out, Quinn plucked Mr. Ochi's sleeve. "I hope you picked up some tips about love," he said gravely. "If you like to wait back, I may be able to arrange for you to see it again."

Mr. Ochi consulted his watch; it occurred to Quinn that it might be an aid to concentration. "Unfortunately, there is little time before sleep," he said. "Perhaps Woody Woodpecker?"

But when they returned to the hotel lobby Mr. Ochi sauntered over to where Ruby Ho sat alone, retouching her lipstick. "My name is Mr. Ochi," he said, bowing carelessly. "I think we should speak together about our lives."

Quinn fled; Millithorpe was not in their room. From the window, he could see him down at the main gate talking to young students and workers who waited there each day and night to practice their English on the foreigners as the West flooded back. Because the tide *was* flooding back; the factories would spread from the Hong Kong border through the rice paddies to form China's southern Ruhr next century, and they'd make all the mistakes the West had made in the process. It was hypocritical to care! A salvo of cheeseburgers over the Kremlin wall, an injection of Coca-Cola in Peking—weren't they preferable to missiles and bacteriological warfare? He flicked a cigarette into the darkness. Perforated eardrums from rock music were better than bloodied, broken old professors.

And yet he did care—not because Communism was losing, but because it was consumerism, not socialism, that everyone wanted. The Americans had not lost in Asia any more than the Japanese had before them; the true war memorials were not the monuments in country towns—the marble soldiers and gray howitzers and rusting machine guns, the fighter planes in parks, the toad-tanks squatting among municipal delphiniums. They were the armies of Colonel Sanders', the clans of McDonald's marching across the globe; they were the jeans factories, the record stores, the purveyors of artificial needs. Doyle and his father had helped make the world safe for business diversity.

He undressed hurriedly and switched off the light. Down below, Millithorpe laughed and fluttered out a hand, tentatively touching a young man on the shoulder. Christianity, too, was making contact again; what promises of glory Millithorpe could unfold in his next dispatch!

He pretended to be asleep when Millithorpe entered, but the reverend was undeterred, switching on his reading lamp. "Remarkable young people," he enthused. "Their thirst for knowledge is boundless. Tomorrow night I've promised them a Bible."

Quinn stirred falsely as if he had been tugged from the edge of sleep. "That's nice," he murmured.

"One of them told me he had been arrested a couple of years ago, just for talking to foreigners. That's all over now, thank goodness—the Gang of Four."

"All they've got to worry about now is the Reverend Millithorpe, the Gang of One."

"Oh, you're incorrigible," Millithorpe joshed. He was in very high spirits; Quinn imagined him flushing with pleasure over his little triumphs, all resentment cast aside. "One of them had read the New Testament already."

"He'd do better with a pamphlet on lathes."

"Quinn!" Millithorpe admonished him happily. He was as excited as a young girl treasuring her first compliments. When he went into the bathroom he missed the side of the bowl and piddled loudly in the center of it.

Quinn pushed his head under his pillow and grinned to himself. Poor meddlesome old bugger; it was wrong to bait him. And he had meddled himself by alerting Mr. Ochi to Ruby Ho, altering the course of their lives as lightly as if he had pushed a stick into an ants' nest.

He decided to dream about the budding romance of Mr. Ochi and Ruby Ho so that he could go to sleep, but when he closed his eyes it was Porter's burning building that he saw, Ming squealing with fear, the old man with the custard eye dangling before him like one of Keh's rubber spiders; it was the skeletons lying a few kilometers away in the bean field. China's insanity was entirely predictable; the shifting pattern of his own life was more incomprehensible.

"TELL ME ABOUT Quinn."

"What Quinn? You know about Quinn. Nut case."

"I don't just mean the Christmas cards. Is he a friend of Milady Hippo too?"

"I'm not discussing anything with you when you go on like this."

"All right, I'll try again. Does she know Quinn?"

"She doesn't know him."

"She doesn't know him. Then let me ask you something else. Are we going to meet Quinn, too, on this mystifying little holiday?"

"I don't know. Yes. Maybe. I guess we might. I will, anyway."

"Good. We're going to meet Quinn. And that awful little Lancelot?"

"What about him? It's business."

"Am I going to meet him too?"

"He's small fry. Arranging a deal . . . No point in you meeting him."

"Well, you seem to find him fascinating. You spent two hours with him this afternoon. Still, it gave me the opportunity for a little chat with Lady Earnshaw."

"You didn't—I told you I'd fix up a meeting."

"I got tired of waiting."

"What did she say?"

"Oh, she thinks you're a cute little guy. Not that she's got much taste."

"Oh? She's OK."

"In fact, the last time I saw her she was going up in the elevator with half a dozen African basketball players . . . What are you doing?"

"Going to bed."

"I told you. You sleep over there."

TWENTY-SIX

QUINN WANDERED AROUND THE HOTEL the next morning. It was a tall modern building, but already becoming scruffy: a foreign toy that was serviced but not cherished. The neglect seemed to be working through from its core, the dirt surfacing, not settling; the pens and ink in the rooms, the ancient Par Avion stamps in the lobby post office, were artefacts of the pre-jet age, the pre-package tour. He found himself in a minimum-security jail with views of the river—and segregated tourist dining rooms permitting no contact with a populace forbidden to enter the grounds. When he inquired at the desk about taxis and buses, a bland girl informed him that Kweilin had none. Large coaches loomed in the forecourt, their mobile prisons, while chirpy warder-guides ran around counting untrustworthy heads.

He had a few days up his sleeve; now that he was so close to the Retreat of Radiance he hung back, postponing decision, appraising the ground ahead. There was no need to see the Retreat again, for that matter, Winifred obviously had burned the eye-

251

witness declarations of the massacre, but he still had the film, his notebook; he could still lay his account before the local authorities to trigger an investigation that would embarrass Keh at the least and topple him at best. Picked up by the English-language press, the old blot on his escutcheon would close palace doors (and racecourse boxes) in England; the noble guardians of children and wildlife might return Keh's checks, his drug underlings decide that he had become too dangerous to live. The heads of the local Party branch could easily set it in motion; they were bound to take some action worth publicizing. Meanwhile, he hesitated, testing the earth for firmness before he leapt over the cliff.

There was little cold logic, anyway, in his actions; he could have set a spark under Keh from Sydney if it were only revenge—not the desire for courage, the need for atonement—that drove him on, his compulsion to return to the scene of the crime. And if it were not for his guilt, which he had not learned to rationalize like more sensible men—the bomber pilots who had buried families in the rubble of Europe and now dug their nightmares in among the roots of their roses, the infantrymen who had shot at small shadows in the corners of their eyes and crouched over the tiny corpses of their own innocence. It was ironic: he had never even had a nightmare. His guilt crawled like a sick cockroach around the walls of his sleep; it was bearable. But he had borne it long enough; standing up, shrugging it off, he was ready—if he lived—for a bigger load.

It was perhaps the peace that made him hesitate, not concern for his own safety. He had never relaxed in the ragged coastal bush of Australia; he knew it too well. Alone, he had always awaited an interruption there, fixed in the invisible eyes of the madman, the murderer, the lizard, the snake, his haunted imagination—fear scraping around the perimeter of vision. On sunny mornings, when it did not oppress him with intimations of danger (or his own mortality) he had tried to love it, but it was a passion that expired quickly, the ersatz love one inflicted on a prostitute too old and gaunt for kindness. The living form there was an intrusion, not a component of the whole, but here . . . here, man blended naturally with river and field, peak and sky, slowly absorbing their deep truths while the bureaucrats frantically planted their lies. The peace that submerged Kwangsi surmounted dogma, the parrotting of production yields, the bloody power game in Peking. It made Millithorpe sleepy.

"I can't keep my eyes open." He was drooping apologetically in an armchair in the foyer as the group waited to embark on a river cruise, a cheap Instamatic camera dangling between his knees. "It's so restful here." His skinny old neck poking out of his collar.

"I thought you were going to rush out and evangelize," Quinn smiled down at him gently. They'd just finished breakfast and the old bugger looked ready for bed again. "Anyway, it won't be a torrid day."

"It should be beautiful," Millithorpe sighed. They were cruising down the Likiang to the town of Yang-shuo—eighty-three kilometers, Mr. Huang had advised them, many pictures for the cameras. "I have some old photographs of the Yangtse. This time I'll be able to take them in color."

Quinn had seen some of his photographs of the Yangtse in an old album left open on his bed—blurred shots of naked haulers snaked from a prewar ship's rail as he and his young chums journeyed through the gorges after their literary saints. Mrs. Millithorpe's Cross. A Niagara of assholes. The poor old closet-cleric before his time.

"There should be some nice views," he said, jiggling his old rolls of film in his pocket; it was only one view that interested him: his excuse for surrendering the day to the outing. From the boat, he could pinpoint the presence of the Retreat of Radiance and study the way to reach it, for already he had decided that he was going to have to walk there.

EVERYONE WENT ON the tour except Ruby Ho; she sat in the foyer awaiting her family—wild-eyed with alarm as Mr. Ochi tenderly made his farewells. Other tour parties were already ensconced when they boarded the ferry, more Americans and Germans perched high in front around the bridge, ready to shoot anything that did not move.

"You have set me a great task of love," Mr. Ochi confided as they went aboard. "I have discovered one imposing difficulty."

"What's that?" Quinn's eyes began raking the river and its banks, gauging landmarks, distances, preparing to estimate how long the walk might take.

Mr. Ochi cupped his fingers like a camera and took a mock photograph. "Already she has a husband."

"Oh, that. A mere technicality." Quinn hid faint alarm that Mr. Ochi appeared to be taking his pursuit of Mrs. Ho so seriously. He paused. "Perhaps you'll have to find a single lady then."

Mr. Ochi stepped back dramatically. "Never!" he declared. "If necessary, I shall ask him to release her to me."

"Mr. Ochi," Quinn said, "I'm beginning to think you're madder than I am," and he patted his arm and pushed his way up toward the prow.

It was a pleasant few hours' cruise—memorable even, for its tranquillity. They puttered gently through a landscape that the world had celebrated for centuries, a fatty white particle traveling down the vein of the Likiang into the ancient heart of Kwangsi. He had painted it badly; he had forgotten so much of what he had glimpsed in such fear and loathing—his water shadowy-blue, his black peaks too tall and glacial-sharp, his sky an ominous white glaring down at the cracked brown bean field. It wasn't like that at all; shame and distance had slashed it into the cruel angles, the pitiless heights and depths of nightmare; memory had darkened and elongated it in poor imitation of the Sung masters. His had been a statement of his guilt—he had twisted it into the wrong shapes; it shrieked all the wrong colors. The Likiang was green and gentle in the sunlight, the sky blue, the knobby limestone hills clothed in thick green vegetation. Peace, not terror.

Mist covered the tops of the higher hills; the ferry glided between grassy banks and orange cliffs streaked black with minerals as if calligraphy had run in the soft rain. They slid between clumps of feathery young bamboo trailing in the water, curved roofs of crumbling slate, crooked steps climbing from the river. Occasionally, too, there were humans: a lone man seated in a sampan, as if an artist had dropped him there for effect; a fisherman poling a slender bamboo raft with three cormorants perched up front; and once, a little girl who squatted alone on the bank and clapped gently as he waved to her. I will remember that child, he thought, when I have forgotten everything else.

He did not inspect Yang-shuo with the other passengers. He had seen all he wanted to see not long after they had chugged out from the center of Kweilin: a glimpse of the white walls of the

Retreat of Radiance behind a torn fragment of mist, a green fold of hill, and beneath it the slate roofs of a village.

THAT EVENING THE tourists were driven to an auditorium to watch a play in Chinese about a comical magistrate; with no English description given beforehand, it was quite incomprehensible. They filed back into their coach after the performance, pestering Mr. Huang to know what they had seen. He laughed nervously. "The moral of the story," he said, "is if you talk too much you go downhill."

Millithorpe loped down to the main gate with his presentation Bible when the coach dropped them back at the entrance of the hotel that night. The youths were waiting eagerly to practice their English: shadowy shapes beside the pillars of the gate, under the trees that lined the road, down at the edge of an artificial lake. Millithorpe stooped above them, trailing a little band behind him as he crossed the road to gather in more disciples. The lucky winners of the Book were in for some free instruction before they were allowed to bear it away.

Mr. Ochi was the first to enter the foyer, but Ruby Ho was too quick for him; she fled for the elevators as the coach nosed in, leaving her old relatives to gather up their bundles. He bowed to them languidly as they hobbled past him and then sprinted for the stairs to try to intercept her.

When Millithorpe returned to the room later he did not turn on the light, and he spent longer than usual on his knees by his bed.

Quinn lay coldly awake, listening to the creak of his old knee joints, the thump and thankful groans as he finally settled into bed.

He might have grown old like Millithorpe, crouching up on West Ridge trickling the past through his fingers, but *that* Quinn seemed so remote, so *aged*, that he found it difficult to believe that he was ever him, that man meekly contemplating oblivion. The only nobility for lesser beings was to oppose; he was opposing.

"HULLO, LUVVY!"
"For God's sake! She's in the bathroom!"
"That's all right. We're old friends. We had a lovely chat about you yesterday. I wanted to ask you . . . Where's Swaziland?"
"Where's what?"

"Swaziland, darling. Africa, isn't it?"

"Africa. Look, what did you tell her?"

"I met these charming chaps—very sexy. My God, I don't know how they're going to *play* today. I'm dead!"

"Thanks for letting me know."

"Oh, poor Ed. I'm sorry. I thought you'd be interested."

"Well, I'm not. The whole goddamn trip's going down the drain."

"Oh, cheer up. It's not as bad as that . . . She's very nice, your Donna, isn't she? Not like I expected at all."

"She's not my Donna. Look, she'll be out of the shower soon. I can't talk now."

"Their hands—I've never seen such hands! And guess what? Oh, it doesn't matter."

"What doesn't matter?"

You'll only sulk. Promise me you won't sulk."

"I promise."

"Guess where they're going after here?"

"If it's Taiwan, I hope they crash."

"Oh, don't say that, luvvy, or we'll all go down."

TWENTY-SEVEN

"YOU'LL HAVE TO HURRY," MILLITHORPE advised, "or you'll miss breakfast." He was pulling his braces over his shoulders to hold himself together; his exuberance of a couple of nights ago had diminished.

"I think I'll miss out on the program today. Bit off color," Quinn said. "I'll stay in bed for a while. Take it easy. Will you tell Mr. Huang?"

"I feel a bit shaky myself." Millithorpe sat on his bed and tried to wriggle his foot into a shoe, but it slid away. Wearily, he lowered himself to the marble floor and thrust it on, wheezing and grunting. "Not as young as I used to be."

"I've got some stomach thing. Don't feel like trudging around caves." Quinn watched Millithorpe struggling to fit on his second shoe. "I didn't hear you come in last night."

"You were asleep." Millithorpe staggered to his feet and plopped down again on his bed, his face crimson, the blood in his eyes. "I didn't put on the light." He seemed distracted, staring away into a corner.

"It should be interesting today," Quinn said cautiously. He didn't want Millithorpe reporting sick as well; Mr. Huang might summon a doctor. "I'll be all right with a few hours' rest. Probably something I ate."

"I must say I'm a little disappointed in the food," Millithorpe said absently. "Far better in Hong Kong." He jerked his eyes away from the corner and rubbed a hand over his face. "Interesting people here, the young ones, a challenge."

"Why don't you just relax and enjoy it? You don't have to carry the banner everywhere, do you?" The old bugger looked washed-out.

"The banner? Oh, I see." Millithorpe tried a deprecating little laugh and rubbed his face again, this time with both hands. He sighed. "I'm quite looking forward to the caves, anyway," staring vaguely again at the floor.

"Did you give them the Bible last night?"

"Oh, yes." Millithorpe straightened, summoning up what brightness he could. "Yes, indeed. We had an interesting discussion."

"I'd have thought some of them might have been against it."

Something flickered in Millithorpe's old red-flecked eyes. "Oh, one or two. You have to expect that," the words dying away. He planted his hands on his knees. "So I'll tell Mr. Huang you're not coming. Would you like me to bring you up some food?"

"Best if I don't eat. Just tell Mr. Huang I'll be all right after a bit of rest, if you don't mind."

It seemed an interminable time before the coach pulled out; Mr. Ochi, bowing with insouciant charm toward the foyer, was last up the steps. Quinn showered quickly, averting his head to avoid a pair of Millithorpe's socks that hung on the rail. Then he went downstairs.

Ruby Ho caught him as he was sauntering casually out the entrance, trying to look as if he were contemplating a convalescent stroll around the grounds.

"That Japanese man! What you say to him?"

"Mr. Ochi?" Quinn pretended surprise. "What do you mean? I didn't say anything to him."

"He follow me, all the time bowing, talking. Crazy man. I am married woman! I have two daughter."

"You are a beautiful woman. I suppose he admires you. Who knows the ways of the heart?"

"Heart!" She spat it out like a dollop of salt in honey prawns. "You crazy too."

"Well, I'm just telling you what I think," Quinn said mildly. "It's between you and him," and he strolled down to the main gate, spuriously inspecting the sky, the tops of trees, the streams of cyclists swishing by. Nobody ran after him with hypodermic needles or leg chains as he turned into the street.

The rest of the party would be away until lunch; they were to inspect Reed Flute Cave, the subject of a brochure left in their rooms—the vast limestone vaults, the pillars and stalactites and stalagmites drenched in lurid colored lighting, the delicate formations likened to sensible proletarian goals: here a power station, there a pumpkin, a field of workers . . .

Remembering the caves without colored lights, he began walking along a wide road beside the river.

A STRING OF small children followed him for a short distance, calling out merrily; they fled in delight whenever he turned on them playfully and pretended to chase them. He went on alone, inexorably ignoring the adults who watched him pass. Gradually the grid of streets petered out, but he strode out firmly along a track by the river to show that he was there with purpose and authority, the protective blessing of the state upon his head. All around him now, on both sides of the river, rose the rich green hills that had withered so falsely in his memory, and he felt perfectly at ease, at peace with the earth, mature enough now to bring shared understandings to strangers. Besides, the penalty for attacking a foreign guest in China no doubt was a cautionary bullet between the eyes.

He wasn't quite sure why he felt so happy: perhaps action itself was enough, to be *projecting* when he spent so much of his life *receiving*. And the grand unreality of what he had begun to do still partly shielded him from the risks that lay ahead when he blew the gaffe on Keh; he felt like an extension of himself, walking along there by the river, marching toward the one moment of courage that awaited every cautious man, the marsh-light that glimmered in front, always a little way off.

Near the bank, a man was fishing with a hand line through a gap in a logjam of thick bamboo rods that had been floated down stream; birds flicked out of fissures in the rock-faces on the opposite side and skimmed low over the water. Socialism had failed, but it was One World anyway; he could have been roaming along a creek bank near Wongbok. He followed a narrow track winding away from the river toward a screen of trees; he was hot now and slung his coat over his shoulder. Small white butterflies jerked past him clumsily, and roosters crowed faintly somewhere ahead. The village.

He emerged beside a rich green checkerboard of rice fields laid at the feet of the furry hills—Cookie Monsters awaiting a game, an image of Sesame Street supplanting Shiozawa. Mopping his face, he trudged along the edge of the rice fields, skirted a small limestone pinnacle, and there it still was, half-hidden from the river: the monastery perched behind white walls on a crag above the village with misty green peaks crowding behind it as far as he could see. The Retreat of Radiance, a symbol of horror, drowsing comfortably on a sultry spring morning. As ominous as a classification of the National Trust.

Quinn stood for a while beneath the shadow of a tree, watching it; once or twice he thought he heard music in the air. It was smaller than he had imagined—he had been prepared for that—and the upraised black characters on its walls, whatever they had been, had been painted over. Two black loudspeakers now sprouted on top of the walls; the blue of the roof had faded to the watercolor wash of Millithorpe's eyes, and one dragon on a corner lashed savagely without a head: a victim, perhaps, of the Red Guards. Otherwise it looked the same.

It was the village that seemed to have changed most. Solid white buildings with black slate roofs stood where the half-ruined hovels had staggered along the narrow alleys, and the mangy curs that had infested the site had disappeared with other useless mouths; there were slim pickings here yet for the pet food manufacturers. Cement paths curved around the houses, and on three sides stretched the neat bamboo trellis-work of the bean fields.

HE WALKED QUIETLY down a track between the rows of beans,

heading toward the farthest field beneath the monastery. Nearby, two women knelt, singing, in a row. Mr. Huang could not have arranged it any better himself—"Happy Members of a Production Brigade Building the New China." They did not even look up; neither did four toddlers playing seesaw outside the village on a board placed over a log. He passed the houses, still surprised that no dogs pelted out to attack him. A swallow swooped by, trailing a long piece of straw.

In the bean field below the crag, four more women crouched busily at work; one of them spotted Quinn and joked to her companion—he heard a quick ripple of words, a laugh. He passed the edge of the field gravely, watching for a tooth, a fragment of jaw, in the rich orange clay. The narrow track twisting up to the crag was exactly where he had remembered it—overgrown, as it had been then, damp and slippery, broken limestone to cling to sticking out of the clay like bone. He climbed where Keh's troops had slid and tumbled down to do their murders, grasping tufts of grass, hauling himself up by gripping the shards of limestone. Thunder rumbled like guns, heralding a sudden rainstorm, but the music had begun again, drifting down from the monastery. He stood listening in the mouth of a mossy cave halfway up, catching drips of water in his foolish hat before he clapped it on again.

On top, high above the plain, he stood against the wall looking down at the geometric village, the bamboo bean poles stacked neatly against walls, the women chatting where the skeletons had sung, choking on clods. Then he trudged around to the entrance of the monastery, slipping in the grass.

He had expected it to be almost empty—one or two old peasants, perhaps, burning joss sticks, or a few suspicious militiamen or commune leaders carefully inflating production yields in sparse offices hung with the Marxist gods. A cheerful ingenuous wave and he'd be off. But now a new bitumen road curved up through the peaks from the plain, and along it streamed a bright river of children with painted faces—red lips, rouged cheeks, the red scarves of the Young Pioneers at their throats, squads of them flowing up from the plain into the monastery. They were attending a Children's Day concert.

He went to the main door of the monastery and looked inside.

It was already crowded noisily with mothers and small boys and girls who were watching six painted tiny tots singing on a stage where the Buddhist god had stood on his jewelled elephant; they had gone, and so had the lesser gods who had lined the walls. Little girls in white blouses and flowered skirts pressed around him giggling—as his own daughter had giggled at concerts long ago, electric with excitement, awaiting her turn, darting from doorway to backstage, backstage to doorway, anxious to be seen. He had been to this concert many times in another country, another dimension—God save the Queen or Communism, what did it matter now? All that mattered were the black pits of the singing mouths, the light dying in their eyes; the final retreat of radiance.

MR. HUANG WAS very cross when he got back to the hotel—soaked in a brief downpour during a long walk down the road to the city. He darted toward Quinn as soon as he squelched into the foyer.

"Where you go?" he hissed. "You get lost! Cause trouble!"

"I wasn't lost. I didn't feel well. I went for a walk."

"You should have come to Reed Flute Cave! Everyone stay together!"

"Mr. Huang, foreigners are paying money for this. You won't be able to keep them all together all the time. They won't take it."

"You are sick—you pretend to be sick. Then you go walking."

Quinn paused. "Well, Mr. Huang, that's what I want to talk to you about. I'll tell you why I went walking."

Mr. Huang hovered before him in his agitation; he seemed torn between the need to upbraid him and a desire to flee before he heard bad news. "Always troublemakers," he complained.

"Come over here," Quinn said. He drew Mr. Huang aside and sat gingerly on the edge of an armchair, plucking his damp trousers from his thighs. "I want to tell you something. You'll be able to play a little part in history when I tell you."

"I'm busy man!" Mr. Huang protested. "You cause trouble. I send money to my wife in Shanghai. What if no money?"

"Mr. Huang, you'll be a hero of the Revolution when I'm finished. Now I'll tell you something. I went to a place I remember from the Civil War."

"Old monastery!" Mr. Huang snapped, and stopped abruptly.

Some minor functionary must have dogged him through the fields.

"So you knew all the time. Well, there was a massacre there during the Civil War."

"Civil War, Civil War—long time ago!" Mr. Huang exploded. "Many people die in the war."

"The Nationalists buried them. Some of them were alive. They came from the village under the monastery."

"How you know this? Massacre—many massacres!"

"I was there. I saw it. Not fighting. Just . . . observing. I know the man who ordered it. His name, were he is. He's on Taiwan."

"You were a soldier in the war?"

"No, just a civilian. But I was there. I want to see justice done. I want it all brought out into the open."

"Trouble for everybody," Mr. Huang moaned. "Better forget."

"I'm not forgetting," Quinn said firmly. "If you won't report what I say I'll get someone else to do it." He stood up.

"OK, OK." Mr. Huang laid a hand on his arm. "I see what I can do."

"I want to talk to some of the government leaders here—the chiefs of the Party Branch or whatever. I want to put it all in front of them. The names, the date, everything."

"I see what I can do." Miserably, he tried a last throw. "Maybe not good for you, all this. Bad for me. I lose my position."

Quinn shook one sodden shoe. "They'll raise a statue to you. Huang the Great. But I've only got a day or two. You'll have to do something pretty quickly."

"I do something," Mr. Huang replied in a small voice.

"OK," Quinn said, and he sighed deeply. The die was cast. "I s'pose I'm late for lunch . . ."

He turned on his way to the elevators. "Mr. Huang," he said, "I'm going to stay in my room this afternoon to dry off. See if you can arrange a meeting tonight?"

TWENTY-EIGHT

MR. HUANG TAPPED AT HIS door before dinner. He had swapped his white shirt and trousers for a blue Mao suit. There was a small lumpy patch in lighter blue on one knee; it looked as if he had sewn it on for effect.

"I arrange a meeting," he said. "Important officials. We must go very quickly."

"I'm ready." Quinn's suit had been dried and pressed; his shoes, although still damp, had been warmed. "I've scribbled a few notes to refresh my memory." Gathering them up, he found that he was tingling with nervousness. "Like sitting for any exam," he joked.

Mr. Huang watched coldly as Quinn shut the door and they walked in silence along the corridor. To Quinn's surprise, a room boy was holding an empty elevator for them; they were getting the royal treatment.

"I would be most grateful . . ." Mr. Huang began when the doors closed on them. "I give instructions that the foreign visitors must remain together . . ."

"Don't worry," Quinn assured him breezily. "I'll tell them it was my fault. I'll tell them you are a very excellent guide."

He did not feel as breezy as he sounded. He had falsified his application for entry by declaring that he had never visited China before; that knowledge might have delayed his arrival while they investigated, and it might delay his departure now that they knew. And he had been present during a crime against the people. He'd have to play the innocent, box clever—but then he'd been doing that all his life.

"When we go in," Mr. Huang continued, "I am the interpreter, that's all. I know nothing! Just interpreter."

"Sure." They crossed the lobby. "Who are we seeing?"

"They send a car," Mr. Huang replied. He made it sound like a treat.

A highly polished black de Soto waited at the entrance, the driver behind the wheel. Two Americans were circling it slowly with cameras, saying "Whooee" softly and shaking their heads in wonder as they focused on the flying Indian.

Mr. Huang and Quinn climbed into the back; Quinn felt faintly foolish, like a teenager on a merry-go-round. "Nineteen forty-nine, I'd guess," one of the Americans said; Quinn craned forward and saw 123,766 miles on the clock. He leaned back on floral seat covers; it was in such spotless condition that they probably carried it across intersections. Sedately they drove out the main gate.

Twenty seconds later the car stopped, not at a government department or Party headquarters, but at the cinema on the next corner. Bewildered, he climbed out behind Mr. Huang, and they mounted the steps into the building and went upstairs to a door beside the projection room. Mr. Huang knocked.

Inside, three men sat smoking cigarettes at a desk at the side of a small office, with two chairs drawn up before it in the middle of the room. The center man was grossly fat, with a cropped gray head and flesh bulging over his blue collar; as warlord or landlord, he looked perfect casting for a movie career in propaganda productions. The other two were thin, middle-aged and deferential; they sat a little behind him, leaning forward to ash their cigarettes with stained fingers. None of them looked at him.

The fat man flipped open a folder; if he did the Long March, thought Quinn, he probably finished it last week. He tried to concentrate.

The four Chinese spoke together for nearly five minutes; he could not pick up any of it. The two thin Chinese sucked in smoke until their cheeks were hollow, allowing it to trail out their nostrils; their leader dropped ash on the folder and pushed it away with a beefy hand onto the knees of the man on his right. Quinn looked down at his notes, awaiting his cue.

Mr. Huang startled him. "Why you not say you come to China before?"

"Ah well," Quinn said smoothly, shifting on his chair. "I haven't been to the *real* China before. The People's Republic. The true history of China began in 1949." When this branch liberated its car.

Mr. Huang translated. When the fat man lifted a sweaty hand to puff his cigarette one of the papers in the folder stuck to it. He plucked it off and dropped it back on the desk.

There was more talk while Quinn gazed around the room. A window behind him looked down on the auditorium; there were no pictures on the walls, but there was a spittoon against a filing cabinet that he began to ignore. A makeshift meeting place, this: perhaps Mr. Huang was fobbing him off with a few relatives.

"Why you come to Kweilin at this time?"

"Now, you mean, or in 1948?"

"Why you come to Kweilin in 1948?"

"I wanted to see the Revolution. Watch the triumph of socialism. I had heard of the . . . excesses of the Kuomintang, and I wanted to see them for myself. Get some firsthand evidence." He gazed earnestly at the three men as he spoke, pumping fake sincerity through the blue cloud which enveloped them.

"What is your occupation?"

"I'm retired. I grow flowers. I used to work on a newspaper." He leaned forward to dismiss further inquiries. "Look, do you want me to give my description of what happened that day? The man who did it is free. He should have been punished."

"Give your description," Mr. Huang said.

Quinn launched into it, glossing over only the reason for his own presence. The eyes of the thin men suddenly lit up. I'm getting through to them, he thought, but it's the big fellow I have to convince. He was a secular archbishop, he decided, not a warlord, the repository of truth in a church turned inside-out.

Quinn plunged deeply into a long staccato discourse, halting each sentence for translation; he consulted his notes carefully, determined to leave nothing out. But three quarters of the way through, the fat official began stirring restlessly and grumbling quietly to his henchmen, and he began to lose the thread of what he was saying.

"Keh," he said, "is now a very important man in Taiwan," but before Mr. Huang had finished translating this the No. 1 man cut him off.

"He has a big amusement park," Quinn continued lamely. "A very rich man." The thin men continued to gaze brightly in his direction, but he began to feel that they were concentrating on a point beyond him, absorbed in more weighty matters.

"This is not new information," Mr. Huang told him. "All the details were reported to the Party."

"Then something should be done. He should be declared a war criminal. He's junketing around the globe." Quinn wondered immediately how Mr. Huang would translate that. He needn't have bothered: Mr. Huang didn't. Quinn watched the beefy hand reflectively flopping at the ash on the desk in front of him.

"Why should he get away with it?" he protested, but he became uncomfortably aware that he was talking to himself. "Tell them I'm prepared to make an official report under my own name."

"Mr. Huang translated, and the two thin men's eyes lit up again. They respect me for that, he thought. "I'll carry the can," pressed Quinn, "but I'd like the Party to act on it officially. It would give it some weight, internationally."

He leaned back, and it was at that point that one of the thin men began to laugh. The fat man spoke curtly to him without lifting his eyes, and the thin man got up and began pulling down a blind on the window. When Quinn turned he caught the bottom half of the baggy pants, the cane, the Chaplin walk: The Kid was doing his stuff for the Party.

Mr. Huang cleared his throat. "They say this matter is well-known. It is not, umm, appropriate at this time to raise the matter with the province of Taiwan. And now we must finish. Other business."

268

Quinn stood up slowly and walked out into the corridor without speaking. He was standing at the top of the steps, waiting angrily for Mr. Huang, when he saw the fat official push open the door of the projection room and grunt an order.

He could guess what the other business was. He was telling the operator to start the movie again.

TWENTY-NINE

AFTER DINNER, MR. OCHI SAT in the foyer pretending to read a magazine while his eyes roamed over to his beloved.

"She will not speak with me." Mr. Ochi whispered. "This is torture. I cannot make my endearments while we are running along."

"She's shy," Quinn assured him. "Romantic. I know the type. On the outside they are a little tough, like the *lichi*, but inside . . ."

"I understand. She has not met someone such as I. The Big Bad Wolf."

"Exactly. Write to her. Push it under her door. Something she can mull over. Put it under her pillow!"

"I believe," Mr. Ochi said, "that you have hit upon it."

"I'm sure I have," Quinn said.

He still felt angry and edgy: rock-hard Ruby was as good a passing target as any. He left Mr. Ochi and went up to his room; bicycle bells tinkled faintly down in the dimly lit streets, and the lamps of the cormorant fishermen flared out on the river. They were not so different, Millithorpe and he, neither of them relevant to the present.

He could begin to feel a love for China now where once he had hated it because he had hated himself—yearning for an impossible transformation like the old madman in the Empire: "Look at me! Arrayed in white robes!" But the thin atmosphere of loss was his natural climate; the gray coastal rocks and eucalypts reflected his essence more truly than the sucking mouths of the rice paddies, this rich green river. He was an anachronism wherever he was; he had spent his life fiddling with the dials of the wrong decade while Today jostled past his door. An enemy of his own land, a stranger in China; the perennial outsider. Standing at the window, jerkily smoking a cigarette, he fretted to be gone.

Millithorpe almost fell in the door. He stood there swaying, exalted, as if he were drunk: his eyes shining, his hair awry, two livid red spots stamped on his sallow cheeks. He was breathing heavily.

"What have you been up to?" Quinn watched him clumsily shut the door, leaning on it with both hands. His shirt was ripped, his collar gone.

Millithorpe made his way to his bed and sat down on it heavily, patting his chest while he regained his breath. "The most wonderful . . ." he gasped. "Beyond my wildest . . ." Pat-pat-pat, struggling to smile.

Quinn went into the bathroom and got him a glass of water. He gulped it, impressing a faint red film on the rim. When at last he smiled, Quinn saw a thread of blood around one large yellow tooth.

"What happened?" he asked. "Who knocked you around?"

"That's the least of it," Millithorpe managed at last. "There is such a thirst . . . I've never preached before to such . . ."

"You don't mean you delivered a sermon down there?"

"Not a sermon, of course. More a little talk." His head reared back as he expelled a long shuddering sigh.

"Wait till you get your breath," Quinn said. He took the glass into the bathroom and refilled it, and then brushed his teeth to allow Millithorpe more time to recover. When he came out he handed the glass to Millithorpe silently. He took it in trembling hands.

"I shall tell you tomorrow," he said, and the glass actually clattered against his teeth. "I have so much to absorb . . ."

"OK." Quinn went to the window again; no shadows now drifted under the trees or around the entrance. "You look like you need a decent sleep . . ."

Millithorpe put the glass on the floor by his bed and eventually heaved himself up and shambled into the bathroom, dragging his braces down from his shoulders. "Socks still wet," Quinn heard him mumble, and then surprisingly, there was the quavering snatch of a hymn before the toilet flushed. He went out, quietly closing the door.

Quinn walked up the dark street in front of the hotel, tagged by a blob of white shirt in the gloom. He wandered into the nearest store; two small girls were buying thin little exercise books, their faces flushed with delight as if they were now the proud owners of luxuries beyond their wildest dreams. "I have a daughter like you," he wanted to say, "and I had two sons." But he merely turned and left.

Down by the lake weak fire rockets were fizzing up into the darkness, and Millithorpe had switched off their bedroom light.

THE GROUP FLEW back to Canton the next day on the return trip to Hong Kong; Mr. Huang avoided his eyes at the airport, and he avoided Ruby Ho's. Mr. Ochi was ecstatic; he dived into a seat beside Ruby, who appeared to withdraw into a catatonic trance. Mr. Ochi assured her that he was a patient man, and leaning over the aisle, he asked Quinn to recommend a hotel in Melbourne. Henceforth, he said, he intended to take all his holidays there.

Everybody frowned and made little murmuring noises that morning when they learned that Millithorpe had died in his sleep, but by the time they got to Kweilin airport he was pretty well forgotten. He had gone over, passed on, been taken up with his secrets, and it was refreshing for Quinn to have a room to himself in Canton, remembering with more distaste than pity the old camel-corpse he had woken to find beside him.

Awaiting him at Kai Tak airport, where he changed planes for Taiwan, was a scribbled note from Rushton on police notepaper: Lancelot Ming had disappeared.

Quinn went cold. His office was just as he had left it, Rushton reported; everything apparently in its place. It looked like homicide without a body; that, anyway, was how the Wanchai detectives had treated it at first.

"But I decided to have a look myself," he added, "and I found the photographic gallery of horrors had gone from his filing cabinet. That's enough for me—he wouldn't move without his dirty pictures.

"He'll bob up again one of these days in Bangkok or Singapore or Honolulu and set up his old stand. The little bastard's indestructible. Trust you're O'Keh."

THIRTY

IT WAS RAINING IN TAIPEI—a hard slanting rain that cleared the wide black streets around the railway station like gunfire. It soaked factories and tenements as the express uncurled through a wasteland of suburbs; soaked Auto Parts and Coca-Cola and the Hollywood Photo and Fashion Center, three egrets in a swamp by a foundry, a rocking horse on a barred veranda; a relentless rain that scoured the gritty corners of the city in a foretaste of the typhoons to come. The express flattened out on the run south to Tai-chung, a yellow diesel dragging its long blue body from the hole of the city, sliding past a Seiko sign on a roof, a giant National TV placard in a rice field, the armchair graves of ancestors looking down from the sodden hills. Keh Country.

"Did you say you went to Changsha?" It was a myopic American woman whom he had met at Kai Tak while changing planes for Taiwan; she had seen him in Kweilin, she had told him then. Now she stood in the aisle beside him: freckled, middle-aged, her skin hanging in folds.

275

"No, I didn't go there," he told her for the third time. She never listened to his answers; she was forever rummaging in her bag, as she rummaged now, holding up documents close to her face: a passport, a boarding card, a tour itinerary.

"There was a 2,100-year-old woman floating in formaldehyde," she informed him again, squinting at her train ticket. "All her organs you could see—the heart, the liver."

Quinn stirred restlessly; he had not wanted to know the first time. "You mean she was transparent?" he asked, but he was thinking of another Changsha, another age: Punch popping up from an armored car.

"No, in bulk. Floating beside her. I was fascinated."

"I suppose I'm trying to forget bodies," he said. "Well, I think I'll take a bit of a walk . . ."

He stood up, and she fumbled on down the aisle with her bag; it was large enough to hold several dozen hearts and livers. He walked through to the dining car and ordered a beer; the lush island was a white blur, a rushing brown stream, a pile of river stones beyond the rice-pattern of rain drops on the wide picture windows. He watched the dragon-spines of trees on shaven hills; there were new concrete houses with flat roofs arranged like cassette boxes beside the rails.

The middle class, the feeding class, was spreading its fat; no contorted faces to admire here as the grandmothers hauled loads; the whispering of worthy bicycles on the mainland was supplanted by the splutter of the Suzuki. It was sad in a counterfeit way: in absorbing Taiwan, China would release a little more of the West's new opium into its stringy old veins. And so he bathed in regret as shallow as the schmaltzy American film music that had played everywhere since his arrival in Taiwan—from loudspeakers, from TV sets, from the dining car intercom itself. Wailing "The Tennessee Waltz," the express fled past a factory licensed by the Pittsburgh Plate Glass Co. while swifts flickered for insects over the cassette boxes and freight yards and funeral urns of the Free China.

Quinn watched them vacantly, truly lamenting only his own broken life. But he was still alive! A carnal itch he had almost forgotten lay at the bottom of his pool of hopeless tenderness while the express switched to "Yesterday." He grinned to himself as a large Northern Chinese at the next table slurped up his soup and contemplated the misty landscape as if it were the next course. Still alive!

He spent most of the trip in the dining car, wondering why he felt so calm; his balance was as fragile as the slender golden vases filled with red and yellow roses that trembled faintly on the white cloths. A young attendant bounded through the train, swiftly pouring tea into glasses from a large silver pot. He envied his athletic grace; lacking speed and strength, he could rely now only on middle-aged authority, on guile. Middle age, like the black suit, the black hat, formed his armor, and although he was riding toward the possibility of his own destruction, his absurd optimism appeared to be growing. Not the old bonehead British pluck, but the devilish merriment of the clown with the craters of Pozières in his eyes, a foot wavering over the trapeze wire, his mouth shaped for triumph or despair.

He left the express at Tai-chung railway station. There were six large sepia photographs in a display case, illustrating to passengers the correct methods to catch trains. The top three pictured men and women stepping decorously aboard; the bottom three featured mutilated bodies scattered on the tracks. An old man stood beside them selling pretty paper fans.

THE BUS TO Green Silk Lake was jammed with students on a weekend visit. The conductress stood in the aisle, chirruping continually on a whistle to inform the driver that the way was clear as it backed out of its bay. Her hair was cut and waved, her blouse and skirt the gray of decay; she teetered on stiletto heels. Later she perched on a seat beside the driver, folding newspapers into fans for the passengers; another Ruby Ho struggling up through an alien chrysalis. The bus trundled through the wet black streets toward the countryside, and the rain fell straight on the Dermatomycosis and VD Control Center, on banana plants and factories and car bodies and pink blossoms piled on tiles, on the gleaming Japanese motorcycles and scooters as their riders cut suicidal swathes through the crowded streets. He imagined Mr. Ochi bobbing up with a bouquet in Melbourne.

The journey took two hours; Keh had chosen the lush center stem of the leaf-shaped island for his kingdom. A narrow bitumen road ran beside swift streams and through tunnels cut in the hills, a misty green landscape shored up with the peanut brittle of round river stones and stitched everywhere with tufts of bamboo. They climbed past fields of banana and sugar cane and young palms as slender as the legs of ostriches; damp ferns now glistened on rocky embankments, and the dark shapes of pagodas and electricity towers arose from the sharp hills, indistinguishable in the hissing walls of rain. Quinn dozed now and again in the humidity, jerking awake with visions of sharp blades in his mind and fingers curling around triggers; the anarchy of the unexpected in a heartland as ordered as a child's drawing of Oz. Everything was stacked neatly in piles for all to see: stones and logs, produce and public loyalties. It had all been cemented in the forties with the Taiwanese blood that Chiang and Keh and the other mainlanders had spilled to crush silly moves for independence. And then the bus began to roar slowly up from the foothills into the high forests where the Magic General ruled, climbing higher and higher until it rattled over a last ridge and descended into a small valley in the center of a range of mountains.

It stopped amid a murky slew of shops and small hotels that huddled in the dusk around the giant gates of Keh's White Horse Gardens amusement park. Outside the gates, on a circular island in the road, reared a mighty white marble horse, and on the white marble horse, triumphant in the stirrups, stood the white marble general, brandishing a golden sword as the dark ranks of the conifers fled away from him up the slopes. There was a proud patriotic curl to his lips: General Keh Shih-kai, Savior of the Free World, conqueror of the cowed hordes of Communism, with a flat belly and false biceps bulging under his marble tunic.

THIRTY-ONE

HONEYMOON COUPLES HAD FILLED UP the small hotels opposite the monument. As Quinn watched them wandering through the narrow cobbled streets, buying trinkets and films, breathing the mountain air gratefully before submerging forever with their souvenirs of silence back in crowded rooms in the cities, he wondered where he was going to sleep that night while he gathered himself together for the morning. Keh owned the sprawling White Horse hotel complex within the park grounds where he had arranged to meet Larsen, but he was not ready to enter it yet; he postponed the moment just as he had switched on the lights on West Ridge to stave off the possibility of confrontation. He needed one more night to prowl the perimeters of an unformed plan. Clutching his suitcase, he drifted past the lovers, feeling the pounding of his heart; summoning up a final spurt of jauntiness to quell his fear. "If I grin," he thought, "if I grin in the darkness to try to screw up my courage—it will be like the opening of a grave." A blind girl passed him, lightly clicking a long white stick from side to side, and night birds began singing harshly in the forest.

A restaurant proprietor who spoke English escorted him to a small police station that let rooms at the same price as the hotels, he said, and Quinn followed him with only momentary hesitation, certain that the local police must be under Keh's thumb, but appreciating the irony of sheltering so uncertainly within the bosom of the law. A policeman took down a key attached to a large sliver of bamboo and motioned Quinn to follow him upstairs, laughing with embarrassment when Quinn addressed him in English. He unlocked a room and made tentative little brushing motions at the cover of a filthy bed, as if he had taken painstaking care to prepare it so perfectly, and then, his pretense completed, he clomped downstairs. From somewhere there was the sound of a scuffle, a blow, a shouting voice suddenly stilled.

Quinn put down his suitcase and gingerly lifted the bed cover: scores of lice were moving on the pillow and sheets. He dropped the cover and looked out the window; a mountain stream was rushing through stands of bamboo behind the building—behind the dirty sink and broken cistern in an adjoining bathroom. He'd have to sit up in a chair all night if he was going to stay here, and the night had only begun; at what cold hour of the morning, he wondered, might the lice decide to march across the room to join him? He left his suitcase on the floor and walked out of the building with a cheery wave; sheltering with the law was even more uncertain than he had imagined.

The rain had stopped; red and violet light splashed from a doorway up the street, and a woman inside was singing—not with the high thin squeal of an alien age he had never known, but rich and gutsy and Western, snarling it more than singing. "That's Why The Lady Is a Tramp"—bouncing it off walls and belting it out the doorway against the big marble horse so that couples paused timidly and began to edge closer around this great gaudy river of sound that poured out into the silence beneath the pines.

"IT'S BEAUTIFUL HERE." Donna laid a painted paper fan on the coffee table and watched Lady Earnshaw sweeping toward them across the parquet floor. "The birds and butterflies. The large mammals."

280

"For Christ's sake, shut up!" Larsen hissed. He writhed to his feet with a pale smile as Lady Earnshaw sailed up like a galleon, her hibiscus caftan billowing. She dropped a bulky evening bag on the table like an anchor. "Hi," he managed weakly.

"Well," she declared brightly, "when does the action start? This place is beginning to give me the creeps."

"You don't like it?" Donna turned up eyes of treacherous blue simplicity. "We think it's such a pretty place. Don't we, Ed?"

"Why don't you sit down?" Ignoring Donna, Larsen motioned fretfully to a chair and Lady Earnshaw dropped into it with a puff of perfume. He looked away quickly as her leg touched his with the stab of an injection.

"It's so peaceful," Donna sighed. "Away from it all. Wonderful to get a good night's sleep. Didn't I say that last night, Ed? It's wonderful to get a good night's sleep."

Larsen darted a savage look at her and flicked a hand lightly over his polished shoes, as if her words were dropping dust. "The food's good," he said, imploring Bertha's approval. "The rooms are OK."

"I mean, the people," Lady Earnshaw complained gazing around the room. "Like little mice. They need someone to jolly them up." She turned on Larsen wickedly. "I might do a fan dance."

Larsen blushed bright red, twitched up his jeans, and then tugged down the sleeves of his casual cream jacket.

"I'm sure he'd love that," Donna interposed sweetly. "Wouldn't you, Ed? Wouldn't you love Lady Earnshaw to do a fan dance?" She had fallen into the habit of addressing him as if he were a child.

Lady Earnshaw trilled her musical little laugh. "He's a naughty boy. You'd think butter wouldn't melt in his mouth. You should hear some of the things he's said to me." And then she paused, artfully returning to Donna her own look of blank innocence. "All in fun, of course."

"Of course," Donna replied. "That's understood," and Larsen sprang to his feet in agitated anger and then sat down again. They were enjoying it.

"You two . . ." he said and trailed off, unable to muster a defense.

"It's just that he keeps so much stitched up inside him, as we were saying the other evening," Donna pursued. She laid a hand on Larsen's head, and he shrugged away irritably; she pulled a face in mock dismay.

"That's not all he keeps stitched up," Lady Earnshaw gushed with another tinkling laugh, and Donna's comic malice wavered; the Englishwoman's crudity was even more deplorable than his treachery. She lit a cigarette defiantly—he hated her to smoke— and blew the blue cloud at them both.

"A problem you obviously don't share," she said at last, smiling brilliantly through her anger at Lady Earnshaw, and she was rewarded by a sly look from the jolly music hall face: a prurient child peeping out. "Nasty mosquito bite you have there—they seem to have jaws like crocodiles."

Lady Earnshaw's hand moved toward her neck and then dropped plumply into her lap. "Oh, that wasn't a mossie, my dear—that was a Swazi," she said coolly. "S-e-x. It happens in all the best circles. No point in keeping it bottled up, is there?" She dropped a contemptuous glance on Donna before turning away.

It was Donna's turn to flush. "Barnyard morals" floated into her head: a phrase her aunt had declaimed in Philadelpia when- ever the English were mentioned. She wanted to make a cutting riposte—to say something about the size of the bottle or the quality of the product—but she couldn't get it out. "Apparently not," she said lamely.

"Rain's stopped," Larsen put in miserably, and he lowered his balding crew cut.

"Well, if you're going to deliver weather forecasts all night I'm off," Lady Earnshaw said, and she grabbed her bag and wriggled upright. "See if there's anyone alive."

Donna rallied. "Perhaps you'd like my fan?" But Lady Earn- shaw merely smiled and slung her bag over her shoulder. "Not big enough for me, luv, Ta ra." She sailed off toward the lobby.

Donna watched her go; Larsen stared the other way doggedly. "That must be the most amoral woman," she said levelly, "that I have ever met. Are you sure you don't want to go with her?"

"I told you—I'm waiting for Keh," Larsen snapped. "I'm meet- ing him here."

"Yes, this General Keh. Look, I don't know what's going on—I don't think I want to know. But I'm beginning to feel very angry.

You've used me. You're smearing me with your grubby little secrets."

She stubbed out her barely smoked cigarette. "You drag me halfway around the world with some . . . whore you say you don't know to whisper in corners with some little bandit in Hong Kong . . ."

"Ming's not a bandit. He's a detective."

"And now we're skulking around here waiting for some Chinaman who builds statues of himself."

"He was a war hero," Larsen mumbled. "If it weren't for people like that . . . Anyway, if you're bored why don't you go to bed?"

"And leave you chasing Big Bertha around the potted plants? All right, why not?"

"I've got business to discuss with Keh."

They sat for a few seconds in a bristling silence. Larsen jiggled with an ashtray and lined it square with the corner of the coffee table. "That crazy Quinn, spreading lies . . ."

"What lies, precisely? Or shouldn't I ask that either?"

Larsen brushed his jacket. "In the Civil War—I knew him in the Civil War. He says that Keh is responsible for . . . some things. In the heat of battle. Crazy. A crazy man."

"So why should you worry? What's it got to do with you? Unless you were responsible for 'some things' yourself."

"You'd like that, wouldn't you? You'd love to see me ruined by some nut spreading a lot of garbage."

"On the contrary. You'd be amazed how detached I am. What I'd really love is a cup of cocoa and the *New Yorker*."

Another silence; Donna stood up. "There isn't much future for us, is there?" she said quietly. "I'm going to bed."

There was nothing to say—and Larsen forgot her instantly, anyway. Out in the lobby dark forms were darting to and fro against the floodlit horse and rider in the square. General Keh had arrived.

THIRTY-TWO

THE NIGHTCLUB WAS NEARLY EMPTY. Young Japanese and Chinese couples sat in a candle-lit crescent around a small dance floor, and a few waiters stood behind them in the shadows stonily watching the European entertainer. Now she was shouting "Heartbreak Hotel," stamping and flicking a microphone cord like a tail, a dark, once-beautiful young woman who was violently shaking an osprey feather headdress, her breasts, her buttocks, while a thin roll of belly-flesh quivered unbidden beneath a tight black satin gown slit to the thigh. Her long hair was thick and tangled, her lipstick smudged—a ruined copy of Ava Gardner; her raw voice blasted desperately over wrong notes while she grimaced with ersatz anguish to hide them. Behind her, a doleful Filipino trio echoed the boredom of the waiters, moving hands, unmoving faces.

Quinn sat at a table beside a pillar; it was the most inappropriate performance he had ever seen. "Thank you," she gasped bitterly, "Thank you," for there was no applause, and prowling up and down a tiny stage, lashing the cord, she descended into her patter: borrowed material that should have been buried; echoes of third-rate clubs and pubs and restaurant revues that she had plundered in her search for imperfection.

"I used to be Snow White, but I drifted!" she confided, her ice-blue eyes sweeping scornfully over the closed faces, and she dropped her head and laughed ruefully to herself for a moment before her eyes rose again, probing the gloom like searchlights.

"This is where I fall flat on my face like Bette Midler! She only thinks she's got tits!" Throwing it at them defiantly, going down fighting, and Quinn lifted his hands and clapped loudly to punctuate her misery.

The eyes swung toward him. "Thank you, sir!" Any advance on one?" she cried, stalking up and down the stage, looming over the waxen heads. "No? No takers? Well, we'll take a little break." She fitted the microphone back on its stand, turning to hiss at the trio. They lifted their hands pallidly in a windup, a final squeal and rattle as she plunged behind a red velvet curtain and someone switched on a disco tape.

Quinn drank Suntory whisky; two or three Japanese couples began dancing, and the waiters commenced sauntering around the tables, released from the oppressive spell that had imprisoned them. He wriggled deep into his chair, preparing for a long stay before he was forced to return to the other chair by his bed; the liquor should anesthetize him against the chill of early morning and the decision he had to make. Sitting there, he felt quite detached; he seemed to view the warm sea of life now from a cold island—a nub of granite in the syrup in which he had bathed for so long. All his life had been an intention.

A hand fell on his shoulder; instantly he thought of Doyle, of Hong Kong a lifetime before, and looked up at the singer's breasts, a face that had coarsened before its time.

"Thanks for the applause," she said. "You're the only live one here."

"You were great," Quinn lied. He rose to drag out the chair opposite, but she had done it before him, thudding down and plunking her feet on an empty chair opposite, leaning against the pillar. Her gown slipped from her golden legs, and she flicked her fingers imperiously at a waiter. "Cigarettes," she ordered. "You want to buy me a drink?"

"Whatever you're having," Quinn said. She was having a double whisky; she ordered the waiter to bring the bottle, and he smiled at her, knowing what Doyle might have said if he were there: "You bite like a bloody shark."

"It's only money," he added.

She drummed long fingers on the table, awaiting the drink. "Dump," she said. "I wish I could get out of here. Get my own place. What're you smoking.?"

He looked at the packet in front of him. "Silver Starlet," and pushed them toward her. "Better than nothing."

She took one without a word and leaned sideways over a candle. "And beer," she said as the waiter set down the whisky. "Make sure it's cold."

"Australian?" Quinn asked, and she nodded briefly.

"Long way from home. Are you singing again?"

"To hell with them." She tossed down a whisky and then swallowed a beer in one smooth, continual process: the liquid disappeared swiftly, as in a TV commercial. "Band's lousy. No acoustics." She poured another whisky.

"So now you can relax." The lice-bed floated into his head. "You live around here?"

"Upstairs." She wiggled a shoe absently on her toes and then raised her foot gently into the buttocks of a waiter bending over the next table; he straightened quickly, but did not look around. "Rat hole. Get my own place soon."

"You're a terrific performer."

"I'm shit house. Only in it for the money. Boyfriend's in jail."

"You mean you've got to bail him out?"

"Are you kidding? For his meals. Can't eat the slop they give them. He's lost forty pounds already."

"Where's he in jail?"

"Bangkok," she said, and he did not need to ask her the charge. Heroin in a suitcase, perhaps, some beefy secondhand car salesman who was confident he could outsmart any Chonko.

"Ah well," he said, and there was nothing else he could say; he'd squat there for years in leg chains, shitting in buckets and nobody could say he hadn't earned it. "You know General Keh?"

"Keh?" She looked at him hard for the first time. "You a friend of his?"

Quinn pulled a Silver Starlet from the packet and leaned back,

287

sighing deeply. "No. I know him, that's all—used to know him a long time ago. I've no reason to like him."

"What's that supposed to mean? No, don't tell me." The bottle swiftly emptying.

He ordered another. A large Englishwoman in caftan swept in with an entourage of three Nationalist Air Force men: tall graceful Northerners in silky American-style uniforms, with American-style twangs; they looked like they had stepped out of *Terry and the Pirates*. Quinn watched her making a great fuss about a table; the waiters finally squeezed one in against the dance floor. When she got up to dance, she dragged all three of them with her, crushing them in turn against her capacious bosom.

He was getting drunk. "No dough," the singer was saying. "Bastard said he'd set me up here in a nice place. A joke."

His mind fumbled back, watching the large woman whooping and giggling. "Who said he'd set you up?"

She jerked a thumb toward the floodlit statue. "Showed me the development plans. Convention center, nightclub. I had it better in Bangkok."

But here you're under his thumb, though Quinn. The boyfriend, no doubt, was in the network; Keh probably had some further minor use for her.

"I went to Bali to commit suicide once," she said. "I was going to take some pills and swim out to sea."

He looked at her curiously. "Why did you go to Bali to do it?"

"I thought I'd have a bit of a holiday at the same time," she said, and he started to laugh, but she was solemnly stubbing out a cigarette. "Anyway, I had the kids."

He didn't want to know about the kids. "A beautiful woman like you," he said. "You could go into movies, modeling . . ."

"I used to do some modeling."

"Do it again."

"Are you kidding, love? I'm thirty-four. This was when I was eighteen, nineteen . . . Tennis star. I beat Evonne Goolagong once."

"You must have been good."

"Could have won the State Final, but I had a miscarriage." She lifted the second bottle, pushing a damp strand of hair from her lips. "Got an offer to coach in the States . . . Too much hassle, with the kids. Maxine Black—I used to be in all the papers."

"Maxine Black," he murmured, pretending to remember.

"Headlines," she declared, sketching them in the air; headlines growing larger each year. "Newk told me once—ah, who cares?"

She waved a fresh cigarette toward Keh's statue. "He's kinky, you know, Keh. Likes to watch women piss."

He didn't want to know about that either . . . The waiter brought him the bill; she instructed him to add another packet of cigarettes.

THEY STUMBLED UP a dark flight of stairs behind the club, laughing and clutching bottles like teenagers; a rat moved sluggishly in the shadows of a landing. Light gleamed through a cracked panel in a door, and when she threw it open with a bang he saw two children asleep on a couch before a hissing TV set. She switched it off.

"What are you kids doing up?" she demanded. "I told you to go to bed."

A small girl in a nightdress sat up querulously, her face squeezing out a protest. "Kenny wouldn't go to sleep," she complained. She looked about seven.

Kenny lay beside her in a dressing gown too large for him, his sister's untied moccasins on his feet. When his mother shook him he shrugged her off, burrowing deeper into the couch.

"Wake up!" she ordered, tugging him upright; he began to grizzle and struck at her hand, still half-asleep. She tossed a bottle onto the couch and slapped him on the cheek.

"Now you be quiet! Watch your manners! What have I told you about going to bed? What have I told you?"

Quinn felt that he was conniving at their destruction; swaying there, suddenly sad, he was witnessing a minute slice in their dismemberment. "I didn't know they were with you."

"Now you're up you can make us a cup of coffee," she continued. "Go on! Take Kenny with you." She tossed her headdress on the TV set and kicked off her shoes. "Kids!" Turning her back on them as they stumbled out.

Quinn sat down on the couch, all at once very tired. This was the way his life was petering out; the disintegration that had begun on West Ridge to be repeated endlessly, wherever he was. An aging toddler desperate to prove that all womankind did not reject him, as his wife had; picking up strangers in bars after a thousand drinks, staring solemnly into each other's eyes, pretending to find meaning. Awaking after desperate impotent nights in tangled bedrooms with willing young divorcees who laughed at his jokes and did not realize how low his flame was burning; awaking to a new roar of traffic, a new chuckle of harbor water, a new set of song birds, but always the same old conversations: "You're beautiful . . . Don't be silly . . . Would I be here if you were just another body?" (The final light kiss, the final lie, and off.) Awaking in inner-city terraces shaken not by his passion, but by the container trucks rumbling up from the wharves; awaking to the cold grave stares of children whose minds he mutilated by his presence, whose eyes spoke silently from their mothers' bedroom doorways: "So this is my future too." Awaking to flick through strange books on urban planning and herbal medicine and soil science, through T. E. Lawrence and Kate Millett and Erica Jong while liberated librarians and the part-time assistant directors of documentaries made coffee downstairs in damp kitchens, switching on FM radio and reassuring him kindly: "Don't worry about it . . ." Awaking in Balmain, Newtown, Taiwan.

The singer went off to the bathroom; he heard a squeal from the kitchen, the clatter of cups, the rattle of a spoon. When the child put the cups on the floor by the couch she rubbed a small burn on her arm.

"I wish you wouldn't make me do this!" she cried tearfully at the bathroom door, but when her mother flung it open she fled.

"Off to bed!" The singer swept out and flung herself on the floor beside him. Through the windows he could see Keh's marble cap, the upraised sword; presumably the statue remained flootlit throughout the night. "And go to sleep!"

She sighed. "No good for them here. When I'm organized I'm sending them back to private schools."

"You'll have to put their names down."

She looked at him blankly. "Little bastards," she said. "I'm going to get my gear off," dragging a cushion from the couch. It was wet with her son's sleep-spittle; she turned it over and punched it into shape. "How about filling a couple of glasses?"

He went into the kitchen with a bottle and poured two more whiskies. From there he could see the girl tucking her brother into bed, but when he poked a friendly face at her, inflating his cheeks, she turned away. He went back into the dining room. She had flung aside her gown and sprawled on her stomach in filmy red panties, flicking a broken nail at one of the steaming cups. The old tennis muscles swelled in her legs.

"What did you come to Taiwan for?" she asked quietly.

"I'm not sure yet. Going to look up Keh tomorrow. Just talk. I haven't seen him for thirty bloody years."

"He won't have changed . . . Where are you staying?"

"I left my case over at the police station. Pretty dirty. Lice on the bed. I'm booked in at the White Horse from tomorrow."

"You'd better stay here." She dropped her head on the cushion. "Cheer me up. You married or something?"

"I was. Twin sons killed in an accident. Well, bit of a relief, in one way—they had leukemia. Almost funny, isn't it? Wife took my daughter to live in Israel. Pretty crippled."

"Your wife?" She raised her head and downed her whisky, the coffee forgotten. "Give us a bit of a massage on that left leg, will you? Gives me hell."

He slid to the floor and began kneading the golden flesh. "No, my daughter. We got hit by a drunk driver—no license. But I blame myself. I should have seen him. Funny, life. Kids were singing. I was thinking of Keh at the time—I had my fingers around his throat."

"There. Press a bit harder."

"Don't remember my wife—trained myself not to. Think of her face and it's just smooth flesh—well, most of the time. Reckons I'm a sort of Yasser Arafat of the Antipodes, anyway. But my daughter, I'm sad about her."

"Take mine. You can have 'em both."

"I went to Tel Aviv a few years ago—got a Credit Union loan. Wife married again, some Israeli army officer—she looked happy. Didn't disturb 'em. They didn't know I was there. Went along to my daughter's school. Looked through the wire. She was playing on crutches. Dragging around like a bloody stick insect."

"Keep pressing. That's good. I could sleep for a week."

"Crazy, it was. Copper came up and moved me along. Thought I was a perv." He laughed. "Bloody funny, life, isn't it? Bloody scream."

"Hop down off your cross. You'll have me throwing up."

"Sorry. A man has all this love with no face to fit it. Wind up clutching shadows."

"You're not doing much bloody clutching here tonight." She half-turned, her breasts hanging full and rich beneath her drained face, as if the last of her essence had lodged there. "Tide's gone out," she said, holding up her empty glass.

He got up and filled it absently from a second whisky bottle he had placed on a lacquered cabinet. In an open top drawer, beneath a Harold Robbins novel, an automatic pistol lay amid a scatter of brass bullets with snub steel noses. Playthings for the kiddies. He sank down again at her feet, remembering Doyle's pistol among the scatter of cards.

"I should have been a war hero like my old man," he said. "I had the Digger cunning—it was just the courage I lacked."

He sipped his coffee and returned to the whisky. "Might as well get pissed. Don't have to brave the lice." But he was already preparing the ground so that he would not have to make love.

"Know what I did once? Gallipoli, First World War? I tossed eighty-three Turks and a German officer into the Aegean in fifty-seven seconds—never forget it. Each one described a perfect arc in the air—the corpse flies rose like bees."

"You're around the fucking bend! I thought I was the entertainer."

"Second World War the same. Remember Wingate? I had to prod him into the jungle at the point of a bayonet. He was gibbering on his knees."

"You need a bloody keeper. Try the other leg."

"Yeah, I know," he sighed. "Tell you the truth, when my mates jingled off to the Crusades I stayed behind and drove the death cart. I was the unit sniper with a drooping licorice gun."

"You can say that again. No wonder your wife pissed off."

"Unkind, unkind. I was only trying to cheer you up . . ."

He hauled himself to his feet again and began to pace around the room, cradling his glass. This should annoy her. "I'm too Australian, that's my trouble—too much grave-dust in the old head."

"Sit down. You make me nervous."

"Where were you from? The country or the city?"

"Beautiful Bankstown."

"I'm country. You know what I've got in my head?"

"I've got a feeling I'm going to find out. Do you always crap on like this?"

He swung around, slopping whisky from his glass. Solemnly, he poured another.

"I've got cart tracks in my head, scored down the creek banks. I've got dented cream cans and nettles around the dunnies, and the red bellies of the black snakes. Don't you understand? I'm lost. I'm the earth. I'm all and nothing."

She raised herself on one elbow. "I'll kick you in the balls if you try any rough stuff."

"I'm not like that, for God's sake—I'm trying to communicate. I'm a ring-barked paddock in the moonlight. I'm the silence in the bush after the rails stop quivering. I'm a broken bottle in a creek bank at Coopernook. I'm a back-street in Bourke on Sunday night. I'm the fizz of a faulty fish shop neon at Padstow."

"That's in the city."

"You don't know what I'm talking about, do you? I'm my land. I'm the painted fighters on Sharman's tent. I'm a cricket beyond the glow of the farmhouse. I'm a diatom beneath the hoof of a Friesian."

She smiled faintly. "Let's face it, darling, you're a dud fuck. Come and sit down."

He lowered himself again to the floor and absently began squeezing her leg. She shook her hair forward over her face; he noticed a small fresh red scar on the back of her neck, imagining a phantom arm around her throat, a knife pressing into her flesh.

"You must meet some bastards in your game," he said.

"No, they're all the strong silent types, like you."

"How did you get that scar on your neck?"

She swung around fiercely, knocking his hand from her leg. "Get your grubby fingers out of my brain! All right? In fact, how about pissing off?" Strained and white, reaching for another cigarette, tossing aside the box.

"You can't condemn me to the lice."

"OK, stay. But don't go on with that shit." She dragged the cushion beneath her head and lay on her back, blowing smoke at the high dark ceiling. He grasped one of her legs roughly to inform her of his lack of sexual intention, squeezing the flesh firmly between his thumbs and fingers. After a time his spine began to ache; he gave a final little pat and sank back against the couch.

"One thing worries me, though." He tensed for her reaction. "Won't the kids get at that gun in the drawer?"

She scrambled up hurriedly, knocking over her coffee cup. "You want it?" she demanded, grabbing it from the drawer. "You want to kill someone? Murder Keh? Blow your brains out? Take it! Go on! Take it!" She pushed it into his coat pocket. "You want some bullets? Here are some bullets! Now what else do you want? Do you want a screw now? Or can I go to bed? Cheesus!" She kicked the cup out of her way.

"You're lovely when you're angry," he said, "twirling your parasol."

"You're unreal." She pushed a damp strand of hair from her lips. "I'm going to bed."

"I'll doss down here." He watched her pad toward her room clutching the cushion, the light shining on her scarred golden body. A minute later he walked after her to the doorway; she had fallen prone on an unmade bed, clutching the cushion beneath her cheek.

"I'll get away early in the morning," he said softly. "Fling on a fig leaf and be gone."

"Try a tea leaf," she murmured. "And turn off the light."

He placed his coat carefully on a chair. The gift of the pistol had immediately contaminated him; already he began considering where he might dump it. He lay on the couch listening to the rats scuttling in the walls as they had scuttled in the monastery on Hua-shan. A pale film of light from the statue glistened on the ceiling.

His mind was clear and cold. He had lived his life on the edge of memory, treasuring the inconsequential: a pale face intently watching the darkness, without the gift of understanding, the discipline of self-knowledge, aware only of a faint luminosity like fungi in a wood, too weak to light the path. The krill down in the Antarctic had more purpose than he, ascending and lowering themselves to the currents that bore them away. And yet somewhere, dimly, he began to see a pattern.

294

THIRTY-THREE

AT NINE O'CLOCK THE GREAT BLACK gates of Keh's amusement park swung open as an attendant pressed a button in a control room above the turnstiles. Quinn got up from the base of the monument and followed a few honeymoon couples inside; they joined queues of students who were already clicking through the turnstiles—occupants of a low-slung youth hostel tucked in beside the hotel in the outer grounds. The sun shone weakly in a pale sky, and mist still hid the higher forest around them.

He felt frail and hungry, holding his arm close to his side to obscure the bulk of the pistol. Beside the turnstiles, gift shops displayed trinkets and holiday gear: T-shirts and baseball caps emblazoned *I'm O'Keh!*; plates and ashtrays and hair clips bearing the motif of the rearing horse. The stallion was everywhere: on flags and pennants drooping above the turnstiles; on the helmets of tall sullen guards in snappy uniforms, with pistols and walkie-talkies at their webbing belts. Pushing through a turnstile, he avoided their eyes; ahead lay a pea-green pond decked with lotus, and in its center, on an artificial island, was a large gaudy pagoda. A willow-pattern bridge arched over the pond to its entrance.

The pagoda was Hollywood Chinese, the sort of curlicued backdrop that Holden and Wayne and Peck had charged around in front of for years to demonstrate the superiority of the straight Anglo-Saxon line. Teenagers clustered on the bridge to photograph its phoney tranquillity, and Quinn squeezed past them, gazing down at the water; the swollen bodies of carp moved obscenely like the bodies of the drowned. A guard stood outside the pagoda as if he were on duty at Keh's old military HQ itself—ready to defend it until the last moment, the final bribe.

And that was what it was, in essence: a sort of HQ glorifying the Magic General's fictitious courage in war, his fake geniality during peace. As Quinn entered, walls began sliding up from recesses in the floor and soft lights glowed in the sudden gloom; a tinny martial fanfare shrilled as a giant color photograph of Keh was flung on the wall before him—Keh and the dead Chiang Kai-shek staring over the boulders of Quemoy at the Mainland. Then the commentary began, a chirping slur of Mandarin he could not grasp, but its intent was obvious: here was a reverential documentary capturing the high points in the great man's life, a clumsy montage of movie film and stills according him his unrightful place in history. Sepia photographs of his childhood and youth gave way to flickering newsreel shots of him during the Second World War and the Civil War; they ended with another fanfare, a stirring shot of the Nationalist flag snapping in the breeze.

More lights came on; now a giant copper mural of China gleamed on another wall, studded with tiny winking red bulbs representing Keh's alleged victories against the Communists. Earphones hung from a rail, offering explanations in Chinese, Japanese, and English. Quinn joined a queue, dropped his hat on the floor, and fitted a pair over his head.

"General Keh fight many battle in the Civil War," a Chinese voice yelped; the words exploded like bullets. "Many enemy soldier run away when he charge on his famous horse! You see the bottom li'? This represent the Battle of Ningsiang, north of Chang sha.."

Quinn gazed at the bottom light, his memory beginning to stir.

"General Keh is leading a spearhead north against the Communist armies!" *North?* "The Communists attempt to ambush him, but he turn the tables in a mighty victory! . . . General Keh strike into Szechuan. Here the Communists commit many atrocity—people skinned alive! He vow vengeance! The White Horse Division gives chase to the bandits, crushing many enemy troops! He traps Communist army on Hua-shan and then swings east into Shansi . . ."

Quinn listened three times to the commentary. Keh's staggering effrontery was comic; he suppressed a wild desire to laugh. Keh had taken the war communique and twisted it into outrageous parody. Each glorious military fiction contained some tiny germ of truth—but each larger lie illustrated his supreme contempt for mankind at large. It was almost as if he didn't care a damn whether people believed him or not; his lunatic lies were as subtle as his old tin inkblots, as unobtrusive as the macaw-nose of Punch. For Keh had reversed his line of flight, for a start—from a pell-mell retreat south (to avoid the war's crucial battles) into a courageous drive north to get into the middle of them. He had not included his gallant victory at the Retreat of Radiance—perhaps that was a little too far south of the main conflict for even him to falsify—but the earlier incidents were there, magnified, turned upside down. Each victory was like a puzzle box with a hidden spring: find it and the lid flew open on the eunuchs sobbing shrilly as he overturned their tables and chairs on the road near Ningsiang; the straw-stuffed human Communist dummy (now a group of patriotic Nationalists) in southern Szechuan; the murdered monks of Hua-shan, miraculously elevated after death into a Red army. No more Punch and Judy in a makeshift armored car for an audience of musty apes: he had built *his* fantasies into mass entertainment for the family, fertilized his ornamental gardens with corpses that the world had not missed. That was the most barbarous joke of all. Keh's lies had grown so large that nobody could see them; Punch, who had once peeped so slyly from the wings, had planted himself permanently in center-stage, with nobody to pull him down. Nobody, apparently, except Quinn.

Quinn walked out of the pagoda and crossed a second bridge leading to the other side of the pond. A string of youths ran ahead; laughing, they began climbing a ladder clamped to a ten-meter cement replica of Hua-shan while recorded shells exploded, hidden Red machine-gun nests spat sparks. When they reached the top, plastic Communist soldiers popped up from the rocks with their hands raised.

He turned away down a path that skirted the miniature mountain. Picture signposts pointed to pony rides and walking trails; there were space games in a silver rocket-shaped building set incongruously amid ornamental flower beds, and a painted ape with dripping fangs presumably indicated a house of horrors. From somewhere above he thought he heard lions or tigers roaring, the screech of jungle birds. He chose another path, which led into a large triangle of rain forest.

He walked only a short way. Just off the track he found what he needed: a rotting tree trunk, lipped with white fungus, standing among ferns still glistening with dew. He wandered around it, affecting a keen botanical interest, and when he was sure that he was unobserved, he took the pistol from his pocket and dropped it inside on a bed of leaf mould. Then he picked up a mossy rock and dropped it on top of the pistol. It could rust in that tree trunk for years, just as his key was rusting under the brick on West Ridge.

Quinn strolled back up the path, idly jingling the bullets in his pocket; he'd scatter them after he had checked in at the hotel—somewhere children could not find them and strike them with hammers. He felt almost carefree again with only his brain and his hands as his weapons; one did not need real props to act out this fantasy. For fantasy it might remain: even now, at the eleventh hour, he had still not decided which role he was going to play. Unless Keh decided for him.

He walked back past the model of Hua-shan; a guard at its base was ordering two youths to climb down from the roof of a miniature monastery on a concrete ridge, but he felt the man's eyes on him, and when he turned, pretending to inspect a flower bed, the guard was unclipping his walkie-talkie. Quinn quickened his pace.

Keh's tongue-in-cheek daring was astonishing: perhaps this whole complex, bristling with clues to his infamy, was the expression of a subconscious he longed to reveal just as Quinn had painted his own guilt in his clumsy landscape of Kweilin. He trod back over the willow-pattern bridges, instinctively seeking someone from the past with whom he could share this new revelation of Keh's ghastly glee—the dead Doyle or the broken Rushton; even Porter or Veitch or the sleeping Maxine; Mr. Ochi or Winifred—anybody whom he could grasp by the elbow and say: "Don't stop me. You've never heard this one."

But when he looked up only one person from the past stood before him. It was Larsen.

LARSEN WAS STARING at him: dapper now, almost elegant in his casual gear, but unmistakably Larsen—a sneer in the memory.

"Well, if it isn't Larsen!" Quinn pushed his fists into his coat pockets and looked him up and down. "You look quite snappy. What happened to the old Bombay bloomers?"

"You're going to regret this." Larsen almost hissed it. "There are laws to protect people's reputations from maniacs like you."

"I used to like old Bombay bloomers. Set you apart in a crowd. Disappointing, really. You look almost trendy."

Larsen took a step forward. "Do you realize what you're doing, you crazy bastard? Meddling in people's lives?"

"Is that what it is?" Quinn smiled in his face. "Well, we can't always expect the truth to stay buried forever, can we? Bit of suffering might be good for the soul."

"If anyone is going to suffer . . ." Larsen stopped abruptly.

"It's going to be me? You may be right. But I'll tell you one thing, chum . . ." He could hear Doyle snapping it: "chum!" "If there's going to be blood on the walls, it won't all be mine."

He sauntered off toward the hotel; the performance had embarrassed him, but it might rattle Larsen. It *did* rattle Larsen; he heard him following.

"What do you mean, blood?" Larsen asked. There was a new edge of anxiety in his voice.

Quinn turned around. "How would I know? I'm crazy. I'm a maniac. I'm the sort of person who'd wander in here with no idea what I'm doing, aren't I? No protection, no evidence, no safeguards. No plan." He walked on: if Larsen only knew.

"We've got to talk." Now it was Larsen following him as he had followed Larsen through the streets of Shanghai. Quinn the shrewd, tough schemer; he had never felt so phoney in his life.

But he was angry too. He wasn't going to take another threat, another insult, as long as he lived.

"We've got to sit down and talk. Thrash this out once and for all." Larsen paused. "Keh's not unreasonable . . ."

"You mean money. I don't remember mentioning money."

"Of course not." Larsen seemed relieved to have the subject out in the open. Issuing long-distance murder instructions to Ming from New Jersey was one thing; bribery was obviously a much more pleasant (and safe) alternative now that he was on the spot.

"Whatever," Larsen said. "We have to find common ground."

Quinn thought of the crop that Keh had sown in the bean field: if ever there was common ground, that was it.

He stopped on the steps at the hotel entrance. "Larsen, I don't have to find anything . . . By the way. Our friend Keh. He hasn't grown, has he?"

"Grown?" Larsen gazed at him testily.

"Yes, I mean, he's not shot up to eight feet with matching chest? It's just that his horse—remember that little horse? Wouldn't rear if you shoved your arm up it. And look at it now."

He nodded at the statue.

"For Christ's sake! Don't you understand?" Larsen gripped his sleeve. "Don't you know how big he is?" He dropped his hand. "Look, I'm sorry about what happened. I was young—you do crazy things you regret! Everybody does."

"Like shooting pumpkins. Well, I didn't spring nobly in front of the firing squad. It was just your . . . enjoyment."

Larsen surprised him. "You don't know," he said. "My background. I was a coiled spring. Yes, I admit it. I wanted to shoot. Until I squeezed the trigger. I couldn't eat for a week."

"They were *kids!*"

"You don't stop to think. I've had to live with it . . . Nobody knows what I've had to put up with."

"You play very nice violin." Quinn hated himself, hearing the cardboard words of the actor, the private eye; beneath the layers of his own ambivalence, inside the soft center, there had never been a rigid core like Doyle's. He had cloaked his timidity as reason and made a virtue of it—hiding, like Keh, behind his humor. Now, he knew, he was beginning to forgive Larsen, not

300

only because forgiveness was the easy way out, but because in Larsen, calibrated more cruelly, he saw himself.

"I'm going to check in," he said. "We'll talk later," and he left him standing on the steps and went in to the reception desk. He had hated him for so long—or thought he had: the bloodless face, the rasping voice, the dry rattling laughter at the expense of others, as if he harbored the cold interior of a reptile in a human body—Larsen, some dreadful genetic mistake on the asembly line while God was tinkering with plans for the Kansas Dust Bowl. But now he did not hate Larsen at all. They were both victims.

He did not even hate Keh—not a boiling bushfire hatred that consumed everything in its path. Sometimes, he suspected, Keh merely supplied the body for the crime: a final dollop of guilt for a prudent life in which he had failed the major test. He had never loved enough.

"I left my suitcase over at the police station," he said to the clerk. "Will someone pick it up?"

THIRTY-FOUR

"YOU HAD ME UNDER SURVEILLANCE, didn't you?"

"You're damn right, I did!"

Quinn and Larsen sat in a long lounge of the hotel late that afternoon looking down on Green Silk Lake. At one end hung a huge framed photograph of Chiang Kai-shek, at the other Sun Yat-sen; between them, beaming against the backdrop of the lake, was a slightly smaller picture of Keh. A lesser figure perhaps, but a mighty mortal, nevertheless—hogging the spot calculated to draw most attention.

"Knowing you," Quinn said, "I wasn't sure at first whether it was ASIO or the Mafia. When nothing happened, I assumed it was ASIO."

"They did a good job." Larsen began to smirk, but thought better of it. "They've come up with enough to discredit anything you say."

"They did a lousy job," Quinn said. "I knew when they were

303

around." That sudden knowledge in the early-morning darkness, and later the creeping car, the cigarette butts in the garden . . . The ambiguous signs of the secret police.

"Maybe," Larsen said. "But they got enough," and Quinn knew that he was right: they always did. No charges laid, no thundering on doors at dawn; the condemned men continued to eat hearty breakfasts.

"So they can smear me," he countered. "I've been smeared all my life." Execution delivered in a brief executive aside (fellow traveler, Commie nogood, bleeding heart, long-haired conservationist—the words all meant disloyal); psychic death by sealing in a folder, by smothering in a significant silence in the boardroom. Suspicions he could never confirm, judgements rustling in the leaves.

"Paranoia," Larsen said. "You had a breakdown once, didn't you? But there's no need to go into this. I told you—Keh is looking for a solution. We had a long talk here last night, and I'm sure he'll see reason. He doesn't need this sort of publicity."

"Doesn't enhance the image, does it?" Tourist launches were puttering over the lake; sunlight flashed like Morse on the windows of Keh's home above the rain forest. "Fake Hero's Drug Millions. *'I Killed Kids,' He Confesses.*"

"Shut up, for God's sake! Do you want to get us killed?"

"I thought he was a reasonable man."

"Tell me what you want. I'm seeing him again tonight up at his place. Give me something to take to him! I told him I'd talk to you."

"Ah yes," Quinn murmured. "Find common ground. Chums to the end. You know what you can do with your common ground."

"Am I interrupting something?"

Larsen looked up sullenly. "My wife, Donna," he said. "Quinn."

"Well, well," Quinn got to his feet. "I didn't realize your good lady would be with you," affecting old-world gallantry. But he was startled. Larsen's wife was a slender blonde with blue eyes—middle thirties, no more.

She regarded him steadily. "But I'm not," she said. "His good lady, I mean. I'm his bad lady."

"Drop it!" Larsen rasped, the color flooding into his face.

"His *good* lady is flouncing around somewhere in a large tent. You can't miss her. She's English—Lady Earnshaw. Follow the hibiscus."

"I think I saw her last night," Quinn said. "This is a joke, I take it?"

"Oh, it's no joke." She looked splendid in a lilac sweater and stretch jeans; her eyes sparkled with malice. "Ed thinks Big Bertha's very attractive. Don't you, Ed?"

"Are you going to have some coffee?" Quinn asked. The dreaded Larsen was shriveling under his eyes.

"For once, I feel like something a little stronger than coffee. You don't mind if I join you, do you, Ed?"

"We're talking business."

"You *were* talking business. Now why don't you be a good boy and run off and play with your balloon? Before the Africans grab her. I'll talk to Mr. Quinn."

"You bitch!" Larsen sprang to his feet. He looked as if he could kill her. Then he stalked away furiously, cannoning into a chair.

"That's better," Donna said brightly. "Now I can breathe. So you're the infamous Quinn. You've been giving my husband nightmares."

"Really?" Quinn widened his eyes, his innocent look. Suddenly he regretted his black suit, the absurd black hat on the floor by his chair. "I can't imagine how anyone could have nightmares with you."

"Oh he can, I assure you. You want to sit on here?"

Quinn looked around. Off the lounge was a bar with a giant tiger's head built around the entrance—rubber fangs painted silver, two green lights burning fiercely in its eye sockets. "Let's try there," he said. "Looks appropriate."

They entered the warm gloom of the bar; a bartender was rubbing tipsy Japanese graffiti from a fang. Keh's taste, as usual, was execrable: mock tiger-skin stools and seats, real hides decorating the walls. They chose a booth at the rear.

"I'm sorry about that little display. I just can't stop myself lately."

"Can't be helped."

"I wouldn't mind so much if he preferred somebody . . . normal.

She appears to have such disgusting sexual appetites. You don't mind me talking about this?"

"Of course not." Something was stirring in the back of his mind.

"I've given up so much for him. Drinking, smoking. Do you have a cigarette? I'd love a cigarette."

He lit one for her; her cheek was as smooth as silk. He ordered whiskies in a quick aside without consulting her, and leaned forward, holding her to her story.

"I don't know you." She puffed inexpertly like a young teenager; her tension showed in each jerky movement. "What's going on, Mr. Quinn? Why have you brought Ed here?"

"I didn't bring him. He wanted to come. What has he told you?"

"That General Keh is a great hero and you're trying to bring them down. Some connection with business—you could ruin them both. Nothing precise. Are you really as unpleasant as he says?"

Quinn leaned back and smiled. "No, and I'm sure you're not a bitch."

"Oh, that." She waved away smoke. "No, I'm not a bitch. Ed's the bitch. I hope you don't mind me talking like this? I find it best to be frank, don't you?"

Quinn smiled again. "I've never tried it. My mob are cursed with convict caution. We're still afraid of the guards."

"I'm serious. What is there between you and Ed?"

"I don't know how much I should tell you."

But he told her.

"We were both . . . loathsome. The only difference between us is that I'm doing something about it after all these years. Facing up to it."

She sipped her drink—quick little sips like a bird at a dangerous water hole. "I didn't know he'd ever had a gun. I won't have one in the house."

"It was a long time ago." He paused. "And I wouldn't want you to be hurt."

"Then why go ahead? When you might be hurt too, Mr. Quinn?"

"Atonement, maybe. Revenge. Disguised suicide—I don't

know. I've waited till I had nothing left to lose. The old hand reaching up out of the grave for the dice."

"Everybody has something to lose." She ashed her cigarette. "I suppose it's noble of you, offering your life for those children. It was so long ago."

"I'm not offering my life for them." He smiled at her again. "I'm merely bequeathing them a small piece of my death. Your husband thinks I want money—that I'll settle for a bribe. I don't give a damn about money. I want . . ."

"What do you want, Mr. Quinn? You know, I'm enjoying this—I feel free for the first time in fourteen years."

"Oh, the old cliché, I suppose. To stand up and be counted . . . That Englishwoman? I just saw her going past. You're not serious that he's pursuing her?"

"Very serious. It seems he's known her for some time—we came over on the same plane. Her husband's a big businessman in New York." She paused. "I had no idea."

"He must be mad." He signaled for more drinks. "Big Bertha, eh? Fancy that. I'll be back in a minute."

"EXCUSE ME. LADY Earnshaw?"

She was bending over a display counter of Taiwanese aboriginal crafts, a strong scent of musky perfume around her, her bright aqua eye shadow beginning to trickle. Her hand flew coyly to her cleavage: here it is, spoke her large blue eyes.

"Yes, luv. What can I do for you?"

"My name's Quinn. I'm a friend of the Larsens. I wonder if I could have a word with you for a minute?"

She looked guarded. "What about?"

"It's a bit confidential. I'm with Mrs. Larsen at the moment. Could we pop around this corner for a minute?"

"What's the mystery?" She planted herself truculently in front of him. He realized that any man who was not her admirer was her enemy.

"I'm sorry. There's no mystery—not really. I was just wanting to do a good turn for Ed, but he's his own worst enemy. He'd be annoyed if he thought I was speaking for him." He paused. "He thinks you're terrific."

The compliment mollified her. He backed around the corner and she followed.

"I was just talking to him," he said. "He's going up tonight to see General Keh—the man who owns this place. A millionaire—billionaire probably. I'm not sure how to say this."

"Say what?" She dabbed her plump neck with a small padded handkerchief.

"Perhaps I shouldn't mention it—but, hell, I'd like to help him. You won't tell him that I've talked to you?"

"I haven't got anything to tell him, have I?"

"It's just that he's so proud—it would blow it if he found out. Anyway, Ed badly needs a lift with his firm. It would be a real feather in his cap if he could get all General Keh's advertising and PR business in the States. I've found out that much from talking with Mrs. Larsen—Donna."

"So what's that got to do with me? I don't know the first thing about business."

"Neither do I. I'm not much help to him. But, well, you're a very attractive woman, and I know that General Keh has a thing about titled English ladies. He's always at Windsor, meeting the queen and so on. So I thought, maybe if you went with Ed and charmed the General it might help him."

"Well, I suppose I could . . . Met the queen, has he?"

"Often, apparently. He's big on horses. And, you know, he might be a very good contact for your husband. Ed tells me he's a pretty big businessman in New York."

"Perhaps he doesn't like ladies who are generously endowed." She dimpled prettily; a plump hand hovered again at her cleavage.

"He likes any ladies—and he'll love you," Quinn said.

The baits laid; perhaps he was certifiable, after all.

"You must be a very good friend of Ed's?" she said. "Poor little bugger," her innocent eyes twinkling.

"Very good," Quinn said. "Very good. You won't say anything to him, will you?"

"Of course not, luvvy." She tugged Quinn's tie gently. "Black suits you. I'll let you know how it goes."

IT WAS TWO hours later in the dining room; Donna swept up to his table, flushed and slightly unsteady. Her eyes sparkled more brilliantly than before.

"Ed's checked into another room. Next door to you, I think. He left a waspish note."

"Good. Don't worry about it."

"He said he was getting away from evil forces." She laughed. "He told a woman on the Short Line once that she was an agent of the Devil—she beat him to a seat. Her husband threatened to punch his nose."

"I don't know how you put up with him. America's warmed me all my life—the songs. He's so cold."

She picked up a menu. "Ed's father turned up an ivory paper knife once with a plow in Iowa. Sometimes I think they're the same, Ed and the paper knife."

Or the skull of a kneecap, he thought, remembering the jolting drive from Shanghai. He reached for the wine, hating his own shallow artifice. "Which leads me to a question. How did he turn up a jewel like you?"

"Ed?" She pondered the clumsy compliment gravely. "I was a secretary. He used to leave me flowers. I think he needed a wife to get on in the business."

"He's a lot older."

"And set in his little ways. I suppose it impressed me. I'd never met anyone who was, you know, anyone before."

He watched her gazing around her brightly. Waitresses decked in striped dresses and white aprons were moving around the tables like grim little Victorian servants, maids' caps perched on their European perms; the ubiquitous piped music quivered on the edge of his memory, stirring childhood images of the Wong-bok Odeon. He felt a moment's tenderness. She was a clear white screen that revealed his own spidery image to him boldly for the first time in his life: the spiky shadow-cluster of the banksia, a hair across the lens.

"I'm glad we've met," he said, and this time it was not pure deceit. But deceit, nevertheless.

"I THINK I'VE had too much to drink."

"Well," he said, "It's still raining. We don't have to go out anywhere."

"You're leading me astray, Mr. Quinn. You're an evil man."

"My strength is as the strength of ten because my heart is pure. Evil enters through a vacuum—the absence of good." He gazed at

her steadily, balancing to throw the dart. "The absence of someone to love."

"You've no one to love? That's a shame." She looked away
wildly, borne up by the liquor on the wings of an impossible
thought. "Love me!" she laughed and immediately bumped to
earth again in Bergen County. "I don't mean that, of course. I'm
sure you must have plenty of women friends."

"No," he said, selecting another dart. "And, to be honest, I've
never met anyone quite like you before. You seem unsullied by
life." (Like a new doll on a shelf). "And yet . . ." he struggled not to
laugh, ". . . you have a sadness about you."

She seized the cliché eagerly. "You've noticed, have you?" She
twiddled her glass. "Well, I guess married life sometimes, you
know . . ."

"I know."

"Not that Ed hasn't been a good provider. I've never had to
work."

"But it's not enough, is it? What would you do, if you went out
in the world again?"

"Me? Oh well, I guess it might sound stupid to you . . ."

"It won't." He touched her hand lightly: premeditation disguised as impetuosity.

"What I always wanted—you'll think me crazy . . ."

"No, no. Go on."

"I've always wanted to be a singer. Nightclubs, you know, Big
TV specials. I told you it was stupid."

"You'd be great," he said, shutting out Maxine, the children
huddled on the couch. He picked up his glass, pretending it was a
microphone. "I'd like to introduce you to a little lady . . ."

She laughed and drew back. "No, no. I'd be too shy, anyway . . ."

"You'd be great," he repeated gravely. "You've got the looks,
everything . . ." He filled her glass.

"You seem so much wiser than Ed."

"I'm not wise. A bachelor with echoes. Failed painter, failed
poet. I used to send verses to little magazines. Open my mouth
and bleed typography. Three guineas, thanks."

"I bet they were beautiful."

"My mother was highly disturbed—all that adolescent love
and desire. The righteous thunder of an Anglican organ, that was
my mother."

310

"And your father?"

"A ghost-gum paddock, a boxing match, a ruined barn . . . What about yours?"

"My mother died when I was born. We lived in Walker Valley, New York—you wouldn't have heard of it. I remember I used to sit up in bed—there was this wallpaper with big yellow sunflowers—and I could see the log cabin down in the woods that my grandmother had lived in. I've never gone back. I'm afraid there'll be a supermarket there."

"Is your father alive?"

"I think so, he's Canadian. He left when I was little. I don't suppose he could cope. An aunt adopted me."

"Why don't you go and see him?"

"I did once. He rents a couple of cabins up at Lake Louise. Ed took me to a convention at Jasper Park Lodge, so I wrote to him. I was unpacking when there was a knock at the door, and there was this poor little old man."

She blew her nose loudly; there was another opportunity to comfort her when she had finished. This time Quinn left his hand on hers for several seconds.

"Jesus," he said. "I'm a depressing bastard. I'm sorry. Here we have this stolen time, and we're sitting around crying like orphans of the bloody storm . . ."

"It's all right."

"I wonder what exquisite tortures your husband and Keh have been cooking up for me."

She gazed at him wide-eyed. "You don't think they'd . . ."

"I don't much give a damn what they're doing. By the way, I didn't tell you. I sent Lady Earnshaw up there with him."

"Whatever for?"

"I thought I'd wheel out the heavy artillery. Worth a try. When you mentioned Big Bertha I remembered that gun the Germans had in the First War. Big Bertha—softened up the enemy. I thought she might soften up Keh."

She giggled, brushing her wet lashes. "I don't know about softening. She might squash him."

"Wash your mouth out with soap," he said gently.

311

THIRTY-FIVE

"HERE IT IS." QUINN PUSHED open the door.

She weaved in before him, waving her shoes in one hand; she probably saw that entrance in a movie, he thought. He took the shoes from her and dropped them on a sofa, aware that a sudden thump on the floor might jolt her conscience. Then he kissed her, gauging the distance to the bed.

"Wouldn't it be great," he asked, "if we could just take one hour out of our lives?" (Mainly your life.) "Just to be loving human beings who understand each other? Suspend the past?" He kissed her again; she responded while gently pushing him away.

"There'll be no Liberty Hall tonight," she declared, and she broke away and flung herself on the sofa.

"No Liberty Hall tonight!" He smiled down at her. "That's terrific. I haven't heard that for years. I'll get the drinks."

He was mixing whiskies and soda when she called over her shoulder: "I haven't told this to anyone before, but I think Ed wears my clothes."

He put the drinks on a coffee table and moved the shoes so that he could sit beside her. "You're joking. How do you know?"

"Sometimes they're put back in the drawers differently. And I keep finding these strange publications in his attaché case."

"He was always locked in. Well, you can relax. I'm not going to flounce around the room in dresses."

"Perhaps if I'd had a baby. But the thought appalls me . . . It's cozy here, isn't it, hearing the rain?"

She jiggled her glass nervously. "I was so innocent when I met Ed. He'd read all these books on politics, Ayn Rand and so on. I was twenty. You won't laugh if I tell you what my favorite TV program was?"

"What was it?"

"Captain Kangaroo! I was twenty! What hope did I have?"

"You're just a slow beginner. And if he was a kangaroo he must have been all right. You can jump into my pouch any time." Wincing as he said it.

"Do male kangaroos have pouches?" She had a way of looking through him gravely, considering his words as if they hung disembodied in the air.

"Of course. But they don't get to use them that much."

"That's sad," she said solemnly. "I find that very sad."

"It is sad," he said.

QUINN AWOKE SEVERAL times during the night; raising his head from the pillow, he lay watching the delicate curves and lifts of her nose and lips, the cupola of her forehead—a mosque on the Bosphorus, he decided, shadowed against the misty white moon of the wall. The green lake lay deep in the darkness beneath his balcony, and now and again he ran his hand over her silky body, remembering the long line of kind women who had done their best to comfort him. "Go to sleep," she murmured each time, smiling drowsily.

Once she sat up suddenly; he was afraid that she was about to flee back to her room.

"I've just realized," she said. "I don't even know your first name!"

"I haven't got one. Quinn. People just call me Quinn."

"You must have one."

"OK. It's Harley. Now forget it. My old man had a sense of humor—once." A crooked grin and the wheelchair, dissolving together in the dim space between the bed and the wall.

At midnight, Larsen tapped on the door. "Is Donna there?" he grated. "I'm looking for her."

Quinn half-rose again from the bed. "She's not here. She's probably gone for a walk or something."

"I've looked everywhere. She's not in her room. If she's there . . ." He stopped. "I'm going to call the police."

"She'll turn up. Look, I'm trying to get some sleep."

"I'm next door," Larsen threatened. "She's my wife."

"So that's *your* problem. Don't bother me with it. Go to sleep!"

Twenty minutes later he spotted Larsen clinging to the marble balustrade of his balcony. He tossed the blankets over Donna, strode to the French doors and flung them open.

"Look, you stupid bastard! I told you—I'm trying to sleep. Piss off or I'll call the cops myself!"

Larsen stared at him wildly. The rain had soaked him; he wavered above the drop, his knuckles as white as his face. For several seconds he tried to speak, and then he edged miserably back to his own balcony.

Quinn locked the French doors, pulled the curtains, and then fell back into bed. Donna lay stiff and silent beside him as they listened for further movement. There was a muffled thump from the next room, as if Larsen had fallen over a chair. Then silence.

Gradually they relaxed. I've done my suffering, you bastard, Quinn thought. Now it's your turn, and he slipped his arm beneath Donna's head.

"He's probably got his foot caught in your garter belt," he said at last, and slowly she began to shake with a deep sobbing laughter which went on and on, as if it were rising from the most secret pit of her being; a truth entombed too long, released now forever.

"Hey," he whispered after a while, resting a hand lightly against her lips. "Slow down. It wasn't that funny," and she pushed her head into his chest and quietly began to weep.

It startled him, suddenly finding the doll programmed as a human. He held her in his arms until she had stopped shaking, and then he turned toward the wall, drawing her arm across him

315

and anchoring her hand against his stomach. "Go to sleep," he said.

But he lay awake, marveling at her warmth while it was there; marveling that it should be Larsen's wife with whom he had discovered such rapport.

"I feel I've known you a long, long time," she sighed.

"Go to sleep," he repeated, but he did not want to sleep himself. He wanted her to sleep so that he could be alone again as he would always be alone. All he had ever truly understood was the emptiness, the perimeters of life, the back streets where he sought fulfillment because there he was least likely to find it; it was too late to change now.

There was a penalty for love, and he could not pay it again. Each moment of happiness contained its opposite; each affair harbored the germ of its own destruction, the ecstatic lunacy of discovery dissolving into the sick loss he most deeply desired so that he could remain true to his aloneness.

He stirred. Only pain and pleasure lay ahead, pleasure and pain: no coherent philosophy, no faith—merely jokes in the dark. It was what he wanted.

"OK," he said, turning suddenly. "Let's do a Schottische," and clasping each other, laughing, they moved their feet to and fro beneath the sheets. Soon he'd regain what he had set aside— what he found most difficult to endure.

QUINN PULLED ASIDE a curtain. Misty rain still blurred the surface of the lake, half-obscuring crocodile snouts of rain forest that poked into the crumpled green water. As he watched, a helicopter rose from the roof of Keh's house and slid away into a hidden valley. Somewhere a bell was tolling.

"What time is it?"

"Our time," he said. He closed the curtain in case Larsen was about to attempt a morning constitutional along the balustrade. "It's early."

"I must look a mess." She rummaged for a mirror in her handbag and sat up in bed, peering into it doubtfully, smoothing imaginary lines around her eyes with her fingers. "I wonder if Ed's up yet."

"I'm making some coffee," he said. "Forget about him for a while."

"I wish I could. I wish I'd met you a long time ago."

"Well, you've met me now for better or worse." He went into the bathroom and poured boiling water onto instant coffee. He had brought it off. He had decided the punishment for Larsen and carried it out: The guilty man had received his sentence by osmosis, clinging to the rail of the balcony, seething all night in his cell next door. And yet a strange sad urge to love lingered in him like the misty rain, obscuring the edge of his intention.

He emerged smiling brightly, holding two steaming cups. "I think I'll learn to love," he said, handing her one.

She smiled softly. "You don't have anything to learn."

"No, I don't just mean that. Stones, trees, people, enemies. I'm almost past judgment of others. I'd probably find something very endearing in Hitler."

"That's the nicest compliment I've ever had."

He laughed. "No, I mean your husband. I don't care about him any more. He doesn't bug me."

"So you won't do anything to hurt him?"

"How could I hurt anyone?"

She sipped her coffee. "I was hoping you'd say that."

A slender black cloud seemed to drift through his chest: for the first time the possibility that she had been using him occurred to him. But, if so, at least it freed him. The gentle disengagement could commence; the morning minuet of grave promises and protestations to mask the banality of mutual exercise.

"I won't hurt him physically, anyway," he said. "Perhaps I'll try to steal you away from him. I'll get you your own cabin in the woods."

"I can't stand spiders—any crawly things. That's one thing Ed and I have in common."

"That's about all you have in common. OK, what about a yacht encrusted with jewels?"

"I get seasick."

"I'll take you to Bratislava. There's a secret corridor under a stall in the market square. Runs right through to a meadow in Walker Valley. We'll dance along it."

She raised an eyebrow, regarding him coolly over her cup. "The Schottische?"

"Ah, I suppose you're right." He felt depressed. He sat down on the bed. "I'm emotional, confused—it's not my time. The age of the cardboard cutouts."

"I like you very much."

"Thanks," he said. "Second prize." He wanted them to part. He wanted them to stay together forever. "I'm only comfortable on the losing side."

"You're not a loser. Not really. You endure."

"Yeah," he said. "You're right. I box clever." And he saw Doyle again, head up straight, life's blows chopping away at his face, the flesh flying from around his eagle eyes.

She placed her cup on the floor. "I've decided to leave today," she said quietly. "There's an early bus to Tai-chung."

"Back to America? Don't go." He looked around the room. "All I've got left is bloody ghosts."

"One day we might meet again."

He stood up and pulled aside the curtain; the swifts were flicking through the rain-mist, darting down across the lake. Back from West Ridge.

"There is no 'one day,'" he said. "One day we might meet dribbling mash in a twilight home. Ah, the ecstasy! Our wheelchairs touched! Don't I know your face? Lift your spoon a minute. Ah, yes!"

He dropped the curtain and turned back into the room. "There is no 'one day.'"

She sat looking at him solemnly, the bedclothes drawn up to her chin. "I'm sorry."

He sat on the sofa and pulled out a cigarette. "OK, I suppose it's for the better. You'll probably meet some eight-foot-tall Marine sergeant."

"I don't like eight-foot-tall Marine sergeants."

"All right, then. A Jamaican radio announcer in a yachting jacket—frayed gold thread on the coat of arms. You'll meet someone. Someone will find you now."

"Not in Bergen County, they won't."

"So you *are* giving up? This is your one little tilt at life? Then back into the suburban tomb?"

"It's Ed. You don't know his background."

"Fuck his background." His anger surprised him. "It's your foreground that interests me."

She leaned over again from the bed, scrabbled in her handbag, and handed him an old black and white snapshot. It showed a man and a woman standing in front of a barn. A boy of about three or four stood with them holding a toy rifle.

"He'd kill me if he knew I had this. I found it in an old box," she said.

"So what? This is him and his parents when he was a kid, I presume? What's she nursing?"

"That's his mother. I never saw her. Those are her arms. They're withered. They're about the size of a doll."

"So he had a mother with withered arms." He flicked the photograph onto the bed. "Poor bastard," he said softly. "That explains why he was always on about Indian arm wrestling."

And then he returned to the attack for the last time: a final show of force to mask his retreat.

"But let him cope with it. We've all got to cope." The fragments of bone flew into his brain. "He's paid it back, for Christ's sake! And you know where the journey ends, don't you? Old photos. Floors for the silverfish."

She was silent for a few seconds. "Perhaps he'll meet someone else," she said at last. "Another Lady Earnshaw."

"Yeah," Quinn said savagely. "Well, I hope you don't get too many lines around your eyes while you're waiting."

Later, at the door, he kissed her forehead. "Good luck," he said. "I'm glad we had this time, anyway."

She looked at him uncertainly. "Perhaps you could write to me sometime? Or give me a call?"

"Yeah," he said. "Perhaps I will."

He closed the door softly after her and stood for a long time, looking at the crumpled bed. There were tears in his eyes. There were also a million Donnas.

THIRTY-SIX

LARSEN PUSHED A CURT NOTE under his door while he was in the shower. He'd meet Quinn in the lobby at 11:30 that morning; Keh wanted to see them up at his house at noon. The handwriting was small and almost indecipherable, as if his mother's tiny hands were guiding his pen.

Quinn dressed in black for the last time; clapping his hat jauntily on his head, he left the room, quietly closing the door behind him. Passing the dining room, he saw Larsen sitting alone among the parties of Japanese; he was lifting a dripping breakfast egg, morosely, on his fork.

There was no sign of Donna; already she was an ache, another ghost. Crossing the polished parquet floor to the lobby, he saw his past strung over the gulf behind him like a shattered suspension bridge, each missing slat someone he had loved. He might have loved her, but now a tense, troubled frustration moved him; this new anger stirring beneath his old wariness. He sat in the lobby to write a brief letter.

"Dear Mrs. Steinway," he wrote, "There is one thing I didn't tell you. You said Tony had known a woman who died—I assume you're aware that it was an overdose. She wasn't high society perhaps, but she helped him when he first signed off in Hong Kong, and he never forgot it. She was the closest he had to family, I suppose, in the days long before he met you. Vera Koshnitsky—Rushton can give you the details.

"It's not clear what happened—nothing *was* with Tony, as you know. But I can guess part of it. Keh incriminated him in his heroin imports and Vera was sucked in accidentally or deliberately (Rushton said he wouldn't put it past Keh). He might even have threatened you if Tony didn't go along with him. I don't know, but I do know that Tony took the hat around for Vera when she died—she had a baby son then (Eurasian—father unknown). It was the sort of thing he'd have done—screwing his old mates' arms, threatening to punch their skulls if they didn't kick in! Characters from his Empire Hotel days, scattered around the globe. I saw the records at the Precious Psychiatric Centre in Kowloon, and I think I remembered some of the names.

"They've been sending money for years, but they've dwindled to one: a man in Hattiesburg, Mississippi, who seems to be having a hard time himself. What I mean is, the boy is still there, obviously getting no treatment. So I'm dumping the problem on you, being a minor wheeler-dealer myself . . ."

SURREPTITIOUSLY, HE POSTED the letter in a box beside the desk and paid his bill, arranging to return later for his suitcase. There was nothing of worth in it anyway: Keh's minions—probably the local police—had carefully removed the three rolls of film from his old Vest Pocket Automatic Kodak. It seemed almost funny.

He walked down the steps. The sun was shining; it was a lovely day to kill time. He was lighting a cigarette when a taxi swept up and Lady Earnshaw stepped out grandly.

"You shouldn't have waited up," she declared with a bright smile. Her hair was a mess, her caftan crumpled and ripped under one arm, but triumph shone in her eyes.

"You're just getting home?" Quinn dropped the cigarette. "How did you leave our friend?"

"Our friend," Lady Earnshaw said, "is a little weary. Bit past it, really. I think it'll be a long time before he gets it up again."

She turned as the first bus from Tai-chung drew in behind the taxi; three tall black men stooped out first, peering around them eagerly. One carried two basketballs in a string bag.

"Mes amis!" Lady Earnshaw cried, arms flung wide, and they swung around, eyes lit with adoration, knees bent as if about to bow.

Quinn saw Larsen watching bitterly from the dining room: a white blur behind the glass.

THE LAKE LAY still and deep to its rim below the sloping hotel gardens. Quinn took the bullets from his pocket and flicked them in lazily, one by one, like pebbles. Then he sauntered along the edge of the lake until he was out of sight of the hotel, hidden by the rise of the earth and an ornamental hedge that enclosed the hotel grounds. The hedge also obscured the turnstiles at the entrance to the amusement park; Larsen could be watching from the hotel.

Quinn entered the park with a jostling group of elderly Japanese women—gnarled little humans who hobbled awkwardly in clusters, like banyan roots torn from the wet pink earth. He crossed the willow-pattern bridge, idled for a few minutes in the Keh-display to allay suspicion, and then wandered past the mock Hua-shan. Over to his right he heard laughter; the grotesque head of a demon rose from the trees, as large as a two-storeyed house. Children were waving handkerchiefs from its barred eyes, and lines of them were sliding down its glistening red tongue into a sand pit.

He turned into the triangle of bamboo and rain forest that swelled up to the knoll capped by Keh's circular house. Through it rushed the crystal stream that tumbled down behind the police station, but the foliage was so thick that he glimpsed it only now and then. He found the path he had taken to dump the pistol and followed it as it curved up.

The forest was sparkling after the rain. New signs bearing the botanical names of each bush or tree or variety of bamboo were planted on each side of the path, but the heart of the forest was old, its trees rich with rotting, yet topped with young green growth, or sprouting ferns from their wounded sides—a symbiosis embracing the spores beneath his shoes, the insects dancing in the air, a celebration of life and death that was more exquisite than either he or Keh could ever attain. Small birds flitted low through the clumps of bamboo, and vines draped ancient boulders, splotched with velvet orange fungus, which had fallen in some forgotten slide. He swung on a vine, and the raindrops showered down; he brushed through the bamboo and let the silver beads fall on his hat, his sodden coat. High above him strange birds cried in the sunlight, and insects he did not know stopped signaling as he approached, like tape recorders clattering to the end of a spool. And yet there was an electric loveliness in there that was familiar; once again, it seemed, it was not the earth that was alien. The faces of his sons lay as pale as dishes in the leaves, awaiting his offering.

Quinn sucked the earth-tang up through his nostrils and brushed aside a glistening spiderweb that spanned the path: nobody had been up this way yet. Mossy stone steps ascended in gentle sweeps toward dark swathes of pine that flowed around the knoll, and he climbed them slowly, wondering what he was doing—his mind moving between love and violence, sentimentality and aggression while the patterns of light and shade shifted ceaselessly on the forest floor. Once a small brown frog hopped away from him into a cluster of tiny purple flowers, and the single frond of a fern shook in the still air as if warning of his approach.

Up ahead, the steps curled off to the right and left, beckoning walkers out over sunny thighs of open land before they returned to the center of the park. Quinn ignored them both, pushing straight up into the somber ranks of conifers that bristled above. A stillness embraced him now, but not a peace: it was the enclosed tension of a vacuum awaiting a fork of electricity. He climbed, slipping on pine needles, carrying the toy hotel below him in his head, the dwindling cluster of shops, the lice-infested police station, the dubious protection of other humans. Far down through the pines, on his left, he could see the lake and the road to Tai-chung climbing out of the valley. The morning bus back from Green Silk Lake was crawling up the road; he watched it labor over a ridge and hang for a moment before it dropped out of sight.

A high steel-mesh fence enclosed the knoll—or he thought it did at first. He walked along it and found that it was still under construction, with coils of mesh and steel stakes lying among the rocks at its base. He skirted it and climbed more zigzag mossy steps, wondering if Keh had set his gallant veterans to work while they were awaiting their glorious Return to the Mainland. Now he felt nervous and exposed, with only the ammunition in his head to guard him: a burst of Doyle's bravado, a clip of his own cunning. For it was Doyle who climbed with him, urging him up, his eagle eyes glinting as he barked jovial threats and vowed vengeance—Doyle and then, briefly, the ragged mist of his father trailing over a shattered lone pine at the top of the steps. A power saw lay beside it on a pile of branches; Keh had never let anything stand in his way.

Quinn crouched behind the branches, getting his breath. White pigeons were strutting among nervous spotted deer in a small enclosure; beside them, in a large cage heaped around and on top with tubs of orchids, two tigers were prowling. Fifty meters away the circular tower of Keh's house rose from the knoll with an open lawn between them; beyond it, tiny red pennants fluttered gently on a golf course. Sunlight shone on the curved empty windows of the house, but two of Keh's helmeted guards stood talking in front of it beside three trucks loaded with steel mesh. They did not look up as a helicopter thudded into view and hung over the roof.

The presence of the helicopter—and the tigers—unnerved him: Keh's playthings had magnified since his rubber spider days; his tin inkblots and mock dog-turd and hideous Punch with the nose beak of a macaw. It was absurd to have clambered up here alone with no clear plan—no certainty, from one moment to the next, what he was going to do himself. And so he shrank against the earth as the helicopter sank to the roof and squatted there with its whirling blades above him: Don Quixote now, not Doyle, preparing for a ludicrous charge at the windmill, or a precipitate flight; the white Gurkha, with knees pumping high.

He decided on flight, but instead when he rose he found himself walking casually toward the house. The guards spotted him at once. Both of them pulled weapons from their belts and ran toward him, shouting; he stopped and held out his empty hands with a faint smile which was meant to reassure them. Then, quite detached, his mind lifted like the helicopter and gazed down curiously at this man in black who stood so calmly on the lawn; he saw the guards rush up around him—one punch him on the jaw. Well, that didn't hurt, his mind remarked coolly, hanging in the air above his body while the hands jerked at his clothes and patted them and threw him to the grass.

Quinn sat up immediately, angrily pushing aside a fist that gripped a revolver. "What the fucking hell are you blokes doing?" he demanded, but he remembered to temper the question with another smile.

One of the guards placed a boot on his thigh; Quinn jerked his leg away immediately. "What's going on?" he protested. "What the hell are you doing?" But "acting" was the word in his head: a superb show of confidence to beat the revolver.

"I'm a friend of General Keh," he said. "Old friend. General Keh."

One of the guards cocked his revolver; it triggered in Quinn a ridiculous exhilaration—exhilaration could turn aside a bullet. But he hid the flame.

"Look," he said reasonably, "if you fire that thing off there's going to be an awful mess, and I can see that you're a neat man."

The revolver nosed back to his head; he dropped his eyes for a moment, awaiting the impact. Then he tapped one of the man's American-style gaiters.

"Beautiful," he said. "Snowy white. No point getting them all splattered, is there?" He looked up with another smile. It was vital to stand up—to get up out of animal level.

The guards solved that problem by hauling him roughly to his feet. His legs were trembling; a muscle was fluttering violently in a thigh. But he felt better now: he had survived.

"Relax," he said. "General Keh. Take me to General Keh." And: "Cool it," he said. "Cool it. OK," as they hustled him across the lawn. Wooden words to keep himself alive.

The guards walked him around the side of the house to the main entrance overlooking the road that zigzagged up from the valley. Gripping his arms tightly, they steered him into a cool marble anteroom decked with ferns and hanging baskets of orchids, and then they pushed him into a bamboo chair. One of them flung his hat on the floor at his feet.

"What's all the fuss?" he protested. He thought of reaching for the hat but left it there, remembering Winifred's mad dog, the danger in sudden movement. Instead, he leaned back and crossed his legs. "Do any of you speak English?"

Both the guards were big men; they scowled at him and spoke to each other briefly. One of them looked at his wristwatch and strode out, pushing his revolver back in its holster. The other backed into a chair about three meters from Quinn and sat watching him stonily, his revolver resting on his knees.

"Do you speak English?" Quinn asked again, but the man did not reply.

"Apparently you don't," Quinn murmured. His bravado was flooding back; it was important now to maintain his anger or pretend to be completely at ease. Pretending to be at ease seemed safer—imparting a confidence in his continued existence that he did not feel. They obviously knew who he was.

"Nice place," he said. At least his words hid the pounding of his heart. "My name is Quinn. Quinn," pointing at his chest. "General Keh wants to see me. Someone get General Keh, uh?"

Still the man did not reply, and Quinn reached slowly now for his hat and began to push it into shape, grateful for the commonplace task. Twice other guards came to the door and looked in, and each time he leaned forward. "General Keh?" he asked. "Is someone getting General Keh?"

Nobody answered. The man continued to glower at him.

"Jesus, you're not very talkative, mate, are you?" he asked mildly, but now and again he looked away from him up at the orchids so as not to provoke him too much, imagining that Doyle stood chuckling beside his chair, imagining Donna's honey-blonde head resting against the window of the bus.

He tossed his hat cheerily onto the floor. "OK, who sang: *'I came uninvited, but I found you, so thrilled and delighted, With somebody new . . .'*? Give in? Mercedes McCambridge. Now let's see—every child on the watershed can tell you how *who* died? No? How *Gilbert* died . . ."

But then he felt sick in his stomach and blinked his eyes, for behind the swaggering poem of the bushranger he could see the mangled bodies of his sons in his mangled car, and he could see his daughter dragging herself across the Indian Ocean to Tel Aviv—plunking her crutches, step by twisting step, in the deep blue water that miraculously supported her. She was turning her head away happily toward Africa; he could see the light in her eyes through her skull, and passengers were gazing down at her tenderly from the rails of passing ships as she splashed along, smiling through their tears, as he tried to smile through his.

THIRTY-SEVEN

GENERAL KEH STOOD SHAKILY AT the doorway in a stiff peacock-blue gown that swished on the marble floor: he was rubbing his eyes like a child who had awoken from a nightmare. Once he had been as round and firm as a beach ball, but age and excess had deflated him. The fat and vigor had leaked steadily from him down the years, exposing the bones of his once-pudgy little face and shriveling his neck. Lady Earnshaw must have very nearly finished him off.

Keh weakly limped a few steps into the room; the guard sprang upright as Quinn rose with mock eagerness. "General Keh!" he greeted him brightly. "It's been a long time!"

He stuck out his hand and grasped Keh's; it contained all the robust warmth of a mummy's. "So, Quinn," he said. "You come early."

"I was out walking when your people jumped on top of me. I'll come back later, if you like." Or perhaps not at all.

"No matter." Keh vaguely waved away the suggestion. "I get Larsen up here now."

Keh turned and began to hobble from the room with a soft aside to the guard; Quinn was struck by his tiny frailty. The guard grasped Quinn's arm, and they followed Keh slowly into an elevator that ascended only one floor. When they got out the guard once more patted Quinn's clothing while Keh made for his desk. The guard pushed Quinn gently toward a sofa and stood back beside the elevator.

They were in Keh's ferny office-aerie above the rain forest, the golf course, the conifer mountains. In a glass tank near Quinn, a Siamese fighting fish spat eggs into a nest of bubbles and swayed into a courtship dance while the female floated belly-up, releasing them from its body. Donna might be arriving now at Tai-chung railway station—yearning for love, journeying as he did where she was least likely to find it . . .

Keh lowered himself into a chair and swiveled around slowly to face him. He was done in. He held a folder limply against his chest, but the old cunning gleamed in his eyes. "You have some tea? Maybe a drink? Scotch?"

"No. Nothing for me," Quinn said. A little undetected poison might nestle at the bottom of Keh's box of tricks. He patted his stomach. "Gastric trouble."

Keh pushed a couple of pills into his mouth and nibbled at a glass of water. It slopped on his chin.

"Busy man," he said. "I just return from England. Many duties."

Keh swung back to his desk and leafed quickly through the folder; whatever the pills were, they were recharging him fast. "A very strange letter you send me," he said, holding it up and letting it drift to the floor.

Quinn rubbed his face nervously, genuinely embarrassed. "I was in a very strange mood. It's not very important. Don't bother about it."

There was a silence while Keh again pushed through the papers in the folder. "You are a very poor man. No money. No friends."

"I've got friends," Quinn said firmly, but Keh was right: his friendships now blossomed only in bars. "And I'm not interested in money."

Keh smiled his disbelief: the concept obviously was beyond his experience. "I have very much money. Very great friends."

Quinn looked at his photographs. "So I see. I saw your picture the other day with the queen. They must think you are a very great man." (Who will not sully your reputation by stooping to harm a nobody like me.)

"Of course. You see what I make here? A park for the people. One day bigger than Disneyland. Biggest in the world."

Quinn rubbed his jaw ruefully. "The rangers are a little heavy-handed . . . I just wanted to talk."

"Talk about money, uh? Blackmail? You think anyone believe you?" Now the eyes stabbed at him; Quinn felt a small shock of fear. He decided to play along with Keh for a minute.

"Look, I'm not interested in blackmail either. How can I put it? I'm a simple man. You've achieved so much. In the war—then with your tanker fleets—now this. Photographs with Reagan and so on."

"Ah yes, photographs!" Keh opened a drawer and pulled out a tangle of negatives and a stack of faded prints. He dropped them carelessly on the floor on top of the letter. "The Police give me your films."

"I thought they would. They were of that massacre in Kweilin—remember? How did the prints turn out?"

"Very old—bad picture," Keh said, and it occurred to Quinn that he was probably right: time had bleached them, like the images in his head. They were as useless as his memories.

He reached into his pocket and took out the diary he had scribbled the next morning in the cave. "You'd better have this too. It's something I wrote at the time. I don't have any copies." He got up and put it in Keh's hands.

Keh glanced at the scrawl and tossed it on to the desk. "You have more gifts? Damaged merchandise? Expensive items?"

"I've told you. They're free. I don't want them any more. I want to get it all off my mind."

Keh frowned. How can he understand me, Quinn thought, when I do not understand myself? He fished out a packet of cigarettes and pulled out the last one. It was bent. He broke it in half and lit up.

"I'm not your enemy," he said. "I just want to understand before I die. I'm not talking about this to anyone else."

Keh sat looking at him while Quinn shook the burnt match and pushed it back in the box. "For instance," he said, "you remember Doyle? Why did he kill himself?"

"Doyle?" Keh frowned more intensely. "Who is this Doyle?"

"You don't remember Doyle?" Quinn lifted his eyebrows innocently; he felt the anger spurting in his brain. "Oh well, I don't suppose it matters." He smiled warmly. "Nothing matters much, does it?"

He stood up, taking in the sweeping view, the tiny jungle in which Keh squatted like a bony toad: I'm O'Keh—I've paid a fortune for my respectability; I'm unassailable now.

"You don't have to worry about me," he lied. "I've always admired you very much. Those tricks you used to do . . . That rubber snake in the cigarette packet! Brilliant!"

Keh smirked; he began to look a little like his merry, murderous old self. "You wait," he said. "I show you something."

He limped away from his desk past banks of TV screens, two telex machines half-hidden by ferns and palms, and pressed a switch in the wall behind Quinn. A curtain slid back, the wall blossomed gently with soft orange light, and Quinn saw that it was glass. Behind it, a slender shadow stirred as Keh tapped to arouse it.

"Come closer," Keh instructed, beckoning him urgently; half-turning toward Quinn with his old Mickey Mouse smile—that queasy Mickey Mouse smile that he had left hanging in the air behind him after he had withdrawn so deferentially from so many war-rooms in the days of his spurious glory: the all-purpose smile of all those Nationalist generals who had not lived to fight, like Doyle, but who had fought to live; who had set themselves up again in Taiwan and California and New York and Virginia on sprawling estates a short drive from Arlington, where Marshall still simmered in his narrow grave. The smile of the corrupt general in Nationalist China, South Vietnam—it was all the same. The deserters.

Quinn rose slowly. "What have you got in there? Rats?"

Keh giggled. "Not rats." He pressed another button, and the glass slid back, and looking over his shoulder, Quinn saw an

Indian cobra slowly swaying up from its coils, its neck inflating into a hideous hood. Keh cuffed the cobra's head with his hand and it weaved higher before he shut the glass and mockingly poked forward his own head.

"We take away the poison," he said, and giggled again. "He love Lady Earnshaw. Follow her everywhere."

Quinn breathed with relief as Keh closed the curtain. He hovered by the sofa, wondering if other serpents lay coiled beneath the cushions—a lovable African mamba, perhaps, a cuddly coral. It was safer to stand; Keh's box of tricks now spanned the continents.

"Doyle, you say?" Keh said suddenly, cocking his head sideways. "I remember Doyle. 'Drunk Man'—my staff call him 'Drunk Man.' I see memos—Drunk Man do this, Drunk Man do that. Ah-ha!"

He hurried to the windows near his desk; down below, the tigers were roaring. "You see this!" he called again, and when Quinn looked down this time over his shoulder he saw the great cats copulating noisily. He turned away, but Keh watched intently; Quinn knew that his eyes were glistening.

"The tigress is on heat!" Keh whispered. "This is the first time!" And he stood there quivering in his sexual jungle, soaking it in to nourish his own fading spasms like some old sire of mythology straining for a wild cosmic ejaculation of earth and trees, orchids and air, which might return him, mysteriously, to his source. Then he plunked down on his chair to rest his gouty foot—Keh astride the globe like a pygmy.

"In six months you see what I do!" he gasped, and Quinn's spirits lifted: there might be time, then, to do what he himself had to do. More time to delay.

"What other developments are you planning?" he asked, barely concealing his pretended admiration.

"Developments? I go into electronic games with the microchip. You know Black Knight, Flash Gordon? Mine better. Put them everywhere in the park. But up here . . ." He shook his head gently, impressed by his own genius. "Up here for myself I make the biggest game in the world."

He rolled his chair to the windows again and pointed at the loaded trucks. "You know what I do with that?"

333

"You're building fences."

"Not fences. I tell you—a game! Electronic. I use the tigers and the deer. Build the tunnels all around—in the forest, up the rocks. Every twenty meters—little gates. I press the buttons up here and the gates open, gates close. Maybe tigers feed. Maybe tigers hungry."

"Ingenious," Quinn observed. Keh playing like a child with his own live pinball machine, flipping spotted deer to their doom. No doubt he'd toss in a discarded drug courier or two if he could get away with it. "Something for you to do on rainy afternoons."

"Simple!" Keh scoffed. "One day I use holograms with the laser. Then I have Buckingham Palace here, Sistine Chapel, White House, everything! I am dead a thousand years and everywhere, in every country, I am still riding my horse! Three-dimensional!"

Quinn shook his head with feigned wonder. The prospect of a three-dimensional General Keh popping up around the globe to eclipse Colonel Sanders was remote, but not beyond the realms of nauseous possibility: the ultimate trickster, assuming new images forever. He was not only crazy; he'd be bloody near indestructible if he could last a few more years while they perfected the process.

"I think I will have a Scotch," he said slowly. "Then maybe I could look around the golf course before I push off . . ."

He sat on the edge of the sofa while Keh slowly ascended with the guard to the top floor to change. He was a long time. Quinn got up and poured a second drink for himself, but it did not warm his brain; he sauntered stiffly around the room, anxious to be out in the fresh air—to be gone, if that were still possible. Like Keh, he had played too many games for too long in his head; acted so many roles to please others that he had forgotten his own. He had been the clown in his father's greatcoat: the cautious antipodean Celt dancing merrily along the precipice of life—a good distance in from the edge. Clowns were not heroes; they mouthed for the moon, but they did not jump off tall buildings to reach it. They hoarded their skin as others hoarded old family scrapbooks; they expired of fatty degeneration of the heart.

He had been content to bleed quietly, at bay on West Ridge, his ignominious Olympus; Quinn MM, rusting like a forgotten grenade. But he was not going to bleed alone.

THIRTY-EIGHT

"NOW WE GO," KEH SAID, when the elevator descended. He wore jodhpurs, riding boots, and a long-sleeved pink silk shirt with a white horse on the pocket, and in one trembling hand he carried a riding crop.

Quinn couldn't help smiling. It was probably his warrior-at-play garb, his meet-Prince-Charles-and-Mark-Phillips-menswear, but it reminded him vaguely of George Brent in some half-forgotten movie: Keh playing hero opposite Maria Ouspenskaya, perhaps, in a manic remake of *The Rains Came*—slopping his drinks and dribbling his dinner while wizened little Maria squinted at him shrewdly, mumbling words of gummy wisdom. The scenario fired him with such exhilaration that for a moment he feared he might laugh aloud. If he whacks his leg with that riding crop, he thought, the bastard will fall over.

He squeezed solemnly into the elevator, rejoicing in his secret lunacy; for all his long obsession with China, he had attracted only Chinese who were bizarre and incomplete—a quixotic mur-

derer, a tin-pot private detective, a Szechuanese from Cambridge
... He hadn't known one normal Chinese, one whole European,
then or now: they stuck to him like metal shavings to a magnet—
the dislocated and despairing, the mad and half-mad, the comic-
strip people who thought they were real. When nothing in the
world now was real and anything was possible: the criminals
patriots and the patriots criminals; the shadow reality and reality
the shadow. His sons lay in the leaves, his daughter was the
scrape of a shoe.

Outside, Keh mounted what appeared at first to be a golf
buggy, but then he saw that it was a battery-powered wheelchair
with a padded bucket seat and armrests. It had small wheels and a
handgrip like a scooter, and somebody had pasted the ubiquitous
white horse over the brand name.

"For my foot," Keh explained. "Very sore," and he turned the
wheelchair and jerked off at a fast walking pace toward the golf
course while Quinn quickened his steps to keep up with him. The
guard stared after them and called to Keh, but Keh waved a
dismissive hand, and he went inside. They were alone.

Keh rode up a cement path onto a grassy rise, and there before
them lay the golf course, a dew-fresh mat spread among the
mountains, with cliffs on three sides. A brisk breeze was whip-
ping up; the pennants were snapping. "Championship course,"
Keh declared. "Open soon."

"It's quite a setting." Quinn found himself contemplating the
lawn cemetery on the plain beneath West Ridge; the pale headlights at noon, the anonymous end that had awaited him there.

"Tournaments on satellite TV," boasted Keh. "All the top
player." With the "tiger hunt" presumably suspended during
transmission.

"You really think big, General." Quinn laid a hand on his back;
it was a cage of bone. "You've certainly come a long way since
your old Punch and Judy days. Is it all right if we go down?"

He started off ahead: as much as anything, he wanted to get
away from the shadows of Keh's staff before Larsen arrived—to
walk in the sunlight for a few minutes while he decided what to
do.

He walked past the first green; Keh zipped up beside him as
they headed down a fairway, and it seemed like a dream that they

should be setting out so companionably together when he had spent so much of his life with so much death in his head; so many years mildewing in his crumbling cottage, compressed beneath age and resignation, when now he strode forth so freely on top of the world. Keh floating over his roof had been a jolly symbol of evil; Keh clinging to the tiny machine beside him was a dry leaf that might whisk away on the breeze.

"I went back to Kweilin the other day," he said. "Remember those bean crops in the village beneath the monastery? They look better than ever."

"Good fertilizer," Keh chuckled, but he glanced slyly at Quinn. "Maybe I offer you a position."

"I'd be interested," Quinn smoothly pretended. "I'd like to try something new. Make a clean break."

Far down to the left of the fairway was a cluster of small trees, and he sauntered toward it instinctively; remembering the dark copse he had dreamed of in the European Hostel in Hong Kong after meeting Winifred and her dog; the shadowy figure with the small black coffin humming in his hands. The gaunt face of his dream, he now suspected, had been his own.

"We talk about it later." Keh was swinging the wheelchair around to go back when he stopped: one of those blips in the brain which spell death or salvation. He completed the circle and once more tootled down the fairway after Quinn. Ahead rose the twin peaks, the glassy staircase of rice ascending between them under the sky. "The next stage," he said.

One more evening with Lady Earnshaw might really finish him off, Quinn thought, or a cobra will get him or a tiger shake him like a rag doll, chewing the buttocks, gnawing the shrunken head at its leisure. Perhaps a horse will kick him while he's awarding a prize, or drug enforcement authorities somewhere will clap him in prison, or the Triads or Mafia or some ambitious underling eventually will blow him away. And perhaps he'll drag for twenty more years around my brain with my dreams of death and separation and loss—because I can't kill him in cold blood, I know that now. A tooth began to ache: he patted his pockets vainly for cigarettes.

He stood on the lip of another green at the end of the fairway, pretending to admire the view, but it was Keh who lay in his head.

When he looked back he saw that he was stuck in the rough beside the copse, twisting the handlebar and kicking weakly with one boot to try to get free.

"Here, I'll help you!" he called brightly, and he walked back to join him. "You get off, and I'll pull it out."

Keh propelled himself from his bucket seat as Quinn held his elbow to steady him. "Switch if off, and I'll get it onto the smooth stuff," Quinn instructed.

Keh pressed a button and stumbled out of the rough. Then he lurched away up onto the green.

Quinn dragged the wheelchair from the rough and pushed it up onto the edge of the green near the cliff. The drive belt had become detached; it seemed like a sign.

He was looking at it when he heard a shout. Larsen was hurrying down the course toward them. The breeze plucked his shirt; he jerked like a puppet on an invisible wire.

"Larsen's coming," he said, but Keh did not turn around. He was gazing at the twin peaks.

"Next stage the big one," Keh mused. "Very much work."

"I'm sure it'll look beautiful." Quinn spoke cheerily, but the old sickness was in his belly. A few meters beyond the green was the cliff edge; there were postholes dug for a fence.

"Make them all struggle hard," Keh giggled. "Two, three year, finish!"

"That's the way to do it." Quinn's heart was thudding. His voice came from the air somewhere near his head. "Larsen looks upset," he said.

Larsen was enraged. He stalked around a bunker and stopped in front of Quinn. He was shaking, his lips tinged with mauve.

"You bastard!" He sprayed spittle. "You *were* with my wife last night! Deny it!"

"Don't be ridiculous." Quinn was aware of the drop behind him. It wasn't the time to complete Larsen's humiliation.

"I heard her laughing! Anyway, I checked your room! There were two dents in the pillows!"

"I'm schizophrenic. Look, you'd better calm down. You know what happens when you get excited." He shifted another step away from the cliff, balancing himself on the balls of his feet.

338

"Always the smart guy, aren't you? I never liked you, you bastard! If I had a gun . . ."

Keh turned. He dropped his riding crop and took a tiny gold automatic from beneath his pink silk shirt. "You have a gun," he said.

Larsen stared at him. "I warned you, General! He's got no intention of keeping quiet!"

"So you take the gun and kill him. Nobody bother us here."

"There are laws." Larsen gazed wildly at the gift that Keh offered. "We were going to talk."

"Better he die." Keh lifted the pistol and pointed it at Quinn's chest. "Finish the problem."

"Come on, there'll really be problems if I die," Quinn said, but who would be left to fight for him if Keh obliterated his presence? No public burial this time; no records left of his brief visit to Green Silk Lake. "You'll ruin everything you've built up."

"He's bound to have told people he's here," Larsen said. "We can't take the risk. There's got to be something else!"

Keh turned slowly and mounted his little machine as he had sat on his little fat horse to supervise so many executions in China. He seemed almost absentminded; assassination had become a bit of a bore. And he had had a long night.

"OK," he said, switching on the engine and smiling his last impish smile. "Maybe better you both die," and once again Quinn saw that murder was a matter of minor detail, not damnation, to Keh—a mental shrug, no more. The copulating tigers, the cobra—they were important. He and Larsen were merely administrative trivia.

"You're not serious," Larsen said, but Quinn knew that he was. Slowly he took off his hat and held it against his heart.

"Give me time for a little prayer," he said, and he flung the hat at Keh and sprang after it, knocking him from his seat. The gold automatic fell on the green. Keh scrabbled for a walkie-talkie clipped to an armrest.

Quinn grabbed him and thrust him back into the seat. Then he aimed the wheelchair at the cliff, spread his hands on Keh's back, and pushed him. It was the most perfect, the most complete action he had ever performed in his life. Keh sped across the green on his last little charger—vainly stabbing the reverse button, groping for the hand brake, slewing sideways too late. He flew out into space, framed by the twin peaks, and then dropped into the rain forest.

Quinn threw the automatic after him. Larsen had fallen to his knees, his arms locked around him. He looked like a marble carving: Man In Extreme Shock.

Quinn looked up the fairway toward the house. The sun still shone. The birds were singing. The little red flags fluttered briskly in the breeze. Nobody was in sight.

"You'd better tell them it was an accident. Safest thing, isn't it?" Quinn said. "Otherwise it might look worse for you than for me, the way you barged into the place . . ."

Quinn picked up his hat. "I'm off," he said, and he walked into the copse and stood looking up at the house while his heartbeat subsided, ready to run forward, waving his arms in utter distress, if anybody pelted down to investigate. Then he straightened his tie and coat and creased his hat and walked back along the edge of the knoll toward the house, looking for a way down, praying that no one had been watching.

He found a small slide thirty meters short of the house and began climbing down toward the road that twisted up the side of the knoll. He was halfway down when a large bus crawled around a hairpin bend beneath him and roared up to the house. It stopped in a turning circle outside the grounds, and a crowd of passengers got out. A few were Europeans, the rest Japanese bristling with cameras, and they all wore identifying discs over their hearts.

Quinn climbed back up the slide and looked over the edge of the golf course. The group was surveying the placid greens and fairways; several were taking photographs, and others were jotting down notes. As for Larsen, he still had not moved. Quinn ducked out of sight, climbed down to the road, and waited. Ten minutes later the passengers began drifting back toward the bus, and he walked casually up the road toward them, keeping close to the rock wall, mingling with them as they emerged.

One of Keh's guards was strutting around the driveway, slapping the walkie-talkie on his belt with boredom; when he turned away, Quinn stooped behind two Europeans who were chatting together as they crossed the road to the bus. "International tournament," they said, and "color TV"—the English phrases surfacing from a broken jumble of German.

He stood beside the bus, trying to read the identity discs as the group filed aboard. Many of them were Japanese clergymen wearing the collars of some Christian denomination: four of them stood around him, their eyes gleaming with interest.

"Could I get a lift down with you?" he asked, and they smiled and motioned to the steps. He climbed in and edged down the aisle, averting his face from the guard. "Is this a church group?"

"One half church, one half travel agents," one of the Japanese said, and then he smiled chirpily. "Same business."

Quinn gazed at him with respect: another Mr. Ochi to superimpose on Shiozawa. But his hands were trembling, and his tooth was jumping; he ground his jaws together and felt it crumble. He huddled in a corner seat at the rear, grateful as the foursome squeezed in beside him. He was desperate to be gone.

"How far are you going?" he asked. "I don't suppose I could get a lift with you if you're leaving here? I've missed my bus, everything . . ."

"WE GO TO Taipei," the clergyman said.

"I'm going to Taipei." The bus began rolling down the hill; he bent his head and pushed his hat under the seat, sizzling with a wild hope. "I have money. I could pay . . ."

"Not necessary." The clergyman's eyes glowed kindly; he had a plump, pleasant face. "There is the empty seat."

"I'm very grateful." He sat in silence until the bus descended to the valley, shrinking back from the window as it turned away from the village. And then slowly, in his mind, he began climbing the vast jade staircase, flinging away his black hat like a frisbee; shedding his black suit as he had once dreamed that he could leave his old self crumpled behind him. Except that now he knew that all his doubts and fears and indecisions were heaped inside him forever: the love and the violence, the jokes in the dark, the new scar of murder; the shadow of a second wheelchair by the orange tree of his childhood.

Later he took off his coat and pushed it down beside the seat to alter his appearance. "Name's Muggeridge," he said, sticking out his hand. "Same as the Englishman. The Flesh Become Word."

The clergyman shook hands. "I'm sorry," Quinn apologized. "That's a joke. I'm afraid I don't have much faith."

"But you are a fellow traveler," the clergyman said, and they laughed together as they began jolting along a half-finished road through fields of sugar cane.

He bumped wildly against Quinn. "I think maybe we are all Buddhists anyway, Mr. Muggeridge," he gasped. "Apart from vibrations there is nothing."